"What were you doing when you lit that fuse?"

Anne-Marie whirled in frustration. "I didn't! I told you before—"

"Deny it," Eli dared her, pulling her close to him. "Look me in the eye and deny it."

"Let me go!" She pulled away as she had the last time, but this time he had the strength to hold on.

"Look at me," he repeated, his voice harsh and low.

They were so close, she could feel his breath upon her skin when she turned toward him. His eyes were almost black, and in some way she couldn't fathom his gaze was both cold and hot at the same time.

"Let me go," she whispered. But he made no response, just kept staring at her with those haunting eyes.

Dear Reader,

This month we bring you award-winning author Patricia Hagan's latest Harlequin Historical, *The Desire*. The novel is the sequel to *The Daring* (HH#84) and tells the story of Belinda Coulter, a troubled young woman who finally finds happiness as a Confederate nurse, only to come face-to-face with a man from the past.

Columbine is the second book by Miranda Jarrett, one of the first-time authors introduced during our 1991 March Madness promotion. The story sweeps from busy London to the wilds of Colonial New England, where a disgraced noblewoman finds a new life full of hope and promise.

Theresa Michaels's *Gifts of Love* is an emotional tale of a grieving widower and an abandoned woman whose practical marriage blossoms into something far more precious than either of them could ever dream.

Lucy Elliot has been writing books for Harlequin Historicals since the introduction of the line. *The Conquest,* her eighth book, is a sequel to *The Claim* (HH#129). It's the story of a tempestuous Frenchwoman and a cool-headed American soldier who fall in love against the backdrop of the American Revolution.

Four intriguing heroines. Four unforgettable heroes. We hope you enjoy them all.

Sincerely,
Tracy Farrell
Senior Editor

The Conquest

Lucy Elliot

Harlequin Books

TORONTO • NEW YORK • LONDON
AMSTERDAM • PARIS • SYDNEY • HAMBURG
STOCKHOLM • ATHENS • TOKYO • MILAN
MADRID • WARSAW • BUDAPEST • AUCKLAND

Harlequin Historicals first edition October 1992

ISBN 0-373-28746-1

THE CONQUEST

Books by Lucy Elliot

LUCY ELLIOT

is a happily transplanted Easterner living in Northern California with her husband, son, dog and any neighborhood cat who wants an extra meal. She has been making up stories for her own entertainment since earliest memory—full of romance, adventure and, of course, happy endings.

To Dora Fink, who lived in Vermont a good
deal later than the events described in this
book; a remarkable woman and the greatest of
great-aunts.

Chapter One

Quebec City, New Year's Eve, 1775

The attack was on. Eli Brownell and his four companions
groped their way through the driving wind and snow,
counting the minutes until their rendezvous. Above them,
unseen through the blizzard, loomed the cliffs and stone
walls of Quebec. The American army didn't have the artillery to breach those cliffs and walls, so they'd been waiting
for a storm they could use as cover to conceal an attack.
After two restless weeks, the snow had begun this afternoon, and at midnight General Montgomery had summoned his officers to headquarters to give them their
orders.

The plan was straightforward. Montgomery and Benedict Arnold would hit the Lower Town on two different
sides, while Colonel Livingston would attack the Upper
Town from the Plains of Abraham. Each attack would be
launched at four o'clock sharp, and by dawn, if God was
with them, they'd all be inside.

Eli had received special orders after the others had gone.
Before the attack was mounted, he and his tiny column
would be let into the city by a spy, who would lead them to
the magazine where the British gunpowder was stored.
From there, they would take enough powder to blow up the

Saint Louis gate so that it would be open when Livingston arrived. In giving them their instructions, Montgomery hadn't minced his words: the outcome of the entire venture depended upon their success.

The path was slick and narrow even in the best of times, with the ice floes of the Saint Lawrence groaning and creaking to their left and the steep walls of the Lower Town rising to their right. The five men stayed close together and near the wall, imagining the sentries stationed above peering down through the howling blizzard for any telltale sign of movement. The American camp was as rotten with spies as Quebec was; without doubt the British knew an attack would be coming now that there was snow. Hopefully they didn't know exactly when and how.

Eli had been counting windows since they'd reached the Lower Town. Eighteen, nineteen, twenty... At the last he stopped, signaling to the others to flatten themselves on the wall while he gathered snow into a ball and threw it as hard as he could. He thought it hit the high shuttered window but he couldn't be sure. Holding his breath, he waited, hearing nothing but the swirling snow and the moaning wind.

Arden leaned forward and whispered hoarsely, "Maybe you should try again." But just then the shutters opened and a rope appeared.

Up they went in rapid succession, awkward in their bulky clothes and with their blanket-wrapped muskets bouncing on their backs. Eli went last. By the time he vaulted the sill, the room into which he tumbled was steaming and stank of wet wool. The only light came from the fire, which had burned very low—just enough for him to make out the four shadows of his men huddled around a fifth, who would be their guide.

In the next moment the window was reshuttered and the rope had disappeared and they were moving into the hall, then down the stairs, out the door and back into the snow again. They followed their guide, jogging and slipping, through a labyrinth of narrow streets that twisted through archways and alleys and scrambled up slippery steps leading up to the plateau on which the Upper Town was built. As they went, Eli was hoping that nothing happened to their guide, because if anything went wrong, he feared they'd never find their way back out of this maze.

The ground beneath his feet leveled and he knew they'd reached the Upper Town. It sat high above the river, protected on three sides by cliffs and on the fourth by a man-made wall. The French had lost Quebec City sixteen years before because they'd let the British tease them into quitting the fortress and fighting on the plains, but in this round the British wouldn't make the same mistake. General Carleton, Quebec's commander, was smart enough to stay holed up in the city with six months' worth of supplies and let the knife-sharp Canadian winter whittle the Americans down. The Americans had no choice but to attack.

Their guide led them past houses, larger and lower than those down below, until they reached the cluster of barracks where the British troops were housed. Those troops would be sleeping lightly, muskets at their sides—unless they'd been alerted and were watching for the attack. The guard led them past the barracks to the rear of a low brick building, which Eli realized must be the powder magazine.

Gathering them close together, the guide spoke for the very first time. "There is a guard of two persons posted in the front. They must be made unconscious if we are to get inside." His English, though heavily accented, was easily understood and his voice was surprisingly pleasing, despite his low muffled tone.

The others looked to Eli, who gave orders rapidly. "Noah, Connor, Arden, go around the other side. The rest of us will come from here. At the count of one hundred, we both attack—and fast, before they can fire a warning shot."

With a quick nod, they disappeared. Counting, moving slowly, Eli edged around the building with the guide and Spencer just behind.

"Ninety-six, ninety-seven, ninety-eight, ninety-nine..." He was already moving when he whispered the last word. His musket butt struck the guard on the back of the head. As the bulky form went down, Connor loomed up through the snow, with Noah and Arden just behind him, dragging the other, also unconscious guard.

The door was padlocked, but Eli jimmied it and then they were all inside, peering at the piled barrels in the faint and shadowy light.

Spencer whistled. "Just think of what all this could do!"

Noah's teeth flashed in the darkness. "I guess we'd wake up the redcoats if we set all this off. Hell, I guess they'd hear it clear up in Montreal!"

Eli gave Noah a poke in the ribs. "Three barrels will do us for now. Two men to a barrel. Roll them outside and wait at the edge of the last barracks until we're all there so nobody gets lost crossing the field to the gate."

They did as he commanded, Spencer and Arden first and Connor and Noah second.

"Our turn," Eli said to the guide, who made no response. He was gazing up at the piled barrels, and although the hood of his cloak hid his face, Eli could sense his awe. "Let's go," he murmured, touching the guide on the arm.

"*Oui, oui,*" the man muttered, and bent to lend a hand, but when they reached the others, the guide turned back again. "Just a moment," he muttered, and was gone before Eli could reply.

"Where's he going?" muttered Noah, but Eli had no response. He felt the cold chill of betrayal creeping beneath his skin.   — -

"I'll go check," he told the others. "You wait here. If I'm not back in a minute, go on and we'll catch up. No matter what happens, we have to blow the gate."

"I don't like it!" he heard Spencer grumble as he moved away. He didn't like it, either, but he had no choice.

The magazine door was open; crouching, he slipped inside. The first thing he heard was the breathing of the still-unconscious guards. Listening more closely, he heard a different noise toward the back, a sound like a mouse scratching—or like a flint striking steel.

Ducking between rows of barrels, he saw the guide down on his hands and knees. What was the fellow doing? Then he saw the glow of fire. The guide was lighting a slow match to blow up the whole magazine! Whatever he'd expected, it hadn't been this. The fellow must be demented—he'd blow the top off Quebec and all of them with it!

"What the hell do you think you're doing?" he demanded, shocked into speech.

The guide froze at the sound of Eli's voice, but he kept his hands cupped around the fire he was coaxing from the fuse. He said, "I'm killing British. Isn't that why we're here? This will wipe out most of Carleton's army."

"And us with it," Eli replied, moving forward as he spoke. "And even if we manage to escape, it won't do our cause any good. This is cold-blooded murder. The whole world will turn against us."

"I don't care," the guide said calmly, coming to his feet. He had a pistol pointing at Eli, while on the floor behind him the fuse burned steadily. "I don't care for the world. I care for justice. Now quickly, get outside!" He held the gun forward and waved it at Eli's chest.

Reacting without thinking, Eli reached out for the gun, lunging for the barrel with his right hand and for the man's wrist with his left. He managed to catch the wrist but he missed the gun, which flew from the guide's grip with the force of his assault. It hit something solid and thudded to the ground. The guide scrambled to catch it, but Eli dragged him back. The guide's eyes glittered in the darkness as he angled his head toward Eli's arm.

"Ow!" Eli yelped in pain as the guide's teeth clamped down on his wrist. He let go for an instant, but in that instant the guide was gone, scrambling on all fours in the direction of the gun. Eli flung himself forward, tackling him from behind, then flipping him over in an effort to pin his hands.

The guide fought back with more fury than physical strength so that Eli had no trouble in keeping him down. But even as he pinned him, alarms inside him were going off. Something was the matter. Something was very wrong. The body writhing beneath his was too soft and fine, and the hair that sprang loose from the fallen hood was as long and as shining as silk. Raising his head slowly and with mounting dread, Eli looked down at the furious face—the face of a woman, and a beautiful one at that. Even in their contortion, her features were exquisite: high brows, huge dark eyes, luminous white skin.

On a night of many surprises, this was the greatest one.

"What—" he muttered hoarsely. Then he muttered, "Why?" Inhaling to clear his mind, he breathed her scent.

She made no attempt to answer. Her eyes were burning with hate. "Let me go!" she whispered.

He stared into her eyes, trying to see their color, but there was no light. Perhaps blue, he was thinking. Then he remembered the fuse.

He held her firmly until he had the gun. She stood with her arms wrapped around her while he stamped out the fire and yanked up the fuse.

"It's none of your business!" she muttered, then added something in French, tossing her hair back from the paleness of her face.

He didn't bother to answer; there wasn't any time. The others would already be halfway across the field, no doubt looking over their shoulders and wondering what had gone wrong. He pushed her before him as he found his way back to the door. They'd hardly reached it when he heard the shouts. The woman froze in the doorway, then bolted into the storm. He reached out to catch her, but she was already gone.

Fire exploded—the shots of guns, coming from the barracks across from the magazine. He flattened himself against the wall, peering through the blizzard for a glimpse of the other men, but he saw nothing. Suddenly, fire exploded again and an awful twisting pain ripped into his arm and leg. He felt himself slipping into darkness, and just before he went, he remembered to toss the fuse he was still holding into the deep drifting snow.

Chapter Two

"My dear, you are not eating." Henri de Beauville, Sieur de Saint Vallier, set down his knife and looked at his ward with concern.

"But of course I am!" Anne-Marie Doucet assured him, reaching for a slice of bread and buttering it with an energy she hoped he would take for eagerness. At least her hands had stopped shaking sometime after dawn, and the fire she'd built in her chamber had mostly dried her skirts and cloak. Not that the condition of her clothes mattered a whit, since the servants were in such an uproar over last night's attack that they wouldn't have noticed if she'd come to breakfast naked as the day she'd been born. And as for the dear sieur, he probably would have frowned in his kindly way and called the maid to add wood to the fire so that she wouldn't catch cold. Anne-Marie took a bite of buttered toast and forced herself to chew.

"Jam? It's strawberry—very good." The sieur offered the dainty dish. "Of course one feels guilty eating jam and butter when the siege has restricted most of our fellow citizens to biscuit and salt pork, but what is the point in having jam and not eating it?" Saint Vallier, the estate from which the sieur took his title, lay past the American lines; so it was fortunate that he also owned this fine house in Quebec.

"Butter is fine," said Anne-Marie, taking another bite.

"Then again," the sieur continued, following his own thoughts, "after this morning's events, the whole city may be eating jam, or else the Americans may be enjoying ours, after they've thrown us in jail. Everyone who rushes out after the true facts comes back with a different tale—battles in the Lower Town, battles on the walls, the Americans defeated and all of their officers dead!"

The sieur shook his head and helped himself to more tea—a necessary expedient since the maid had disappeared, no doubt to rush about after more rumors along with the rest of the staff. Setting down the teapot, he said to Anne-Marie, "If you ask me it's a miracle that the Americans haven't seized our butter and jam long before now. A month ago, when Montreal fell and General Carleton fled here to try to save Quebec, I wouldn't have bet half a bottle of new brandy in favor of our troops holding out against the Americans for above an hour, and now, not only have they held out over a month, perhaps they've even defeated them. I call that remarkable. But the most remarkable of all is you, sleeping through all the excitement!"

"Ah, but you know I've always slept soundly," Anne-Marie returned with a teasing smile, as though the reason for her sound sleeping were the greatest joke. It wasn't, not a bit. She'd learned the trick during those horrible years after she and her mother had fled their native Acadia and been hunted by the British every step of the way to Quebec. Anne-Marie had been terrified of the wild woods, but her mother had promised to keep watch over her while she slept. And so her poor mother had, every night for four years, until at last they'd had the luck to reach the sieur's estate at Quebec.

And what an arrival—Anne-Marie hardly more than a starveling and her mother so gaunt and ill! Her mother had never recovered, and when she'd died the sieur, a softhearted bachelor, had taken Anne-Marie in and he had been doting upon her ever since.

Her smile all but faded, Anne-Marie wondered for the thousandth time if another kindly savior had taken care of her brother, François, who'd been lost in the confusion of their exile and never heard from again. The sieur thought that François was dead, but she refused to believe it was so. Not only did she believe François was still alive, she believed that wherever he was, he was fighting against the British just as hard as she was right here.

She abandoned her toast, half-eaten. "Who told you that all the *Bostonnais* officers were dead?" she asked, using a popular, if derogatory, term for the Americans.

Saint Vallier threw up one hand. "That worthless Catherine! Instead of helping the cook with breakfast, she's spent most of her morning dashing out into the snow and rushing back with any rumor she hears. You know how rumors are—those who know the fewest facts invariably have the most to say. Anyone with real knowledge is certainly too busy at this moment to spend time gossiping at back doors. But never mind. We'll sit snug and tight by the fire until we find out the truth, and then . . . well, whatever it is, we'll make the best of it." He frowned as he added, "You aren't eating again, my dear."

Anne-Marie dutifully retrieved her toast, but before she could take a bite, the dining room door flew open upon the errant Catherine, red cheeked and bursting with the news that she'd run into Captain Massey coming up the front walk.

"Massey!" At mention of the captain's name, Saint Vallier perked up. "If Massey's coming to visit, things can't be so bleak. Besides which, he'll certainly be able to tell us what's what!" He glanced toward the empty doorway. "Where have you left him, foolish girl? Show him in right away! Then set another place at the table since I'm sure he'll want to eat."

"There goes the jam," murmured Anne-Marie, but she didn't really care, since the sieur was right about Massey.

In his position as General Carleton's aide, he would know the truth.

Massey came in a moment later, still shedding clots of snow from his thick scarlet overcoat.

"Catherine!" cried the sieur. "Come and take the captain's coat and set him a place for breakfast, then bring us some wine. Or would you prefer brandy?"

"How kind, but I really can't stay. Wine, please," Massey added as Catherine disappeared beneath the bulk of his dripping coat. Massey was square and ugly, with a square ugly face, though he wasn't quite as stupid as most of the British Anne-Marie had met. He'd come to Quebec with General Carleton just over a month ago and had become Anne-Marie's best source of information almost immediately.

Massey returned her smile with his complacent leer as he accepted the chair directly across from her. He rubbed his hands together. "I say, what a day—what a night!"

The sieur cleared his throat, attempting to restrain his curiosity. But as Massey only continued to leer at Anne-Marie, he finally gave up. "Do tell us what's happened," he urged. "We've had nothing but the wild stories Catherine brings home. We were just wishing that someone would come and tell us the truth and here you are! You're the answer to our prayer—isn't he, Anne-Marie?"

"Yes indeed." Still smiling, she looked away, mainly to hide the avidity in her eyes. She'd spent a frantic half hour blundering home from the magazine, only to pass the rest of the night berating herself for cowardice. She'd run at the first sign of trouble, which wasn't like her at all. Had she been afraid of the gunfire, or had it been that man? That man. If she closed her eyes now she knew she'd be able to feel the hard length of his body pinning her to the floor, and she didn't like that feeling. She didn't like it at all.

"They attacked at four this morning," Massey began. "Our spies had told us that they'd be coming, so we were prepared for everything except the magazine caper—"

"Magazine caper?" Anne-Marie broke in.

"How nice!" Massey's face dissolved in pleasure as Catherine reappeared bearing a platter of assorted meats, such as were rarely seen in the city these days of the siege. "And your wonderful Burgundy!" he added, catching sight of the bottle of wine. He held his glass to be filled, smacking his lips as he drank. "Here's to the victorious partnership of Great Britain and Canada!"

"Here, here!" echoed the sieur.

Anne-Marie was not drinking. "You were saying?" she urged.

"They attacked in three columns." Massey's words were thickened by a mouthful of meat. "One came across the plains up above, the other two came from two different directions down below. All three were supposed to be simultaneous, but as usual the Americans made a mess of things. The three attacks were hopelessly piecemeal, which meant that we were able to pick them off like sitting ducks."

He paused long enough to swallow and refill his mouth, then he continued. "General Montgomery and all his aides were killed in the first round of fire, after which his own men ran off and left the bodies there. We've got Montgomery's body up at the Ursulines."

"What about Colonel Arnold?"

"He was shot, too, but I don't know if he's dead. He was carried away by a small party of his men, while the rest managed to get themselves trapped between two barricades down in the Lower Town. We took about four hundred of them prisoner and those who got away are probably running back to Boston right now with their tails between their legs. What is this—venison? Excellent, excellent!"

"And the magazine caper?" Anne-Marie repeated doggedly.

Massey paused long enough to swallow. "A bold but a foolhardy plot—happily for us. Someone from the city guided a group of Americans up to the powder magazine near the Saint Louis gate. As near as we can guess, their goal was to steal enough powder to blow up the gate, but they never got there before they were caught. We're holding four of them prisoner. The fifth one is dead."

"Dead!" exclaimed Anne-Marie.

"Do you have the one who let them in?" the sieur asked.

"Not yet." Massey shook his head as he helped himself to more wine. "Sieur?"

"Yes, thank you." Saint Vallier held out his glass. "Any clues as to who he may be?"

"Not yet, but we will. With the right sort of coaxing, no doubt one of the four Americans will oblige, and in the meantime we'll be on the lookout for anyone trying to leave. We've held on to our city and we'll get our man. To triumph!" he toasted, lifting his refilled glass.

"To triumph!" the sieur echoed, and the two men drank while Anne-Marie swallowed the lump of panic rising in her throat. Only one of the five men had seen her. That one, with the dark eyes. What if he told them? They'd hang her as a spy! But maybe he couldn't tell them, maybe he was dead. One of the five had been killed; maybe it was him. She knew she ought to hope so, but she could not. Instead the thought of him dying sent cold chills down her spine. Not knowing was the worst part. What was she going to do?

Massey drained his second glass and the sieur offered him a third.

"I can't," he said with true regret. "I've already stayed too long. They've got all the wounded prisoners over at the hospital and General Carleton wants me to go over there to be sure they're being treated like proper royalty and not like the laborers and tradesmen—and enemies—they are!"

Anne-Marie was still too agitated to react, but the sieur raised a brow at Massey's bitter words. "You don't think they should be well treated?"

"Oh yes, of course I do. You know me. You know how much I respect the general. He snatched this city out of the jaws of the Americans and now he's kept it safe from them.

But I wish he wouldn't be so soft on the Americans. This fighting isn't about any legitimate border dispute. This rebellion is out-and-out treason and I think it ought to be treated that way! Carleton's willing to hang the spy who broke into the magazine, but he'll spare the Americans he led. It doesn't make any sense.''

"Maybe it does," said Saint Vallier in his mildest tone. "A dozen years ago, when England took Canada from France, she might have treated us harshly, but she did not, and now we join with her in a common cause against the Americans. No doubt Carleton believes the same policy should be pursued with the Americans. Once they realize that they cannot win this war, the general's kindness will provide the groundwork for reconciliation and future peace."

"Maybe," Massey allowed, pushing back his chair. "But not every Canadian is as loyal as you and Mademoiselle Doucet. There are plenty of Canadians who didn't help us. If they had, Montgomery wouldn't have taken Montreal. And despite all of Carleton's kindness, there are still spies in this very city who would stab us in the back."

"But not for long," Saint Vallier said comfortingly, rising with his guest.

Anne-Marie rose with them. "Captain Massey, I'd like to go along." She spoke so abruptly that both men turned to her.

"Like to go where?" asked Massey.

"To see the prisoners. You said that you were going and I'd like to go along. If you don't mind," she added, flashing him the smile that never failed to get her what she wanted from a man.

Massey tried to resist it. He gave her an appraising look. "It won't be very pretty."

"I'm not afraid. And if I see something that upsets me, I'll look at you." What am I doing? she wondered, smiling at him again. If that man is there and if he sees me, I'll be walking right into his hands. He can point me out to Massey and then what will I do?

But the thought of not knowing—of hiding—was infinitely worse, especially after the way she'd skittered off like a guinea hen last night. "Please?" she entreated.

Massey relented. "I suppose it wouldn't hurt. What about you, Saint Vallier?" he added, to be polite.

The sieur appeared astonished that he would even ask. "What—go out in this snow and cold to look at wounded men? No, I'll stay right here and later perhaps you'll come back and we'll open another bottle of wine and play a game of chess. The wind is blowing. Dress warmly, Anne-Marie."

The colors were blurry and so were the sounds: murmurings and moanings and shufflings mixed in with the swishing of skirts. Skirts? Eli wondered vaguely, watching the colors swirl. The browns and the reds receded and the blacks and whites came near. A face floated above him, thin lips, a pointed nose, dark eyes and eyebrows all encased in a circle of flesh. No ears, no hair, no body; then he saw the hands, also disembodied, holding out a bowl.

"Monsieur?" the lips murmured. French. She was speaking French. He wasn't dreaming and the woman was a nun.

He let his breath out slowly. "I thought I'd died and gone to heaven—and it was Catholic." He smiled weakly.

The nun didn't smile back. She held the bowl closer; it was steaming and smelled very good. He nodded his head to show that he was willing, so she set down the bowl, propped up his head on the pillows, then held the spoon to his mouth.

He spilled most of the first spoonful but got a fair amount of the rest. "Where am I?" he asked her when he'd had enough.

"They don't speak English," a hoarse voice said to his right. It belonged to the man in the next bed, whose head was thickly bandaged and whose pale cheek was bisected by a long streak of dried blood. Beyond his, there were more beds, all filled with wounded men.

"Where are we?" asked Eli.

"It's a hospital," said the man. "It's called the Hôtel Dieu. We're in Quebec City."

Eli remembered that much. The nun had taken the empty bowl and moved on to the next bed. As Eli turned to watch her, his neighbor spoke again. "I'm sorry, I didn't hear you," Eli said, turning back.

"I said I guess they got your arm."

His right arm was splinted. So was his left leg. "I . . . I really don't remember."

"You're lucky," his neighbor said. "Me, I lay there for four hours wondering if I'd freeze before I bled to death. Guess I didn't do neither, but it was mighty close. By the time the redcoats found me I was so covered up with snow I wouldn't have blamed them if they'd taken me for a drift." He patted the mattress on which he was lying. "I ain't saying I'm glad I was took, but still, I ain't slept in a bed since I left home six months ago. Back in Cambridge, when I took sick, they laid me on the ground."

"Who were you with last night?"

"Colonel Arnold," he said. "I marched with him from Cambridge, straight up through the Kennebec—three hundred miles of uncharted land, some of it places no white man has ever seen. It's a miracle we ever made it—those of us what did. But it's too bad we couldn't drag our artillery along or we could have taken this damn city the day we arrived, 'stead of having to wait around for Montgomery to get here from Montreal."

The man's eyes closed briefly. "They got him, you know."

"Who—Montgomery?"

The blood-streaked face hardened. "Killed him in the Lower Town. They got Arnold, too, in the leg. He was bleeding pretty bad when they took him away."

"What about the others? Did anyone get through?"

"We could have," the man said bitterly. "We come through the first barricade and we could have come through the second if'n we'd set it afire, but the officers said if we did that we'd keep Montgomery from getting through. Montgomery!" He snorted in despair. "By that time he was dead and those girls he had for troops was all scrambling back to camp. So there we was and the redcoats caught us— came out the Palace Gate and around behind us, bottled us in that stinking street like a bunch of rats!"

"Were there any Grants men with you?" Eli was thinking of his brother, Zeke, and the other Green Mountain Boys from his regiment.

"Can't say either way, but you'll find out by and by—if they ain't been shipped off to England before we get out. What about you? Where'd they get you?"

"In the Upper Town."

"No kiddin'!" The man whistled. "How'd you get up there?"

"It's a long story." Too long, at least for his present state of pain and fatigue. Closing his eyes, Eli felt the frigid wind again and shivered in the cold damp of the magazine. He saw the rows of barrels and smelled the sharp powder smell. Then he saw the woman with her pale face and lustrous hair.

His arm and his leg were aching, clouding up his thoughts. That face. Where did it come from, and what was it doing mixed up with his memory of last night? He pushed his mind backward to the trek below the wall, the rope up through the window, the trip to the Upper Town. The guards, the barrels... There was that woman again. Something about a slow match and a struggle over a gun.

What gun? he wondered, sinking toward welcome sleep. What slow match? What woman? That silky flow of hair. That lush, writhing body. The faintest hint of scent. A dream, he was thinking. A vivid fever dream. It scattered into fragments as he drifted toward the dark.

* * *

He didn't know how long he'd been sleeping when he was shaken awake by the sound of a man's voice speaking somewhere nearby.

"...proved their worth in the French and Indian wars—or should I say that they proved their worthlessness!" The voice grew louder as it approached. "Back then, when we fought together, the Americans were always the first to break and run, and I guess last night's debacle shows they haven't changed. Mark my words, *mademoiselle,* this so-called revolution will be over before next winter begins."

"They didn't run in Montreal," observed a softer voice. "Or when they met your troops in Boston, according to the reports."

That second voice was familiar. Eli opened his eyes and found himself staring at the scarlet of a British officer's coat. The officer and his companion were walking the length of the ward, the officer declaiming with his hands behind his back. Of the woman who was his companion, Eli could see only the hem of her skirts. The officer's considerable girth blocked the rest of her from his view.

"Flukes!" the officer said harshly as they came even with Eli's bed. "In Boston and Montreal they caught us unprepared. But once we've gathered our reinforcements, we'll beat them back. You'll see," he promised as he passed the bed.

The woman passed with him, but after she did, she glanced back. Her eyes skimmed over Eli, moved on, then jerked back again—or so it seemed to Eli, frozen in shock as he was. She was the woman, the one from his fever dream—the one who writhed beneath him, with the masses of silky hair! That hair was primly bound now and tucked beneath the collar of her cloak, but as much of it as was showing was a bright coppery brown, and her eyes fixed upon him were a cool silver gray.

The officer was droning on about the Americans. He'd pulled ahead of the woman and she must have realized, because she turned quickly and hurried after him. Eli continued watching as they moved down the aisle. A few beds farther along, she turned to look back again.

He watched her retreating back, shocked even beyond awareness of the aching of his wounds. Had she known him? Was that why she had stopped? If he hadn't met her somewhere, how had she gotten into his dream? He waited for her to look back as she moved down the ward, but she kept her eyes forward until she'd reached the door, which the officer held open for her to pass from the room. But no more than a minute later she reappeared alone, coming down the aisle quickly to stop beside Eli's bed.

"*Monsieur,* you were looking at me strangely. I would like to know the reason why?" Her voice, though low and urgent, held a defiant note—the same note he remembered from his fever dream.

"I—I'm not sure," Eli answered. It was hard to think clearly with her standing so near. She was so close that he could have touched her only by moving his uninjured hand. His dream hadn't done her justice: she was magnificent. "Maybe we've met somehow...?" Maybe before the war?

She shook her head vehemently, dislodging a curl of bright hair. "No, *monsieur,* you are mistaken. I am certain I have never seen you before. Never," she repeated, and turned to leave.

Without thinking, he reached out to grab her as he had in the dream, and he heard her startled gasp as his hand closed on her wrist. She glanced beyond him quickly, down the long aisle of the ward. "*Monsieur,* what are you doing? Let me go!"

"Not yet," Eli said. He didn't want her to go until he understood. "I must have seen you somewhere."

Again she shook her head, her attention darting to his bandages and back. "*Monsieur* has been wounded. Sometimes the pain causes the mind to drift. I am sorry if *monsieur* is confused, but you must let me go. If not, I will have to call the guard and *monsieur* would not like that," she said, twisting her arm.

His weakness and his position kept him from holding on. In an instant his hand was empty and she was hurrying down the aisle, the tap-tapping of her heels echoing beneath the vaulted roof. Sweating from his exertion, Eli watched her go.

Had he been dreaming? No matter what she said, he couldn't have imagined that face. Where had he seen her? He shook his head. If he wasn't so fuddled from the pain and the drugs, he knew he could figure it out. In the meantime he had nothing but the memory of her clear eyes and her rapid-fire voice. In a few days, when he felt better, no doubt he would understand. But now he had no choice but to drift and sleep.

He was still watching the doorway when the nun reappeared with a wooden tray of steaming broth for the prisoners.

Chapter Three

"Here is the list of the prisoners as you requested, sir." Massey clicked his heels as he handed the written sheets to General Carleton. "Four hundred and twenty-six, counting officers and men. About eighty of them are still in the hospital. From what our spies tell us that's a good third of their men, and what's left would probably turn tail and run like rabbits if we came out after them."

"No doubt," murmured Carleton, accepting the lists and taking them to the window, where there was better light. Two days after the battle the snow had stopped falling, but the wind was still restless and the sky an unfriendly gray.

Massey watched Carleton's powdered head bend to the columns of names. In Carleton's position he would have gone after the Americans two days ago and made his reputation as the man who'd saved Canada by bringing those upstarts into line. But Carleton wouldn't do it because he was afraid that taking the offensive might stiffen the rebels' resolve. He wanted to kill them with kindness instead. In Massey's opinion it would be better to kill them with grapeshot and be done with this so-called revolution, instead of wasting everybody's time playing footsie with a bunch of farmers and shopkeepers, which was really all the Americans were.

Carleton wasn't skimming the lists, he was reading every name. Massey's eyes drifted to the window and his mind to

Anne-Marie Doucet. According to local gossip, men had been following her in droves since she'd come of age, and the most they'd gotten for their devotion had been a mouthful of the Canadian dust kicked up by her heels. But since he'd met her in mid-November she'd been feminine charm itself, which he couldn't help but take as a personal compliment.

He wondered what his mother would say to a popish daughter-in-law. But Anne-Marie wasn't really popish, if Saint Vallier could be believed, and there was no reason to think he could not—apart from the obvious fact of his being French. Yet some Frenchmen were almost as trustworthy as their English counterparts.

According to Saint Vallier, Anne-Marie's father had been not only English but a member of the Queen's Own Buffs. He'd been posted to Nova Scotia—or Acadia, as the French had called it when it was theirs—sometime before the last of the French and Indian Wars. He'd met and married Anne-Marie's mother and they'd had Anne-Marie, but unfortunately he'd died just before the last war had begun and Lawrence had deported the entire Acadian population to keep them from giving secret aid to the French.

Without the father to protect them, Anne-Marie and her family had been swept up with the rest. An older brother had disappeared and Anne-Marie and her mother had spent several unpleasant years wandering about before finding their way to Quebec and Saint Vallier. Admittedly, the experience couldn't have been much fun, but on the other hand, Anne-Marie's father had been a lowly sergeant in the Buffs, while Saint Vallier was a lord whose estate she would most likely inherit when he died. So one could say that the adventure had worked out to her benefit—and also to the benefit of the man who married her.

Carleton looked up from his reading with a pensive frown. "One of the names on this list seems to ring a bell, though I can't quite remember why. Where's the file of my correspondence with America?"

Massey produced the file and watched as Carleton thumbed through the sheets one by one.

"Here it is!" he declared, holding a letter up. "Lieutenant Eli Brownell. Only he wasn't a lieutenant when this was written. He was just plain Eli Brownell last June when he appeared before the Continental Congress along with a delegation from the New Hampshire Grants for the express purpose of securing the Congress's permission for the Grants to form their own regiment."

"The Green Mountain Boys," said Massey.

"The Green Mountain Boys," Carleton agreed. "Who had already been formed and fighting since '71."

"But not fighting England."

"No, they'd been fighting New York, over land both sides insisted that they owned. New York said the land was hers, but the Green Mountain Boys claimed that New Hampshire had owned it and had sold it to them."

"Didn't the king issue a ruling?"

"He most certainly did. He said that the Grants—as the land came to be called—had always belonged to New York. The Green Mountain Boys didn't like that. King or no king, they meant to hang on to that land, so they formed themselves into a renegade army to keep the New Yorkers off it by force."

"I've heard they were holy terrors."

"They still are." Carleton sighed. "Only now they've declared a truce with the New Yorkers and they've become a terror to us, which is a great pity. If the Boys weren't fighting England, they'd be damned useful to us. And we, Captain Massey, could be damned useful to them."

Carleton tapped the letter he was holding. "Listen to this. According to my correspondent, Brownell and his friends didn't go all the way to Philadelphia just to ask for a Grants regiment. Their real purpose was to gauge Congress's support for the Grants declaring itself a separate colony, independent of both New Hampshire and New York."

"How much support was there?"

"Not enough," Carleton said. "New York is dead set against it and Congress can't afford to alienate New York. So I was thinking..." Carleton's voice trailed off, then shifted briskly to a different thought. "According to this list, Brownell is recovering from wounds."

"Yes, sir. He was injured by grapeshot through both his arm and his leg. He led the party that broke into the magazine. He's also got a brother—"

"Yes, by the name of Zeke. He's the hell-raiser, but Eli is the brains and it's the brains I need for what I've got in mind. As soon as Brownell is recovered enough to be moved I want him transferred to a private home."

"What sort of a home, sir?"

"A good one." Carleton was pacing the floor, looking from window to window but thinking of something else. All at once he snapped his fingers. "I know. Saint Vallier. I want Brownell quartered with the Sieur de Saint Vallier."

"Saint Vallier?" Massey repeated, thinking of Anne-Marie and trying to dredge Brownell's face out of the rows of wounded men. Not that it really mattered what Brownell looked like, since he couldn't imagine Anne-Marie taking an interest in an American, especially one of the rabble-rousers of the Green Mountain Boys. And if Brownell was housed there he'd have to check up on him, which would give him an excuse to call as often as he pleased.

Carleton was speaking. "Check the hall for eavesdroppers, then lock the door and I'll tell you what I've got in mind."

"A prisoner?" Anne-Marie held her hands out to the warmth of the fire. She'd just come back from calling on Madame Arsenault, whose husband was the city's most powerful and most secret pro-American. It was he who had assigned her as the guide to the magazine, and she'd called on him to apologize for having let him down. Monsieur Arsenault had assured her there was nothing she could have done and that he'd let her know her next assignment once he'd reestablished contact with the depleted Americans. "A prisoner staying with us? What sort of a prisoner?"

"An officer," said the sieur. "He's also a lawyer, which comes as a relief, since I understand the Americans are led by hairdressers and butchers—useful trades, to be sure, but not quite what one would hope for in a long-term guest. And he must be something special or General Carleton wouldn't want him here. Captain Massey was not any more specific about the man, however.

"By the way, Captain Massey was very sorry to have missed you when he called and made me promise to tell you that he hopes he will see you tomorrow morning when he comes with the prisoner." Saint Vallier looked at Anne-Marie fondly. "It gives me such pleasure to see you receiving your beaux instead of mocking their peculiarities then locking yourself in your room."

"You always laughed at my imitations."

"They were hilarious. But I would give up more than laughter to see you let go of the past. I don't mean for you to forget your poor mother or your heritage, but when you hold in resentment too long it festers like a sore. In the end, forgiving your enemies is the thing that sets you free." He patted her shoulder.

She cringed inwardly with guilt. She'd deceived him and he'd always been so good. But forgive the English? Not in a million years! If she thought it would help free Canada, she'd kill Massey with her own two hands. She didn't feel much fonder of the Americans, but she'd do what she could to aid them in throwing the British out, not just from Quebec but also from Acadia. Then she'd find her lost brother, François, and they'd go home and reclaim their farm. That had been her dream since she'd been old enough to think, and not all the sieur's kindness could make her give that up. Never, no never, so long as she was alive! She meant to have both her revenge and her heritage.

"There's something else," said Saint Vallier, breaking into her thoughts.

"Something?"

"About our prisoner. According to Captain Massey, he was the leader of the raid on the magazine. He was wounded during his capture and at the moment he can't walk, but even so, Massey asks that we put him in a room we can make secure. I was thinking of the blue room at the end of the second floor—or do you think it's too small? The green room is larger, but there's a portico beneath the window, and when his wounds are mended I suppose he could climb down onto it. What do you think, my dear?"

But Anne-Marie wasn't thinking of rooms. Her mouth was hanging open as she gaped at Saint Vallier. It couldn't be! she was thinking, but at the same time she knew that it was, which brought back all too clearly that hand around her wrist and that low voice raising gooseflesh on her neck. She hadn't told Monsieur Arsenault about the American. Blowing up the magazine had been her own impulsive idea, and if he knew she'd even tried it, he'd probably never trust her again. Besides, she'd been hoping that the American had believed her story about a fever dream, mainly because she had no alternative. If he did accuse her, she'd planned to deny it up and down, supported by her reputation and Massey and the sieur. But now...

Despite the warmth of the fire, she shuddered with sudden violence. Of all the American prisoners, why were they sending him? Was it merely an awful coincidence, or had he already told? Did Carleton suspect her— And Massey! How much did Massey know?

The sieur saw her shudder and reached out to touch her arm. "My dear—"

Caught in her mounting panic, she clutched at his hand. "No! No! You can't let them! You can't let them bring him here!"

"Anne-Marie, what is it?"

"You can't let them bring that man here! Please, please don't let them!"

"My dear, what are you saying? What is it? Are you ill?"

Ill! In the midst of the maelstrom, she seized upon the word. "That's it! That's what I'm afraid of!"

"What is?"

"Falling ill! I've heard that smallpox is sweeping through the Americans. If this man has had it, he could pass it on to us. You could die—we can't risk it! When you were ill with pneumonia last spring I was beside myself, and you know the doctor says you're still not very strong. We can't risk it. Please say you won't let them!"

His hand was stroking hers. "Poor Anne-Marie, I can see that you're upset. You've forgotten that we were inoculated by that Swedish doctor two years ago. We both had the symptoms, which means that we're immune. If you're worried about infection, you can keep away from him, and if he does get it, we can send him back. But we can't refuse him. We'd be insulting General Carleton if we did. You know we would," he said gently.

She knew that he was right, and that she'd only arouse his suspicion if she continued to object. Maybe it was just an awful coincidence, and if it wasn't, her best hope was to face the American and deny whatever he said. Her trying to avoid him could easily look like guilt. But to live in the same house with that voice and those eyes . . .

"Having him with us might even be nice," mused the sieur, following his own train of thought. "If he's a lawyer, he probably plays chess, which would be cozy on these long winter nights. And, oh, I forgot to tell you. Massey told me his name. It's Brownell. Eli Brownell. How very American!"

Brownell. Eli Brownell. Anne-Marie stifled a groan. Knowing his name somehow made everything more real. Calm down, she cautioned herself silently. You've gotten yourself into an uproar and you're thinking the worst. You're treating him as though he's a monster, but he's not.

He's only a man and you've been handling men all your
life. You'll treat him just the way you did at the hospital.
You'll deny his accusations and the sieur will swear that you
were home on the night of the attack. When Carleton re-
alizes that he's lying, they'll take Eli Brownell away. Maybe
they'll hang him as a spy or maybe they won't, but either
way you'll be safe. The thing is to be calm until you know
what's what. Get a good night's sleep and in the morning
you'll be ready for anything.

That night she slept terribly, when she slept at all,
dreaming of endless chases through narrow, snow-covered
streets. Her head was aching the next morning at nine as she
took her place beside the sieur to watch Eli Brownell being
carried up the front steps from the cariole, as the brightly
painted wooden sleds were called in Quebec. Massey led the
procession, halting the orderlies with the stretcher in the
front hall so that the prisoner could be properly introduced.

"The Sieur de Saint Vallier and Mademoiselle Doucet."

"Very pleased to meet you," Eli was saying as his eyes
came to Anne-Marie. For the first instant they remained
coolly impersonal, but when he recognized her they re-
layed shock. "Mademoiselle..."

"Doucet," she repeated, her voice commendably calm.
He wasn't faking his reaction, he was genuinely surprised.
He hadn't known whose house he was coming to, which
meant that he hadn't betrayed her to Carleton. Not yet, in
any case.

He had already recovered but his eyes hadn't left her
face. "Doucet," he said slowly. "I don't believe I've heard
the name, and yet I have the strangest feeling that I have
seen the face. What makes me think that Mademoiselle
Doucet and I have already met?"

"I couldn't say," sniffed Massey, rocking back on his
heels.

Meanwhile, Anne-Marie's body had frozen into ice. Was this why they had brought him? Was it to happen right here?

"I'm sure," Eli said slowly, his eyes fixed on her face.

Anne-Marie's heart ceased beating. She knew she ought to deny it, but she couldn't speak.

"Perhaps it will come to you later," suggested Saint Vallier. "In the meantime you will be more comfortable settled in your room."

"Up you go," Massey said to the orderlies, nodding them in the direction of the stairs.

Go! Anne-Marie was praying. Go now, before he speaks.

The orderlies started moving. Eli's cool voice rang out. "Wait. I've got it. I've just remembered where we met." He paused. They all waited. "It was in the hospital. Mademoiselle Doucet was walking through the ward."

She thought her legs would buckle purely from relief. "That's right," she said faintly, touching Massey's arm. "Remember, you took me with you to see the prisoners."

Her legs were still shaking as the orderlies carried the stretcher upstairs, but a hot wash of anger was already replacing her fear. Of course the whole scene might have been innocent, but she had the feeling that it hadn't been. She believed he'd scared her on purpose, and if he had, that meant he knew that she wasn't any delusion from a fever dream. He knew and, damn him, he was playing games with her! Right now he was probably upstairs laughing himself silly about how badly he had frightened her. And she had let herself be frightened like a brainless goose, not only this morning but the other two times they'd met.

Damn him! she repeated, resolving to make up lost ground and show him once and forever just who was in control. She didn't know why he'd been sent here, but she meant to find out and she meant to teach him the meaning of self-defense.

Meanwhile, as always, the sieur was coaxing Massey to stay. "You're sure you couldn't, not even for one glass?"

Massey looked regretful. "I wish I could, but I'll join you later when I come back to see Brownell."

"Why not stay and see him now?"

"I've got another appointment at ten. Besides, I thought I'd wait to let Brownell get settled in before I delivered Carleton's message. Until then, *mademoiselle.*"

But Anne-Marie couldn't let Massey get away until she'd discovered how much he knew. She tucked her hand firmly beneath his bulky arm. "If you're leaving, Captain, I'll walk you to the cariole."

"You'll catch cold," the sieur cautioned.

"Captain Massey will keep me warm!" Before the sieur could say more, she'd bustled him out the door.

"I hope you don't mind the inconvenience of having to put up with Brownell." Massey's polished boots crunched on the freshly packed snow and his words rolled from his thick lips in great gusts of steam.

"I'm happy to help," she lied. "I know that General Carleton wouldn't have asked unless he had a very good reason for wanting Lieutenant Brownell to be at our house."

"A very good reason," Massey agreed.

Goodness, would he tell her nothing? Desperate, she pressed on. "A very *good* reason or a very *secret* one?" She fluttered her lashes and made her voice teasing as she squeezed his arm. "I can't imagine such an undistinguished-looking man as Lieutenant Brownell being so important to you."

"He isn't much to look at," Massey agreed, obviously pleased. "But believe it or not, he could be of great use to us—and Carleton's convinced that if we treat him well, he'll give us what we want. I know it won't be amusing to have someone like him in your house, and I do appreciate you being so gracious about this—you and the sieur both. I'll try to make up for the burden by calling as often as I can."

"How lovely!" She smiled, silently groaning inside. Both Massey and Eli Brownell—how would she survive? From what Massey had said, she could guess exactly what Carleton wanted from their guest. How would she keep Eli Brownell from betraying her?

"Brrr!" Massey shivered. Despite all the flesh he had to keep him warm, he hated the Canadian cold. "You'd better get back inside before you freeze! Tell the sieur I'll be back as soon as I can manage it."

"He'll be so happy," she assured him, and ran back to the house.

The sieur was in the hall, watching the orderlies bringing the empty stretcher down the stairs. "Watch the wainscoting," he cautioned as they came. "He seems rather well-spoken," he added to Anne-Marie. "When he's settled perhaps I'll go up and ask him if he plays chess."

"I could ask him," she offered.

"Don't tell me you're going up? I thought you were afraid of smallpox."

"As you yourself pointed out, we have nothing to fear. And I promised Captain Massey..." This was not quite a lie.

The sieur smiled with pleasure. "Good girl," he approved. "You may even find him amusing if you give him half a chance."

She opened her mouth to respond to that but really there was no point. She settled for shrugging her shoulders as she started up the stairs.

The blue room, where they'd put him, was at the end of the hall, two doors beyond hers. It was locked from the outside, so she turned the key and went in. She couldn't see him clearly past the hangings that draped the bed. She shut the door and moved up closer.

"Lieutenant?"

He didn't answer. She realized that he was asleep, his splinted arm lying outside the covers and his bandaged leg making an awkward lump underneath. At the sight of his wounds, she suffered an unexpected pang of guilt. None of this would be happening if she hadn't run away. If she'd stayed with him instead of bolting away from the magazine, she might have led him to a safe hiding place then smuggled him out of the city and back to the Americans. If she hadn't panicked, he wouldn't be here today and she wouldn't be in danger of being exposed as a spy.

The gray light from the window illuminated his sleeping face. In it she saw reflected not only the strain of his wounds but the harshness of the conditions of the American camp. She doubted his face had been so thin a year ago, or the line of his jaw so sharp. She wondered if the scar above his right eyebrow had come from this fighting or before.

The nuns must have shaved him but they hadn't cut his hair, which was thick and ragged and as dark as the fringe of lashes lying against his cheek. Thin lines of exhaustion traced the edges of his mouth and left smudges beneath his eyes, and the bridge of his nose listed a little bit to the right as if it had once been broken.

Thin as his face was, and tired and scarred, it was nevertheless handsome, almost disturbingly so. Standing in the dim room three feet away from the bed, she felt the same irrational fear she'd felt at the hospital, a fear that went beyond betrayal, to something she couldn't name. She felt that now familiar warning prickle down the length of her spine.

The smart thing to do would be to leave. Holding her skirts to keep them quiet, she took a backward step. She'd come and see him later when he was awake. There was no point in having him open his eyes to find her gawking at him. She moved silently backward until she reached the door. She'd already twisted the doorknob when suddenly he spoke.

"What do you want?"

She was so startled she actually jumped and let go of the door. But in the very next moment the rush of her anger returned. *What do you want?* he had asked her in that imperious cool voice—as if he were the master of this house and she were some sort of sneak!

His eyes were open as she stalked back to the bed, reining in her anger, which wouldn't help with him. "I am sorry if *monsieur* was sleeping and I awakened him. I came to be sure that the servants had made him comfortable."

"Did you?" His eyes looked at her slowly and carefully up and down, but with none of the appreciation she was accustomed to from men. "Captain Massey described my hostess as a proper Canadian lady, so you were the last person I was expecting to see. I'd be interested to know your role in my being here."

"*Monsieur* has the mistaken impression—"

"Save it." He cut her off. "That day in the hospital I was groggy from the drugs so I half believed what you said. The whole thing was so fantastic, I believed I'd made it up."

"I'm sorry that I do not know what *monsieur* is referring to."

"It's not *monsieur,* it's lieutenant, and you damn well do know. You let us into the city and you led us up to the magazine—and you would have blown us sky-high if I hadn't stopped you. I've had a lot of time for thinking since that night, enough to be sure of what's real and what's not. I'm not interested in hearing any more of your denying the truth. What I want to know is why you're denying it."

"Because I don't trust you!" she was about to explode, but she caught herself just in time and bit back the response. "*Monsieur*—that is, Lieutenant—we Quebecois take great pride in our hospitality. General Carleton wishes for us to take you in, so we welcome you in our home. If there is anything you need to make yourself comfortable, I hope you will not hesitate to ask."

"Anything?" he repeated as one dark eyebrow rose. "What about a ride back to Colonel Arnold's camp?"

"Pah!" She let her guard down and spoke with frank disgust. "From what I've heard about conditions in the

American camp, I assure you that you will be far more comfortable here."

"That depends on your idea of comfort." His eyes left her to glance around the room, and brief as his survey was, she had the feeling that when he'd finished he would be able to close his eyes and describe it, right down to the little blue Chinese vase on the mantelpiece. She didn't think there was much that Eli Brownell missed and that increased her feeling that he was dangerous. But the last thing she intended was to show him her fear.

"I hope that this room suits you," she said sarcastically.

His eyes swung back to hers abruptly. "Why did you light that match?"

The question was so sudden she'd opened her mouth to answer before she saw the trap. "*Monsieur,* really! I wish you'd let this go. All this useless question and answer is becoming tedious!"

"Lieutenant," he corrected. "Are you afraid that I'll turn you in? Is that it?"

Anne-Marie tossed her head. "Is it the habit of all *Bostonnais* to be so rude?"

"It's our habit to be honest," he fired back, while his cool dark eyes bored into hers. He wasn't at all like the other men she knew—like Massey and the others, who buzzed around her like gnats. If other men were insects, this one was a wildcat who paralyzed her with his stare as he moved in for the kill. She wanted to step backward, but she wouldn't let herself. Then his spell was broken by a chorus of sleigh bells in the street below.

Released, she went to look out the window.

"What is it?" Eli asked.

"A procession. A funeral."

"Probably for General Montgomery. They're burying him today. The troops will miss him. He was a good general."

"Then for his sake I hope he died before he saw the men he was leading turn and run like frightened sheep!" She spoke with anger and scorn, her eyes on the carioles, the first of which held the coffin and the second Lieutenant Governor Cramahé and General Carleton. She looked for Massey but didn't see him.

Eli spoke from the bed. "I suppose you would have stayed there to face the cannon fire."

"I would have done my duty, knowing others depended upon me."

"Is that what you were doing when you lit that fuse?"

She whirled back in frustration. "I didn't! I told you before—"

"And we both know that you're lying."

"How dare you call me a liar!" She was so angry she practically yelled.

"You're a liar," he said calmly.

She wanted to strangle him. "And you, *monsieur*, are a—a—" Groping for the right word, she advanced toward the bed, foolishly forgetting the lesson he'd already taught her twice. And sure enough, as soon as she was close enough, his good hand shot out and clamped around her wrist.

"Deny it," he dared her, pulling her close to him. "Look me in the eye and deny it."

"Let me go!" She pulled away as she had the last time, but this time he had enough strength to hold on.

"Look at me," he repeated, his voice harsh and low.

They were so close she could feel his breath upon her skin when she turned toward him. His eyes were almost black, and in some way she couldn't fathom his gaze was both cold and hot at the same time.

"Let me go!" she whispered, or at least she thought she did. But maybe she didn't, because he made no response, just kept holding her, and staring at her with those haunting eyes.

The tingle of warning was rushing up and down her spine and her heart was pounding so hard she thought it would crack her ribs. Something was happening that she'd never felt before, something overwhelming and dangerous. She remembered vaguely that she had meant to take control, but at this moment control was nothing more than a tiny dot dissolving in his eyes.

She felt her eyes drawn lower. They faltered and moved to his lips. Her own lips parted slightly. She was thinking about a kiss. In the midst of this nightmare, she was thinking about a kiss! She was thinking of kissing this monster who might betray her as a spy! The shock shot through her with a force that jerked her arm hard enough to break his hold.

She was panting as if she'd been racing and her whole body was quivering.

"I do deny it!" she whispered, and she whirled and ran out of the room in such a hurry that she almost forgot to lock the door. It was hours later, when the sieur brought it up, that she realized she'd neglected to ask the prisoner about playing chess.

Flat on his back and sweating with pain, Eli was panting, too. The move and this last exertion had aggravated the ache in his arm and the razor-sharp knives that sliced up and down his leg. They'd left his medicine on the dresser where it was out of reach. If he rang the bellrope he wondered who would come. Certainly not Mademoiselle Doucet, not after what he'd just done.

He closed his eyes and remembered the tremor that had passed from her body into his. She was wilder than he'd remembered; he supposed he ought to feel glad that he'd managed to grab her gun that night, because if he hadn't he didn't doubt they'd both be dead today. One thing was for certain: no matter what she said, she'd been the silk-haired fury he'd struggled with on the floor of the magazine.

Why was she so adamant in denying the truth? Was she afraid that he'd betray her, or was it something else? She'd never answered his question about whether she'd had any role in his being sent to this house. Could it have been her doing, and if so, to what end? Why had she run off so quickly on the night of the attack? She didn't strike him as a coward—unstable and impetuous, but not cowardly. Could she have had some other reason to flee? Was she working for the British as well as for the Americans?

The key grated in the lock. A servant, he thought with relief, casting a longing glance toward the medicine, and yet in the back of his mind he was thinking of *mademoiselle,* seeing that pale creamy skin and those wide silver eyes.

It was neither. It was Captain Massey. He must have left his coat downstairs and he was wearing a dress uniform. He shut the door firmly behind him and looked around the room.

"Nice." He nodded, taking in the hangings and the ornaments. "They've set you up very nicely, and the sieur will also feed you well."

I'll bet he's fed you well, too, Eli thought to himself, and wondered how far the captain had gotten with *mademoiselle.* Stop it, he cautioned. There was no point to that line of inquiry. Besides which, he had other, much more important concerns. Massey was waiting for him to say something, so he said, "What does Carleton want?"

At his bluntness, Massey's broad nostrils flared, though whether in approval or objection, Eli couldn't tell. "You have your spies, Brownell, and so do we. We know things about you. We know that you're not only a lieutenant with the Green Mountain Boys. You're also a lawyer and a highly intelligent man."

"You flatter me."

"Yes, perhaps." Massey ignored his sarcasm. "We know that you are not like the other Green Mountain Boys, who like to rush around yelling and firing guns. You've got a sharp mind and you use it, which is why you realize that the British may not be your biggest enemy."

"If not the British, then who?" asked Eli, thinking of Mademoiselle Doucet.

"New York, of course," said Massey, pulling up a chair and making himself comfortable next to Eli's bed. "We know how you petitioned Congress about the New Hampshire Grants becoming a separate colony. New York blocked the petition, and since then, while you've been stuck up here, she's been busy in Philadelphia consolidating her support. By the time you manage to get out of Quebec, Congress declaring the Grants a part of New York will be a fait accompli."

Eli raised one eyebrow. "You speak French. I'm impressed. Permit me to guess the trade Carleton has in mind. If the Green Mountain Boys come over to England's side, Carleton will see that the king makes the Grants a separate colony."

"Who told you?" demanded Massey before he could catch himself.

Eli's eyes glinted. "No one. Remember, I'm highly intelligent. In any case, it doesn't take a genius to see the difference the Grants could make to you right now. The Grants could give you a supply line for marching from Montreal clear down to Albany. Some people believe that's all it will take to beat the colonies. Is that the whole proposition, or is there more?"

"Just one thing," Massey admitted, shifting in his chair. "In addition to your promise of loyalty, the general also wants the name of the man who let you into the city and led you up to the magazine."

"I see." Eli nodded. She couldn't be working for the British, or Massey would know; that meant she must be worried that he'd give her away. Massey was watching him closely. "Suppose I did agree. What makes you think the rest of the Boys would agree to desert the common cause? What makes you think they'd be willing to take up arms against their brothers in the other colonies?"

"Their brothers!" Massey snorted. "Do you think the New Yorkers will ever be brothers with you? And even if they were, do you honestly believe you can beat us without shoes and ammunition, let alone without unity! You've got eyes, Brownell. You saw what happened here on New Year's Eve, and from now on the same thing will happen every time our two armies meet. Your victories at Boston and Montreal were flukes. You caught us off guard, but now we've got our balance and there's no way on God's earth that you can stop us."

He leaned forward toward Eli. "Listen to me, Brownell. At this very moment the king is sending us more troops than the colonies could possibly raise if they drafted every man and boy over the age of fourteen. As soon as the spring thaw comes, we'll have twenty thousand new soldiers, well armed and ready to fight. And what will you have to throw against them? Pox-ridden scarecrows, half of whom don't even have guns! By this time next winter your Rebellion will be history and every man who took up arms against England will be wishing he'd never heard the name George Washington!

"There'll be a new order," Massey continued, his face flushed red, "and if you help us, you'll be at the very top. If the Grants goes with us now, she'll be rewarded then. She'll rise above both New York and New England, and you'll rise with her!" He dragged out his handkerchief to mop his scarlet face.

Propped against the pillows, Eli hadn't moved. "And if I'm fool enough to turn down this marvelous offer?"

Massey stuffed his handkerchief back into his pocket and his pale eyes went hard. "I'm afraid you've been misled by the favor the general has shown you in having you transferred here. You're not our guest, Brownell. You're our prisoner, and you're also a rebel traitor. You're the lawyer—you tell me what that means."

"That if the general chooses, he can send me to England to be tried."

"To be tried and hanged as a traitor! And not only you. We can send your brother, too. Oh yes, in case you were wondering, he's our prisoner, as well. We caught him with

Arnold's men down in the Lower Town. We're holding him with the others at the seminary."

"That must be a treat for his jailors."

"A British soldier does his job." Massey's eyes left Eli to glance around the room. "I've instructed the sieur that your door should be kept locked, though I have no doubt that a locked door will pose only a fleeting problem to a man of your wit and skills. As your condition improves, you may contemplate attempting to escape, so let me make this clear. We are holding your brother as security for you. If you leave this city without permission, he'll be sent to England and tried in your stead. Tried and punished," he added, lest Eli might have misunderstood.

"You've heard our offer." Massey pushed back his chair. "Now it's up to you. For your sake I hope you're as smart as the general thinks you are!"

Eli's leg was throbbing as Massey slammed the door, locked it and stomped off down the hall. He reached for the bellrope, thinking briefly of *mademoiselle* and wondering how much she knew about why he was here.

Then his thoughts switched to Zeke. He knew how his brother would react to Massey's threat. Zeke would roar, "Damn them—let 'em hang me, but don't you give in! If we want our independence, we'll win it for ourselves, and to hell with Carleton's offers and guarantees!" But Zeke was ruled by emotion and spontaneity, whereas Eli had been blessed, or cursed, with the cooler mind—cool enough to realize that on many points what Massey said was true.

He'd been with the army at Cambridge before he'd left for Canada, and a scruffier, sorrier bunch he'd never seen. Two months of camp life had turned respectable farmers into ragamuffin vagabonds who were dying faster from disease and hunger than they had been under enemy fire. The ones who did survive didn't want to stay; when their times of enlistment came up, they wanted to leave. And what could the army offer to make them stay? There was no food, no blankets, no shoes, no pay to send to their families who were starving back at home.

Congress was even worse. He'd been to Philadelphia and he'd seen for himself. Congress was ruled by the petty jealousy of small-minded men who worried more about personal favor than the greater good. And the big-minded ones were dreamers, full of great plans that probably couldn't work even if their fellows weren't constantly voting them down. As for the amorphous "people," as far as Eli could tell, most of them just wanted Parliament to repeal some of the hateful laws, in exchange for which they'd be more than happy to lay down their arms and go back to being ruled by England again.

Shifting his leg in search of comfort, Eli sighed. To an impartial observer, Massey's assessment was right and the odds were that what he'd offered was the best that the Grants could do. But Eli had tried enough cases to know that there was often evidence the impartial observer missed—such as the looks on the women's faces back in Bennington when they'd bid farewell to their men, telling them not to worry and that they'd look out for the farms. Such as his neighbor in the hospital ward, who'd followed Benedict Arnold through the untracked Maine wilderness—through swamps and over mountains that no white man had ever seen, starving and dying but never turning back in the effort to surprise the British and seize Quebec.

He thought again of Zeke. Through the haze of his throbbing wounds he could hear Zeke roaring, "You *what!*" In spite of the pain, he smiled. Life was simple for Zeke: better to hang as a traitor than to make deals with your enemies. Although the odds were against them, you could never tell. Besides, Eli had the habit of supporting the underdog, in part from practice and in part from pure Yankee stubbornness. Unless things changed dramatically, he couldn't accept Carleton's deal, but it wouldn't hurt to string Massey and his master along for as long as possible. Being here and in contact with Carleton, he might be able to gather information that the Americans could use—when and if he managed to get out of here.

He reached for the bellrope. His leg was on fire. As he pulled it he recalled the condition about naming the *mademoiselle*. He wondered if Carleton would settle for that alone. He thought the reverse more likely. Carleton would be willing to forgo learning the name of the spy if Eli would guarantee him the loyalty of the Grants.

At last, someone was coming; the key turned in the lock. Raising his head, Eli saw a red-cheeked maid. He felt a ripple of disappointment, which was lost in a flood of relief, for she could fluff his pillows and give him his medicine, then leave him to the dubious comfort of his pain-racked dreams.

Chapter Four

Two days later Anne-Marie paused outside the door to the blue room. She smoothed her skirts and touched her hair before she caught herself. She was acting like a chambermaid applying for a job! What was there about this man that made her react this way? She still didn't know for certain why he was here. She could guess, but given the potential danger, guessing wasn't good enough. And not even flattery and smiles could worm the truth out of Massey. With no choice, she'd determined to try Eli again. This time she'd remember to keep her distance from the bed.

She opened the door and went in.

He was awake, propped up on the pillows with sun shining in through the windows and the remains of his breakfast on a tray. He looked better than when she'd last seen him, his face less lined and drawn, and there was a vitality about him she could sense all the way from the door. There was also a change in his expression when he saw who his visitor was.

"Good morning, Lieutenant."

"Bonjour, mademoiselle."

"You speak French. How delightful."

"I speak enough." His eyes flickered over her in a way she tried to ignore. "You can take the tray away if you wish. Don't be afraid. I won't try to grab you if you come close."

"I'm not afraid of you," she retorted, snatching up the tray. She set it on the dresser where his medicine was arranged.

He saw her eye the bottles. "I'm due for a spoonful of the bigger one—that is, if you're up to it."

"I can open a bottle, if you can open your mouth."

"Wide enough for what you want," he answered, and looked mildly amused when she shot an instinctive glance at his lips. "I won't ask you to change my bandage," he added as she filled the spoon. "Careful, you're spilling."

"I'll dump this whole bottle upside down on your head if you don't watch your tongue!" She thrust the spoon forward so roughly that half of it spilled on the sheets. She heaved a breath, refilled the spoon and held it out again.

"Thank you," he said politely.

"Is there anything else you need?"

"Now that you offer, I could use a shave."

"A what!"

"A shave," he repeated, rubbing his cheek with his good hand. It was rough with a thick stubble the color of his eyes. "One of the sisters shaved me the day before I came here and it's beginning to itch." Still rubbing his cheek, he let his eyes linger on the medicine stains on the sheet. "On second thought, perhaps I should wait for someone with a steadier hand."

"So long as you keep your mouth shut, my hand is as steady as yours."

"And if I don't?"

"I may just slip and cut your throat." Her anger broke as she said this, and to her surprise, she smiled. Exchanging barbs with him was like dancing with a sure-footed, light-handed man. If she wasn't careful, she'd forget who he really was.

He smiled back. "I'll risk it. I wouldn't mind a little bit of excitement after so much lying in bed."

Her cheeks were flushed as she left the room in search of a razor she could borrow from the sieur. My goodness,

what a change! Thus far she'd seen only the lieutenant's
coolness and resolve, but he seemed almost playful now; he
also seemed to have stopped harping on the night of the
attack, though that was most likely temporary. In any
event, he was clearly in a talkative mood, and getting him
to talk freely was just what she'd hoped to do. Maybe this
would turn out better than she'd thought. Maybe she could
coax him to tell her Carleton's request, and then once he'd
told her—well, she'd have to see.

Her color was back to normal by the time she returned.
He watched as she filled the basin from the kettle at the fire.
She carried the basin to the table beside the bed, along with
two thick towels, the razor and the soap. She'd been so busy
thinking of other things that it wasn't until she'd gotten
everything assembled that she realized just what shaving
him would entail.

"Well?" said Eli.

She was standing there holding the towel as if she were
waiting for someone else to come. But no one else was
coming. There was only her—and him. You'll be fine, she
told herself. Just remember to keep your mind on your
goal.

"Let's get this around you to keep you dry," she murmured, businesslike as a nun as she slid the towel behind
him and around his shoulders, crossing it in the front. She
held her breath as she did this, though she couldn't have
said why. She told herself to pretend that he was the sieur.
She worked the soap into a lather then spread it on his face,
trying not to react to the sharpness of his stubble or the
sharper heat of his skin.

"Stay still." She lifted the razor. Her cheeks were hot
again. Don't be a ninny, she remonstrated. He knows
something you need to know and if you turn silly you'll
never find out what it is.

At least her hands were steady as the razor cut a swath
down the length of his cheek. She dipped it in the water
then cut another swath. He stayed still as she'd cautioned,

so still that he might have been carved of stone. But he wasn't, he was made of flesh and blood; of this she was reminded in a dozen distracting ways.

It wasn't only the contact between her fingers and his skin; there was the nearness of their thighs and the way her breasts thrust toward him when she raised both her arms—her right arm to shave him and her left to hold his head. There was the rhythm of their breathing, the rise and fall of his chest. Finally, there was the fullness of his lips, which stood out all too vividly against the whiteness of the soap. Pretend he's the sieur, she repeated, but it didn't help. The sieur's thigh didn't burn like fire right through the covers and the sheets.

Rinse and stroke, rinse and stroke—like rowing a boat. When he shifted even slightly she could feel the warmth rising from his body, mingling his manly scent with the perfume of the soap. When her palm accidentally grazed his lips, her stomach contracted so violently she almost cut his throat.

"You're not half-bad at this," he commented as she rinsed the razor slowly to give herself time to collect her wits. "You're better than a lot of barbers I've known."

To her surprise, she found herself almost blushing at his praise. "Last spring the sieur had pneumonia. I had to shave him for a month."

"You call him the sieur, not 'my father'?"

"He's not my father," she said. "My father died many years ago and the sieur adopted me."

"And your mother?"

"She died, too." Much as she disliked discussing this aspect of her past, at least it served to return her to a state of calm. She shook dry the razor and lifted it again. "By the way, Captain Massey sent a note to say that he is busy all day today, but he'll come tomorrow to hear if you've reached a decision on what General Carleton proposed." She paused to rinse the razor. "Have you decided?"

In that familiar cool voice, he answered, "Wouldn't you like to know."

Damn! He was watchful as a cat, but she wasn't about to give up. "No, not particularly." She shrugged as she raised the razor. "Of course I know what Massey asked you. Turn your head the other way."

"The hell you do," he muttered as he turned his head. "If you knew, you wouldn't be here trying your hardest to worm it out of me. Ouch!"

She dropped the razor into the water and blotted his cheek with the towel. "*Oo-la!* It's your own fault. I told you to keep still."

"I was answering your question."

"You could have waited until it was safe. And for your information, I'm not trying to worm anything out of you. I'm just making conversation to pass the time. There, it's stopped bleeding." She took the towel away. He didn't intend to tell her. What was she going to do?

She shook the razor, but when she raised it, he moved away. "Can't you guess what Carleton wants without having to ask?" Without waiting for her to answer, he said, "He wants the name of the man who led us up to the magazine. If I named you, I suppose you'd deny it."

She was so surprised she feared she couldn't hold the razor without slicing her own hand. "Of course," she said calmly—more calmly than she felt. "And the sieur will give his oath that I was here all that night."

One dark brow lifted. "Then we'd have to see which of us Carleton believes—the lovely lady or the American."

"The desperate American," she amended, matching him tone for tone.

His arched brow flattened and he continued to watch her so steadily that she didn't trust herself to touch the razor to his face. She didn't know what she would do if he asked her why she'd stopped.

He didn't ask. What he did instead took her completely by surprise. In the same reflective voice, he said, "I'll tell

you what Carleton really wants. He wants me to guarantee
England the loyalty of the Grants.''

"The Grants?'' she said blankly.

"The New Hampshire Grants. That's what we call the
land between Lake Champlain and the Connecticut River.
A lot of it is wild mountains, but there's also some of the
best farmland you've ever seen. Those farms could supply
an army marching to New York.''

She frowned. "What sort of an army?'' What was he
talking about?

He put it all too clearly. "With the guaranteed support
of the Grants, the British could sail down Lake Champlain
to the Hudson River and straight on to New York. They
could drive a wedge between New England and the other
colonies, isolate the two halves and defeat them each sep-
arately.''

"And you—one man—could do that? You could assure
that support?''

He shook his head slowly. "Not just like that. But if I
talked the idea up, it might take hold.''

"Why? Are the people who live there in favor of the
king?''

That made him smile, as if she'd made a joke. "When it
comes to being governed, Grants people are only in favor
of themselves. They don't like the idea of anyone lording
it over them—not the King of England and not other
Americans.''

"But if they don't want—''

"Hush. Listen and I'll explain. Right now the Grants
people are in a bind. Because the land lay between New
Hampshire and New York, both colonies believed they
owned it and both sold titles to the land. Grants people
took from New Hampshire, but after they'd moved in,
along came New York and insisted the Grants belonged to
her. So Grants people formed a sort of army to protect their
claims. They're called the Green Mountain Boys—maybe
you've heard of them.''

"Maybe I have," she said vaguely. She set the razor beside the basin. She was beginning to see. "So if the Grants people promise to help England, in exchange the king will let them keep their land. But what if the British lose the war with the Americans?"

He shrugged. "Then Carleton's promise won't be worth very much. But if the Grants go with England she'd be hard-pressed to lose."

"And the people would do that? They'd turn on their own comrades and make peace with the enemy?"

His eyes glinted with what—amusement? "Terms like enemy and comrade are misleading if you consider the history. A year ago if you'd asked a Grants man who was his enemy, he'd have told you New York. Now that both sides are fighting England they've formed a sort of truce, but New York is still claiming the Grants belong to her and Congress seems more than willing to back her up.

"If the colonies ever do manage to win this thing, it's more than likely that they'll try to force the Grants to submit to New York. On the other hand, Carleton is not only offering us good title to our land. He's guaranteeing us preferred status if England wins the war. In view of that, you'd have to admit we'd be smart to take Carleton's deal."

Her fist came down on the table. "I'd admit no such thing! I'd call you all traitors to do such a thing—to betray the cause of freedom and take sides with the British swine!"

Her words, sharp and angry, echoed sickeningly in her ears. The silence that followed was even worse.

"Swine, are they?" Eli clucked his tongue. "That strikes me as a very strange way to speak of friends. Is this some Canadian custom I'm not familiar with, or could it possibly be your admission that I was right about you all along?"

Her hands still clenched, she rose and stood looking down at him. She was desperate to deny it, but she saw there was no use. "Congratulations," she said with a bitter smile. "General Carleton will be pleased. No doubt you'll be richly rewarded for your help."

"You honestly think I'd tell him?"

"Why not—wouldn't it be 'smart,' to use your word? I believe you'd betray your own mother if you thought it might serve your ends."

"My mother's dead," he said flatly, his face showing nothing at all. His voice was just as flat when he asked her, "Why did you light that fuse?"

"I told you already—in the magazine."

"Yes, to kill the British. Why do you hate them so much?"

She looked at his dark eyes, so cool and self-possessed, and in her mind she heard him laying out the case for betrayal with such clarity. How could she begin to tell him about her past and the tumult of feelings it had instilled in her? He would think she was overreacting and, of course, that she wasn't smart. "Smart" would be to forget everything that had happened to her and to support the British, who'd preserved the sieur's wealth. "Smart" would be to marry some man that she didn't love, to live quietly ever after, to forget about François. "Smart" would be everything she detested and despised.

Eli was still waiting. She gave her head a shake. "It isn't worth the effort. You wouldn't understand." She turned.

"Where are you going? You haven't finished shaving me."

"I'll send the maid. You've had your excitement, what more do you want?" But before he could answer, she was gone from the room.

"Why?" Eli murmured aloud after she was gone, and he knew that the question concerned a good deal more than the fuse.

Why had he come here? To be with Zeke. Left to his own devices, he would have preferred to have spent these past six months promoting the Grants' interests in Philadelphia. But he'd been worried about what Zeke, the greathearted and impulsive, might do on his own. Zeke's wife, Sarah, had also asked him to go with Zeke, but even if she hadn't, he would have gone anyway. When they'd been children, Zeke had watched over him, and ever since then he'd been returning the favor as best he could.

He wasn't doing very well at the moment. At the moment it was clear that Zeke would be a hell of a lot safer if he, Eli, had gone to Philadelphia or even stayed in Bennington. And the danger didn't only come from Massey's threat. The danger had stretched to take in the hot-tempered *mademoiselle*. He didn't have to close his eyes to conjure up the swell of her breast or the hint of her fragrance, which drifted from her hair.

Something had sprung up between them the first time they met, and every time they came together, that something grew. Even though he hadn't seen her for two days, there hadn't been an hour when he hadn't been conscious of her presence in the house. In the best of times he was wary of any woman's influence and it didn't take a genius to know that this wasn't the best of times. He was playing with fire, in more ways than one, and only control and clear vision would deliver both Zeke and him.

And the Grants? His forehead furrowed as he considered Carleton's deal. Only a witch or a fortune-teller could guess how this war would come out, and if he had one with him at this moment, he wasn't sure that he'd want to ask.

Sleigh bells jingled in the street below. His face itched from the soap. He pulled the towel from his shoulder and ruefully wiped his cheeks, trying not to remember her fingers' fleeting touch. Fire, he was thinking. Quebec was fire and ice, and he was walking down the middle with a bum leg, trying to keep to the path.

"You are very good to meet me," Anne-Marie said to Monsieur Arsenault. They were walking along the low wall that overlooked the broad Saint Lawrence and the roofs of the Lower Town. The air was frigid but the sky was clear and the sinking sun turned the ice on the river magnificent shades of gold. Except for them, the walk was deserted, which was why they had chosen this place.

Anne-Marie's mother had lived through only one Quebec winter and she had hated it. Acadia, with its ocean currents from the south, enjoyed a milder climate than the rest of Canada. No matter how warmly her mother had bundled up, the arctic winds had cut through her padding and into her flesh, making her miserable. Anne-Marie, who had been too young to remember Acadia, didn't mind the cold. She found it invigorating, as did the Quebecois. Even today it lifted her spirits and seemed to offer hope. It was five days since she'd shaved Eli, five fretful days, at the end of which she'd written to Monsieur Arsenault.

"Your note sounded urgent," Monsieur Arsenault replied in his unruffled way. Monsieur Arsenault was never ruffled, which was why all the Quebec merchants trusted him with their gold. The English traders trusted Monsieur Arsenault so much that they probably would have been willing to ignore his pro-American tendencies. Wisely, however, Monsieur Arsenault kept those to himself.

In the months before the American invasion, knowing the weakness of the British garrisons in the north, many Canadians had spoken out in favor of the colonies, but Monsieur Arsenault had been carefully discreet. As a result, in early December, when Carleton had exiled all of Quebec's pro-Americans, Monsieur Arsenault had been allowed to stay, and subsequently he'd become the leader of all secret activities. Unlike a number of others, who saw the potential for financial gain, Monsieur Arsenault had been drawn to the cause by a belief in democracy.

"I have some things to tell you." Anne-Marie looked away, to the hills across the river, then back to him again. "You know General Carleton has lodged one of the American prisoners at our house."

Arsenault nodded. "Eli Brownell. He and his brother are both Green Mountain Boys."

"I didn't know he had a brother."

"He's also a prisoner. I believe they've got him at the seminary. I assume that Carleton wants something from Brownell."

"Yes." She repeated what Eli had told her about Carleton's proposal for trading the guarantee of sovereignty in exchange for the Grants' support. "General Carleton also wants him to give the name of the person who let them into the city and up to the magazine."

"Do you believe he will do it?"

"I don't know. He—he's very calculating. I don't know what he thinks." Before Arsenault could speak again, she said, "There's something more. Something that happened the night of the attack. After we took the powder out of the magazine, I went back to light a fuse to blow the whole magazine up. I—I thought if all the barracks were blown up there wouldn't be soldiers to keep the Americans out." She ventured a glance at his face.

As always he looked calm. "There wouldn't have been much to keep them out of if all those barrels had blown. What happened?"

"Lieutenant Brownell found me and put out the fuse. I—I know I was wrong to do it, but all I could think of was paying the British back for what they'd done, and when I thought of all that powder—" She shook her head. "Now that I've told you, you probably won't want to trust me anymore. That's why I didn't tell you before, which was also wrong. But you see, if Lieutenant Brownell does decide to tell Carleton what I did, he'll probably tell him the whole thing, and I'm afraid that if Carleton hears about blowing up the magazine he'll take real alarm. Maybe he'll think it's a conspiracy and start rounding up everyone he suspects.

"I thought," she continued, twisting her hands within her fur muff, "that maybe we could arrange to help the lieutenant escape."

Arsenault considered this for a few minutes, then he said, "If he were to escape from your house, wouldn't you and the sieur be blamed?"

"I thought we might make it appear to have been the Americans." She looked at him hopefully.

Slowly he shook his head. "I'm afraid that the general wouldn't believe that. What Lieutenant Brownell has told you is true. At this moment the Americans can barely help themselves, let alone sneak into the city to rescue prisoners. Colonel Arnold is too gravely wounded to lead the troops, but no replacement has been sent. He is also waiting for reinforcements, food and supplies. Whole companies are ill with smallpox and morale is very low.

"Beyond this, the risk of smuggling the lieutenant out is too grave. Not only is there a double guard all along the wall, but since Carleton won the battle, civilian sympathies have changed. People who were neutral three weeks ago are suddenly avid supporters of Carleton and the king. Given the circumstances, I think it best to do nothing for the moment but to keep a careful watch. If Lieutenant Brownell gives you some specific indication that he is about to speak, we will act, but not otherwise. I know this puts you under a considerable strain."

"I don't mind. If anything, I deserve it."

He looked at her sympathetically. "When things don't go well, it's all too easy for one to take personal blame. War arouses passions—people act rashly. Sometimes that rashness saves the moment and sometimes it loses it. Only hindsight lets you see clearly which it is. No matter what Lieutenant Brownell says, the war isn't over yet, and before it is, we all may be given a second chance. Go home, be still, and watch carefully. If either of us has news, we'll send word."

"There isn't anything else I can do?"

"Not at the present time." His hand rested on her shoulder. "I'm glad you told me. Now go."

She went as he had ordered, trying to figure out if she was angrier at herself or at Eli Brownell. For one of her temperament, inaction was a curse; and watching, waiting and being careful were conditions next to impossible.

"I say, Mademoiselle Doucet!"

Merciful heavens! If her mood wasn't already low enough, here was Captain Massey stomping straight for her in his high boots. It was too late for her to escape.

As he reached her, he exclaimed, "I can't for the life of me understand how anyone would choose to live in Quebec! It's too cold, there's too much snow and winter lasts too long."

"It's not so bad," she answered, "wnen we're not under siege. People skate on the river and go visiting. You can take a cariole up to Montreal or—"

"And what's worse is the lack of firewood," he went on, ignoring her. "Obviously we can't get it in the city so we have to send cutters out, but as soon as we do, the Americans open fire on them. I don't know why they don't give up. Cursed stubbornness!"

At that, despite her dark mood, Anne-Marie almost started to laugh. "I've never heard a better description of war."

"Humph!" grumbled Massey. "Are you going home? I called on Brownell a while ago but you'd already gone out."

At the mention of Eli, all thought of laughter slipped away. "Has he reached his decision?"

"No, he's still holding us off. Well, let him. In the end he'll give us what we want."

"What makes you think so?"

Despite his loose jowls and big red nose, Massey's look was shrewd. "Many things. For one, he's a realist and not likely to be blinded by sentimentality. He won't lose sight of where his best interests lie and in the end he'll follow them. For another, we've got his brother."

She stiffened. "What do you mean?"

"We'll use him," said Massey, slapping his hands together for warmth. "I've already warned Brownell that if he tries to escape we'll send his brother to England and punish him."

So much for sneaking Eli out of the city, she thought with a sinking heart. "If he's such a realist, maybe he won't care."

"His brother's the exception," Massey said with a little smile. "These backwoods Americans take family seriously. You should have seen his face when I told him. No, we've got him there. Maybe we'll even use his brother to get him to agree—threaten to hang him as a traitor. That ought to change his mind."

She shivered in her warm coat. "Would General Carleton permit such a thing?"

"As a threat? I don't see why not. And what Carleton doesn't know won't hurt him, will it now?" he added, giving her a playful jab in the ribs. "Are you going home? I'll walk along with you."

"No. I'm going to the Saint Fleurs'." Had Massey really found Eli's Achilles' heel? From what she knew of Eli, it was hard to believe. On the other hand, the possibility sent cold chills down her back.

"Saint Fleur," repeated Massey. "Haven't they got a son? A silly fellow."

No sillier than you, she thought, looking at Massey's florid face and his swelled chest. Then she thought of Eli, so pale and lean. A strange current shot through her, like lightning striking a tree. "Yes." She nodded. "He's called Jean Pierre."

"Should I be jealous?"

"No," she said honestly. "I've turned down the last three invitations and I only accepted this time because to refuse would have been too rude. I'd better be going. I'm already late."

"I'll come by tomorrow," he promised. "Remember. Mum's the word."

* * *

"At times I find life a cipher," Saint Vallier was saying as he studied the pieces on the chessboard that had been laid on the table next to Eli's bed.

"In what way?" asked Eli, also studying the board.

Saint Vallier shrugged expressively. "Take my experience. I was born a French subject and therefore a sworn enemy of England and now I have become the reverse, and yet I do not feel that I am a hypocrite. In some ways what has happened is almost logical." His rook was threatened. He moved it out of reach.

This wasn't the first game of chess they'd played. A few days ago the sieur had sent Eli a note inquiring whether he knew how to play and, if so, whether he had any interest in attempting a game. That night they'd played until the sieur had nodded off, and they'd resumed the next afternoon. Eli welcomed the diversion and the sieur's company, both of which took his mind off his own concerns.

"More wine?" The sieur refilled his own glass.

"No, thank you," said Eli. "Logical in what way? Your becoming England's ally, I mean."

"Ah, yes." The sieur paused to take a sip of wine then set down his glass. "To begin with, France never governed very well. The intendant was notoriously corrupt and nothing was ever done for the good of the whole. I tried to remain on amicable terms, but that became increasingly difficult as the years progressed. I dislike corruption. At the time of the English invasion, I was in danger of being stripped of my lands."

"But England let you keep them?"

"Yes, she did. As you can imagine, that alone won my friendship. Beyond that, she has done her best to govern fairly. You're sure you won't have more wine?"

"Thank you, I'm fine. I agree that a good master is better than a bad one. But what about having no master? Isn't that the best of all?"

Saint Vallier sipped his wine and smiled. "Shall I report to Captain Massey that you've tried to subvert me over chess? The truth is, I don't believe things would be better if England were thrown out. If she were, I'm afraid we'd see a civil war between the merchants and the church, and meanwhile somebody stronger would invade and conquer us."

"Such as France?" asked Eli.

"Or America. You know that many Canadians believe that's what your country wants—to make us a part of your United Colonies. A tax-paying part," he added apologetically. "It's what the priests have been saying to the farmers—the habitants—and the habitants are accustomed to believing the priests."

"The habitants stood in the road and cheered us when we marched from Montreal."

"Because you were winning and the habitant is shrewd. When you stop winning, he'll go back to cheering the English. He'll turn his back on you."

Eli didn't answer, but he knew the sieur was right. They both sat in silence until he'd made his move. Then he leaned back on the pillows and asked a question he'd been wanting to ask since the first time they'd played chess.

"How is it that Mademoiselle Doucet came to be your ward?"

Eli had learned to read silence during his years in court; although the sieur didn't look up, he could tell that he'd been expecting the question. Why not? Anne-Marie was a beautiful woman and Eli was a man. Wasn't it only natural that he should notice her?

The sieur sipped more wine and explained, "She'd been exiled from Acadia in 1755. To avoid being sent off by ship, she and her mother had fled to the woods and had managed to elude the British all the way to Quebec. It's a miracle that they made it, since most who fled did not. Most were run down and caught by the British or else they died in the wilderness."

Remembering, he shook his head. "You should have seen them when they arrived, more naked than dressed and nothing but skin and bones. Her mother never recovered. She died within the year. They were living in the village on my estate. Anne-Marie was a lovely child. I'd taken a great liking to her. After her mother died, I adopted her."

"She had no other relatives?"

"None that I could find. There was a brother, who'd become separated during the deportation and sent off on one of the ships. I did try to find him, but it was impossible. There were no records, no rosters, and so many of the Acadians died."

"What about her father?"

"He died after she was born. That was the problem, because he was an Englishman, a soldier who'd been posted to Louisbourg during the war in 1745. Four years later, when the war was over, he'd been posted to the south of Acadia, where he met and married Anne-Marie's mother. It wasn't so unusual in the place and time. There were religious problems, of course, but in this case they were solved by the children being brought up in the Anglican church. This continued even after the father died."

"Then why were they deported?"

The game forgotten, the sieur continued. "They didn't think they would be. That is, the mother didn't think so. The children were too young. Had things been handled calmly, they probably would have been saved. But things were not handled calmly—not by a very long shot. There was panic, terrible confusion, acts of cruelty. When the mother went to plead with the authorities, she was turned away. She continued pleading up until the last moment, then finally she fled." He sighed deeply.

After a minute Eli asked, "But what about her name? If her father was English, why is she called Doucet?"

"Doucet was her mother's maiden name. She took it after her mother died." The older man's hands rose briefly to shield his eyes. "That was a difficult time. She was just a child to have come through such an ordeal, and then to lose her mother, her only relative. She was bitter. She blamed the British—who can say that she didn't have cause? Her father's name hadn't managed to keep them safe, so in anger she cast it off and I didn't try to stop her. That would have been unfair. If anything, I understood."

So did Eli—and not only about her name. Now he had his answer to why she'd lighted that fuse. "What was her father's name?"

"Perkins." The sieur smiled. "It hardly suits her, does it?"

Eli shook his head. Anne-Marie Perkins? It sounded like a joke. He had another question, not because he didn't know the answer but because he was curious as to what the sieur would say. "She doesn't seem to hate the British now. When did she forgive them?"

"Only quite recently. Really just about the time your colonies began their revolt. We've never discussed it—I didn't want to belabor the issue. I was only content that the change had come. But I think that having to choose sides gave her the freedom to admit that the British were no longer her enemy."

A logical explanation, if a wrong one, thought Eli, returning his attention to the board. But he'd lost his concentration. He was thinking of Anne-Marie.

So was the sieur. "It pains me that she must experience this war. I've been afraid that it will bring back all the bad memories. She feels things so strongly." He sighed. "But I can't stop the fighting so I must hope for the best." He reached for his glass then stopped, his hand arrested in midair. "Who could this be?"

Cariole bells jangled as the front door opened and shut. Less than a minute later, they heard Anne-Marie's feet on the stairs.

The sieur frowned. "She's home early." He got up and moved to the door. Opening it, he stuck his head into the hall. "You're home early. Is something wrong?"

"Nothing. What are you doing?"

Eli heard her breathless reply. He could imagine her, bright-eyed and red-cheeked from the cold, tossing her hair back as she spoke.

"We've been playing chess. Why don't you come in to join us?"

Eli knew that she'd refuse. She'd been staying away from him scrupulously during the last five days. To his surprise, however, he heard her footsteps coming near and a moment later the sieur stepped back to let her in. She paused in the doorway, her eyes on him as if she were deciding whether to change her mind.

He held his breath. She didn't change it but swept into the room to fling herself backward into the leather chair.

He'd been right in his imagined vision—she radiated cold. He could feel it flowing from her, tingling on his skin. It must have been snowing because drops of wet clung to her hair, teasing a halo of curls out of her chignon. Her cheeks were flushed and her eyes brilliant—she looked magnificent.

She also looked fed up. With him? Eli wondered, and found that he didn't care. Despite the wine he'd been drinking, he felt wide-awake.

"How was your party?" asked Saint Vallier, coming back to his chair.

She threw both hands up. "Like a storm at sea. I'm lucky I haven't been blown over the edge of the world! Don't smile!" She shook her finger. "It was terrible!"

"Who was the villain this time?"

"Saint Fleur's son, Jean Pierre. He fancies himself a British lord—such airs he puts on! And the snuff! In great handfuls, then he sneezes in my face!" With an economy of motion, she was up out of the chair, one hand held behind her and the other extended limply as she minced around the room, avoiding furniture and lisping, "I say— aren't the British absolutely capital? Oh, my gracious!

Achoo! Achoo! Achoo!'' She sneezed in three directions, like an actor taking a bow.

Eli started laughing, as did Saint Vallier. Anne-Marie scowled from one to the other. "Don't laugh!" she scolded, but then her anger cracked. Surrendering to laughter, she threw herself back into the chair. "I swear, a cow at market is allowed more dignity! Hand on the elbow, hand at the waist, hand on the shoulder—hands everywhere! Sometimes I feel like screaming!"

"Why don't you?" Eli asked.

She fixed him with big gray eyes. "Sometimes I do. That's worse—they find it charming. Charming!" She sneered the word.

"Heaven forbid!" Eli held up one hand as if he were warding off the very thought. The truth was, he raised it in order to block his face so that she wouldn't know from his expression that he also found her charming—and a good deal more. For the first time since that night at the magazine, he felt thoroughly alive.

Saint Vallier was smiling. "I hope you weren't too rude."

"Hardly at all," she assured him. "Not nearly enough! I told him I had to go home to change my clothes." She held out her skirt for inspection. "Happily it isn't too bad. But it would have been ruined if I'd stayed. Snuff is a disgusting habit!" She gave up on the inspection and flopped back in the chair.

There was a discreet knocking. It was the butler. "My lord, there's someone below to see you. A Mr. Wick. Something about buying land. Shall I tell him to come back in the morning?"

"No, no." The sieur stood up. "I want to hear his offer. I may as well see him now. Shall we resume our game later or give up for the night?"

"Whatever you like," said Eli.

"Then we'll see how long this takes. My dear." With a nod to Anne-Marie, the sieur was gone.

He left behind an instant tension that hadn't existed before. Eli felt it and he knew that Anne-Marie did, too. When she pulled her feet in and sat forward, he expected her to leave. He could feel her intention, but she stayed in the chair, toying distractedly with one damp curl of her hair.

Referring to its wetness, he said, "Is it snowing again?"

She looked at him sidewise. "I suppose you hate it, too."

"Hate the snow? Why should I?"

She let go of the curl and shrugged. "I don't know. Because there's too much of it. Because it's too cold."

"We have winter where I come from. Who hates the cold?"

"Captain Massey, for one. I saw him earlier. He was complaining about the weather. He said he'd just been here."

So that was it. He nodded. "He wanted to know if I'd made up my mind. Are you here to make me an offer?"

"An offer for what?" She frowned.

"For giving you an early warning so that you can act before I do." Despite the seriousness of the topic, he almost started laughing again at the change in her face. "You've got to do better than that, *mademoiselle,* if you want to be a spy. Right now you've got confirmation printed across your face."

"Why, you—" She lurched forward, but she didn't leave, just sat there glaring at him for a full minute before she settled back. "Captain Massey told me about your brother."

"The sieur told me about yours."

Another change, just as rapid, but this time she was shutting down. "That's none of your business!"

"I could say the same."

She considered that in silence, while he wondered what Massey had said. He hated the thought of Massey talking to her, and not just because he knew they were discussing Zeke.

"Did Massey tell you what he wanted when he came here today?"

"To—to know if you'd decided."

"Massey's in a rush. I pointed out that there's no hurry, since nothing can happen until the spring thaw anyway. They can't ship me off to England and they can't march on New York."

"He can send you to the prison with your brother and the rest."

"Yes." Their eyes met. He knew what she meant. Massey had the power to remove him from this house so that he wouldn't see her, and whatever had started between them would end. She did feel it. He could see it in her eyes and in her lips, which were parted.

She stood. Was she leaving? Her skirts rustled and his pulses leapt. In spite of himself he asked her, "What else does Massey say? Does he tell you that you're charming while he's pawing you?"

She hadn't expected his question. She tensed, but then she relaxed. "Don't tell me that you're jealous?"

"Do I seem like the jealous type?"

"No, you seem too cold-blooded for jealousy." She was standing at the foot of the bed, surveying him with what she must have wanted to look like disinterest, but which didn't look that way at all. "I don't believe you were an outlaw with the Green Mountain Boys. Outlaws have more passion."

"You ought to meet my brother, Zeke. Anyway, I wasn't an outlaw."

"What were you, then?"

"A lawyer."

She tossed her head. "Yes, I believe it. You're just the type—all cool and collected, sitting back and waiting for other people to betray themselves. I bet you were a very good lawyer."

"I wasn't bad." Their eyes, which had parted, were locked together again. He watched as the tension drew her along the side of the bed. Break it, he warned, but he couldn't.

"You're being modest," she said. "I'll bet you were murder on hostile witnesses. I'll bet you kept at them and kept at them till they cracked. I'll bet you even pretended to soften, to lull them into trusting you, and when they gave you what you wanted—snap! You were stone again."

She'd come within reach now. She was smiling, as if she knew—a fierce little smile that had nothing to do with joy. Did she know what she was doing? Did she know she was daring him? He knew it. Lord, he knew it. He clenched his fist around a handful of sheet.

She wasn't one to back off—he'd known that since the first night they'd met. She kept at him, kept daring, kept moving up the bed. "I'll bet you were even harder on the girls, taking what you wanted and giving nothing in return. I'll bet they called you the heartbreaker of the Grants. I'll bet you left them all crying when you marched off to war. I'll bet—oh! Stop it!"

All at once his resistance snapped and his good hand had her—first her wrist, then the back of her head, pulling her down, holding her against him as his lips closed over hers. She struggled but he held her, forcing her lips apart until he tasted the sweetness of her open mouth. She struggled, at first against him and then against herself. She lost both struggles. Her hands rose to clutch his shirt, then her hands were open, her fingers raking his back.

Their mouths were glued together. He was devouring her, the fingers of his good hand driving deep into her hair, pulling her head back, wanting more and more. She threw her head back farther when his hot lips sought her throat and finally the lush swelling of her breasts where they pressed up from her gown. Any moment she'd come to her senses, but he had her now, and while he had her, he wanted everything.

She was half-slumped against him, leaning on his bad leg; it was aching, but he didn't care. If he hadn't been wounded, he'd have had her in the bed; even wounded, he wanted that. His fingers disentangled from her curls to slip around to cup her breast. He pushed it up higher, toward the heat of his open mouth. She whimpered and clung to him. Damning pain and the future, he used his splinted arm to support her while his good hand reached beneath her skirt, sliding over ankle and bent knee to silken thigh. She trembled against him with mounting violence. When his fingers reached higher, she went rigid and jerked away.

"What are you doing?"

"Proving I'm not made of stone."

"Let me go!" With a violent, angry motion she twisted free.

"I thought you wanted passion."

"Not from you, I don't!" Panting, her hair streaming down her shoulders and over her disheveled gown, she gripped the bedpost as if she would collapse without its support.

She'd moved out of reach of his hand, so he tracked her with his words. "Saint Vallier believes you've forgiven the British, but he's wrong, isn't he? It was revenge you wanted that night at the magazine. You hate the British for killing your mother."

"Stop it! Leave me alone!"

"Is that what you really want?"

"Yes! Yes—I hate you!" With a final cry, she pulled free of the bedpost and ran out of the room, slamming the door behind her so hard that the shutters shook.

Eli flung himself back on the pillows, on fire and so aching with frustrated desire he hardly noticed the pain of his wounds. Cool and distant had she called him? Not by a long shot. He burned for the *mademoiselle,* regardless of any risk. He might tell himself that after this she would surely stay away, but he knew her. She was the type to move toward fire, to act before she thought. And if she acted, he knew that he'd react with the speed and the passion he'd shown them both today.

It didn't have to be. As she'd pointed out, Massey could take him away from this house. He himself could speed up the process by telling Carleton he wouldn't deal, then they'd send him back to prison with the other men. He could, but would he? There were good reasons to stay. Here he had some power, whereas in prison he'd have none. And in prison there was no *mademoiselle*.

His leg was throbbing, but so was the rest of him. She was right, he was careful, but he was also a man and she was a woman. His body could vouch for that, and it had been a long, long time since he'd known a woman like her. Had he ever known one? Right now he couldn't think. He could leave now, but he wouldn't. Not yet. Not yet.

Chapter Five

The Cramahé mansion, the home of the lieutenant governor of Quebec, sat high on an eminence in the Upper Town. When the shutters were open, the windows gave a splendid view of the river and the countryside beyond. Tonight, however, the shutters were barred, as they had been ever since the December evening when a well-aimed American cannonball had come whistling and crashing into the dining room.

As Cramahé told the story, by the grace of God the family had not been dining at the time. They'd been playing cards in the room next door and the explosion had put a sudden end to the game as the guests fell over one another fleeing down to the cellar below. Finding the party cowering amid the racks of his wine, Cramahé suggested that they might put the evening to good use by sampling the excellent burgundy he'd received the month before. The bombardment had ended at midnight or before, but it was well into the following morning before the guests emerged, declaring it the best bombing they'd ever had.

There hadn't been much artillery fire since New Year's Eve, and tonight, because it was snowing, the American guns were still.

General Carleton greeted Anne-Marie very graciously as she came through the reception line. "I am indebted to you and the sieur for taking in Lieutenant Brownell. Captain

Massey has spoken highly of your care and your hospitality and I want you to know that it could make a real difference in how everything turns out."

By the time she murmured "Thank you," the column of guests had progressed and she was thanking the person at Carleton's right, though as she did, the general's words were still ringing in her ears. She felt as if she'd been living in a siege within a siege.

Two weeks had crept by since that scene in Eli's room, and though she'd done her best not to see him, avoiding him was becoming increasingly difficult. For one thing, he was recovering from his wounds, and for another, the sieur, in his regrettable kindness, had determined that Eli needed a change of scenery. So now he joined them for dinner, and three evenings out of four, the two men played chess in the drawing room.

To Eli's credit, he wasn't carrying on a hot pursuit. He rejected some of the sieur's invitations, claiming pain from his wounds, and when he didn't, she made an effort to be otherwise engaged. But there had been meals and evenings they'd been forced to share, and those had been excruciating, to say the least. When they sat in a room together the very air seemed charged. She was surprised that the sieur didn't feel it, not to mention the household staff.

Despite Monsieur Arsenault's advice, she couldn't watch Eli closely for signs of betrayal. She couldn't watch him at all. Whenever their eyes met, she remembered that kiss and the way his hand had felt sliding up her leg. The best she could do was to hope that he'd meant what he'd said about not responding to Carleton either way until spring. Given the Quebec winters, spring was two good months away. Two endless months, she thought with an inward groan.

"I say! What a storm outside!" As she came to the end of the line, Massey, in full regalia, materialized at her side. "It's coming down harder than it did on New Year's Eve. I was practically buried alive just coming here from your house!"

"From my house?" That stopped her. "What were you doing there?"

"Paying a visit on your uninvited guest. Brownell's brother's come down with smallpox and was sent to the hospital. I wanted to be the first to let him know."

She looked at him, surprised. "That was thoughtful of you, especially in the storm."

He cackled with laughter. "Not thoughtful—smart. I've told you that Brownell and his brother are close. I knew he'd ask to see him when he found out he was sick and I promised to take him over to the Hôtel Dieu myself—as soon as he agrees to the general's terms. Dance?" He held out his hand.

She snatched hers behind her back so he couldn't take it. "That was a beastly thing to do! You used his brother's illness to threaten him." She was thinking of François and how she would have felt if Massey had tried to do the same to her. She would have killed him. She would have broken his fat neck.

Her anger only amused him. "You're forgetting that this is a war, in view of which it wasn't beastly, it was damned intelligent. Furthermore, you can be sure that in my position, Brownell would have done the same."

Her stomach churning, she realized that he was probably right. Then she realized the worst part. "Did—did Lieutenant Brownell agree?"

"Not yet," said Massey. "His brother's not ill enough. But let him get a little worse and he'll change his tune."

Fear was shouldered aside by disgust. "Does General Carleton know what you're doing?" She turned her head, looking down the line.

"No. And I'll thank you not to tell him." He put his hand through her arm as if to prevent her bodily.

"Don't worry," she said hotly. "I'm not a tattletale!"

Even so, he continued to hold her. "I don't think Carleton will waste time quibbling over kindness when he hears that Brownell is willing to give him what he wants. I say, they're playing a Sir Roger de Coverley. That's my favorite dance.''

"You'll have to find another partner. I have to go up-stairs."

She practically ran up two flights to get away from him. She wasn't sure which was worse: Massey using Eli's brother's illness to advance his own career, or the very real possibility that Eli might change his mind and decide to tell Carleton everything he wanted to know. She stood at the window, looking out at the pelting snow. Would he betray her after what had happened that night in their room? Would he, after the way he had kissed her and all the rest?

Her cheeks were burning hot. She touched them to the coolness of the window and remembered what Massey had said—that in his position, Eli would have done the same. Eli had demonstrated that he wasn't made of stone, but beneath the flare of passion there was still his steely mind. He might protect his brother, but he wouldn't do the same for her. If she stood between him and his interests, she believed he would strike her down. And what could she do to stop him? What could she do? She closed her eyes and of-fered a quick prayer that Zeke Brownell wouldn't get worse. By that time another guest was at the door, wanting to use the commode.

She came down the stairs slowly, scanning the heads of the crowd. She spotted Massey in the ballroom, dancing with Cramahé's horse-faced niece. Then she spotted Gen-eral Carleton talking with a group of men. Just before she reached them, the group broke up and coincidentally Carleton came toward her. As she watched him approach-ing, inspiration struck.

"General!" she called out. "May I have a word with you?"

He beamed as he recognized her. "Mademoiselle Doucet, and all alone while the music is playing! Should I risk the displeasure of every young man in Quebec by asking you to dance?''

She smiled to show him she was flattered by his compliment, but her mind was on other things. "If you don't mind, General, I'd like to talk to you about something serious. I know how you feel about being good to the Americans, and we've all heard about how many of the prisoners are contracting smallpox and having to be transferred to the Hôtel Dieu."

"It is terrible," the general agreed, cutting her off in his sympathy. "What's worse is that our intelligence tells us things are even more desperate in the American camp. According to our agents, up to one half of all the soldiers in the camp have fallen ill."

"I was thinking," she pressed on, pursuing her own theme, "maybe I could read to the sick men at the Hôtel Dieu—to raise their spirits and help them get well. I've got the free time," she added, catching sight of Madame Cramahé approaching the general with a determined look, "and I've been inoculated, so there's no danger of me getting sick. I could start tomorrow if you think it's a good idea."

"Read to the sick men?" he repeated.

"Yes, sir, read to them—to take their minds off their suffering and help them pass the time. My English isn't perfect, but I can make myself understood." Madame Cramahé was almost upon them. Oh, please let him say she could. Don't let him refer it to Massey, because Massey would say no.

The general smiled. "I can't think of a person more likely to take men's minds off their suffering and win their sympathy. I have no objection, and I can't imagine that the sisters would object. With your guardian's approval—"

"General Carleton!" With a rustle of satin, Madame Cramahé arrived. "Will you do me the kindness of leading the guests into the buffet! With your leave, Mademoiselle Doucet."

"Of course," Anne-Marie murmured, her eyes still on Carleton. "The sieur would approve if he knew you were in favor."

"In favor of what?" Madame Cramahé asked, but she didn't really care. "The servants are all waiting. Sir, if you'll step this way."

"Yes. Gladly, gladly." Carleton let himself be led. "I shall send you permission," he said over his shoulder to Anne-Marie. "And thank you again for your kindness."

"Thank *you*," she replied. She watched Madame Cramahé leading him away with the same guilty feeling she sometimes had with the sieur. Carleton might be English, but he was a decent man and she didn't like deceiving him. But if she didn't deceive him, Eli might agree to his terms and she could be hanged as a traitor and England could win the war. That all sounded melodramatic but unfortunately it was true—and worse, it all might happen anyway if her little scheme didn't work.

As she'd suspected, Massey disapproved of her idea, though to her surprise he didn't link it directly to Zeke Brownell. Instead he attributed it to some misguided maternal urge. "They're prisoners, not babies. Besides which, I don't believe inoculation works!" he grumbled. But since both Carleton and the sieur had agreed, he couldn't stop her from going to the Hôtel Dieu first thing the next morning with a copy of Mr. Swift's *Gulliver's Travels* tucked beneath her arm.

It was easier than she'd imagined to get to see Zeke, and what was more, she didn't even have to lie. She just told the sister in charge that Eli Brownell was staying at her house and she wanted to see his brother so that she could report on the state of his health.

"How is he?" she asked, thinking again of François. Ever since Massey had told her the news at the Cramahés', the comparison had been in her mind. Now, as the sister frowned, she felt a quick stab of fear.

But the sister's words offered comfort. "He could be worse. He's got a very strong constitution, but none of the Americans have had enough to eat these last few months, and before Monsieur Brownell was taken prisoner in this freezing weather, he was sleeping in a tent! You can assure his brother that we're doing everything we can."

"Can I see him?"

"Have you had smallpox?"

She nodded.

"Then I'll take you up. No doubt hearing news of his brother will cheer him up."

"No doubt," Anne-Marie murmured, following her up the stairs and wondering what she could say about Eli that would cheer his brother up.

She also needed cheering up by the time they had walked through ward after ward of tormented men, calling out for water and tearing at themselves in a futile effort to soothe the terrible itching of their sores.

Zeke Brownell's bed was the last in a long, long row, and unlike most of the other men, he was lying almost still. The first thing that struck her about him was how big he was—that and the darkness of his bushy beard. He was so big that at first she missed his skinniness.

"He's sleeping," said the sister.

"No, he ain't," Zeke contradicted, opening first one eye, then the other when he saw Anne-Marie. He whistled hoarsely through his great black beard. "Have I died and gone to heaven?"

Anne-Marie shook her head. "Fortunately—or unfortunately—you're still in Quebec."

"You're sure you're not an angel? I'm sure you're not a nun. No offense, Sister."

That made both women smile.

"I'll leave you now," said the sister, and silently withdrew, hurrying back down the aisle, pausing to murmur a few words of comfort to the moaning men.

When she was gone, Anne-Marie introduced herself. "Your brother, Lieutenant Brownell, is staying at my house."

"I heard he was wounded."

"Yes, in the arm and the leg, but he's doing very well. He can already walk with the aid of a cane and the doctor says that when he's healed he shouldn't have any limp."

Zeke nodded and closed his eyes, running his tongue over his dry lips.

"Shall I get you a drink of water?"

"I'd be grateful if you did."

She filled a glass from the pitcher and held him up so he could drink. He was much bigger than Eli, but their dark hair was the same.

"You aren't afraid of catching smallpox?" His feverish eyes searched her face for evidence of scars.

"I was inoculated a couple of years ago."

"I wish I'd been. This feels worse than burning in hell. 'Course I ain't been to hell yet, so I can't be sure. The thing I can't figure," he added after a pause, "is what Carleton had in mind putting Eli at your house."

"I don't know," she said—too quickly. Despite their fevered heat, Zeke's eyes fixed on her with a sharpness that she knew all too well.

"Damn," he said softly. "It's a treat just looking at you after these scarecrow types I've been seeing every day. As for the sisters, except for up and fainting whenever a man says damn, they're mostly very nice, but those getups they wear still scare me half to death. I suppose they take getting used to, just like everything. Damn," he concluded, and his eyes flickered shut again.

"I have a book." She held it up although his eyes were closed. "*Gulliver's Travels*. Would—would you like me to read to you? It might take your mind off things."

"By and by," he said.

She watched him, thinking that he was drifting off to sleep. "Perhaps I should go," she murmured.

"By and by," he said again. "How do you get on with Eli?"

She wasn't expecting that. "We—oh, we get on well enough."

"That cold-fish way of his'll drive you crazy. I know, 'cause it's driven me, but it's just an act. Down underneath he feels things just as strongly as you and me—maybe stronger, because of his keeping them bottled up."

"You're wrong," she said flatly.

He opened his eyes again. "How hard's he being on you?"

"Very hard," she said. She couldn't believe she'd said that. Zeke's eyes were shut again. "Mr. Brownell?"

He moved his head. "Tired," he muttered. "Come back another time."

"Yes." She nodded. "Yes, I'll come back again." Holding her skirts to keep them from rustling, she moved around the bed and on down the long room in search of a patient who wasn't so out of his mind with thrashing that he might enjoy a book. As she left him, she thought she heard Zeke Brownell murmur something beneath his breath. She thought he'd murmured "patience," but she couldn't be sure.

When she came home, she found the sieur in the drawing room with his lawyer, talking about selling land. "How did it go at the Hôtel Dieu?" he asked when she opened the door.

"I read to a few of the men. But there are so many and some of them are dying." Even in this cozy room she could still hear their groans.

The sieur shook his head in comprehension. "Smallpox is terrible. If only people were more enlightened about inoculation, all those men wouldn't have to be sick. If it upsets you, you shouldn't go back. I'm sure General Carleton will understand."

"I can go back," she said slowly, thinking of Zeke Brownell. "Where's the lieutenant?"

"He's in the library. He's not only a chess player, he's a lover of literature. Given what we know of the Americans, he's quite unusual."

The lawyer nodded at this politely but looked anxious to get on.

"I won't interrupt you any further." Anne-Marie shut the drawing room door, crossed the hall and knocked on the door to the library.

"Come in."

The door was unlocked. She opened it and went in.

"Your guardian trusts me," Eli said when he saw who it was. "He also told me about your latest scheme."

His definition rankled, as did his sarcastic tone, but with business to accomplish, she brushed them both off. "I saw your brother."

He closed the book he'd been reading and framed it between his hands. His right arm was still splinted and rested on the desk. "No," he said in a low voice.

"No what?" She frowned.

"No, I don't want you getting involved with Zeke. I won't have it."

"You? You have no choice. Aren't you even interested in knowing how he is?"

He was holding the book so tightly the tops of his hands were white. If the pressure hurt his injured arm, he gave no sign. "All right. How is he?"

"The sister says he could be worse. I spoke to him. He was weak but he seemed all right—a lot better off than most of the other men."

"I'm glad. Thank you. Now stay away from him. He's in enough danger without you adding more."

"Me adding danger! I don't know what you mean."

"You like to play games. I don't want you playing with Zeke." He spoke softly but the force of his will sliced through the air like a knife. He kept his eyes on the book he was holding as if looking at her caused him pain.

She shook her head slowly. "I can't believe you're saying this. After what Massey told you, you ought to be grateful that I went to the Hôtel Dieu. You ought to thank me for seeing your brother and ask me to see him again, so you can know how he really is without having to accept Carleton's terms."

"No, *you* ought to be glad," he corrected, his hard eyes coming up. "You went out of self-preservation, and don't bother to act otherwise. You went in the hopes that if you told me how my brother was, I wouldn't betray you to Carleton so that Massey would let me see Zeke. All right, listen. I won't tell Carleton it was you. I swear I won't betray you if you'll give me your word that you'll stay away from Zeke. He's in enough danger without you adding more." His eyes, smoldering with anger, bored into hers.

"Never!" she retorted. She was angry, too. No, she was more than angry. She was furious at him for calling her purely selfish and for ordering her around. "I may not want you to tell Carleton who led you up to the magazine, but that's not the only reason I went to the Hôtel Dieu. I'm not like you and Massey. I don't think of people as pawns. I feel sorry for your brother and I will see him again—I'll see him whenever and as often as I please. And as for your betraying me, go ahead if you want. I'm sick and tired of being threatened by you.

"Go ahead and tell Captain Massey anything you please. He'll never believe you—especially not now. He'll think you're doing it just to see your brother, and so will General Carleton. You sit there issuing ultimatums and insulting me, but you're not the commander of Quebec, you're just a prisoner and you have no rights. No rights!" She tossed her head. "So go ahead and try to stop me. I'll laugh in your face."

She whirled, intent on leaving, but his words caught her at the door.

"You're angry because I kissed you," he said in that same quiet voice.

She stopped as if he'd slapped her and she made herself turn around. "No, I'm not. I'd forgotten all about that until you brought it up."

"I'll bet you did. You're lying."

"How dare you—"

"Because I do. You haven't forgotten what happened any more than I have. You still feel it every time we end up together in a room, and just like me you're wondering when it will happen again."

"It won't happen," she answered, but her voice sounded very faint.

"The hell it won't." Her stomach seemed to leave her body as his eyes flicked over her. "We both know as long as I stay here, it's only a matter of time. I ought to tell Carleton and Massey both to go to hell just so they'll get me out of here."

Her mouth, which had been opened, shut with a little snap. "You—you'd do that?" she stammered.

"I ought to," he said again.

"What's stopping you?"

"Me." He drew a breath. "And you."

She closed her eyes. Her legs were shaking. She thought she was going to faint. For two weeks she'd been fighting the memory of that kiss, but now it swept up to wrap her in its fierce unyielding grip. She wanted to plead with him, only she didn't know what for. To go? To stay? To hold her the way he had done before—hand pressing on her bodice, fingers driven in her hair; hard corded muscles; hot insistent mouth.

"Please," she whispered.

"Please what?" His voice was hoarse.

Her body was yearning. Her will was caving in. If she took one step forward she knew where it would end.

She took a step backward, groping for the door. Her fingers grazed the handle. When she had it she opened her eyes.

He was still looking at her, his eyes dark.

"Do what you must," she whispered, and turning, fled the room.

The next day, bright and early, she went to the hospital. The sister met her with a worried face. "I'm sorry to tell you that Monsieur Brownell has taken a turn for the worse."

"How much worse?"

"The doctor is not sure he will outlast the day."

Her legs were shaking as she made her way upstairs. This time, Zeke didn't greet her with a joke. He was piled with blankets but still shivering, while rivers of sweat were pouring off his face. One of the nuns was wiping the sweat with a dampened towel. Anne-Marie hardly recognized him. In the day since she'd been here, his face had swelled up until he seemed ready to burst. His skin and his lips looked like old leather, brown and parched and cracked.

"Water!" Zeke muttered. "Sally, give me a drink!"

"He doesn't know where he is," the nun said to Anne-Marie.

"How long has he been like this?"

"Since the middle of the night."

"Why didn't anyone tell me?" she demanded. The nun gave her a puzzled look. Of course, she remembered. Zeke wasn't her relative—in fact she had only met him the day before. Then why this awful feeling, as though this were really François? "Here, I can do that," she offered, reaching for the towel. The nun handed it over, glad of the relief.

"Water!" Zeke moaned. When he tried to raise his hand, Anne-Marie realized it was tied down to the bed.

"To keep him from scratching," the nun explained. "If you're staying here, I'd better see to the other patients. There are so many," she said, moving off.

"For God's sake give me water! Sally, I'm on fire!"

She dipped the towel in cool water and squeezed some between his lips, but he kept on thrashing and moaning for a drink. Then she thought of Eli. My God, what if Zeke died without Eli ever seeing him again?

She didn't stop to think about what had happened yesterday. What did that matter if Zeke was about to die? What if this were François, she thought, wringing out the cloth.

But what about Massey? What about his rule that Eli couldn't see Zeke unless he agreed to Carleton's terms?

"Damn Massey," she muttered. What if Massey didn't know? What if she brought Eli here on her own? If it were her brother, she'd want the same. If this were François and Eli were sitting here, she'd never forgive him for not sending for her—and some instinct told her that he'd do it, too.

"Sally, I can't reach you!" Zeke strained at the ropes so hard that the whole bed groaned.

"It's all right," Anne-Marie murmured, laying the towel on his skin. "I'm going to get Eli. You hold on until I get back."

She grabbed the first nun she came to and dragged her back to sit with Zeke. "I'm going to get his brother. Please don't let him die until we get back." She left the nun looking bewildered and ran out through the ward.

Eli was in his room, reading, when she burst through his door. "What—"

"No questions. Zeke is very bad. I'm taking you to see him. Hurry, we haven't much time. Have you had smallpox?"

"I'll be all right." He was already moving with the assistance of his cane. She took his arm to help him.

"Massey won't like this."

"I don't care. Don't you want to see him?"

"Yes, I do," he said. "Thank you for coming."

"You can thank me if we're in time."

She grabbed a cloak from the front hall and swung it around his shoulders, over his splinted arm. "Watch the steps, they're icy. I've got a cariole."

He crept down the walk at a snail's pace, but at last they were in the sleigh and whisking along to the Hôtel Dieu. Anne-Marie pulled the cloak's hood close over his head and prayed they wouldn't run into Massey on the way.

They didn't, and in only five minutes they arrived, though it took that long and longer for Eli to get upstairs. With the assistance of one of the nuns, Anne-Marie practically carried him, though he walked when they got to the ward. When they came within range of Zeke's bed and she saw the nun still there, she almost fainted with relief. They wouldn't be wasting time on Zeke if he were already dead.

She clutched Eli's arm tighter. "He's alive, thank God!"

Eli didn't answer; he seemed unaware of her or of the other patients as he walked to his brother's bed. When the nun saw them, she stood up and left silently.

"You'd better sit down." Anne-Marie led Eli to the chair but he shook her off and moved up close to Zeke.

Zeke hadn't changed since she'd left him; he was still tossing and bathed in sweat. She was so relieved to find him still living that it took her a while to realize that Eli's silence was shock. He was staring at his brother as if he'd never seen him before.

"It's the smallpox," she said softly.

Eli started at the sound of her voice and raised his eyes to give her an endless, anguished look. His eyes, usually so collected, were shattered with fear and such pain that she reached out her hand without thinking and touched him on the cheek.

"I'm sorry," she whispered.

Eli covered his eyes with his good hand. When he dropped it a moment later, she saw that he'd regained control. "We've all changed," he said shortly. "I guess that's the nature of war."

"Sally, where are you?" Zeke groaned, straining against his bonds.

Eli touched him on the shoulder. "Zeke, it's Eli."

"Sally!"

"Sally's not here. She's home with the baby and Archie. You're in Quebec with me. You're sick. You've got smallpox."

"Water, please, Sally!"

Anne-Marie dipped the towel and dropped some water between his lips. "Sally's his wife?"

Eli nodded. "They'll be married three years this fall. The first time I met her, I defended her in a trial for the title to the land she and Zeke both claimed."

"You defended her against Zeke?"

"He's the one who asked me to. We almost won, too, but the judge was afraid of Zeke." His mouth turned up in a crooked smile. "He couldn't run her off that land, so finally he married her. She's about the only woman who could put up with him." He spoke with deep affection. For the hundredth time Anne-Marie thought of François and felt a pang of longing for the brother she'd barely known.

"They built a house way up on Lake Champlain. You ought to see the view. They've hardly got any neighbors but they're happy there. They've got a baby—I guess she's almost two by now. I promised Sally I wouldn't let anything happen to Zeke."

"She won't blame you for this."

"No, maybe not. But I'll blame myself."

"Water!" Zeke muttered.

Eli took the towel from Anne-Marie and gave Zeke a drink. Then he bathed his forehead with a gentleness that almost broke Anne-Marie's heart. "He does a lot of threatening and shouting, but down underneath his heart's as soft as a feather tick. That's always been his weakness, thinking with his heart. It's gotten him into trouble more times than I can count."

"But if he'd spent his life being careful, what would he have in the end? Maybe the satisfaction that no one had taken advantage of him, but what's that compared to the love of his wife and his family?" Her voice shook with emotion.

Eli wiped Zeke's face tenderly. "Not much, I guess," he admitted in a voice Anne-Marie had never heard.

"I'm sorry," she whispered.

A voice, outraged and familiar, exploded in her ears.

"If Colonel Arnold knocked on the front door, I suppose you'd ask him in! And if General Washington came calling, you'd probably give him a guided tour of the wards!"

Captain Massey was striding toward them, past the rows of writhing men, with a distraught-looking Mother Superior trailing after him.

"Where is he!" Massey was shouting, when he saw Anne-Marie. He reared up and stopped so abruptly the nun crashed into him. "So!" he fumed, advancing with angry, measured strides. "So, this is how you show your gratitude for all I've done for you!"

"*You've* done!" His statement surprised her so much she almost choked.

But Massey had no time to listen. "What kind of a stunt is this? Of all the empty-headed, idiotic—you knew I'd set conditions for Brownell to see his brother and yet you willfully ignored them with no regard for the mischief you were causing by bringing him here!"

"His brother might be dying!"

"I don't care if his brother dies!" Massey exploded without so much as a glance at the bed. "Can't any of you get it through your silly female heads that this isn't a tea party? This is a war, and war is about men dying. How else do you think one side wins?"

"Captain, please!" entreated the Mother Superior, laying a hand on Massey's arm.

Massey ignored her, still ranting at Anne-Marie. "You're lucky he didn't take you hostage and try to get through the gates! You could have been injured or worse! But do you stop to think of that? Do you stop to think?"

Anne-Marie's face was almost purple. Her fury choked her throat so that when she tried to answer, she couldn't find the words. In desperation, she turned to Eli. Damn it, why didn't he speak! Why didn't he defend her instead of standing there like a block of ice? Had she imagined he cared for his brother? Had she seen pain and fear in his eyes? She must have been mistaken—he didn't care at all; not for her, not for his brother, not for anything but himself. Why else would he stand there and let Massey humiliate her as if she were a mongrel dog?

Massey also turned to Eli and grabbed him by the arm. "Let's go, Lieutenant. I'm taking you back to bed. I'll deal with you later," he added to Anne-Marie.

Before Massey could drag him two paces, Anne-Marie was blocking their way. "What's wrong with you!" she pleaded with Eli. "This is your own brother, your own flesh and blood! Aren't you even going to put up a little fight? Don't you care at all?" She didn't realize she was crying until she heard her voice. When she put her tongue out sideways, she tasted the salt of her tears.

Eli's face was carved in granite. "You care," he said. "You stay here and watch over him." When he added, "Let me go," she moved aside to stand with the tears streaming down her cheeks as Massey dragged him away.

"I don't care."

"The hell you don't! You worked hard for that book. I know how much wood you chopped and carried to pay for it, and now he's going to burn it unless you stop him!"

"You know I can't stop him."

"Damn it, you can try! I'll try if you don't!" Zeke's voice was young but it came to Eli strongly across the intervening years.

"Don't," said Eli, but Zeke was already gone, out of the barn into the yard where their father had built the fire in order to show Eli once and for all that he really meant no more school. From the wall against which he was sitting with his back to the yard, Eli could hear Zeke pleading with their father to spare the book.

"I'll do his chores for him," Zeke was saying, "if you think he's not doing enough. I'll—"

Eli put his hands over his ears. It was better not to listen, better not to feel, better to think his way through this to a better time. The book was gone; so be it. He would get another one. There was no point fighting his father, who was bigger and stronger than him, and he hated to hear Zeke pleading on his behalf. He could smell the pages burning, the pungent stink of cloth. If he took his hands away now, would he still hear Zeke's voice, or would Zeke be gone forever? Was he already gone?

He took his hands away and heard a sharp sound—the sound of a fist knocking on a door. He opened his eyes to darkness.

"Who is it?"

"Anne-Marie. Can I come in?"

He sat up, his mind whirling as it sorted out the scenes: the past, the present, what was yet to come. "Please," he answered.

The door opened and she appeared, her face reflecting the light of the candle she held. Even in the dimness he could see the strain of exhaustion smudged beneath her eyes, darkening their silver to pewter gray.

He came to his feet, hardly noticing the weakness of his bad leg. "He's dead."

"No! No." The flame leapt and guttered as she shook her head vehemently. "The fever broke. The doctor thinks he's going to live. Watch out!" she cried as Eli's leg suddenly gave way.

He managed to catch the table before he went down in a heap, and by that time she was with him, lowering him to sit on the bed. Even at such a moment he was conscious of her scent.

"Did Massey hurt you?" Her eyes flashed at the thought.

Relief and longing mingled and swirled in his chest. He wanted to reach up with his good hand to stroke her hair and her cheek. He wanted to, but he didn't. Instead he shook his head. "It doesn't matter. Tell me about Zeke."

"There's not much more to tell. After you left, he seemed to get worse and worse. We kept on bathing him with cool water and trying to get him to drink. Then all of a sudden, he was soaking wet. The fever had broken and his body was cool. He's still very weak, but the doctor says in most cases the fever doesn't come back. If it doesn't, and nothing else goes wrong, the doctor says he'll live."

They were sitting side by side on the bed. He was conscious of her beside him as he dropped his head to his hands and caught the whiff of burning pages, the echo of Zeke's young voice. He couldn't remember being so grateful in all his life.

After a long time she shifted away from him and asked, "Why didn't you say something when Massey was yelling at me?"

He raised his head and looked at her. "It wouldn't have helped. If I'd come back at Massey, he would have gotten angrier. At you, too," he added, in case she hadn't understood. "And in his anger he might have forbidden you to stay with Zeke."

"He might have tried, but he couldn't have done it," she said with a toss of her head.

She was lovely, but unrealistic. "Yes, he could," he said. "At that moment he could have done just about anything, whereas nothing I could have said or done would have convinced him to let me stay. The best I could do was to get him out of there so that you could stay. If I'd caused a scene he would have called a guard, and if Carleton heard I'd turned violent, he would have had no choice but to take

Massey's side. This way Massey won't dare go to Carleton, because he won't want Carleton to know that he'd tried
to keep me away from Zeke. Massey will have no choice but
to let the whole incident drop.''

As he spoke, she listened intently, her face half-lighted by
the candle and her hands loose in her lap. After he finished, she sat unmoving and silent for so long that he
thought she wouldn't reply.

But she did after several minutes, in a tone of hushed
disbelief. ''Was that what you were thinking while Massey
was yelling at me? You were working through all the an-
gles—all the risks and the benefits? Your own brother
might have been dying two feet away, but you were thinking like a lawyer in a courtroom, figuring everything out.''

He brushed away a sharp barb of anger. ''You're tired
and you're being unfair.''

''Don't tell me what I am! You let me and your brother
down.''

He sighed in frustration. Would she ever grow up and
stop being blind? ''I suppose you would have liked it better if I hadn't thought. You'd probably have preferred if I'd
called Massey a bastard and punched him in the nose!''

Her hands were no longer loose now, they were curled
tightly into fists. ''Maybe I would!'' she retorted.

''It wouldn't have done any good.''

''But it would have done something!'' she cried, springing up from the bed. ''It would have been better than
standing there like a lump! Don't you ever act on your
feelings? Don't you have any feelings at all? If that had
been my brother, I'd never have left unless they'd knocked
me unconscious and dragged me out by the hair!''

''Which they would have done, I assure you.''

''I don't care! That's not what matters! Don't you understand?''

She was standing before him, magnificent in her rage,
but at the moment he was too angry to appreciate any of
that. ''It's you who refuses to understand,'' he said with

deceptive calm. "You cling to empty gestures because you don't want to know—"

"Empty!" She seized him by the shoulders, her face only inches from his. "What about your brother?"

"My brother wouldn't have known. He was delirious from the fever, if you'll recall. I thought it would help him to get Massey out of there."

"You thought! You thought!" she shouted, shaking him in her rage until he grabbed her hands and forced her back down.

"Hush! You'll wake the whole house!"

"I don't care!" She twisted to break free but he wouldn't let her go. Her hair, already loosened, had come tumbling down over her shoulders, glinting red in the candlelight.

Anger and desire were only a hairbreadth apart. Even as he held her he could see himself pulling her down beneath him, full breasts, responsive mouth, long, long legs and magnificent cape of hair. She'd fight him with a passion and her yielding would be fierce. They were so close he could do it.

"Damn you, let me go!" She bent her head and he remembered how she'd bit him that first night they'd met.

"No you don't." Before she could do it, he pulled her back by the hair.

"You're hurting me!"

"It's your own fault. Be still and listen now. You think you're so fine and heroic because you never stoop to sordid things like planning ahead or taking care. You think there's a glory in shooting and punching your way through life, but while you're punching—and shouting and bombing—people are getting hurt. Some of them might deserve it, but others are innocent—"

"Like Captain Massey?"

"I was thinking of the sieur. I was thinking of how he'll suffer if anything happens to you. You may be brave and fearless, but you're also immature. You're a headstrong, spoiled child and it's way past time that you grew up!"

"I hate you!" she sobbed, twisting away, and this time he let her go. When she raised her hand to strike him, he didn't move.

"Go ahead," he dared her. "Slap me, then run away just like you always do. Very brave and fearless."

She dropped her hand, clearly enraged by his words. "I wouldn't dirty myself by touching you! I'm sorry I took you to see your brother! You don't deserve a brother! You don't deserve anything!"

She took two steps away then stopped and turned back. "You may think you're invulnerable. You may think you're made of iron, but nobody really is. You're made of the same flesh and blood as everybody else, and one day, sooner or later, you're going to do something that's not completely 'smart.' You're going to do something stupid, and when you do, I hope you'll remember me!

"I'm not running away because of what you said. I'm leaving now because I don't want to be here with you. I don't care if you do betray me to General Carleton. I don't care if you sell your damn Grants to England, if that will get you out of here!"

She didn't slam the door behind her. She closed it quietly, and he wasn't surprised in the least when she didn't turn the key.

He leaned back against the pillows. All right. The door was unlocked. There was nothing stopping him from walking out of here, nothing but his bum leg, and he could manage that. He could get a knife from the stables and hitch up the cariole to drive to the Hôtel Dieu. When he got there, he'd force the nuns to help him get Zeke out. He'd take one of them hostage to get them both out through the gates. Better yet, if he could get Zeke up on the wall he could drop him and then jump over into the deep snow. He could—

He could go to hell. The plan was worse than desperate, it was ludicrous. He'd barely been able to get up those steps with help, not to mention the fact that if he dragged Zeke out in the snow tonight, he'd kill him for sure. Here he was, doing exactly what she'd accused him of. He was thinking like a lawyer to block out everything else.

What was so goddamn wrong with thinking? What was he supposed to do—throw open the windows and howl at the Canadian moon? Would she be happy if he howled out to the whole city just how much he wanted her?

He'd be damned if he'd do that, for her or for anyone else. Once, he'd given his heart to a woman and she'd kicked him in the teeth. It had taken him a long, long time to get back up from that, and when he had, he'd sworn to himself never again.

He got up and limped to the window. The sky was growing light and all of the stars had been swept away except for the few brightest ones. Thinking wasn't a weakness, it was a strength; right now, if he followed impulse, he knew where that would lead. His plan had been desperate, but he could mold it into one that would work. When his leg was stronger and when Zeke was well, he'd be able to come up with a way to get them both out. He would stay where he was for the present and he would use his head. He'd be smart—the thing she hated—and he'd survive. And when he got away from here, eventually he'd forget.

Chapter Six

The soldiers on the parapet saluted as Carleton and Massey passed on the walkway below.

"Can you see springtime coming from up there?" Carleton joked with the men.

"Not quite, sir!" The soldiers' breath clouded in the frosty air.

"Well, winter can't last forever, and then we'll see," Carleton said. "Any trouble from the Americans?"

"No, sir!" The soldiers shook their heads.

One made a face of scorn. "They toss us a ball every so often so's we'll know they're still alive, but they can't hurt us. We'll go out there and get 'em anytime you want."

"That time will come," Carleton promised, saluting as he and Massey walked on.

"The men are eager," Massey said unnecessarily. "You've read our spies' reports. The Americans are just barely keeping body and soul together. We don't have to wait for the reinforcements to come with the thaw—we've got more than enough men in the city right now to drive them out."

"Perhaps," Carleton mused. "But why take a risk? Lord Germain writes that Parliament has authorized another ten thousand troops. They'll be sailing from England any day, and once they can come up the river, we'll have all the strength we need to deal with the Americans. Besides, in the meantime we have enough supplies to last, and they haven't got the men or artillery to come in, so there's no point in taking the risk."

"But—" Massey began before he caught himself. But you can't get ahead without risks, he'd been about to say, quite a presumptuous statement coming from an aide.

Carleton saluted again as they approached the next parapet and exchanged greetings with the soldiers on patrol. When they were out of range, he said, "Speaking of biding one's time, I don't suppose Lieutenant Brownell has made up his mind?"

Massey shook his head. "He's also waiting for the thaw."

Carleton gave Massey a thoughtful, sideways look. "I understand you crossed swords with Mademoiselle Doucet at the Hôtel Dieu last week."

Massey felt himself flushing with annoyance but not with surprise. Why should nuns be different from other women when it came to gossiping? "Lieutenant Brownell's brother was ill with smallpox. Mademoiselle Doucet took it upon herself to take Brownell to visit him."

"You objected?"

"Yes, sir, I did. By doing what she did, the *mademoiselle* put herself at risk."

"You believe Brownell would have left without his brother, knowing what would happen to his brother if he did?"

"Sir, the brother might have been dying. Then Brownell would have been free, and he could have used Mademoiselle Doucet as a hostage to get through the gates."

"Fortunately he didn't."

"That's true. But he might have."

"I see . . . ."

Massey glanced at Carleton, trying to read his mood. He couldn't, but on impulse he spoke anyway. "Sir, since you've broached the subject, there's something I've been meaning to say. After what happened, I'm concerned about keeping Brownell at Saint Vallier's. I'm afraid he might be gaining undue influence over Mademoiselle Doucet. I'm afraid he and his brother might try to use her as some sort of go-between, especially once his brother recovers and goes back with the prisoners."

"Undue influence, eh?" Carleton rubbed his cheek. "That's difficult to imagine with Mademoiselle Doucet. I'd have said the danger lay in the other direction." He seemed almost amused, but his next words were thoughtful and serious. "I know you and I have differing opinions about the best way to proceed with the situation here. No, don't apologize, Captain. I'm glad you disagree. You show me things from a different perspective and that helps to keep me clear."

He paused, and Massey thought he'd continue or at least return to the discussion of Brownell, but Carleton said nothing more except to suggest that since they'd done their duty to the guard, perhaps they could repair to a tavern for something warm to drink.

There was such a tavern just below the wall. The landlord recognized Carleton and led them to a table agreeably near the fire, saw them seated and took their order himself. After he'd left, Carleton returned to Zeke Brownell, asking if Massey knew when he might be released.

"I suppose it could be any day," Massey replied, sensing that far from dropping the subject, Carleton had been pondering it.

"We've got agents among the prisoners, don't we?"

"Not many, but a few. We had more to begin with, but the men sniffed them out and after that it wasn't safe for them to stay. On the other hand, you could say that only the good ones are left."

"I hope so," Carleton said. "When Zeke Brownell is returned to the seminary, I want you to see that our best spy is put in with him. That way, if there's a plot hatching, we'll be the first to know."

Massey didn't answer until after the landlord had filled their mugs with brandy and cider, left the pitcher and withdrawn. Then he said, "What about Eli Brownell?"

"Nothing for the present. I want to leave him where he is. If he is in league with his brother, we'll know from the brother's side."

"And if Mademoiselle Doucet is involved?"

"We'll know that, too," Carleton said, looking pensive but also distinctly grim.

Zeke was awake and bright-eyed when Anne-Marie arrived. "It's good to see you again—hell, it's good to see anyone! I understand you were my angel of mercy when I was at my worst."

"It was nothing." She smiled. He looked as thin as ever, but all sign of the fever was gone.

And he was grinning. "That's not what I heard. I heard you had a knock-down fight with that lobster-back Captain Massey over your bringing Eli here."

"I'd prefer not to discuss it."

"I'll bet!" Zeke guffawed. "From what I heard, he chewed you out something powerful before he dragged Eli out by his ear. Well, never mind. It's the effort that counts and I do appreciate it."

"I'm glad someone does," she muttered.

Zeke's eyes gleamed with a knowing light. "You aren't referring to brother Eli by any chance?"

She felt herself flushing. "Are you always so direct?"

"Sometimes I'm directer." He shook his head. "I don't envy you having to put up with him. He can be the devil to deal with, especially if you don't happen to be the reflective type, and you don't strike me as especially reflective. I don't mean that to be insulting."

"I'm not insulted." That was mostly true. She wasn't half as insulted as she was surprised at how effortlessly Zeke seemed to have read her mind. She had *Gulliver's Travels*

with her, intending to read, but Zeke was clearly more interested in pursuing the subject of Eli's character.

"My father had a terrible temper and he was about twice
as big as me, least that's how I remember him. He'd shout
and he'd holler and I'd shout and holler back, but not Eli.
He'd shout at Eli and Eli wouldn't say a word, just clam up
tight and stony, no matter how bad it got. Later on I'd ask
him how come he didn't fight back, and he'd give me this
sort of are-you-joking look. 'What's the use?' he'd say.
'You yell as much as he does and it doesn't change his
mind. Yelling makes him stubborner, if anything.'

"'Course, I knew that as well as him, but that didn't
change a thing. When he hollered I got so angry I had to
holler back. But not Eli.''

"No, never," she agreed.

Her tone was bitterly sarcastic. Hearing it, Zeke grinned.
"I was right, then. You've been crossing horns with him."

"I was a couple of weeks ago, but not anymore. To tell
the truth, I haven't spoken to him since just after I brought
him here."

"That bad, eh?"

"It isn't bad at all. As you say, we've got totally different ways of viewing the world. I'm not going to change the
way he thinks and he's not going to change me. I've
brought *Gulliver's Travels.*" She held up the book. "Would
you like me to read to you?"

He'd been prepared to comment but for once he held his
tongue. He nodded. "Yes, please. I'd like that."

She opened the book and read. He lay there so quietly
she thought he might be asleep, but when she glanced over
she saw he was watching her face.

He didn't give her any time to wonder what was on his
mind. "Eli's not half so bad as he seems. I know sometimes he acts like if you cut him he'd bleed ice water instead of blood, but I've seen him cut, and believe me, his
blood's as red as anyone's. I guess life manages to knock us
all around some and it's up to us to figure out how to take

the blows and keep on going. I do it by making a hell of a fuss. If I've got a problem, folks in three counties are likely to know.

"Eli's the opposite. When he's hurting, he pretends he's not. He just digs in and holes up inside. But that don't mean he's disappeared. He's still there and he knows everything that's going on. You may not believe this, but he sees a hell of a lot that other people miss. And when he sees something wrong he ain't above rousing himself to set it right."

"I'm sure he's been a model citizen." She looked down at the book.

"I'll give you an example," Zeke said, without missing a beat. "Take when I first met my wife. We didn't hit it off real well together, if you know what I mean. She thought I was a terrible bully and I thought she cared about all the wrong things, and if it hadn't been for Eli we'd have gone on thinking that way until the end of time. Eli was the one who made us see that we weren't nearly so far apart as we'd thought."

"How nice," she said tightly.

Zeke's beard twitched as he hid his smile. "He traveled two hundred miles in three days to be with us when our first baby came. We named her Elizabeth, after him."

"Look, Monsieur Brownell—"

"Everyone calls me Zeke."

"Look, Zeke. You seem like a very nice man and I'm sure you have great loyalty to your brother, but I'm afraid you don't know the half of what's going on."

"I don't, eh?"

"No, you don't." She shut the book and faced him, meeting him eye to eye.

He relented, and faster than Eli ever would. "All right, then, why not tell me? Lord knows, I've got nothing but time. And don't worry about us being overheard. Old Wally's deaf as a dormouse." He looked over to the next bed, whose grizzled occupant was watching the ceiling with a pleasant smile. "He was a gunner in the French and Indian Wars. Burst his eardrums so many times they gave up on growing back. Ain't that so, Wally?" he asked loudly, but Wally's eyes didn't even flicker at the noise.

Zeke turned back to her. "All right, then, tell me. What's going on?"

Of course she couldn't tell him. In the first place, it wasn't any of his business, and beyond that, she owed him no explanations about Eli or anything else. That's what she meant to tell him when she opened her mouth, but instead the whole story just came tumbling out, like linen from a cupboard when you pack the shelves too full.

"General Carleton had your brother put at my house because he wants to make a deal. If Eli will help lead the Grants over to England's side so that England can win, in exchange Carleton will guarantee that the Grants will be made an independent colony, and one more powerful than New York."

Zeke whistled softly. "Well, I'll be damned. I guess Carleton's smarter than I thought. What did Eli tell him?"

"He hasn't said anything yet. He said there's no point in him deciding before the thaw since nothing can happen until then."

"Smart man," said Zeke. "And in the meantime he's sleeping in a soft bed and enjoying good company. So to speak," he added at the expression on her face.

"I believe he may do it."

"And why is that?"

"Because it's smart," she said, wrapping the word in all its bitter irony. "Consider the condition of the Americans. If you believe the rumors, Howe's kicked the Americans out of Boston and New York and ten thousand British troops will be landing in Quebec as soon as the river thaws."

"If you believe the rumors, twenty thousand American reinforcements are on their way to Quebec right now."

"If they are, they'll be down with smallpox before the end of the month. Besides, if the Americans do win, your Congress will continue to side with New York against the Grants. The way your brother sees it, your only chance of gaining independent title to your lands is by going along with Carleton."

"He may see that, but he won't do it."

"How can you be so sure?"

"Because I know him," Zeke said, looking at her just the way Eli would have done. After a moment his expression turned thoughtful. "You're with us, aren't you?" he asked softly so that only she could hear.

She opened her mouth to deny it, but Zeke shook his head. "Never mind. I don't really have to ask. The truth is, I guessed it the first day you came up here. Don't look so worried. It's not as if it's printed on your face. Some people are thinkers, others are feelers. I'm a feeler myself. You can bet that drives Eli crazy."

As he said this he grinned, but Anne-Marie could tell that his grin was perfunctory. He might be a feeler, but she could almost see his brain working beneath his mop of hair. "I'm just about recovered so they'll be discharging me pretty soon. If they send me back to the seminary, do you suppose you could get permission to come read to me there?"

As if they sensed danger, her fingers gripped the book. "You don't seem very interested in the reading."

"Oh, I am. I am." This grin was full of humor. "So are the rest of the boys. We're always looking to improve our minds. Do you think you could do it?"

"I don't know," she said. She knew what he was thinking as if she'd read his mind. He was thinking she'd be helpful in planning an escape. What's more, she knew that he was right. And if she did know it, why was she holding back? Why? She knew the answer.

So did Zeke, whose good-humored expression had long since disappeared. "You're worried about Eli, aren't you?

You're worried about him knowing. You don't have to be. I'd bet my life on his holding steady.''

"That's your right. I'd bet mine on my own brother, but I won't bet on yours.''

He seemed about to protest but then he changed his mind. "You don't have to," he said quickly. "You don't have to tell him a thing, not even that you're coming to read to me. It gets mighty lonely over there with nothing but the same ugly faces day after day. Will you do it? Will you read to us?'' This time his dark eyes were full of mute appeal.

His eyes were too much like Eli's; she turned her head away. "Is this how you got your wife to give up her claim to the land?''

"How the hell—'' he began, then he realized who'd told her the tale. He chuckled softly. "No, not exactly. With her, I had to try something a little stronger than a simple plea. What do you say, Annie?''

Annie! She turned to him and saw that he was grinning his most endearing grin. Half-exasperated, she relented. "All right. If General Carleton permits it, I'll read to you, so long as you promise that we'll keep Eli out of it.''

"He's out," Zeke vowed, holding up one huge hand.

Carleton looked up from his writing as Massey closed the door.

"You wanted to see me, General?''

"Captain Massey. Have a seat.'' He waited until Massey was seated, then he said, "I wanted to hear your report on Zeke Brownell.''

Massey shrugged his broad shoulders. "There isn't much to tell. As you know, he was returned to the seminary two days ago. We put him in with a few of the other men from his regiment and also with our best spy.''

"Anything yet?''

"No, nothing. I believe it's still too soon.''

"Yes, of course.'' Carleton nodded, holding a letter out. "I wanted you to see this.''

Massey took the letter from him. The handwriting was
familiar. The note was from Anne-Marie, asking the general's permission to be allowed to expand her charitable
activities to include the prisoners at the seminary. Thanks
to excellent care, many of the men she'd been reading to
had recovered and were being returned to the seminary.
Many of them had asked her if she could read to them
there. Massey read further.

I know them. I know that their minds will be even
more restless now that they are well, and I can't help
but think how useful it would be to have them occupied at least for a few hours a week. I know that my
request is unusual, but I trust that it will be favorably
considered by a mind as broad and forward-looking as
yours.

Massey looked up from the letter. "What are you going
to do?"

"I'm going to allow it," Carleton replied. "And I'm going to hope for her sake that it's as innocent as it seems."

Massey frowned deeply. "I'm sure it is innocent—now.
They'll want her safely in position before they go to work.
Sir, with your leave I'd like to persuade her not to go to the
seminary."

Carleton looked at Massey for a long moment then he
shrugged. "As you wish, Captain. I have no objection to
your trying, so long as you don't mention our suspicions."

"Sir, that is understood."

"Good luck, Captain."

"Thank you, sir."

Massey had seen Anne-Marie several times since the
scene in the hospital and they'd managed to patch together
a sort of truce. He'd apologized for his tone of voice and
she'd apologized for being rash. The sieur had done his best
to promote the peace, but a wariness remained between

them that only time would resolve. Massey knew that his trying to dissuade her from this new plan wouldn't help, but he couldn't stand by and allow the Brownell brothers to lure her into a trap. He couldn't imagine a greater waste of womanhood.

He called on her at home and found her doing a bit of needlework in the drawing room. As he'd foreseen, when he broached the subject, she was adamant.

"But why shouldn't I read to the men? I've been doing it for over a month and there hasn't been any problem. Why should it be any different reading to them when they're well?"

"For the obvious reasons," he explained, wondering how women could be so naive. "Men go to the hospital because they're wounded or ill, and sick men don't pose any physical threat."

"Why should the prisoners hurt me?" In and out her needle went, while the maid fluttered about, clattering cups and saucers as she presented tea. "It's not as if they're criminals. I already know them. They're just ordinary men."

"Ordinary men can get desperate, especially in jail."

Her head was down, her mouth set with a stubbornness he recognized. "I'm not afraid. Besides, General Carleton has already said I can read to them if I want. He set the condition that the men will have to give their parole that I won't be harmed in any way, so I can't see that there will be any problem."

"*Mademoiselle,* if you do this I believe you'll regret it," he said earnestly. It sounded very close to a warning, so he wasn't surprised when she looked up.

For a long minute, her wonderful eyes searched his. Then she said, "Thank you for your concern, Captain Massey, but my mind is made up."

Short of reiterating his warning, what else could he do? He said, "Then be careful. We'll talk about this again."

* * *

After Massey had taken his leave, Anne-Marie sat alone, no longer sewing but thinking of what he'd said. She'd expected him to try to discourage her. She'd expected he'd scold and bluster as he had when he'd heard about her going to the hospital. But this time had been different. Why? Did Massey suspect? Was that the point of his warning—did he know something about Zeke?

An uncomfortable chill of suspicion crept its way up her back. Was she about to stumble unwittingly into a trap? Was that what Massey had been saying? Looking down at the neat pattern of her needlework, she remembered Eli's biting words about hurting innocent people when you acted before you thought.

She was thinking. If there was a trap, no one was forcing her to walk into it. She'd only agreed to read to Zeke, whatever he'd understood. If he wanted more and she sensed danger, she could always refuse. As long as she had her eyes open she'd be able to avoid a trap. She was rethreading the needle as Catherine appeared.

"*Mademoiselle,* the lieutenant would like a word with you."

"Damn!" she muttered as the thread slipped away. "Where is he?"

"In the library. What should I tell him?"

Tell him if he wants a word to talk to himself! she wanted to snap. But at the same time she was curious as to why Eli would want to see her. He'd made it clear enough that he hadn't wanted to ever since they'd fought about Massey and the scene at the hospital.

"Tell him I'll be in shortly," she said, going back to her work. She didn't want him to think that she'd drop everything and run when he called.

She made three uneven stitches then poked the needle into her thumb. "All right, all right!" she muttered, thrusting the needlework away and briefly checking her appearance before she went across the hall.

As always, he was reading. She would have liked to know what, but she had no intention of getting up close enough to see. She stood in the open doorway. "What is it you want?"

"Please close the door," he said calmly, waiting until she did.

"All right. It's shut now."

"What did Captain Massey want?"

"That's none of your business."

He didn't even blink at that. "Are you still seeing Zeke?"

"That's not your business, either. I don't see the point in this."

"Stay."

It was just one word, but it kept her in the room. When he stood, she took one step backward till her shoulders touched the door.

He didn't miss her reaction; he paused before he spoke. "I know they've moved Zeke back to the seminary and you intend to continue to read to him there. After what Massey told you, I think you should give it up."

"How—"

"The maid told me. She overheard. Look," he said quickly, before she could respond. "I know you don't like me interfering with your affairs. Believe me, I don't like it any more than you do, but this is important. If Massey's trying to trap Zeke, you could not only get caught in it, you could spring the trap and catch him, too. You say I don't care for my brother. Here's the proof I do. I'm asking you, for his sake, to stay away from him."

His words, coming back-to-back with Massey's, shook her more than she cared to admit. But at the same time they touched an already sensitive nerve. "You don't trust me, do you? You believe I'll endanger your brother with my carelessness—with my need to be heroic and punch my way through life."

He winced slightly as he recognized the words. "I'm sorry I said that—"

"But you still believe it's true. You do, don't you?" She was angry, but her voice was calm. "You don't trust me, do you? I don't really care, because I don't trust you, either, so we're even."

"Anne-Marie—"

"No." She shook her head. "You wanted to tell me something and I've heard what you said, but I can make up my own mind."

"Will you do one thing?"

"What is that?"

"Will you at least tell Zeke? Tell him that Massey warned you not to come, and tell him I think it's a trap. Will you tell him?"

She wanted to say no. More than anything, she didn't want to honor his wish. But she wasn't quite as childish as he believed she was. "Yes, I'll tell him," she said. "But after that, whatever happens is strictly between him and me. Agreed?"

He didn't like it, but there was nothing he could do, so in the end he nodded. "All right. Agreed."

Chapter Seven

The seminary was a large squarish stone building with an inner yard. Before the arrival of the Americans, a visitor at the front gates would have been quizzed by the aged watchman, then admitted into the maze of halls to find his way as best he could past knots of earnest young men.

But now all that had changed. The priests and their students had been crowded into the first two floors, while the upper two had been taken over as a military jail. Red-coated soldiers halted Anne-Marie at the door to demand her business and frown over Carleton's note.

"Vetter, fetch the sergeant, he can deal with this. Best step inside, miss, so's you don't freeze."

The sergeant, duly produced, seemed put out by the note. "We've got a hundred and forty-seven prisoners upstairs. I don't suppose the general means for you to read to all of them?"

"Oh, no. He understood I'd read to one group at a time, starting with the men I've been reading to in the hospital."

"And who would that be?"

She took a steadying breath and on the exhale answered, "One of them's Zeke Brownell."

Uneasy about Massey's warning, she was watching the sergeant's face, but he showed no reaction other than the irritation he'd shown from the first. "If that's what the general has in mind, Vetter, you might as well take her up."

Vetter led her up four flights of stairs and down a series of turning halls, depositing her in a guardroom where three soldiers were playing cards around a stove. None of the three wanted to leave either the warmth or the game, but when Vetter explained Anne-Marie's business, one of them got up begrudgingly.

"I don't know what the general's got in mind," he grumbled as he led her down another hall. "The hospital's one thing, but this is a prison and I can't very well lock you in alone with a bunch of men. I guess he expects me to stay with you."

"You don't have to," she said, too quickly, but the guard was ignoring her. He'd come to a stop at one of the doors and was pounding on it with his fist.

"You men, there's a lady come to read to you. Make sure that you're decent!"

"We're decent!" called back a voice she recognized as Zeke's. "At least as decent as a body can be in this infernal place."

"As if they'd be better off in their own camp!" the guard muttered as he unlocked the door. It opened inward, giving a view of a room that might have been spacious if it hadn't been so full of men and beds. Four pairs of bunks were stationed along the walls, with cots wedged in between them closely, leaving very little open space. At the present, most of the standing space was filled with standing men, who had all come to attention at the sight of Anne-Marie.

"Why, if it ain't Mademoiselle Doucet!" Zeke beamed when he saw whom the guard had brought. He spotted the book under her arm and his smile grew. "Don't tell me you've brought along Mr. Swift. Fellers, ain't that something?"

They all agreed it was, shifting their feet and looking as awkward as schoolboys on the first day of a new term. The room smelled of unwashed bodies and smoke and whatever they were cooking in the kettle on the stove. The smells and the closeness weren't exactly her ideal, but they were far more pleasant than those of the hospital.

Zeke's enthusiasm had a poor effect on the guard. Anne-Marie suspected he was still thinking about the game of cards going on without him at the far end of the hall.

"I don't know," he grumbled, looking around the room and clearly reevaluating the entire idea.

She beat him to the conclusion. "I'll be fine sitting right here on this bed." When she pointed at a cot nearest the door, the men tripped over one another in their rush to shake out the blanket and spread it carefully.

"Lucky you chose that one," Zeke pointed out. "It's just about the only one where the rope's not torn and dangling. With most of these, you sit down and you're sitting on the floor."

The guard made a scornful sound. "As if you had any beds to sit on when you were with the Americans!"

"Maybe we didn't, but if we'd had 'em, they would have worked."

"As you'll see—" Anne-Marie raised her voice before the guard could retort "—in his note, General Carleton asks that these men give their parole that they won't harm me or try to escape while I'm reading to them. Once they do that," she added, "you're perfectly free to leave."

"I don't know," Zeke grumbled as she handed the note to the guard. "I don't like to give the redcoats anything, let alone my parole, so I guess this one had better stay. Clear another cot, boys—if you can find one that'll hold him up."

"Just a minute." The guard looked up from Carleton's note. "According to the general, if you don't give your parole, the lady don't read to you."

"Not if you're staying," Zeke shot back. "If you're staying, you can watch us to make sure we don't do those things. You can have it one way or the other, but you can't have it both. Which will it be?"

The guard looked baffled. "But I thought you said—"

The fog lifted and Anne-Marie saw what Zeke was trying to do. "We're wasting time," she announced to the room in general. "And you," she added to Zeke. "I came here to read to you, not to listen to a debate, so why don't you just give your word and let him go?"

Zeke's eyes twinkled briefly as he gave a mighty shrug. "What do you say, boys, are you willing?"

They reckoned that they were, so Zeke raised his hand and led them in a solemn, if garbled, vow not to harm the *mademoiselle* or try to escape while she was reading to them.

The guard was still reluctant. "Listen here, you men, I'll be checking regularly, and if I even imagine you're up to something, I'll have you all hauled over to the Dauphin jail and clapped in irons! You'll be all right, miss?"

"Just fine," said Anne-Marie. "These men may be *Bostonnais*, but they're not criminals. They're soldiers, just like our men—though perhaps not quite as skilled." Zeke made a sound like a strangling ox; she ignored him and held up the book. "This isn't Mr. Swift. This is *Robinson Crusoe*, by Mr. Daniel Defoe. It's about a man stranded on a desert island with nothing but savages."

"Sorta like us," someone said. Still grumbling, the guard slammed the door.

Anne-Marie started reading as she heard him stomp away. When he'd gone, she thought Zeke might stop her, but he didn't, and when she glanced up with her question, he was settled back in his bunk looking like a man well on his way to being lost in an absorbing tale.

Had they all been mistaken about Zeke's motives for wanting her here? Maybe he really did just want the diversion and company. To her surprise, she felt a wave of disappointment at the thought. But her disappointment faded as she became caught up in the book. She was so engrossed in the story that at first she didn't feel Zeke's hand on her arm.

"You can stop now, but don't lose your place. If Harry gives the signal, you'll start right up again." He nodded at a thin man who was listening at the door.

"We was just gettin' to the good part!" complained a man from an upper bunk. "You ought to let her go on!"

"She'll leave you the book when she goes, Jed, so's you can read ahead on your own."

"Hell's afire," Jed protested. "You know I can't read."

"Shut up, will you?" The man on the bunk beneath him gave him a poke in the back. "I'll read you to sleep every night, once we get out of here."

"That was pretty fancy footwork we used with that lobster-back guard." Zeke gave Anne-Marie a broad grin. "Redcoats are a contrary bunch, so you've got to tell them the opposite of what you want. If you want 'em to leave, you tell them to stick around. You've got to confound them—which isn't very hard."

He chuckled, then he got down to business. "Listen. We've got a plan to get out of here, but to do it we need three things—candles, a flat-headed file and nails about this big." He showed her on his index finger. "We'll need a dozen to be safe. Can you bring them with you next time?"

"I—ah..." She swallowed and looked around. There were a dozen men, all listening to every word. If there was a spy among them, he'd have an easy job.

Zeke read her expression. "Don't worry about these fellers. I can vouch for each of them myself. Jed and Noah down below him are from the Grants. Harry's from Rhode Island. He's the one standing by the door. If you ask Carleton, Harry's the redcoats' number one spy. That's why Carleton had him put in here. He's supposed to watch me and see if I'm planning to escape. Ain't that so, Harry?"

"That's so." Harry grinned. He was gap-toothed, with a sprinkling of freckles across his nose.

"But meanwhile," Zeke continued, "Harry's really on our side. He feeds Carleton wrong information or stuff that he'd get anyhow. For instance, Harry'll report that we're considering tying our blankets together and going out the window, but then he'll say we've decided it's way too dangerous. Then he'll say that we suspect him, so he's got to lay off for a while. He's been stringing the redcoats along since we got in here, and meanwhile he's uncovered a half dozen of their real spies."

Harry made a sudden movement. "Guard's coming back!"

"Read!" Zeke ordered, and Anne-Marie began to read.

The lock in the door rattled and the guard's head appeared. "How's it going, miss?"

"Very well, thank you." She looked up.

"It's a good book," Zeke added. "Maybe after we take this city and we've got all you lobster-backs locked up, she'll come and read it to you."

"Big talk!" the guard muttered, and the door thumped shut.

Zeke gestured. "Keep reading."

She read for a while, but this time she was hardly seeing the words that she pronounced. She hadn't been mistaken. This was all about escape. Had Massey warned her because of Harry? It seemed certain that he had. Then there was less danger than Eli and Massey had feared. Zeke was still waiting for her answer. What would she do?

Zeke's hand touched her sleeve again. "Coast's clear. You can stop." He didn't say any more, he didn't have to; everything about him showed what he was waiting for.

She focused on him and tried to ignore the other men. "Captain Massey warned me against coming here. He said I'd regret it. Eli warned me, too. He believes Massey and Carleton are setting a trap."

Zeke shook his head in contradiction. "Carleton's trap is Harry, but Harry's with us, so you can tell Eli that we're safe. Will you help us?"

His eyes were brown like Eli's, but with a sparkle of fun that stirred something ticklish at the very bottom of her spine. The tickling worked its way upward and she knew what it was: the excitement of adventure and of taking risks. Eli was certain that Zeke's plan would fail, but this was her chance to show him that her way worked. She wanted to do it. It even sounded like fun—thumbing her nose at the British and getting away with it.

"What about your parole?" she asked Zeke.

"That only covers while you're here. We never said we wouldn't try to escape when you weren't." He didn't repeat his question, but it was hanging in the air.

She could hear Eli's reaction as if he were right in the room. She squared her shoulders. "I'll bring you what you want."

A palpable sigh swept the men; she almost sprawled off the bed as Zeke clapped her on the back. "Good girl! You won't regret it, and one day we'll return the favor, if we can."

The rest of the men nodded. She looked around at them: Harry from Rhode Island, Jed and Noah from the Grants, possibly others from other places. Might one of them possibly know...

"What is it?" Zeke asked.

She looked at him, and before she could think of a reason not to, she said, "I—I wonder if any of you have ever met a man named François Perkins."

"François Perkins," Zeke repeated, looking around at the men.

"He's a relative. We lost touch a long time ago and I thought he might have gone to one of the colonies."

"Anyone?" Zeke said, but the men were all shaking their heads.

"It doesn't matter," she said quickly, pushing hard at the bitter disappointment so that it wouldn't well up in tears. "I didn't think you would have. I don't know why I bothered to ask. I'd better keep reading...."

Zeke touched her on the arm. "If you like, when they let us out for exercise, we can ask the other men. There are men here from just about all of the colonies. We'll ask them about your François Perkins if you want us to."

She wanted to tell him to never mind. She hated the disappointment, but if there was a chance, how could she resist it? "Yes, thank you," she said softly, and began to read again.

The guard came back a few minutes later, saying it was time for her to leave. In his hearing, she promised the men she'd be back.

"I'll be wondering what happens," Jed called out as she closed the book.

"I'll tell you," said Noah. "In the end the redcoats lose!"

The sound of their laughter followed her down the hall.

"Can't see why you bother," the guard grumbled.

She smiled. "Charity."

From the seminary, she went to the Arsenaults'. Monsieur Arsenault was with clients when she arrived, but she drank tea with his wife until he was done. When she told him what she'd undertaken, Monsieur Arsenault looked concerned.

"Even if this spy is on our side, something can still go wrong. Getting out of the seminary is only the first part of escaping. They will still have to get to the wall and then beyond it and the guard is very tight. And even if they do get away, when it is learned how they escaped you may be implicated in the attempt."

She'd thought of that. "I'll deny it. I'm willing to take the risk."

He looked at her steadily in silence, then he asked, "What about Lieutenant Brownell?"

Her cup clattered against the saucer as a tremor passed through her hand. "His brother and I have agreed that he won't be involved."

"Perhaps his brother would agree to excluding him, but I can't believe that the lieutenant would agree to it." Arsenault's disbelief showed clearly in his face.

"He'll have no choice. If nobody tells him, how can he be involved?" She concentrated on holding her saucer still while Arsenault considered this.

"You honestly believe he'd betray his own brother if he knew of the plan?"

She took a breath and released it, then she answered, "Yes."

There was a moment of silence. She looked up at Arsenault, trying to gauge his reaction, but as always he appeared serene.

"In that case," he said slowly, "he shouldn't be told. But you must be very careful."

"I will be."

"Then good luck."

The bell in the cathedral was ringing six o'clock when she got home, and the last long golden fingers of sunlight were stealing across the snow. When the stretcher-bearers had carried Eli up the path from the cariole in January, the sun had set at half past four. Now it was almost April, and if you listened at the city walls, you could already hear the groaning from the river as the ice began to crack. Soon the ice would break off in great pieces to crash and twirl away and the thunder of racing water would reach as far as the Upper Town. Soon the great fleet from England would be able to sail to Quebec, and the Americans would be forced to stand and fight or turn and run. In a month, six weeks at the longest, everything would change. Then Eli would have to make his choice whether to serve Carleton or the colonies.

She shivered as the words "nearly over" crept into her mind. When the river was open everything would change. The siege would end one way or the other and Eli would go away. The sooner the better, she thought fiercely, trying to ignore the pang that started deep within her and pushed up through her chest as the fingers of sunlight shrank farther and farther back. She pushed open the gate and hurried up the front walk as the sunlight disappeared.

"Where is the sieur?" she asked the servant who answered the door.

"His lordship is in the salon playing chess with Lieutenant Brownell."

"If his lordship asks, please tell him I've gone up to my room."

"Very good, *mademoiselle.*"

In her room she took off her cloak and hung it on the hook behind the door, then sat at her dressing table and began to brush her hair. Her reflection stared at her from the mirror; her eyes looked distressed. She had told Monsieur Arsenault that Eli might betray Zeke. Did she honestly believe he would, or was she letting other emotions influence her thoughts? She remembered the tingle of excitement she'd felt when she had told Zeke that she would help, and how her next thought had been that this would give her a chance to prove that Eli was wrong. Was she acting from conviction in excluding him from the plan, or was her true purpose to get back at him?

The brush moved with more spirit as another thought came to mind. What if one of the American prisoners had heard of François? She knew that hoping invited disappointment, but it was her nature to hope, just as it was in her nature to take risks. Zeke had said that the prisoners came from every colony. What if someone knew him? She closed her eyes and imagined Zeke saying, "Good news! There's a man down the hall who knows your François." He'd tell her which cell and she'd go there and the man would say, "Yes, I know him. He's—"

She heard a small sound behind her. She opened her eyes and her breath stopped when she saw Eli standing just inside the door. The brush fell from her hand to the carpet with a muffled thud; she left it where it lay as she turned to face him.

"How did you get in here?"

"Your door was unlocked."

Her heart was knocking wildly. "I thought you were playing chess."

He completely ignored the statement. "Did you tell Zeke?"

"Yes, I told him."

"And?"

"And that's for me to know. I told you I'd tell him. I told him. That's all."

She thought he'd come back with a new thrust and was braced to parry it. He didn't. Instead of talking, he looked around the room with the same meticulous interest he'd shown the first day he'd arrived. Except that these were her things he was inspecting and fixing in his mind. She didn't like him looking; it made her feel undressed, as if he were looking inside her as well as inside her room. Her cloak was hanging near him; when he touched it, she drew back. "Why won't you tell me what happened?"

"That's my affair."

He ran his finger along the fur collar of her cloak so gently that she shuddered, but she couldn't look away. "You believe I'd betray my own brother. You're the most—" He stopped himself with an effort she could see but could not understand. Dropping his hand from the cloak, he turned to face her. "Do you know what I think?"

"I don't care what you think." The truth was that she was afraid to know. Frissons of warning were running up and down her spine.

"I think you don't want to tell me because you don't want me to leave. Whatever excuses you're making, the truth is you want to keep me here."

"That's a lie!" Her cheeks were flaming with the force of her own words.

"Is it?" he asked softly. "I know you say you hate me. I even believe you do. But I also know what happens whenever I come near." As he spoke, he began to move toward her.

"Don't!" she gasped, a wave of panic gripping her.

"Why not?" He kept moving. "Are you afraid? You're afraid, but you want it. Don't you?"

"No! Stay away." She pressed back against the table. She wanted to flee but she couldn't. Her legs were good for nothing but shaking hopelessly.

"You're lying," he almost whispered as his finger touched her chin. She knew he felt her shudder as he slowly pulled it up.

"No!" she pleaded hoarsely.

"No what?" he breathed, but before she could answer, his lips were over hers.

It wasn't like the last time he'd kissed her; the same violence was there, but this time it was repressed. It seethed threateningly beneath the surface. His lips were relentless and the force of their caress seemed to pull her upward as it sucked away her will.

As if he controlled them, her arms came up and around his neck, linking at the wrists to support her, since her legs were shaking too badly to hold her up. His hands pressed lightly against the base of her spine as his kiss bent her backward until she was gasping for breath.

Breaking away was out of the question, so was saying no. Until the moment he'd touched her, she hadn't realized how much she remembered and how much she'd been longing for him. What she was doing was wrong and against everything she'd resolved, but if her life depended upon it, she couldn't ask him to stop. He was right; she'd been lying. She wanted this.

His hands opened, pressing her to him until she could feel him through her petticoats. His hips were moving slowly and hers were moving in time. It was shameful but she couldn't stop it; she was beyond caring about shame.

She gasped a deep gulp of air when his lips finally let hers go, then she released it in a shivering explosion as his lips burned a slow path down her throat, nibbling, nudging her backward until her head touched the looking glass. She gasped again and went rigid as his hot lips found her breast.

His tongue teased hotly, slowly. She pushed closer, wanting more.

"Tell me," he murmured.

"What?" Her voice was thick, her mind miles away from thought.

"Tell me what Zeke said."

She remembered. "No."

She pushed back but he held her. His head dipped back down, his tongue delving deeper and deeper beneath her bodice hem, finding and teasing, starting the terrible ache that she remembered from the last time. She clung to him and whimpered, moving restlessly.

He stopped.

"Don't, please!"

"Tell me first. Tell me what Zeke said." His lips were at her throat, burning and whispering words she couldn't hear. "Tell me," he murmured.

She closed her eyes and whispered swiftly, "They're planning an escape. They need candles, nails and a file. Carleton's planted a spy in with them but the spy's really on their side."

"He wants you to bring him those things?"

"I said I would."

She was still bent backward and they were touching everywhere. She could feel from his body that he was still aroused and she held her breath, hoping that he'd heard enough. His eyes, dark and smoldering, lingered on her breasts, and the heat of his look stirred her almost as much as his touch had done. She felt like molten metal waiting to be poured.

His hands loosened their hold and he straightened, straightening her, as well. In a cool voice he said, "I want you to tell Zeke you told me. Tell him I said to be careful and to keep in touch. Will you tell him?''

She wanted to refuse. She wanted to scream or to slap him, but she knew there was no point. Her arms felt like lead when she unlinked them and they fell to her sides. ''I hate you,'' she whispered.

''I know you do. Will you tell him?''

''Yes!'' she said bitterly. ''Yes, I'll tell him. Is there anything else?''

''Yes. Be careful.'' Just that, and then he left, shutting the door behind him as softly as he'd opened it.

She crumpled slowly, slumping into the chair and leaning forward against the table to bury her face in her arms. She was torn between shame and fury and her body was still on fire, still aching with the deep ache she had begged him to satisfy.

What had happened? What was happening to her? She hated him, truly and with her entire soul, and even so she knew that if he came through the door again she'd be back on her feet, eager and willing to pick up what he'd broken off.

She raised her head and looked at her reflection in the glass. Her hair was wild, her bodice was open, and her eyes were asking ''Why?''

''I don't know,'' she whispered hoarsely, and the words caught in a sob. She shut her lips tightly. She'd already done enough. She couldn't undo what had happened; the best that she could do was to make sure that it wouldn't happen again.

She, make sure! That was a bitter joke. All Eli had wanted from her was a messenger. He'd only used her body to conquer her will, and so long as she did what he wanted, he'd leave her alone. She didn't have to worry about keeping him away.

He was wrong if he thought she wanted to keep him here. All she wanted at this moment was for him to be gone. She'd bring Zeke the things he'd asked for and she'd carry messages; she'd do whatever she could to expedite the escape. She'd move heaven and earth if she had to to get Eli past the walls and on his way to wherever she'd never see him again.

"Never again," she vowed fiercely to the looking glass, and she meant it as much as she'd ever meant anything in her life.

That Thursday when she went to read, she carried the things Zeke had asked for tied up in a cloth and fastened beneath her overskirt. She passed them to him after the guard had gone and within instants they were safely stowed away. That surprised her. "Aren't you going to work while I read?"

"We gave our parole not to try to escape while you were here and someone could say that popping out nails from the lock was part of trying."

"Is that how you're going to do it?"

He nodded. "The plan is to use the file to take out the nails that hold the lock on the door in place, then we'll replace them with the ones you brought. The ones you brought are smaller and we'll hold them in with wax. Then, at the last moment, we'll be able to pop them out."

"What if the guard notices that there's something wrong with the lock? What if it moves or falls out before you're ready?"

"It won't. We'll leave enough of the old nails to hold it in place. And just before we go, we'll put all the old nails back so they won't be able to see how we did get out. That way they won't be able to blame it on you."

"How will you get out of the city?" she asked, voicing Monsieur Arsenault's concerns.

"We've got a guard who's agreed to help once we get into the yard. We're a pretty crafty bunch. Among us we've gotten out of a heap of scrapes. With luck we'll get out of this one."

"Guard coming!" warned Harry.

She lifted the book and began reading randomly as the key grated in the lock.

"You all right, miss?"

"Just fine."

"You missed a part," Jed complained after the guard had gone. "Before he was in the ship and now he's on the island—"

Zeke took the book from Anne-Marie and handed it across. "Here, Noah, you read for a minute. If you boys will excuse us, the *mademoiselle* and I have a couple of things to discuss in privacy."

Noah did as instructed, while Zeke took Anne-Marie by the arm and conducted her to the farthest corner of the room, where they took seats side by side on the lower bunk. The privacy was far from total, but it was the best they could do.

She was braced to tell him about Eli, but he beat her to the punch. "We've asked around about your François Perkins."

"Yes?"

"Nobody's heard of him. I'm sorry."

"That's all right." She looked away so he wouldn't see the tears that stung her eyes.

He didn't see them but he sensed them. "Don't give up," he urged her in a gentle voice. "There's a far sight more men outside the walls and once we get out of here we can ask them, too. If he is in the colonies, somebody's bound to have heard of him, and as soon as we know anything, we'll get word to you. In the meantime, keep your chin up."

He was really very kind. Why was his brother so different?

His brother. Her heart sank but she forced herself to speak. "I told Eli what you're planning."

"But I thought you—"

"I changed my mind. He said for you to be careful and to keep in touch." She tried to make herself look up but in the end she could not.

"I see," he said slowly. After a pause he added, "We'd better get back to that book."

She continued to read to the men twice a week. Each time, Zeke reported on the progress of their planned escape and she passed each report on to Eli. She delivered them to him in his room, her back against the closed door and her hand resting on the knob so she could run in case he moved toward her. He never did, and when she felt herself minding that he didn't, she called herself a fool.

The plan was set. On the day of the escape, Zeke and the men would break out of the seminary and Eli would leave the house to rendezvous with them in the Lower Town. They would escape through the same window through which Eli had come in that stormy predawn four months before. The house belonged to an old couple who were both deaf and hopefully would be unaware of the men passing through.

Chunks of ice crashing into the river had cleared a channel three rods wide when Zeke told Anne-Marie that the escape was set for the following day.

"You're sure Eli's leg can take it?"

She nodded wordlessly, struggling to swallow the panic that welled up in her throat. Panic for what reason? She didn't like to think. "He still limps, but he must think he can manage what he needs to, because he hasn't said anything."

She didn't add that Eli hardly spoke to her at all. He acted as eager to be going as she was to have him gone. In his room, he listened stiffly and answered her in as few words as possible, and when they were forced to be together at a meal or for the evening, he was pointedly careful to stay away from her. Either the sight of her repulsed him or else it attracted him in a way she didn't want to think about. One was as bad as the other; she walked a thin line between anger and shame as she consciously counted the hours until he'd be gone. But now that the time was upon her, for some reason she felt afraid.

Panic was displaced by another emotion when Zeke took her hand. "I don't know what to say. It doesn't seem enough to just thank you for all you've done."

"You don't have to thank me," she said hurriedly, afraid that she'd burst out crying if he went on. "If you want to thank me, then take Quebec."

"We will if we can," he promised. His beard crinkled as he grinned. "You're sure you don't want to go with us? America's pretty nice, 'specially up where I live. I could sell you a nice piece of land at a real reasonable price. Real reasonable—and you can pay me anytime."

"I can't leave, but thank you."

"Come visit, then. After this business is over, you come anytime you want. I'd like for Sally to meet you."

"Thank you," she repeated, knowing that after today she'd never see him again. "Good luck, Zeke."

"We'll be fine. You take care." He dropped her hand and caught her up in a great bear hug. When he released her, she wiped her eyes. After that each of the men wanted to shake her hand, thank her and wish her luck.

"All right now, boys," Zeke chided when she'd gone through the line. "Buck up. This looks like a goddamn funeral! That lobster-back'll take one look at you and know just what's up. I know redcoats are stupid, but they do have eyes! Read on, Annie."

Anne-Marie read on and presently the guard came and told her it was time to leave.

Half an hour later, she was standing in Eli's room. "Zeke just told me that tomorrow's the day."

"Everything's ready?"

"It must be." It was five o'clock and the afternoon sun filled the room with a mellow light. It filled the space between her and Eli, making it hard to see his face, but she could imagine his expression because she'd seen it often enough. Barely tolerant. Stony. Hurt welled up in her. "That's all," she said quickly and turned, grasping the door.

"Wait," he said softly.

Her heart gave a wrenching thud. She paused, holding tight to the door handle. "What do you want?"

"For one thing, to thank you for your help."

"Whatever I did, I didn't do it to earn your thanks."

"Yes, I know, and I'm sorry that things had to happen the way they did."

"No sorrier than I am."

"Is that so?"

She released the door and turned to face him. "What do you think? Do you think I like to be seduced like a courtesan then treated like I've got the plague?"

"Would you rather—" he shot back in an instant, but then he stopped himself. He shook his head. "I'm sorry."

"The devil you are! These last three weeks you haven't looked sorry to me—except sorry to be here," she added, her voice hard with bitterness.

"What about you?" he asked softly.

"What do you mean, what about me?"

He didn't answer, he just stood there looking at her. Now, despite the sunlight, she could see his face, and what she saw was very far from stony or tolerant. The look in his eyes was like nothing she'd ever seen before. It gripped her and moved her as his kiss had done; it moved her toward him, or else he was moving toward her. This is wrong, she was thinking; this is dangerous. But they kept on moving until not even the sunlight was holding them apart and they were so close together that all she had to do was reach up if she wanted to touch his chest.

His chest expanded and contracted as he drew a deep breath. "I don't think you're a courtesan, or that you've got the plague."

"I don't care." Her voice was low, barely audible. She had to get away. This was exactly what she'd promised herself not to do: not to stand so close to him that she could see the black of his pupils and breathe in his scent; not to feel the heat rising from him in waves; and certainly not to lay her palm on the smooth, hard muscles of his chest.

"I care," he murmured. His eyes were entirely black as he put his hands on her shoulders and bent to claim her lips.

This time there was no violence in his kiss. This time there was even sweetness in the way his lips stroked hers and nudged them apart, as if they were talking, mouth to mouth. He made a statement and she answered him. Their tongues elucidated; his fingers touched her cheek. She'd never been kissed this way, by him or by any man.

Something tight and painful unfolded in her chest. It needed more space than she could afford it; for a moment she thought she might cry. Her whole body heaved in a deep, deep, shuddering sigh. His lips parted and he drew it in; he held it, then exhaled it and it disappeared. Now she felt like laughing; she felt dizzy and airy and light.

He held her, but gently, as if he thought she might break—as though he were trying to show her that he meant what he'd said. If he did mean it, why had he acted so cold? Why had he been so mean? It didn't matter; all that mattered was this.

He held her so gently they were hardly touching at all, but the lightness of their contact focused its intensity. She felt his arousal and she heard his breathing change. His hands left her shoulders to run up and down her arms. She sighed and leaned against him; he turned his head to rub his cheek against hers, murmuring the meaningless words she'd heard before.

"Yes," she heard him whisper. "This," and "Ah!" She thought she heard "Never," but she might have made that up.

Her hands, which were locked together, loosened; one touched his hair. It was soft and curling and even felt richly brown. His hair wound around her fingers, tickling and teasing her. She let her other hand drift down the curve of his back, down below his waistcoat then up and underneath. His skin felt electric beneath the thin cotton of his shirt. He must have felt the jolt, too, because once more his breathing changed.

He held her to him in a way that made her feel satisfied and tortured both at once. His hips were moving in the rhythm she recognized. One hand pressed her to him while the other slid down her flank then up beneath her skirt, bunching it in handfuls until he'd reached bare skin. This she remembered with searing clarity. Her legs, which had been steady, began to shake.

He made different sounds now, soothing and comforting, sounds that you would murmur to a kitten or a skittish colt. The sounds heightened her excitement; her fingers clutched his shirt with such force that she expected the material to rip.

"...need you," he murmured, his mouth deep in her hair. One hand was stroking, the other flat on her back. She curled her leg around him and he held her thigh. They were moving together, but her skirt was in the way. He reached around and pushed it until it was at her waist, then she could feel his breeches against her naked skin.

She shifted, her breasts rubbing on his chest, her arms up high around him so she could feel everything. Half of her skirt was still down and now he was pushing it free, then his hands were beneath her and she was wrapped around his hips and he was thrusting against the barrier of his fall.

She felt him falter as his wounded leg gave way, but before he could drop her, he swung her around so that she was sitting on the edge of the desk. The wood was cool on her bottom, increasing the heat of her fire. His fingers grazed her belly as he fumbled with his fall.

She knew what happened next and she was willing—she didn't care if it was wrong. There would never be another man like him and tomorrow he would be gone. She shifted to give him more room, but his fingers followed her.

She gasped at the contact and instinctively pulled away; he let her go but followed gently, persuading her until she needed no more persuading. Her breath was coming in long uneven pulls, her body was taut and trembling as he nudged her up and up, coaxing her to the border of a miracle. Her head lolled backward, his lips spoke to her neck, nibbling their way up to blow warm air into her ear.

She was in the river, riding a great piece of ice, shooting down the rapids to the edge of the waterfall. She would die if someone didn't stop her, but there was nobody there.

Then she heard a voice speaking, a knocking on a door. *"Mademoiselle?"* the voice was calling. "Captain Massey is downstairs and his lordship asks will you come down and join them for a cup of wine?"

Eli's hand stopped moving.

"No, don't!" she gasped, afraid that he would desert her in the river and she'd drown.

"Mademoiselle?" It was the servant, rapping at her door. She drew in a deep breath of Eli and held it, listening, and a moment later she heard faint mumbling and the sound of footsteps retreating down the hall.

"He'll think—" she began explaining, but Eli's lips closed over hers and she made a soft sound of contentment as his fingers began to move again.

She was back in the river, flying faster than before; now the falls were before her and nothing could stand in her way. With a cry she passed the border; she shot into empty space with the roaring of the river pulsing in her ears. The water she hit was bath warm and she sank into it, cradled deeply in his hand, alive and exhausted, bewildered and infinitely wise.

Her whole body was liquid. She opened her eyes and found his head above hers, his eyes hooded and half-closed, looking down at her.

"Did you like that?" he murmured.

She nodded. She had no words. She had never imagined two people being so intimate. He was touching the most private part of her and she was looking at him, not in the dark of night but in the light of day.

He bent again to kiss her and she raised her head to meet him halfway. In the moment before their meeting, they heard the footsteps coming back.

They stared silently at each other. The footsteps passed her door. This time they were coming for Eli.

"Lieutenant Brownell? His lordship asks if he may have the volume he lent you last week. He wishes to show it to Captain Massey."

"One moment," called Eli as the key rattled in the lock. At the sound they both realized that the door wasn't even locked.

In one flurry of motion they were apart. Eli had her skirts down and was straightening his clothes while he reached for the volume behind her on the desk. Pointing, he directed her to the spot along the wall where she would be hidden by the open door.

She floated to where he had pointed. Her body felt very strange and she was filled with the wildest urge to laugh. She didn't; she stayed very quiet as the key rattled again as the bewildered servant locked and then opened the door.

"It was unlocked," she heard him saying.

"Was it?" Eli shrugged. "Here is his lordship's book."

"Also, Captain Massey would like a word with you. He asks will you please come down. Otherwise he will come up."

"I don't mind coming down as soon as I've combed my hair. You can wait if you want to, or you can leave the door unlocked." He paused, then added, "I promise I won't run away."

"I will tell the captain," the servant replied, and left.

Eli closed the door behind him and turned to her.

"Don't go," she whispered, leaning against the wall.

"I have to." He raised his hand as if he meant to touch her, but he dropped it before he did. "It's for the best."

"No it isn't."

"Yes, it is. If we'd gone any further, you would have regretted it. More than you will already," he added in a tired voice.

"I won't regret what happened."

"Yes, you will." He spoke with a somber assurance that filled her with a nameless fear. The sunlight had disappeared, and the room floated in the shadows of early evening.

"I won't," she insisted, but her heart sank as she spoke, because she realized that he'd turned back into the Eli that he'd been before, cool and distant and evasive. "You'll be gone tomorrow. We only have tonight." She knew that she was pleading but she didn't care. Maybe if she pleaded he'd change back again, and as she'd told him, they had only one night.

His lashes shadowed his cheeks as he closed his eyes and rested his forehead against the back of the door. She could almost see reason struggling with desire.

"Please, Eli!" she whispered, reaching out to touch his sleeve.

"No!" The word exploded though his voice was low. He took her by the shoulders, but not gently as before. "You hate me, remember? Even when we've been together, you've never stopped hating me. I'm going downstairs now and when I come back up I'm going to bed—alone. We'll say goodbye right now. I don't want to see you again. Do you understand?"

She nodded miserably. He had to have read her expression but he didn't do anything, just stood there looking at her for a long wordless time before he turned away and opened the door.

She closed her eyes and bit her lip so she wouldn't cry. She heard the door closing, but somehow the next thing she knew he was back and his arms were around her and she was lost in the heat of his kiss. He held her for a long breathless minute, then he let her go. Before she could call

out, he was gone. This time, though she waited, he didn't
come back again.

Eli covered the hallway in long determined strides. He
wasn't just walking, he was pulling against a rope. The instant he stopped pulling, he'd be yanked back into her arms
and he'd be doing exactly what he'd sworn he wouldn't do.
How could he walk away when he wanted her so much? If
they hadn't been interrupted he never would have stopped.
What difference would it have made? Would she really have
hated him any less when she woke up and realized what
he'd done—taken the best she had to offer and then deserted her?

He stopped at the top of the staircase. He couldn't help
himself, but the instant he did his senses were overwhelmed by the memory of her. It was more than a memory; she was still in his arms, lush legs wrapped around him,
that beautiful flushed face. He reached out with his right
hand and clutched the banister. Don't do it, his mind was
warning. You're nearly free now, don't turn back.

Free? He wondered if there were really such a thing, or
whether freedom was an illusion that pulled men through
life like a carrot on a stick. Freedom had led him to Quebec and was now leading him back home. Where next? he
wondered.

Behind him he heard a sound. His door was being
opened. He felt her in the hall. He knew that she saw him;
all he had to do was turn, then damn Massey and Carleton, damn wisdom, damn the world. He wasn't breathing.
He saw himself turning back. Before the vision could claim
him, he made himself block it out. Then, still holding on to
the banister, he started down the stairs. He hadn't reached
the bottom when he heard her door slam hard.

Chapter Eight

"In New York City with twelve thousand men," Madame Goselin was saying as she surveyed the cards in her hand. "I, for one, remember Lord Amherst when he was our enemy, and let me assure you that it is a relief to have him for a friend—especially if he is in New York with twelve thousand men."

"I don't believe it," said Madame Revier, helping herself to sugared nuts. "Ah, delicious! I don't know where Madame Cramahé finds such wonderful treats! Our last nuts were gone by New Year's. If only the ice would break more quickly so that the ships can come and rid us of these awful *Bostonnais!*"

"You may have to wait for your sugared nuts," Madame Goselin replied. "Because if the ships have gone to New York with Lord Amherst, they won't be coming here."

"I don't believe it," Madame Revier said for the second time. "I don't believe Lord Amherst has gone to New York at all. I believe that's just a rumor and that he's really coming here. Monsieur Revier says so and I believe he had it from General Carleton."

Madame Goselin raised her brows, which had been unevenly tweezed, giving her an expression of lopsided surprise. "Maybe there are two sets of ships. Maybe Lord Amherst has gone to New York and another commander is coming here. Then they could best the Americans twice as quickly. Wouldn't that be nice! Are you wool-gathering, Mademoiselle Doucet? Mademoiselle Doucet?''

"I beg your pardon?"

"Madame Revier has played her card. It's your turn."

"I beg your pardon." Anne-Marie dragged her eyes from the clock on the mantel shelf and tried to focus them on the cards in her hand. She felt as if she'd been here for hours and it wasn't even ten o'clock. She'd just been imagining Eli and Zeke and the rest running across a field, trying to dodge the bullets a half dozen shouting soldiers were firing at them.

It was a terrible image, but no worse than the others that had been plaguing her all day. She wouldn't allow herself to think about what had happened yesterday. If she did, she knew she'd go crazy, right here in the middle of Madame Cramahé's salon. She'd think about that later, after Eli was gone.

The other ladies at her table exchanged a knowing look and Madame Revier smirked. "True love will blossom even in the depth of the winter and burst into bloom in the spring! Shall we try to guess the name of the lucky man?"

Horror of horrors, they were all looking at her! "I wish you wouldn't," Anne-Marie muttered, randomly playing a card. Naturally it turned out to be the worst card she could have played. "What if everyone is wrong and there are no troops coming to America at all?"

"There are troops," Madame Goselin assured her.

"But what if there aren't?"

"Then the siege will go on forever and we'll run out of sugared nuts!" Madame Revier pointed a plump finger at her. "You're trying to dodge the question. It's Captain Massey, isn't it? Ah, look! We can ask him ourselves. Here are the men coming to join us—Captain Massey, over here!"

"Please, *madame!*" Anne-Marie fixed Madame Revier with a look that would have been sufficient to stop anyone with sense.

Madame Revier only giggled as Massey approached. "Come here, Captain. Mademoiselle Doucet requires your assistance with her hand. For some reason or other her mind isn't on the game. We ladies were saying that she must be in love."

Massey gave Anne-Marie a sharp look, and despite her best efforts, Anne-Marie turned bright red, less from embarrassment than pure, unuttered rage.

For once—miracle of miracles—Massey came to her aid. "Perhaps a turn around the room would clear *mademoiselle*'s mind." When he offered her his arm, she practically vaulted from her chair, trying to ignore the women's knowing smiles as Massey led her away.

"Stupid woman!" she muttered when they were out of range. "Really, she has no discretion!"

"Madame Revier? Ignore her." Massey steered her past the other guests to a little alcove at the far end of the room. "This will give the ladies something more to gossip about."

"Let them. I don't care." Anne-Marie glanced again toward the clock. Good gracious, the hands had barely moved! It seemed to her that it must be at least midnight—perhaps the hands were stuck.

"I have some news to tell you," said Massey. "A couple of hours ago your friend Brownell and his buddies were caught trying to escape from the seminary."

In the moment before he said it, she had a presentiment, which just barely saved her from betraying herself. "Escape—but how?" she demanded. How did she find her voice, since her chest had caved in until her ribs were touching and her legs were giving way? In a moment she'd pitch into Massey and he'd guess the truth.

"They'd gotten a hold of a file from somewhere and jimmied out all the nails in the door." He was looking straight at her; her whole face had gone numb so she had no idea if she looked shocked or was smiling. He took her by the shoulders. "*Mademoiselle*, I need to know—did you have any knowledge of this plan?"

In her mind she saw herself crumpling at his feet. If she did that, he'd have his answer and she'd be lost. Her head weighed as much as a cannonball but she managed to hold it up. "What are you suggesting—that I helped them with this plan?"

"Did you?"

"Of course not!" It was no longer her voice speaking or her head held up. Somebody else had taken over; as for herself, she'd moved aside and was watching with admiration and disbelief. "I am profoundly insulted that you even had to ask!"

Amazing. That seemed to sway him. He said, "I apologize. Please try to understand my position."

"Yes, of course." She lowered her eyes. Now the real question hit her. How had they been caught? Had someone betrayed them—and if so, who? "Did you know about it beforehand?"

He shrugged his shoulders. "We have our spies."

"Was it your spy who suggested that I was involved?"

"No, he didn't." His hands were still on her arms. She wished that he'd release her, since it made her think of yesterday.

Eli! She felt her eyes bulge out of her head. Two hours ago he'd have left for the rendezvous. He'd still be waiting for Zeke and the others to come. She had to go warn him! The thought hit her with such force that she almost broke loose from Massey and rushed out of the room.

Thank goodness she didn't, but caught herself in time. She looked up. "Where are they?"

"At the Dauphin jail. They're all in irons, as a lesson to the other men. I don't imagine you'll be reading to them anymore. I hope you didn't leave them dangling in the middle of a plot."

"They'll have to miss the conclusion," she said, ignoring his smirk of satisfaction at his own great wit. Her head was throbbing. She had to get away, but of course she couldn't with Massey watching her. How much did he suspect her? And what about Carleton? Her life and perhaps Eli's depended upon her keeping calm.

She glanced toward the other guests. "They're all watching us and I can imagine what Madame Revier is saying right now."

She started and recoiled as Massey's finger touched her cheek.

"Shall we gratify their curiosity?" he murmured, turning her back to him.

Merciful saints in heaven—he meant to kiss her now! She was beside herself with worry and he wanted to make love to her! The thought of it was repulsive beyond all imagining, especially after what had happened yesterday. But if she let him, wouldn't he stop suspecting her?

He was bending down to kiss her, as Eli had done. A knife of awful hurt twisted in her heart, followed by a stab of longing too forceful to abide. Don't think of what he's doing. Don't think of anything at all. You can get through this by making yourself numb. She closed her eyes. Their lips met.

It was worse than she had feared. She felt as if someone were pressing a clammy pillow over her face and she had to steel herself not to gag and push him away. Massey's scent made her nauseated and his heat was stifling. Now he was trying to poke his tongue between her lips. Great God in heaven, his hand was on her breast! She felt no thrill of reaction, only the deepest disgust.

"Please, Captain Massey!" She tried to squirm free of his grip but only succeeded in tightening his hold. Her eyes were wide open but his were still closed, which made him look exactly like a rutting goat. A goat rutting on her body.

"Captain, please!" She shoved him so hard she not only broke his grip but almost knocked him down. He might have crashed into the window had the drapes not caught him first. There was a bust of the Sun King on a table at her side. She was swept by a mad desire to smash it over his head, but that would be disastrous if she wanted him on her side. So she swallowed down her revulsion and forced herself to smile.

"My goodness, Captain Massey, you are a very passionate man!"

Massey, the old goat, liked that. He stopped scowling and stuck out his chest. "And you're a very passionate woman, *mademoiselle*."

When he reached out again, she dodged him. "No, Captain, please. We must rejoin the others."

"Why must we?"

She made herself laugh, a high-pitched gay laugh that sounded almost hysterical. She tried to sneak around him, but he blocked her way.

"I'll let you go, but I want you to promise that you'll let me take you home."

Home. Where Eli would not be in his room. What if Massey wanted to talk to him? "I'm not sure—"

"I am. Whenever you're ready, I'll take you home. The sooner the better," he added with another smirk. "And now that you won't be wasting your time reading to the prisoners, we'll have more time to spend together. Tell me, did Madame Revier guess right?"

"What a question!" she muttered, unable even to summon a smile.

To put it mildly, the next hour was hell. She smiled and chatted while inside her head she was listening to herself screaming. Finally she gave in and let Massey take her home, which meant fighting him off physically in the cariole. Of course he wanted to come inside but somehow she kept him out. When she closed the front door behind her she almost fainted with relief.

Her relief was fleeting at best. Now she faced the prospect of going after Eli and getting him safely back—and telling him that his brother was in irons in the Dauphin jail. Moving to the nearest window, she peeked out at the street. Good, Massey was leaving. At least the coast was clear.

She'd change out of her gown and leave right away. It wouldn't take long to get there if everything went well.

She was halfway up the stairs when she saw Catherine coming down with a tray.

"Where did you get that?"

"From Lieutenant Brownell. Since you and his lordship were both out, he took his supper up in his room."

"He's there? You saw him?"

"Yes, *mademoiselle*." Catherine was surprised by her tone of voice. "And he must have been very hungry because he finished everything." She held up the tray to show the empty dishes.

Anne-Marie stared at them. A terrible suspicion was forming in her mind, too terrible to consider. But she had to consider it. "Catherine, did the lieutenant have any visitors today? Did he send any letters?"

Catherine thought, then shook her head. "No, *mademoiselle*. No one. Mostly he stayed in his room."

"I see." But he had seen Massey here last night. He'd left her to see him, but before he had gone he had told her that she would hate him for what he'd done.

"Is there anything else?" asked Catherine.

"No, thank you. You may go."

"Good night, *mademoiselle*," Catherine murmured, but Anne-Marie didn't hear.

She didn't bother knocking when she got to Eli's door. She turned the key and went in. He was on his feet, standing at the window looking out over Quebec, one tall candle burning on the table beside the bed.

He turned sharply as she entered. "What happened? What went wrong?"

She felt a surge of wild hope. Could she be wrong?

"Why are you still here? Why aren't you at the rendezvous?"

"I went, but when Zeke and the others didn't show up, I came back."

"You didn't stay very long."

"I stayed long enough. Tell me what's happened."

"Catherine said you were here all night."

"She's wrong. I called her when I came back in so she'd think that I'd been here."

"Would you swear to it on a Bible?"

"What's this all about?" In two long, angry strides, he'd crossed the room to her and had her by the arms just the way that Massey had held her earlier. "Tell me!" he demanded.

Massey had been here last night, just after she'd told Eli that the escape would be today, and Massey himself had told her he'd learned of the plan from a spy. Eli had gone down to see Massey. Had he told him then? She'd pleaded with him, but he'd left her—had he gone down to betray Zeke?

"Tell me!" he repeated, giving her a shake.

"Zeke and the others were caught trying to escape. Massey said a spy informed on them. I don't believe the spy was Harry or any of the other men."

His eyes glittered from the candle. "What are you trying to say?"

"What did you and Massey talk about when you saw him last night?"

He opened his mouth to answer, then closed it silently. His eyes were black with anger but she didn't look away. She forced herself to withstand their silent violence. "You believe I betrayed him." He gritted out the words. "You believe I was Massey's spy."

"Were you?"

"Do you have to ask me?"

"Yes, I do."

"Then there's no point in my saying anything. You already know the answer."

It hit her in the chest like a fist punching from the inside. She grunted as if she'd been struck, and in the same moment Eli let her go. He turned and walked back to the window.

She watched, caught in the flood of truths fitting together like bricks in a prison wall. She remembered things he'd told her and what she knew of the way he was. She also remembered what he'd said last night. He had promised her that she would hate him for what he had done to her. He'd already known....

Without meaning to, she groaned and pressed her clenched fists against her chest. She wanted to hurt him as badly as he'd hurt her, but short of murder, she didn't see how she could.

"Ever since you came here," she said unsteadily, "I thought the worst thing that could happen was for you to betray me to Carleton, but I was wrong. What you did to me last night was a thousand times worse. You knew... How could you do it?" She stopped before she broke down.

He turned back from the window. She couldn't see his face. She was too angry to look at him.

When he spoke, his voice was clear. "Maybe you were right about me. Maybe I have no heart."

So cold and distant. No excuses. No apologies. He had done what he'd done to her and the whole time he hadn't cared. He was worse than she'd imagined. A monster to be reviled. If she never did anything else, somehow she would pay him back for this, and for what he'd done to Zeke and the other men. Noah, Jed, Harry...she imagined them in chains.

"Why did you do it? What could Massey give you that was worth betraying Zeke?"

"You've got all the answers. Why don't you give me my reasons."

"I've given you enough!" Her voice was rising way beyond the danger point. She felt ill, suffocating. She had to get away. She turned, groping back to the doorway, when she thought of something else. "Why didn't you tell Massey that I was involved—or are you holding on to that in case you need to use it later?"

He made a sudden movement but then he was still. "Maybe I am," he answered in the same flat, frozen tone.

"Then do it!" she shot back. "I don't give a damn. Go ahead and tell Carleton everything you know. At least if they hang me, I'll never have to see you again. All my life I've been afraid of going to hell, but now I think it would be worth it just to watch you suffer for what you've done. Yesterday you said I'd hate you, but I don't. You don't hate garbage, you revile it."

"Get out," he said softly.

"When I'm ready."

"Now!" He began coming toward her.

She felt a wave of fear, but for that very reason she refused to move. "What are you going to do, make love to me? Or hurt me—if there's a difference." When he reached for her arm, she twisted away. "Don't you dare! Don't you ever dare touch me again! I'd rather be touched by a leper. I'd rather die of disease!"

"Will you leave now?"

"Yes, but I'm warning you. If you ever try to touch me or speak to me again, I'll kill you." She opened her mouth to say more but there was no point. Her anger was beyond words. Maybe tomorrow she'd wake up and discover that it all was a dream. Maybe she'd be granted a miracle.

The next morning she went to the Dauphin jail, but no amount of smiles could convince the guards to let her in.

"Sorry, miss, but we've got our orders direct from General Carleton. Nobody's to see 'em."

"Yes. I understand." She wished she could send them a message but she didn't dare. It would be bad enough if Massey heard that she'd been here at all. Maybe it was better that they'd kept her out, since if he'd seen her, Zeke might have been able to guess the truth. As bad as it had been for her, it would be even worse for him. Eli was his brother, and Zeke had once told her that he'd bet his life on him.

* * *

The days lengthened, the sun grew warmer, and at last the thaw arrived. From the walls of the city you could see patches of green on the sunny side of the valley that stretched out to the west. Every day the patches grew until finally there was more green than snow and the good smell of wet earth reached all the way to the Upper Town. In the Lower Town the air rang with the groan and splash of melting ice. The channel in the river widened every day until it reached from side to side, and the only ice remaining was tucked into the deepest shadows at the very base of the cliffs.

All eyes turned to the river, searching for the first sign of the hoped-for British fleet, and every day brought new rumors of sightings, which increased to every hour, until everyone's nerves were on edge and you could feel the tension humming in the damp spring air.

As if they realized that their chances were running out, the Americans opened three sets of batteries: across the river at Point Levis, on the bank of the Saint Charles and to the west of the Upper Town on the Plains of Abraham. Their guns filled the air with thunder but few of the balls found their mark, and the fire returned from the city soon forced them to pull back. People came out of their cellars and began watching the river again.

Anne-Marie watched and waited with a sense of dread, for the coming of a British army would signal the end of her dreams of the wholesale liberation of Acadia. Every once in a while someone would report that they'd heard on good authority that the Americans were sending an army of their own and that they had no intention of giving up on Canada. But even at her most sanguine, she didn't believe they were.

To make things worse, since the evening at the Cramahés', Massey had stepped up his pursuit of her, so that there was hardly an evening when she wasn't fending him off. Almost nightly she was on the verge of expressing her true feelings toward him, but somehow she managed to keep them to herself. Whenever he touched her she thought of Eli, which filled her with bitterness. Instead of fading, the memories seemed to sharpen with passing time.

As outraged as she'd been by Eli's betrayal, she had still thought that after what had happened he would get Massey to move him somewhere else. Clearly his actions meant that he had made up his mind to help the British win back the Grants, so it stood to reason that they would treat him well. But it seemed he lacked even that shred of human decency, because instead of leaving, he stayed.

She redoubled her efforts to keep away from him, and when she could not avoid him, she ignored him. The tension and uncertainty exhausted her, but when nighttime came, she found that she couldn't sleep. For the first time in her life she found no pleasure in the coming of spring.

On the third of May the Americans loaded a ship with dry wood and explosives, pointed it toward the Lower Town and set it on fire. As the terrified population watched from the walls, the flaming ship sailed straight at them. But the crew jumped clear too early and the current caught the ship and swept it away toward the Île d'Orléans, where it dazzled the twilight briefly before it burned out. The next day, after darkness, the bombardment from the batteries recommenced, louder and heavier than ever before. Residents dived for their shelters, and those who ventured out scampered back quickly with the usual wild tales. One was that the American reinforcements had finally arrived and were in the process of storming the city walls.

Anne-Marie heard these stories and grasped at unreasonable hope. Maybe the Americans would manage to win. Maybe twenty thousand reinforcements were coming after all. She wanted to go see for herself, but when she tried, the sieur threatened to have her tied to a chair. Worse, he wouldn't let her stay up in her room but insisted that they all retreat to the cellar. All included Eli, which meant that she had to spend the night and day within spitting distance of him. Eli and the sieur passed the time by playing game after game of chess, while she paced and fretted and tried not to think.

Sometime toward the early evening the front doorbell rang. Catherine, who was sent to answer, returned lighting Massey's way down the steep wooden steps.

"Great news!" Massey cried, his shadow looming monstrously. "The fleet was anchored at Malbaie night before last. If the wind holds in this direction, they'll be here by tomorrow at noon!"

Anne-Marie looked at Eli. She couldn't help herself. In the dim light he looked bitter. What was he bitter about? Didn't this mean the Grants would become an independent colony? He was probably planning on being appointed its first governor.

Massey also looked at Eli. "You and I will have to talk, but not now. I haven't got the time. I'll be back when all this is over."

Over. The word held an awful chill. She felt trapped and hopeless, like a rat caught in a hole. The explosions had diminished. "I'm going upstairs," she said, and left quickly before the sieur could object.

Her room was stuffy from two days with the shutters closed. She pushed one set open and leaned heedlessly out, but even the cool of the evening air didn't temper her sense of being caged. All her life, for as long as she could remember, she'd had only one goal, which was to find her brother and reclaim her Acadian home. Until last year when the Americans had marched into Canada, she'd imagined achieving that goal on her own, which had been daunting, to say the least. Then suddenly, last September, all that had changed and greater events had conspired to offer her a whole new hope. She'd felt as though someone had opened a secret door, and passing through it, she'd found herself on the exact road she'd always hoped to find.

Now, just as abruptly, that road was about to end. The Americans didn't have the strength to turn the British back

in Canada, let alone in their own colonies. The British
would go on ruling Canada until the end of time, and Acadians would never be welcome in Acadia.

It wasn't just the American failure that filled her with
such bitterness. After the way Eli had betrayed her she
couldn't imagine ever trusting another man. It was hard to
imagine ever trusting anyone at all. She felt alone, for-
saken, angry and bitter. Always before, when things had
been bad, she'd found something to look forward to. But
tonight beneath the cold stars even her vow to find François
sounded hollow and improbable.

She sat watching the flash of the cannon as darkness
grew more complete. She listened as the sieur and Eli came
upstairs and went into their rooms. She heard the sieur
locking Eli's door, an empty gesture. As she knew all too
well, when Eli wanted something, no lock would prevent
him from getting it. Why had he come here? If Carleton
had sent him somewhere else she wouldn't be feeling this
way right now. Her dreams had been trampled not once,
but twice.

At some point toward morning she must have fallen
asleep, for the next thing she knew, sunlight was streaming
across the bed and every bell in the city seemed to be ringing at once. The guns were still shooting, but she could
hardly hear them over the bells. She pushed herself up from
the pillows and nearly upended the tray Catherine had left
on a chair beside the bed.

The tray held a pot of coffee, which was stone cold. It
also held a brief note in Catherine's halting scrawl: *"Gon
to the gate with the oters to wilcom the ships."*

The ships. She pushed the tray aside and went to the
window to look. There were three of them, their white sails
fearlessly furled in the wind as they negotiated their way
upriver past the Île d'Orléans. She counted two frigates
followed by a sloop. Doubtless there were many more following close behind. The frigates were firing at the American batteries as they came. Above the boom of the cannon

and the clanging of the bells, she could hear the cheer of welcome rising from the walls.

It was over. Done. She didn't know what would come next, but she knew that something would. She hadn't undressed last night, and though her skirts were badly wrinkled, she did no more than to shake them out, wash her face and comb her hair before she left her room. Whatever was coming, she wanted to meet it face-to-face. Bitter or not, she'd never been one for hiding in her room.

The upstairs hall was empty and the house was still. Had the sieur gone out and left her? And what about Eli? She glanced toward his closed door, which was when she noticed that the key wasn't in the lock.

That was strange. She took a step or two toward his door, thinking of the reasons why the key might have been removed. By accident? Had it fallen on the floor? She certainly didn't see it anywhere. She took another few steps and then she heard the thump. At first she thought it was gunfire, but it sounded different. Smaller. Closer. She walked up to the door and listened. She heard another thump.

"Eli?" she called.

She heard another sound, this one more like the buzzing of a bug caught against a window and trying to get out—the buzzing of a very large and determined bug.

"Eli? Are you in there? What's happened to the key?"

More thumping and buzzing. What was going on?

She tried the knob but it wouldn't open. Who could have taken the key? Never mind, there was an extra in the sieur's room. Quickly she went to fetch it and unlocked the door. Had something happened to Eli? Was he hurt or ill? Hate him or not, she wanted to know what was going on.

"Eli?" She pushed the door open, then stared in mute surprise at the sight of Captain Massey gagged and bound, hand and foot, to the bed.

As much of his face as was showing past the gag was violet with rage and he was shouting incomprehensible words. She knew what he was shouting, so she went and untied the gag. "What happened?"

He choked and sputtered. "Goddamn Brownell! He sent me a note marked urgent, so of course I came, but no sooner did I get here than he grabbed my gun and assured me he'd kill me if I didn't do what he wanted. Untie me, and quickly."

"What did he want?"

"What do you think—for me to write a permission for the release of the prisoners from the Dauphin jail. He would have killed me if I hadn't, I could tell from the way he looked."

"But why would he do that? I thought you two were the best of friends? Wasn't he the one who told you about his brother's plan to escape?"

"Brownell? What are you talking about?" Despite his furor, Massey looked amazed. "Brownell had nothing to do with that—I heard it from a guard. He was supposed to help the prisoners, but he got drunk and talked. Damn, but Brownell's a clever one. I know what he's got in mind—to sneak out his brother in the confusion over the fleet. Quickly, untie me. There's no time to lose. What are you doing?"

She didn't bother to answer, since he could see for himself and she was having enough trouble refastening the gag while he tried to thwart her by jerking his head back and forth. But in the end she managed, then she was out and running down the stairs, the door locked and the key in her pocket. She'd been wrong about Eli. She hoped she wasn't too late.

It wasn't more than a five-minute walk to the Dauphin jail and she made it in even less, though everyone in the city seemed to be in the streets and rushing in all directions with no purpose or goal. As she went, she racked her mind for a reasonable plan, but nothing came to her. How could she plan anything when she didn't know what she'd find? Maybe Eli had a plan. Hopefully he did.

She found him at the front gate arguing with the guards. From the gestures both sides were making, she could tell that the guards were unwilling to honor Massey's note. She stopped, her heart sinking, then inspiration struck. Drawing herself up haughtily, she swept forward, talking as she went.

"Don't tell me you haven't got them yet? Captain Massey sent me to see what was holding you up. Haven't you read the captain's order?" She addressed herself to the guards in the hopes she'd draw their attention from Eli's likely reaction to her bursting in.

"Yes, ma'am," one guard said smoothly. He was the one holding the note. "Only we've got our orders—"

"Orders, do you say? Orders aren't all you're about to have! You're about to have the full force of General Carleton's anger if you don't let us in! Don't you know that Captain Massey is the general's aide? The general wants to see these prisoners and he wants to see them now! Everyone at headquarters has got his hands full today, so I suggest you produce these prisoners immediately!"

"Who are you?"

"Mademoiselle Anne-Marie Doucet. I am the ward of the Sieur de Saint Vallier—and the personal friend of General Carleton. Everyone at headquarters is busy, as you might imagine, so the general asked me if I could come along and see what was holding up the prisoners." As she said this she smiled, a meaningful smile. Let them make what they would of her in their dirty minds. Only let them permit Eli through the gate. She didn't dare look at him for fear she'd lose her nerve.

"We're wasting time," he said curtly. "If this order's not enough, I suggest you go over to headquarters and get whatever you need. Only do it quickly or you'll have to answer to the general."

She could see that the guard was weakening. "If the general wants them..." He took a silent poll of his fellows, but all three of them shrugged. "I'll have to send a guard with them."

"Come yourself," she said. "If you do I can recommend you to the general." She winced inwardly as she said this, thinking it might be too much, but Zeke was right about redcoats, for this one seemed to like the idea.

"All right," he relented. "I'll take you up."

Eli looked at her only once as they followed the guard upstairs. His look held a question and a warning, but there was no time to respond. They followed the soldier up to the guardroom, where they collected a second guard with the keys, who conducted them down the hallway, past the heavy doors of the cells. Unlike the seminary, the Dauphin had been built as a jail, and Anne-Marie's heart sank to think of Zeke and the others in here. It sank even lower when the guard opened the door and she got her first look at the inside of the cell.

There were eight prisoners in the cell, which was probably meant to hold two. They were all lying on filthy pallets and shackled hand and foot, with the shackles around their ankles connected to the wall. Clearly they hadn't changed their clothes or washed since they'd been brought here, for their shirts and trousers were filthy and the one small barred window didn't begin to provide enough air. It was so dark that for the first few minutes she couldn't tell the men apart. She had spent the last weeks feeling sorry for herself because she'd been misused, and meanwhile these men had been locked in this terrible place.

She looked at Eli, but his face was a total blank and his voice was void of emotion when he addressed the guard. "I suppose we ought to leave the shackles on their hands. If you remove the ones on their ankles, we'll make better time."

Anne-Marie felt the first guard stiffen and thought he might object, but the second one was already busy with his keys. By now her eyes had adjusted and she could recognize Zeke, who looked like a wild man with his great beard and matted hair. He was almost as thin as he'd been when he was sick, but his spirit was far from broken.

"Why don't you try them on for size," he taunted as the guard unfastened the shackles from his legs. "The next time I see Colonel Arnold, I'm going to suggest to him that when we take this city we make a pair of these part of the redcoat uniform."

"Aw, shut your mouth," the guard muttered, hard at work. "You'll be crow bait in England long before that day ever comes!"

"Ha! Crows would die of starvation the way you feed us here." Zeke was ignoring Eli but he kept shooting Anne-Marie a sly sideways leer. What was he doing? Did he mean to alert the guard? But the guard seemed not to notice—then she realized that Zeke was simply acting like a normal man who was seeing a woman, perhaps for the first time in months.

It seemed like hours before all the shackles were removed and the second guard back at his post while the first marched the double row of prisoners down the stairs. She and Eli followed behind.

"Where are you taking us?" Noah demanded. He and Jed were among the eight. So were Harry and most of the other men. She hated to have to leave any of the men behind, but in the circumstances she understood they were lucky to have these eight. Or would be lucky, she amended, if they managed to escape.

The guard didn't bother to answer Noah, so Zeke answered him instead. "What do you think? General Carleton's inviting us to dinner so's he can apologize. I hear he's got a good cellar so there's bound to be plenty of wine."

"Shut up!" the guard ordered, and, grumbling, Zeke complied, but not before Anne-Marie realized that he was enjoying himself. Even his wordless grumbling had an ebullient air, and the other seven in the coffle were clearly taking their cues from him.

She suffered a tense moment as they came through the gate, for now there was a sergeant with the other three guards. She was afraid the sergeant might stop them and challenge Massey's note, but it turned out he had something else on his mind.

"Both of the frigates have docked and they've sent up a company from the Twenty-Ninth and a hundred sailors. Carleton's called for the garrison to assemble at the Place d'Armes. We're going out to get 'em!"

"It's about time," said their guard. Then another thought struck him. "If Carleton's having a battle, he may not want these men."

"He wants them," said Eli. "He wanted them two hours ago."

To Anne-Marie's relief, the guard gave up his protest and marched them through the gate into streets even more crowded than they'd been before, since now the men from the garrison were all rushing pell-mell to form ranks so they could march out and attack.

She shot a look at Eli, but his expression was still blank. Zeke, by contrast, was doing his best to impede progress in the street and the others were helping him out, bumping and jostling everything in their path. In this they were greatly aided by the condition of the streets. Last fall, when the American bombardment had begun, Carleton had ordered all the paving to be torn up so that shells that fell in the city would sink into soft earth, where their explosions would cause less harm. Since then, the snow had fallen and melted so that now the streets were churning mud, so deep in some places that a small child could drown. When Zeke brought down his feet hard, mud flew everywhere.

"Watch that! Get over—stay to the side!" The guard was hoarse from shouting, but the men paid him no heed, trying to force all the passing soldiers into the deepest mud. They also whistled at all the women, even the ugly ones. They jostled a very fat lieutenant, who roundly cursed the guard.

The guard glared at Eli with silent fury. Anne-Marie looked at him, too, and suddenly it struck her that he didn't know Quebec. How was he planning on getting them out if he didn't know where he was going, let alone where he ought to go? Did he mean for her to lead them, and if so, to where? Not to headquarters, more likely to a gate.

But to which gate? she wondered. She wished she dared to ask, but there were people all around them and she didn't want to be overheard. Then—horror of horrors!—she heard a familiar voice.

"Allo! Up here, Mademoiselle Doucet!" There was no mistaking Madame Revier's piercing shrill. She was sitting at a window with her fat daughter, Renée. "Where are you going in such a hurry? Why don't you come up and join us? What a spectacle! You know General Carleton's called the men to arms—there's going to be a fight! If they have it on the Plains of Abraham we can see it all from here! Come up!" She beckoned.

Anne-Marie shook her head. "I'll come in a little while. I have to do something first."

Madame Revier pouted. "Hurry back, and bring your Captain Massey."

"I don't think so. I'm sure he'll be tied up."

She hurried after Eli and the others, who'd marched on ahead. Madame Revier hadn't realized that she was walking with them, but the streets were full of people. She could run into anyone and then there'd be questions, problems and delays. They might even run into Catherine or the sieur.

The sieur! She hadn't thought of him, and now that she did her heart sank. What troubles had she brought upon him by leaving Massey tied up and running off to help Zeke and Eli escape? Whatever they were, it was too late to turn back. Massey would never forgive her for what she'd done today, and he was smart enough to realize that she'd been lying when she'd denied helping Zeke.

Eli scarcely turned his head when she caught up. Zeke was exchanging insults with two soldiers on their way to the Place d'Armes.

"I'll shoot you," the guard threatened when the soldiers had moved off. "One more stunt like that and I'll shoot you, Carleton or not."

"My, my!" Zeke quavered in a falsetto. "I'm afraid he will!"

Before the guard could answer, Eli spoke in a carrying voice. "It's too crowded in the streets. We'll do better on the back ways. Turn left into this lane."

"I don't know—" the guard protested, but the column had already turned down the alleyway so the guard had no choice but to go after them. The alley was dark and narrow, like all of the byways of Quebec, with houses so steep on either side they seemed to meet at the roofs, blocking out all but the faintest light of day.

"Left again," directed Eli, and again the prisoners turned, into a channel even darker and tighter than the one they'd just left.

"Now wait a minute," the guard called after them. "You men hold up! I'm not—"

But whatever he wasn't doing remained a mystery as he slumped forward, victim to a crashing blow from Eli's fist. In less time than it took for Anne-Marie to realize what was afoot, Zeke and the others were huddled in a group, stripping the unconscious guard of his uniform as fast as they could, given the awkwardness of their chains. As fast as they had his clothes off, Eli had them on. When he produced rope and a handkerchief, they bound and gagged the guard, emptied out the nearest rain barrel and stuffed him inside.

"What if he dies before someone finds him?" said Anne-Marie.

Zeke snorted through his nose. "If he can't get his gag off first, he deserves to die! I liked what you told that foolish woman about Massey being tied up—I assume it's the truth!" If possible, his spirits were higher than they'd been before. Before she could answer, he turned to Eli, who was buttoning up his scarlet coat. "What now, little brother?"

"We just walk out. We're headed for one of the frigates in case anybody asks, though I doubt they will. We'd better go out through the Palace Gate. It might be easier to get out through the Lower Town, but if we went that way I doubt we'd reach the camp in time."

"In time for what?" asked Anne-Marie.

"In time for fighting Carleton." He looked at her for the first time since they'd left the jail. She could guess what he was thinking: what a wrongheaded fool she'd been. And she couldn't deny it. That was the worst part of all.

Zeke was also looking at her. "What about *mademoiselle?*"

"Never mind about me," she said quickly. "I can take care of myself."

Eli said, "I suppose Massey saw you." His voice was as cool as his look.

She nodded briefly. "I untied his gag, but after he told me what happened I tied it back again."

"She can't stay in the city," Zeke pointed out. "If she does, Massey will have her thrown in jail. You'd better come with us. We'll get you out somehow."

"I can't," she said without thinking, though she knew Zeke was right. "I can't leave just like that, at least not without explaining to the sieur. You go ahead. I'll be all right." She waved them back toward the street as if she were taking leave of them to pay a social call.

Zeke shot a look at Eli, as if urging him to speak. When he didn't, Zeke shook his head. "Your staying here is suicide. You can write your sieur a letter once you're safe."

"But Massey might blame him."

"You can write him a letter, too. Once we're out of this mess, you can write to any damn person you please. Come on."

She still held back. "I'll jeopardize your chances of getting through the gate. What would a woman be doing walking with a guard?"

"What a woman generally does." Zeke's teeth flashed briefly in the wildness of his beard. "If there's any problem, just smile. That'll get you through. Take her arm, Eli. She's coming along with us. Or cut me out of these damn bracelets and I'll take her myself."

"He's right," Eli said quickly, though he seemed far from pleased. "You're in danger if you don't come with us and we've got to get out of here. Let's move out," he ordered, but he didn't take her arm. "Straight through here then to the right. Right again when you reach daylight, then straight all the way to the gate."

Chains clanked as the men started moving. Anne-Marie stood still. She'd spent so many years longing for Acadia that until this moment she'd never realized how much Quebec had become her home. An image of the sieur's kindly face hovered in her mind. She couldn't just leave him. She couldn't walk away.

"Let's go!" Eli's voice, pitched low and stern, cut through her tumbled thoughts. The column had halted and they were all waiting for her. There was no point in protesting; she knew she had to go. The sieur would rather have her gone forever than see her hung as a traitor to the king.

The men waited until she caught up then began to move again, following Eli's direction when they came to the next alleyway. Suddenly she realized that he knew just where he was. "How do you know where you're going?" she asked as they reached the turn.

Without looking at her he answered, "I studied the sieur's maps. When I had questions, I asked the sieur."

Of course. All those companionable hours playing chess, and the use of his library. While she'd been blaming him for betrayal, he'd been laying his plans. She'd been guided by emotion when she should have used her head. She thought briefly of the things she'd said to him the night of the foiled escape and she cringed in shame. If she didn't know Zeke would forbid it, she'd have broken off on her own. She was almost certain that Eli wouldn't mind if she did. Once they were out of the city she'd go on her own separate way—that is, if they did manage to get out.

Now they were back in the main streets again, with the bells ringing and the crowds jostling. Zeke was still making verbal note of everything that passed, but he was also moving at twice the speed he'd been walking before. He whistled at an old woman, who gave him a toothless grin, though her equally toothless husband looked to be on the verge of a fit.

"Sal Bostonnais!" he called after them. Dirty Bostonnais!

"Miss Doucet!"

Anne-Marie's heart sank as a deep voice called her name. She pretended not to hear it, but of course it called again. It belonged to a lieutenant from the garrison who'd challenged Massey's claim to her affections more than once.

"Good day, Lieutenant."

"Good day, Miss Doucet. I say, isn't this fine! They're finally going to let us go after the Americans! We've got a company from the *Isis*." His words came pouring out and he saluted Eli with hardly a glance at him. "I guess you're going to watch the battle. Everybody is. You'd better hurry—it won't last for long!"

"Yes, thank you," she murmured as he hurried off, his polished boots already hopelessly spattered with mud. When she turned she saw that Eli had disappeared. She felt a moment of pure panic, then she saw him up ahead, closing the last distance before the Palace Gate.

The gate had been open to admit the men from the ships, but it was even more heavily guarded than usual. She caught up just as Eli brought the men to a halt. He saluted neatly and called out in a perfect redcoat voice, "General Carleton wants this bunch taken down to the ships."

The sergeant in charge shook his head. "No one passes. You'll have to take them back."

"I can't do that," said Eli. Just then there was an explosion louder than the rest. The crowd near the gate surged forward.

"American shell hit a wharf!" one of the sentries shouted down from the wall.

"Near the ships?" shouted the sergeant.

The sentry shook his head. Eli pointed to Anne-Marie. "This lady's uncle is captain of the *Isis*. The general told me to take her down there when I took these men. I'll have to leave them here with you while I take her down." He took Anne-Marie by the arm and started through the gate.

"Just a minute!" the sergeant shouted. There was another crash.

"Same wharf!" shouted the sentry.

"Sir?" Eli asked, looking impatient.

The sergeant scowled, then he waved one hand at the men. "If the general says so, take them and get out of here."

"Yes, sir!" Eli saluted and went back to the prisoners. "You heard the man, get moving!"

"It's dangerous down there," Zeke grumbled, but he was moving as he spoke, and a minute later they were past the city walls and marching downhill toward the broad sparkling river and the bare masts of the anchored ships.

Anne-Marie walked next to Eli, looking straight ahead. Her heart was racing and her whole body was trembling with relief, as if she'd been delivered into safety and not exiled from everything she knew for the second time in her life.

Chapter Nine

The road to the wharves curved around to their right. To their left were the remains of the palace where the intendant, the French king's representative, had lived. Beyond that, still to the left, lay the suburb of Saint Roque and the American camp. Straight ahead was a short strip of wasteland with a couple of decrepit warehouses and an abandoned wharf.

The guard at the gate and the soldiers on the ramparts were expecting them to turn to the right, but if they did that, they'd end up caught on the narrow shore between the ships and the Lower Town with even less chance than they had now of getting out alive. Risky as it was, they had to turn sharply to the left and hope they could find enough shelter among the palace's rubble to keep them from being picked off by the men up on the walls.

"Whenever you're ready," Zeke muttered without turning around.

"Are they watching us?" asked Eli.

Zeke turned to look back. "Hard to tell for certain, there's so many of them."

"We can't help it," said Eli. "We'll have to take the chance. Hopefully it'll take them a minute to figure out what's going on. Can you make it?"

"Without those damn leg irons, I feel like I could fly. Give the word and we're running."

"Now!" Eli said, and the next thing Anne-Marie knew, his arm was under hers and they were running through the rubble of the ruined palace wall.

A shout rose from the wall behind them. "Keep going!" Eli said, but before he'd finished speaking, she heard the sharp bark of the guns and a handful of grapeshot exploded less than a meter to her right.

"Short minute," Zeke shouted. He was running practically bent in half to give the redcoats less of a target as he dodged from rock to rock.

"Down!" As he said it, Eli pulled Anne-Marie down and she grunted as she skidded along the unforgiving ground. She scraped one hand badly but she barely noticed before he had her up and they were running again. The shots chased them, but she could tell they were falling short.

As if he'd shared her thought, Zeke called over his shoulder. "We're out of range—unless they use the big guns or come out after us."

"They won't," said Eli. He was still pulling her along, though her lungs were burning so sharply she felt as if they might burst. "They won't want to bother, not with the main attack under way. They figure when they come out they'll have another crack at us."

Ahead of Zeke, Noah whistled. They were past the palace now and among the first houses of the suburb of Saint Roque. Before the American invasion, Saint Roque had been a pleasant place, but in the months since the siege had started it had suffered enormous abuse. Those buildings that hadn't been torn apart by shells had been burned by the Americans to prevent the British from stripping them for firewood.

"Looks a sight worse than when we last seen it," Jed panted as they jogged along. "Guess they moved the camp out farther."

"A mile." Eli cast his eyes up and down the ruined streets. "We need to find somewhere where you can get rid of those irons."

At the far edge of the suburb they found a number of houses intact, but nobody answered when they knocked on the doors.

"They're in there," Harry said grimly. "They just ain't answering."

"I'll make 'em answer," Zeke vowed, seizing hold of one door and shaking it until Anne-Marie could hear the hinges groan. "Hey, there—open up!" he thundered, pounding with his fists.

"If you don't stop," Eli pointed out, "they can't open the door."

Zeke stopped long enough to bellow, "You in there—if you don't open up by the count of three, I'll start in again, and once I get the door off I'll be coming after you!"

Jed said, "What if they don't speak English?"

"Then they'll get my drift. I'm counting. One, two..."

The door opened a crack and a wizened face peered out. Zeke cackled with amazement. "If it isn't old man Panet!" With a flick of his huge hand, he pushed man and door both out of his way. "You remember old man Panet. Before the attack we used to drink in his tavern—he filled the pitchers halfway full and always overcharged. Company's here," he added, stomping through the open door. "Remember us, Panet? We're your customers."

Eli let go of Anne-Marie's arm as they came in the door. By that time Zeke was using gestures to show that they needed a file and the old man was muttering as he fumbled through the contents of a drawer. When he produced two files, Zeke slapped him on the back.

"Thanks, feller, much obliged! Now do you s'pose you could rustle up something for us to eat? *Manger*," he translated, murdering the word, but when he made the sign of eating, the old man understood. He spread his hands to show he had nothing, but Zeke pointed to the stove. "Whatever you've got in that kettle, we'll each have a bowl."

Meanwhile, Eli was stripping off his scarlet coat. "I want to see if I can find Arnold," he said to Zeke. "No doubt he'll be anxious to hear what Carleton's got in mind. I'll be back," he added as he vanished out the door without so much as a glance at Anne-Marie.

He hates me, she thought, leaning against the wall, since all the chairs were filled with men drinking soup and filing off their chains. The room was dark except for one guttering candle. The shutters were all locked and barred, no doubt in anticipation of the battle to come.

Why shouldn't Eli hate her? She'd jumped to all the wrong conclusions and accused him of terrible things. In his position, she'd never want to lay eyes on her again. She watched Zeke working with a file. She'd thought that Eli was inhuman not to have gotten Massey to move him to another house, but now she realized why he'd stayed. He'd understood that he was Zeke's only hope of escape and that he, Eli, had maximum freedom where he was. The sieur trusted him, which meant that he wasn't watched and he would be free to act when the right time came.

Eli must have been planning today's escape ever since Zeke had been caught. She thought of his brief response to her question about him knowing the way. He'd been studying maps and planning while she'd believed he was scheming to serve his own selfish ends. All the time, since the very beginning, she'd been wrong about him. But Eli, by contrast, had been perfectly right about her. She was a spoiled child, foolish and irresponsible. And the insults she'd paid him were unforgivable.

"Have some soup, Annie." Zeke gestured to a bowl the old man was offering to her.

"No, thank you," she said quickly.

"You'd better," Zeke advised. "The American army isn't known for plentiful supplies, food in particular. Especially with a battle brewing."

She took the soup and drank it, although she had little appetite. She had to decide, and quickly, what she was going to do. It went without saying that she couldn't stay with the men. Eli had made it clear that he didn't want her and she had no intention of forcing herself on him. If she had had any money, she would have struck out on her own, but she'd left the house without coin or anything she could trade.

One thing was certain: she couldn't stay in Quebec. If Massey ever found her, she knew that he'd see her hanged. But if she had no money, where was she supposed to go?

She looked at the men, busy filing their thick iron chains. Perhaps she could find employment in the American camp. She could nurse and she could translate, and if there was to be a battle, the Americans could probably use a good deal of both. She remembered what Zeke had said about asking around the American camp to see if anyone knew François. If she was in the camp she could do that herself, and if she found him . . .

She drank her soup, and by the time she'd finished, the last of the chains was being filed and Eli was back.

"No Arnold," he said grimly, lowering himself into a chair. He looked as if he'd been running the whole time since he'd left. She wondered how his leg was doing, but of course she couldn't ask. "They sent Arnold to Montreal last month and put Wooster in charge."

"Wooster!" Zeke looked stricken.

"That's not the worst of it. After the mess he made of the fireboat, they pulled Wooster out and put Thomas in his place, only he's too frightened of catching smallpox to keep his mind on strategy. Thanks." He accepted a bowl of soup from the scowling old man and drank it quickly before he went on.

"They're all in battle position up on the Plains of Abraham, but the men I spoke to say they don't believe Thomas has got the stomach for a fight. They're all facing the Saint Louis gate but they're looking over their shoulders so much their necks are getting stiff."

"Yorkers!" Zeke spat with derision.

"Maybe." Eli shrugged.

"Did you see Thomas?"

"No time—he's too far back. I sent a message then I came straight here. The British could come out any minute. I don't think we've got much time. If you're ready…"

"We're ready!" Zeke was already on his feet, the rest of the men with him. Leaving the chains where they'd dropped them, they rushed en masse for the door.

Anne-Marie drew back to the shadows, swallowing her sudden rush of fear. In her mind, she'd seen Zeke taking her to the American camp before he went into battle. What was she going to do? You'll go on your own, she told herself firmly. You're going to go on your own. You have a brain and a sense of direction. You'll manage to find your own way.

The door shut with a clatter. Through it, she could hear Zeke shouting and the trample of hurrying feet.

"*Mademoiselle* isn't going with them?" The old man was looking at her with an expression that made it clear just what he thought of her. Did he take her for a camp follower? Let him think what he liked; at the moment she had bigger things on her mind.

"*Mademoiselle* will find her own way," she told him icily. "Thank you for the refreshment." She took a step toward the door. At that same moment it opened and Eli appeared.

His eyes squinted into the darkness until they located her. "Hurry up. We're leaving."

"I'm not going."

"Of course you are." He made an impatient gesture. "Come on, and hurry. We haven't got much time. It sounds like the British are already through the gate."

She shook her head. "You don't want me and I'll only be in the way. You got me this far safely. If you owed me any obligation, you've fulfilled it. I can go on from here on my own."

He didn't bother to argue. In two strides he'd crossed the room, had her firmly by the arm and was leading her outside.

"Please don't!" she protested, but he paid her no heed.

The other men were waiting. Of course, she thought to herself. Zeke realized I was missing and sent Eli back inside. The thought of it made her feel even worse than before, but by that time they were running toward the Plains of Abraham.

Keeping a firm grip just below her elbow, Eli tossed his musket to Zeke. "Take this, and when we get there, you go ahead and join the lines. I'll take her around to headquarters, then I'll find you wherever you are."

"What about guns for the rest of us?" called Jed.

"Take 'em off the redcoats!" Zeke shouted back at him.

The road from Saint Roque led steeply up, first to the suburb of Saint Foy, then to the Plains of Abraham. Anne-Marie's lungs were on fire by the time they reached Saint Foy and only pride kept her from begging Eli to stop— pride and the feeling that he wouldn't even if she asked. By that time the hillside was shaking with the boom and the roar of the guns.

"Let's go, men!" Zeke bellowed, his long legs eating up the ground. He ran, waving his musket as though it were a weightless twig.

Stumbling and panting, they charged up the last of the hill. Up ahead she saw Zeke arrive at the plateau, with the city marching to his left and the stretch of the plains to his right. She expected that he would keep running, but to her surprise he stopped—in midshout and still holding his musket in the air. Noah, who was running behind him, slammed into Zeke's back so hard that he fell back down the hill with the air knocked out of him.

"What the hell . . . ?" Harry muttered as he reached the top.

Zeke bellowed. "Damn Thomas! This is all his goddamn fault!"

By that time Eli had pulled Anne-Marie up so that she saw the debacle that had brought Zeke to a stop. To their left, from the city, came the British advance: troops in crisp formation, pausing from time to time to fire, their flags and bright facings sparkling in the sun. The rest of the plains were covered with fleeing Americans, shedding knapsacks and muskets and even their coats as they ran.

Noah made a sound of derision. "At least we won't have trouble finding guns."

"Stop, you goddamn cowards!" Zeke thundered, and began to move.

Eli dropped Anne-Marie's arm and caught Zeke as he went.

Zeke spun around, outraged. "What are you doing? Let me go! We've got to stop them!"

"We can't," Eli said. "The best we can do is be killed or be taken prisoner again. The troops won't run forever, and unless Carleton's changed overnight, he won't push them too hard. Arnold fell back to Point aux Trembles before he started the siege, and if I'm not mistaken, Thomas will do the same. We can circle to the northwest and catch up with them there." Glancing at Anne-Marie, he added, "If we cut back through Saint Foy, maybe we can find a horse."

"I'm not going with you," she gasped between labored breaths. It was no longer a matter of feeling. She couldn't stand the pace.

Eli didn't bother to answer and Zeke didn't even hear. His eyes were still on the battlefield and were burning with impotent rage. "Cowards!" he muttered. "Wait till I catch up with them."

"Come on," said Eli. "We've got a long ways to go."

Miraculously they found a horse: a knock-kneed starveling for which the owner demanded thirty pounds. Without batting an eyelash, Eli produced a pocket watch.

"Thief," Zeke grumbled as Eli made the trade.

"Please don't give up your watch for me." Anne-Marie felt miserable, and she only felt worse when Eli shrugged.

If I get through this, she told herself, I'll buy him another watch. Then there will be one thing he won't hold against me.

Eli helped her into the saddle.

"How's your leg?" Zeke asked.

Eli gave the horse a thump on the withers. "Probably better than this nag's."

Zeke laughed with appreciation, but Anne-Marie saw Eli's face. "Why don't you ride?" she said quickly.

"I'm fine." He turned away and she closed her eyes tightly on a sudden rush of tears. This day was a nightmare that she knew she'd never forget.

She was right, but the real nightmare had yet to begin. The trip to Point aux Trembles dragged through the endless day and well into the night along a road knee-deep in mud churned up by the stream of American soldiers who'd lost their companies and their provisions in the flight from the battlefield.

The sides of the road were littered with every manner of goods shed by the fleeing men. Eli and the others picked up as many guns as they could carry, and Zeke searched the knapsacks for anything the local habitants might be willing to accept in trade for food. At first he and the others cursed and traded insults to keep their spirits up, but eventually they fell silent, slogging through the mud.

It had been dark for some time when Eli stumbled and almost fell. He caught himself and kept going.

"Stop," commanded Zeke.

"I'm fine." Eli kept walking.

"The hell you are," growled Zeke. Raising one of the muskets from his load, he pointed it at Eli's leg. "Either you get up on that nag on your own or I'll fix it so you don't have a choice."

"You wouldn't dare," Eli said tightly.

"Oh yeah? Try me and see." Zeke cocked the trigger.

With a muffled curse, Eli passed Zeke his musket and swung up behind Anne-Marie. From his movement alone

she could tell how bad the pain must be. She was sure that
his face showed it, but she didn't dare look at him.

If the day had been bad to this point, now it became even
worse. Eli held himself stiffly to keep from touching her
and she held herself forward as far as she could, which only
succeeded in making the ride rougher than before. She was
as physically exhausted as she'd ever been, and the only
thing that kept her going was repeating in her mind that
when they reached Point aux Trembles, she'd take herself
off his hands. If General Thomas didn't want her services,
she'd think of something else. But she'd never—never—
spend another day like this.

They reached Point aux Trembles in the middle of the
night and found it already full to bursting with filthy, exhausted troops, and more straggling in every minute,
looking for food and a place to sleep. There wasn't much
of either, so men ate what they could find and some slept
where they fell in the street, while others wandered around
dazedly looking for their companies.

They made their way through the mud and confusion to
headquarters, which was alight and buzzing with a desperate energy. "You can't stop here—keep moving!" the guard
bawled when Eli swung down from the horse.

"I need to see General Thomas."

"Ha! You and everyone else. If you want, you can state
your business, but it won't do any good."

Eli did just that, with a force and precision of words that
Anne-Marie found astonishing. Her own brain felt dulled
and befuddled from the lack of sleep, and her body felt as
if it were made of sacks of cannonballs. It was all she could
do to rouse herself when the sergeant reappeared to an-
nounce that General Thomas would give Eli exactly one
minute of his time.

Her legs were so stiff from riding she could barely slide
down from the horse, and her feet felt like two hollow
bricks when they hit the ground. She tottered after Eli and
the guard toward the door. The guard ignored her, but

when Eli sensed her behind him and turned, she said, "Don't tell me not to, because I'm going in." At that, he shrugged his shoulders, but he did hold the door to allow her to enter ahead of him.

Thomas was standing at a table when they came into the room. He'd been in the midst of expostulating to the various officers of his staff, but he broke off to demand of Eli, "How many men does Carleton have?"

Eli gave no sign of finding Thomas's question abrupt. "During the siege he had eleven hundred, but a third of those are Canadians whom he doesn't really trust. Now, with the three ships, he's probably got five hundred more."

"But more ships are coming. We've heard ten thousand men are on their way, led by Gentleman Johnny Burgoyne. And what have I got to throw against them? Three thousand half-trained recruits, half of whom are so ill from smallpox they're barely able to walk, while most of the men with two good legs are using them to walk away. And the Congress wonders why I didn't take Quebec! If they think there's so little to it, let them take it themselves—and let them figure out what they're going to eat while they're taking it! Right now we'll be lucky if we can save what provisions we've still got from being captured by Carleton and hauled back to Quebec!"

"General," said Eli when Thomas paused for breath. "From everything I've heard and observed in the past four months, I don't believe that Carleton will force a confrontation. I believe if we make a stand here he'll back off."

"Oh, you do, do you?" Thomas glared at him. "And I suppose you'd like to take responsibility for the results if you're wrong!" Before Eli could answer, Thomas relented and shook his head. "It's not your fault, Lieutenant. You've done your duty, go and get some rest. We'll be moving out with the first light. By the way, have you had smallpox?"

"I had a light case when I was young."

"You're lucky," said Thomas. "It's a terrible disease. Terrible," he repeated, frowning at the door as if he saw a specter lurking in the night. Then he whirled back to the officers he'd been speaking to before. "Where was I? That's right. We need a full count of everything that floats. Bateaux, rafts, everything, even if it leaks. If it leaks, we can bail it—"

Eli tugged on her arm. "He was right," he said softly, so Thomas wouldn't hear. "The best thing you can do right now is to get some rest. It's no use," he added when she held back. What surprised her more than his tone was the look in his eyes, which showed her understanding buried amidst the disappointment and fatigue.

"Come on," he said, tugging on her arm, and without protest she allowed herself to be led out the door. She knew that Eli was right. She'd do better to see Thomas tomorrow, after she'd had some rest. She doubted he'd be any calmer, but at least she'd have her wits about her more than she did right now. Right now, all she wanted was to lay down her aching body and sleep.

While they'd been in headquarters, Zeke had found them a place to stay. It was nothing more than a barn floor, but at least it had a roof and straw on which to lie. She curled up in the corner and was asleep when she closed her eyes, but in the next moment—or so it seemed—Eli was shaking her awake.

"Get up. We're leaving."

"We just got here. I want to sleep."

"Later. Here, eat this." He thrust something at her, but when she reached for it dazedly, he took her hand instead. "What's this?"

"Nothing. Just scrapes from yesterday." She tried to pull away, but he held on. She thought he looked annoyed. "It's nothing. Really."

Without speaking, he let her go, giving her the food he'd brought her, which turned out to be half a hard biscuit and two mouthfuls of salt pork. It looked disgusting and she was too tired to chew, but she took it and ate it and was hungrier afterward, as if her stomach had just remembered it had gone a long time without food.

She'd barely finished when Eli was back again with a canteen of water and a handful of bandages. He thrust them both at her. "You'd better clean that wound. If it festers, you'll be in trouble."

"Thank you," she murmured, but he was already gone. She cleaned the wound and bound it, chiding herself for feeling hurt at a moment like this. She wasn't a baby stumbling after its mother. She was a woman in the midst of a war. When she was through, she'd go and find Thomas and see if he'd put her to work.

Except that, as Zeke informed her, Thomas had already left for the next destination. Zeke reported this with scorn and added that she'd better hurry up because they were moving on. When she started to explain that she intended to go on from here alone, Zeke calmly informed her that if she didn't come along, he'd hoist her up over his shoulder and carry her. She knew that he'd do it, so she got up and came along. After all, there was no point in staying if Thomas had already gone.

She dreaded another ordeal on the horse, but it appeared they weren't riding but rather going in a boat, a clumsy flat-bottomed bateau that leaked in the rear. Somebody handed her a leather bucket and told her that her job was to bail, which she did at least a million times through the endless day. Her only comfort was that her mind was too numb to assess her body's pain, let alone to worry about what she was going to do.

Their new destination was Deschambault, a nondescript village forty-five miles west of Quebec. Theirs had been among the first of the boats to leave. Nevertheless, by the time they had shoved and splashed their way ashore, they found themselves in the same chaos that had claimed Point aux Trembles last night. Other bateaux were beaching wherever there was room. Anne-Marie watched in mute exhaustion as men in ragged clothing dragged the ill and the

wounded ashore, sometimes on stretchers but more often
scraping and bumping up the rocky beach.

What was she doing? she wondered dazedly. With every
hour she was getting farther from Quebec, farther into this
incomprehensible world of sickness and confusion.

Before she could come up with an answer, Eli was at her
side. "Come on. We've got to find quarters and food."

She was beyond protest, so she followed where he led.
That night's lodging turned out to be a cattle shed and
supper was nothing but a cupful of flour, which they mixed
with hot water into a kind of gruel. It tasted awful, but she
drank it down gratefully and fell asleep exhausted, her
stomach rumbling.

The wind was howling, driving snow into his face. Half-
blinded, he was groping with frozen fingers along a wall.
She was there, somewhere; if only he could see. He couldn't
call out for fear the soldiers inside the barracks would hear.
The others had gone on and were waiting for him at the
gate. Time was short, he had to join them, but he had to
find her first.

Wait. He saw a movement, a bulky shape ahead. Not
far—he almost had her. The snow caught at his legs and
with every step he sank in almost to his thighs. She was
moving quickly. How did she do it in the snow? He'd lose
her if he didn't hurry. He'd—

A flash of light and a muffled explosion. In the instant
before he was hit, he remembered that he wouldn't find her
and would be shot in the arm and the leg. He braced himself for the impact, but this time when it came, it hit him in
the shoulder, knocking him into the snow. Not sharp—a
dull pressure, like something leaning on him. Like a weight,
leaning...

Eli opened his eyes to the smell of cattle and the sound
of men snoring in their sleep. It took him a few seconds to
remember where he was and to realize that his shoulder was
aching because someone was leaning on it. Anne-Marie was
leaning on him, deeply asleep, her hair fallen forward and

covering her face. It was so crowded in the cow shed that they had to sleep sitting up, and somewhere in the last hours she'd slumped sideways against him. On her far side, Noah was snoring mightily.

Shifting to ease his shoulder, he looked around the shed at the huddled, slumping forms. Even after two days of hard going, if he breathed deeply, he could still catch the faintest whiff of roses in Anne-Marie's tangled hair. Or maybe he was just imagining that he could. Everyone else bore the telling signs of hard traveling. The once white guard's breeches in which he'd fled Quebec were now a dullish gray, and he'd replaced the discarded red coat with a homespun one he'd picked up on the road the first day of their flight.

Their flight. The words echoed bitterly in his mind. The smell of this room was the smell of a frightened army in the midst of a headlong retreat. How had it happened? How had it come to this? As if from another lifetime, he remembered his farm in Bennington, everything well taken care of, everything in its place. Before he'd come to Canada, his life had made sense. Even dressing up like Indians to scare Yorkers off the land had had a point.

Zeke had seen the invasion of Canada as one more adventure for the Boys. Eli had seen the experience more realistically, but even at his most skeptical, he hadn't envisioned this room full of hungry, filthy, bewildered men, and he'd never imagined such a failure of leadership. There were plenty of men who found Arnold insufferably arrogant, but not even his worst enemies doubted his courage and he never lost sight of his reason for being here.

He wondered what Thomas intended to do. Regardless of what he himself had told the general, he knew it was too much to expect that Carleton would let them walk away— especially if he had use of ten thousand British troops. Carleton would follow them down the river, and when he caught them it would be the end, unless someone turned these snoring, dirty bodies back into the army they'd been once upon a time. And then there was the smallpox....

Anne-Marie sighed deeply in her sleep and shifted against him, seeking a softer place. As she snuggled closer, her warmth enveloped him, and between one breath and another he forgot the snoring men as his body responded to vivid memory. His leg was aching and his whole body was sore, but he knew that her nearness could sweep all that away. If he let himself, in a minute he could leave war and depression behind.

He turned his head slowly until his cheek touched her tangled hair. Below it, her lips were pouted. He remembered those lips; he remembered their softness beneath the tip of his tongue. He remembered her long legs...he remembered everything.

He closed his eyes. If he bent down and kissed her, he knew what she'd do. She wouldn't just permit it, she would welcome his caress. He knew she was feeling sorry for having misjudged him. She was tired and probably frightened, and she'd be glad to see that he'd forgiven her. Beyond that, she'd respond because her nature was passionate.

He'd never met a woman with her hunger for life. But that was the danger: she bit before she thought. She was heedless and inconsistent, like the rest of her countrymen. The Canadians gave their loyalty to whichever side was winning. Anne-Marie used different criteria but she was just as impetuous. She loved and hated with very little in between, and the changes were swift, sudden and all too often wrong.

And hurtful. She could be hurtful when she drew her claws. She had no idea how she'd hurt him when she'd accused him of making love to her while in his mind he was planning on betraying Zeke. She'd never know what he had really been feeling that night—even now he could still close his eyes and feel her heat and see her face, flushed and eager, half-tilted back.

Even now he could remember the aching in his chest, because he wanted her so much and he knew that he could never have her because of who she was. Even as she clutched him and begged him not to go, he'd known that when the fire died, she would change her mind and very likely blame him for her own desire. But he had never imagined that she would accuse him of using her to betray his own brother. No woman—no person—had ever thought so badly of him.

He still wanted her more than he'd ever wanted a woman before, but if he surrendered to desire he'd get what he deserved. Right now she was feeling sorry because she'd been wrong about him, but he knew her and he knew that her repentant mood wouldn't last for long. Soon enough something would happen and she'd turn on him again. The best thing that could happen was for their paths to part.

She muttered in her sleep. He listened, but he couldn't hear the words. He couldn't leave her yet, not amid all this madness and all these desperate men. Even if he suggested it, Zeke would veto the idea, and he knew he owed her this much for helping them to get out of Quebec. But as soon as he got her to safety he would leave her without a backward look. He knew he could do it. As she would be the first to point out, he was capable of shutting out temptation and doing what was reasonable.

She muttered again, shifting. He sensed that she was waking up. It was too late to move his shoulder, so instead he closed his eyes and pretended to be asleep. He could feel her slowly extracting herself from sleep; he could almost feel her eyes flutter open to puzzle, as he had done, until she'd figured out where she was. He knew when she'd realized because he felt her jerk away, and despite all his resolution, he felt a sharp stab of regret. He'd lost the moment, possibly forever.

He listened to her skirts rustle as she resettled herself; she sighed, and he did, too, as he sat with his eyes closed, waiting for sleep to come.

Chapter Ten

They stayed at Deschambault for a week; one useless, wasted week. Thomas's objective was to collect his forces before moving on, but he even failed at that, because a good number of the men who reached Deschambault hardly stopped to collect their rations before they continued south. In any event, there were scanty rations to collect, since, as the sieur had once predicted to Eli, the same Canadians who had cheered the Americans when they'd been winning had small use for rabble in retreat. Habitants with food or fodder to spare would only sell for gold—of which Thomas and his quartermaster had almost none. So the habitants were hoarding their generosity until Carleton's forces arrived. Then, if the Americans stood and triumphed, maybe they'd change their minds.

Zeke was especially outraged by the deserters. "Hell's fire!" he stormed. "They're as bad as the Canadians. When you ask them why they're going, they whine that they've had enough of the suffering—as though anyone promised them that war would be all fun! If Thomas gave me permission, I'd stand on the road outside of town and shoot every man I caught heading south."

"Dead men don't make good soldiers," Eli observed mildly.

"No worse than deserters," Zeke flashed back.

Eli ignored the comment. "It's not a bad idea. Maybe Thomas would give us permission if we asked."

"Permission?"

"To catch the deserters and put them to good use. We might as well be doing something besides hunkering down in the mud and listening to our stomachs growl."

Thomas granted them permission, though he added that he wasn't sure he saw the point in keeping men he couldn't feed and who would probably be ill with smallpox by the end of the week.

"That's our real enemy," he concluded, his voice rising hysterically. "The men think the enemy's Carleton, but he's mercy incarnate compared to that terrible disease." His eyes swept the room in which they were standing. "God preserve us—what a dismal place to die!"

Eli forbore from replying that maybe they all wouldn't die. He left Thomas and went off to report the good news. Within two days, he and Zeke had organized a guard to log in arrivals and see that every man was assigned to a company. Some of the officers were as bad as Thomas in letting men slip through their fingers, but in many cases Eli and Zeke's efforts succeeded in keeping would-be deserters in camp.

The work also aided Eli in avoiding Anne-Marie. He had barely seen her after their first night in the town. That morning she'd gone to see Thomas to volunteer her services as a nurse, to which Thomas had predictably replied that if she was fool enough to expose herself to smallpox, she had his blessing to nurse to her heart's desire. The number of ill men was only more appalling than the conditions in which they'd been left. Anne-Marie had gone to work and been working ever since. She had also moved out of their humble lodgings to be closer to her wards—or more distant from Eli, as the case might be.

Once or twice, while he'd been passing through the camp, Eli had caught sight of her. On those occasions, his feet had stopped on their own and his body had turned in her direction like a trained carnival bear. Once, before he could break the spell, she'd also caught sight of him. She'd stopped as their eyes locked, then he'd made himself turn away. After that, he'd taken greater care to stay away from the hospitals.

At the end of the week at Deschambault there was nothing left to eat and no gold to buy more from the habitants. Worse yet, after all the waste during the flight from Quebec, there wasn't enough ammunition to hold off the British if Carleton did attack. Thus far he hadn't arrived, but every hour brought rumors of his approach, so finally Thomas ordered the army to fall back again, this time to Three Rivers, another forty-five miles upstream from Quebec. Thomas himself went another thirty miles to the town of Sorel, which straddled the mouth of the Richelieu River, the waterway south to Lake Champlain—and Albany and the rest of the colonies.

"You know what he's doing!" Zeke ranted as they pushed their bateau off from Deschambault. "He's putting himself in position to retreat. Damn it, I say give us Arnold so we can at least attack!"

"Maybe we will." Eli dug his oar into the water, squinting against the sun to see the procession of boats laboring upstream ahead of them. Anne-Marie was up ahead somewhere with her wards. He hadn't seen her when they'd been leaving, but he could sense she was there. She wouldn't stop at Three Rivers but go on to Sorel, since Thomas had ordered the ill and the wounded men back from the front.

"Maybe we'll what?" Zeke asked.

"Maybe we'll attack Carleton before he makes up his mind to strike. I've heard that General Schuyler is sending us four thousand fresh recruits under General Sullivan. Even with the fleet arriving, I don't believe Carleton has half that many yet, so if Sullivan gets here fast enough, there's no reason why we can't beat Carleton at Three Rivers then push back toward Quebec."

"If he gets here," grumbled Zeke, trailing water from his oar. "And *if* they've got guns with 'em, and food to eat— and *if* they aren't too put out by all the suffering! If you ask me, the way things are going, we'll be back in Bennington by July and we'll be lucky if Gentleman Johnny Burgoyne ain't right there with us, nipping at our heels!"

"I say we can best them—if Sullivan comes."

Between strokes, Zeke looked hard at his brother. "For a man who's retreating, you're in a rare good mood. I don't suppose that's because of Thomas ordering the sick and the wounded back to Sorel. I don't understand you. In your position, I'd be glad to have her around. Hell—in your position, I'd probably go after her."

Eli turned back to the river. "I don't know what you're talking about."

"The hell you don't! I'm talking about us going to Three Rivers and *mademoiselle* going to Sorel. I'm also talking about showing a little more charity after all she's done. We'd probably still be in that damn prison if it wasn't for her."

"In case you've forgotten, I got you out of the jail and the city both. If you want charity shown, why don't you show it yourself?"

"Maybe I will," Zeke retorted. Then, realizing he was getting nowhere, he changed his tone. "She may have grown up rich and spoiled, but you can't deny she's been working like a plow horse since we got to Deschambault."

"I never said she was afraid of work. Ever since I've known her, she's been busy as a bee. Besides, she didn't grow up in Quebec. She spent the first part of her life fleeing from Acadia after the French were kicked out."

"No kidding." Absorbing this information, Zeke rested his oar on his knees. "I guess all this retreating must bring back some pretty bad memories."

Eli kept rowing. "We've all got bad memories."

"Yes, I reckon we have. Say!" Zeke's shaggy head swiveled as he thought of something else. "She didn't by any chance have a brother?"

"She did, but he disappeared." In spite of himself, he added, "Why do you ask?"

Zeke's eyes twinkled briefly as he shook his head. "If you were more kindly disposed to her I might tell you, but seeing's how you're not, I'd feel like I was betraying a confidence."

Sharp irritation prickled Eli but he forced himself to shrug. "Suit yourself—and if you can take time out from being righteous, do you suppose you could dip in your oar before we end up smack against those rocks?"

He gestured toward the rocks they were passing, keeping his back to Zeke. So what if Zeke knew things about Anne-Marie that he didn't? That was none of his affair. The less he knew about her the better, as far as he was concerned. He knew it wasn't worth trying to make Zeke understand; the best he could do was to avoid the subject until it had died a natural death.

"It would be bad enough if the men were catching smallpox naturally, but they aren't," Anne-Marie was saying to General Sullivan two weeks later at headquarters in Sorel. "Most of the cases result from self-inoculation—bad self-inoculation." She paused to let her words sink in. "At last count there were two thousand ill, and unless you stop what's happening, those numbers are bound to rise."

"I see," General Sullivan murmured thoughtfully, his eyes scanning the desk, which was piled high with maps and orders and more requests than three generals could hope to address in three weeks.

General Sullivan didn't have three weeks. He was a man with a mission, and the mission was to get the troops he'd brought north with him through Sorel and up to Three Rivers before Carleton had time to prepare. In a stroke of terrible irony, General Thomas had contracted smallpox two weeks before and had been moved farther south, to Chambly, where he'd quickly died. He'd been replaced briefly by Wooster, who'd been replaced by Sullivan. Sullivan had arrived last night with four thousand spanking fresh troops and was already breathing new hope into the shattered settlement.

Sullivan looked up from the piles of papers. "Why do they self-inoculate?"

"They believe they can give themselves a light case of the disease—not enough to harm them, but enough to keep them from being sent to the front, and maybe to get them discharged and sent back home. But in most cases they're wrong. Most of them get very sick and many of them die."

"I see... Since you raise the problem, I wonder if you've got any ideas for solving it?"

"I do have one." Grateful for his interest, she answered rapidly. "I thought you could put new men coming down with symptoms in quarantine and let it be known that when they recover—if they recover—they'll be sent straight to the front."

"Yes, that makes good sense, though with any luck it may prove unnecessary. After we defeat the British at Three Rivers, I believe you'll find the men more willing, if not downright anxious, to fight. Let's wait until after the battle, then if there's still a problem, I'll take the necessary steps to implement your idea."

"Thank you, General," she said, firmly reminding herself that promised future action was better than no action at all, which was what she'd gotten from both Thomas and Wooster.

"Is there anything else, *mademoiselle?*"

She hesitated. "Yes, there is. I know you're very busy, but I wonder if I might have your permission to ask the quartermaster to look up a certain name in his rosters."

From behind the piles of papers, the general smiled. "A sweetheart?"

She blushed. "No, a relative."

"Ah." Sullivan nodded. "You have my permission—if you can find him. I haven't seen him since last night. If you do manage to find him, you could tell him I've been looking for him, too."

"Yes, sir. And thank you."

She walked swiftly down the muddy street, the fatigue and doubt of the past weeks swept away by a fresh surge of hope. The source of her hope was more than the possibility that François's name might be among the four thousand on Sullivan's roster. "After we defeat the British at Three Rivers," Sullivan had said. Wooster and Thomas had spoken in feeble "ifs," but Sullivan spoke in a powerful "when"—and he'd brought four thousand soldiers with muskets and powder and food, not to mention enough artillery to take every town between here and Quebec. After ten minutes in his presence, she believed that triumph was possible and the simple fact of believing felt too wonderful for words.

She ran down the quartermaster near the wharves, where he was shouting himself hoarse above the splashing and scraping of score after score of bateaux that were landing and pushing off on the final leg of their journey north. Carleton was at Three Rivers. He'd been there for a week, and the last she'd heard, Zeke and Eli had gone to join Arnold in Montreal. She wondered if they'd go back to Three Rivers with Sullivan's troops.

"Mademoiselle?" the quartermaster bellowed practically in her ear.

She snapped to attention and delivered Sullivan's message and her request.

"He wants to see me—him and the rest of the world!" the quartermaster grumbled, but he gave her the lists. Despite herself, her hands were shaking as she turned from page to page. Her heart stopped at the sight of "Perkins," but the name was Benjamin. There was also a Judah and a Robert, but there was no François.

The quartermaster nodded vaguely when she returned the lists. The repetition of disappointment didn't make it any easier to bear, and the conditions in which she'd been working were enough to depress even the giddiest optimist. She must have asked hundreds of soldiers in these last three weeks, but she still hadn't found a single one, not one, who'd heard of François.

She hadn't found her brother and she'd lost the sieur, and as for Eli, she couldn't help but thinking that he'd gone to Montreal just to avoid any chance of seeing her. That should have been a relief, since she'd hated those few times their paths had crossed in Deschambault and he hadn't even said hello. Instead, he'd turned away as if the sight of her made him sick. He hadn't even bothered to say goodbye before he left.

Never mind. She wouldn't think of him. She'd think of these thousands of fresh troops eagerly streaming north. She'd think of the battle Sullivan expected to win. If he took Three Rivers, maybe he'd go on to Quebec, and if he took that, she could see the sieur. That was something to hope for, and meanwhile she had two thousand sick men to keep her occupied.

Six days later, the remnants of Sullivan's troops were back, no longer sharp and spiffy but as shattered and bedraggled as the troops they'd come to inspire. They'd landed to the west of Three Rivers, but the guide they'd employed had tricked them and led them into swamps, giving Carleton enough time to rush reinforcements down from Quebec. By the time the Americans had found their way, Carleton was ready and waiting for them. Overwhelmed by the British fire, the exhausted troops had turned and fled, leaving behind all their cannons and two hundred prisoners—including virtually all of their commanding officers.

Anne-Marie thought of Eli and Zeke. If they had been at Three Rivers, she prayed they weren't among the prisoners. If they were, she doubted that even Carleton would show them much mercy; as for Massey, if he was in Three Rivers, he'd be crying for blood. What if they were hanged as traitors? She couldn't stand the thought. She hadn't heard anything definite when the next blow fell: General Arnold had been forced to abandon Montreal and was at that moment retreating to Sorel. Worse, General Carleton had left Three Rivers and was also on his way.

Because of the shape of the Richelieu's shore, Sorel lay on a peninsula, which could be surrounded by Carleton's fleet. If that happened, Sullivan had no artillery with which to defend himself—as Carleton knew, having seized it from him in the Three Rivers debacle. Under the circumstances, only a fool would stay at Sorel, and though Sullivan wasn't generally considered a fool, he was sulking about Three Rivers and hated to give up another town without a fight. His staff tried to persuade him to leave while the troops waited anxiously, and Carleton's sails had filled the horizon before he changed his mind. The frantic retreat that followed made last month's flight from Quebec look like a holiday.

On the map hanging in headquarters, the trip south looked easy enough—straight down the Richelieu River, all the way to Lake Champlain. But even before she laid eyes on it that day, Anne-Marie had heard of the stretch of rapids that lay to the south: twelve miles of white water between Chambly and Saint John, water that would chew up and swallow any man fool enough to navigate it in a boat. If they could get past the rapids, they'd be safe from Carleton's fleet. But Sullivan didn't have the wagons to transport his supplies and provisions, let along two thousand sick men, for twelve miles overland. So how could they get from Chambly to Saint John?

How? The provisions would go by bateaux, not rowed on the river but dragged by ropes from the shore—dragged by phalanxes of cursing, stumbling, groaning soldiers who, in another army, would have been considered too ill for work and who were considered healthy only in contrast to the thousands worse off than they. Their shouts and curses filled the night, rising above the thunder of the rapids, which they battled with their last ounce of strength.

And the sick men? They would have to walk. Those without the strength to walk would have to crawl, and those too weak to crawl would be dragged by those who could. Anne-Marie walked with her charges, coaxing them along with the promise of a drink of water and an occasional mouthful of food, encouraging them when they stumbled, browbeating them up when they fell. She was hoarse, filthy and so exhausted she would have gladly lain down in the mud where she stood, but whatever force drove the tattered army was driving her, as well. The ordeal seemed endless, but when dawn finally came, it found them on the outskirts of the placid town of Saint John. There, the bateaux were pulled ashore and loaded with the ill, then rowed a few miles farther south to a flat thumbprint of an island known as the Île aux Noix.

"What does it mean?" asked one of the oarsmen in Anne-Marie's boat.

"The Island of Nuts," she answered.

"Nuts!" The man cackled with mirth. "Suits us perfectly. We'd have to be nuts to put up with this!"

Anne-Marie would have smiled if she'd had the strength—and if she hadn't been surveying the landscape of their new home, which was flat as a pancake except in the center, where a house and a barn stood alone on a little rise. There were a couple of trees around the house, and some acres of plowed fields, but apart from that the island's vegetation was confined to low brush.

"Where will the men stay?" she murmured, her eyes on the house, which couldn't have begun to accommodate two thousand men. And that number had surely risen after last night's ordeal.

"Maybe tents will rain down from heaven." The oarsman cackled again.

The only thing that rained down from heaven was rain, by the hogshead, and it lasted all night. They turned the bateaux over and put the men under them, where the hoards of mosquitoes found them and added to their misery. Anne-Marie was so exhausted she fell asleep despite the bugs, and she woke up in a mud puddle an hour or so before dawn. After she'd done the best she could with her skirts, she roused the first soldiers she found and sent them back to Saint John with a letter to General Sullivan describing conditions and begging for tents. She was so desperate she urged the soldiers to steal tents if they couldn't find Sullivan. As a postscript she added a request for food. She didn't bother asking for medicine, since she knew that there was none.

The food they received was one barrel of sour salt pork, but at least the tents began arriving that afternoon in time to get a portion of the men out of that night's storm. The next morning more tents arrived—along with a dozen bateaux filled with the men who'd fallen ill on the flight from Sorel. There wasn't anywhere to put them, or even nurses to bring them water, and what water they brought was bad. The storms that came nightly turned the place to a sea of mud; all this and the mosquitoes made the island a living hell.

Out of compassion or madness, Anne-Marie tried to be everywhere at once, falling where sleep overcame her then struggling awake a few hours later to pick up where she'd left off. She sent scouts across to the mainland in search of food, and when they came back with next to nothing, she sent them to gather spring greens, which she made into great vats of soup, flavored with the salt pork and thickened with moldy flour. The brew would have tasted revolting if they hadn't all been so starved; in any case, she was so busy she hardly had time to eat.

Days ran into days and she lost track of time. For every man she managed to pull back from the edge, two more plunged over before she could get to them. Those who re-

covered were soon put to work, carrying water, sweeping
out the tents and picking greens for more soup. Burying the
corpses alone was a full-time job. Men performed it for a
few days then deserted to the south, and plenty of others
deserted as soon as they could walk. Anne-Marie got so
tired of seeing men she'd saved depart that when a man
begged for water, she'd hold the dipper up and demand, "If
I give you a swallow, do you give me your word you'll
stay?"

It was madness. It was all madness. The whole world had
gone mad, and if she stayed here much longer she'd go mad
along with it. Sometimes all of a sudden the swirling in her
mind would stop and she'd have a memory of Quebec so
clear she couldn't believe it wasn't real. She'd stop whatever she was doing and stand there in a daze, struck by the
thought that somewhere normal life was going on.

At Deschambault she'd written a letter to the sieur, begging his forgiveness for what she'd done and explaining that
she meant to find François. She'd given it to headquarters
to be delivered to Carleton, but she had no idea whether it
had ever reached Quebec. If it had fallen into Massey's
hands, she guessed that it wouldn't have. Not knowing the
fate of the letter only increased her sadness and guilt.

Then, as if things weren't bad enough, Carleton's army,
well equipped with wagons, marched overland to Saint
John, forcing the "healthy" American troops to fall back
to the Île aux Noix, so that now there were that many more
bodies to be sheltered and mouths to be fed. For all she
knew, Eli could already be here, or captured, or even dead.
But she was too tired to worry. She was too tired even to
think. She was so tired that one day when an orderly
touched her on the arm, she looked up and imagined that
it was Eli himself.

Of course it wasn't. She was so exhausted that her mind
was playing tricks. Disappointment swooped down so
swiftly that for a moment the world turned dark. Until now
she hadn't realized how much she longed for the comfort of

a familiar face. No, not just a face, but his face, and she wanted to see it so much that she had resorted to hallucinating him, and she couldn't afford to do that, not with so many people depending on her.

She turned back to the man she was feeding and said to the orderly, "You can refill the bucket and after that you can sweep out this tent."

"In a minute." The hand stayed on her arm. "Can you talk for a minute? We won't keep you very long."

She looked back. Was it really Eli? She blinked, but his face remained. And there was Zeke, standing just behind him and looking very serious.

The world wobbled slightly. "Is—is it really you?"

Zeke thrust out an arm. "Pinch me. Go ahead."

She didn't. She just stood there. Eli's hand was still on her arm. "Come outside," he murmured. "You look like you need some air."

"I guess I do," she said vaguely. The world was still wobbling. "I need to find someone to take over."

"I'll do that," said Zeke, and before she could protest, the soup was in his hand and Eli was guiding her gently but firmly from the tent.

She looked even worse in the sunlight, so pale, and the arm he was holding was as thin as a twig. Eli had no trouble guessing what she'd been doing since he'd last seen her, but even so he was shocked. He might not have known her if he hadn't recognized her dress, and he'd scarcely recognized that for its shabbiness.

"Where are you staying?" he asked when he had her in the open air. She blinked like a night creature when she faced the sun.

"Over there." She pointed vaguely. "But there isn't time. We can talk here. Then I've got to get back to work. The last time we counted there were three thousand men. Three thousand, just imagine." Her eyes were wide and blank and the circles beneath them looked as if they'd been drawn in ink.

"Pretty soon," he said gently, steering her in the direction she'd pointed. "Tell me which tent is yours."

"No time," she repeated, but she pointed it out to him and then she let him lead her through the open flap. The single pallet told him that she had it to herself, but from the looks of it she didn't spend much time here. He was half-surprised she even remembered where it was.

"Sit down," he directed, pushing her gently so that she sat.

"Really, I can't—"

"I know. Just lie back, that's right."

She sighed as she lay back. "Where have you been? After Three Rivers I was worried about you. I was worried you'd been captured...."

"We weren't even there. There was a battle at Les Cèdres, to the west of Montreal. The British were outnumbered about five to one, but the American officer in charge panicked and surrendered. He claimed he believed there were swarms of Indians waiting in the woods and that his men would have been massacred if he'd put up a fight." As he spoke he was unfastening her shoes and pulling them and her stockings off.

"Five to one," she repeated foggily. "Were you there?"

"Not then. We went later. Arnold sent us to scout out the possibility of taking it back." When he pulled off her stockings, she sighed and wriggled her toes.

"It feels nice," she said, and giggled, but by the middle of the giggle she was fast asleep, her head fallen sideways, both of her hands lying limp.

Eli set her shoes side by side next to the door, but her stockings he tossed on the ground. He'd find someone to wash them, or he'd wash them himself. If he could peel it off her, he'd also wash her dress. He sat back on his heels, looking down at her silent face. There was a smudge of dirt across her forehead and the marks of dozens of mosquito bites. She'd braided her hair who knew how many days before, and whenever a strand had crept loose, she'd tucked it back randomly. Looking down at the resultant tangles, he remembered perfectly how that hair looked washed and combed. He remembered just as clearly how it felt and smelled.

He looked away, out through the open flap and down the row of tents. She'd fallen asleep before he could tell her what he was doing here. Last night he and Zeke had arrived from their scouting trip. They'd reported to Arnold, but he'd been occupied trying to convince Sullivan to order a retreat. There was no natural barrier between Saint John and the Île aux Noix. There was no barrier at all. For ten days Carleton had been waiting for the cumbersome train of his wagons to gather at Saint John, but he wouldn't wait forever, and once he made his move, the troops on the island were there for the plucking, like ripe fruit off the tree. Eli was here to be sure that Anne-Marie didn't fall into Carleton's hands—or Massey's, to be more specific.

He looked back at her. Her lips were parted and she was breathing deeply and evenly. There would be time to tell her when she woke; from what he'd seen, he knew she could use a few hours' untroubled sleep. He shook his head sadly. She could use a great deal more than that.

He found a bucket in the next tent. From his pocket he took out a strip of cloth wrapped around a sliver of scented soap from Montreal. There hadn't been food to trade for, so he'd traded for soap. At the time he'd wished it was salt pork, but now he was glad it was soap.

She hardly stirred when he washed her face, though he had to scrub in some places. He washed her hands when he'd finished, then he washed her feet. That made her giggle faintly and pull away. She giggled again and she muttered when he stripped off her dress. He did it quickly and covered her with his shirt, making sure he touched her as little as possible. When he came out of the tent with the dress and stockings, he caught an idle soldier across the way watching him with a knowing smirk.

Anger flashed through him. He tossed the soldier the clothes and the soap. "Go down to the river and wash these, and bring them straight back when you're done."

"Yes, sir." The soldier saluted and ambled off. Eli watched till he'd vanished, then went back into the tent.

He found a comb among her few possessions and unbraided her hair, then settled down to the lengthy process of teasing out the snarls. He would have liked to wash it, but that was impossible; for the present, combing would have to do. He sat on the edge of her pallet, her hair spread across his lap. Twilight was falling and bringing a cooling breeze as well as the drone of mosquitoes—promise of things to come. For the first time in a long time he felt a sense of peace steal over him.

Her hair was untangled. Submitting to temptation, he gathered it up in his hands and let it run between his fingers. He'd been worried about seeing her. Part of him had wanted to let Zeke come alone—the wise part, probably. But now that he was with her, he wasn't feeling the way he thought he would. He wasn't feeling either the anger or the desire. More than anything he felt relief that after what they'd been through, they were both still alive.

She twitched her nose and murmured something incoherent: the falling hair had tickled her. He divided it into three strands and rebraided it, then tied it with a bit of ribbon—the result of another trade.

He leaned back and smiled as he inspected his handiwork. Except for being too thin, and the bug bites, she looked pretty good. When the soldier brought her dress back, he'd put it back on and she'd have quite a surprise when she woke up. One of her hands was lying near his knee; without thinking he took it in his. The skin was rough and in some places blistered, and her nails were all broken down.

Gently he stroked her fingers, then he lifted them to his cheek, closing his eyes to feel their warmth before he lowered them to his chest. Looking down at her, he remembered that he'd called her immature and spoiled. She had been both, but she'd grown up since that night in Quebec. He felt proud of what she'd done here, as if in some way she belonged to him.

In her sleep she muttered and pulled her hand away. When he released it, she rolled over with her back toward him. Her braid lay across her shoulder. He reached out to touch it in the warm place just above the nape of her neck. That sense of peace was still with him. He'd sit here while she slept, and when she woke up he'd tell her why he'd come.

Despite his best intentions, he must have dozed off, because the evening campfires were burning when Zeke's voice jerked him awake.

"Good news," Zeke said. "Sullivan's finally given the order to retreat."

"Where to?"

"Crown Point. We're giving up Canada." Lighted by the glimmer of the fire, Zeke's eyes met his. For all they'd both known what was coming, the news was still hard to hear. A year ago it had seemed inevitable that Canada would be theirs. Six months from now they could both be at the end of a British rope. They could all be, Eli amended, looking down at Anne-Marie.

Zeke gave her a quick glance. "Schuyler's sent us everything he's got that floats. You ought to see the selection. They've even got whaleboats they pulled up from Lake George. On the way down, I'm going after Sally and the children. The land's no place for them with the British on the move."

"I'll go with you."

"Bring her, too. If you can find a blanket, we can rig it up as a sail."

"For what?"

Zeke's teeth flashed dimly. "I was figuring on finding us a boat. Nothing special, just some little thing that floats. With a sail and a little bit of luck we'll be there in a day."

Eli nodded. "We'll meet you at the landing as soon as I wake her up."

Zeke nodded and was gone. Anne-Marie was sleeping as soundly as before. She didn't so much as stir when he touched her cheek, so he shook her by the shoulder. "Anne-Marie. Wake up. The British are coming. We're going to Crown Point."

The soldier who'd washed her clothes must have returned them while they'd both been asleep. Dress and stockings were hung just inside the flap; both were still slightly damp, but at least they were clean. She was so groggy he had her dressed before she knew what was happening.

"The British?" she murmured.

He nodded once. "Zeke is waiting at the landing. We'll stop at his land to collect Sarah and the children, then we'll meet the army at Crown Point. Come on, we've got to go now."

He was putting on her shoes and she was watching, still more than half-asleep. "I can't go," she said vaguely. "What about the men?"

"They'll come," he told her. "They'll be loaded on boats and sent on. You can meet them at Crown Point. What do you want to take with you?" But he didn't wait to hear, just threw all her possessions into the canvas bag, pulled her up from the pallet and out of the tent.

Word of the latest order had evidently spread and the camp was full of people running in all directions, orders barked with nobody listening while everyone who was able fended for himself. Eli guided Anne-Marie through the hubbub and down to the landing. They'd almost reached it when she pulled back to stop.

"What's wrong?"

"I can't leave now."

"Everyone is leaving."

"But what about the men? They can't all be loaded to-night, and who'll take care of them until they are? If they aren't taken care of, some of them will die before they're ready to leave."

He looked around briefly at the sea of tents. "You can't fill an ocean with a thimble. Some of them will die anyway. If Carleton's coming, then Massey's coming, too. You know what'll happen if you're here when they arrive."

"Yes, I know," she said calmly. "But they aren't here yet and the men need me. You go with Zeke and I'll meet you at Crown Point. Don't worry. I'll be all right."

"There you are!" Out of the confusion, Zeke came rushing up. "There's a thousand captains grabbing for a hundred boats. I've got one just right for us but it won't be there for long."

"Please come," said Eli.

Anne-Marie shook her head.

Zeke looked from one to the other. "What's going on?"

"We're staying," Eli said. "We'll see that the sick men are loaded, then we'll come. It won't take long."

"You must be—" Zeke began, then stopped himself. Shooting a look at Anne-Marie, he took Eli by the arm and pulled him aside. "What are you doing?" he snapped. "You know what'll happen if they catch her—if they catch either of you. Massey'll have you strung up before you can say your name."

Eli nodded briefly. "That's why I've got to stay. Don't worry. I'll get her out in time."

"You'd better," Zeke said, glancing back at the tangle of boats. He moved back to Anne-Marie. "You take good care of my baby brother. I'm leaving him in your care."

"He should go," she said, looking distracted.

The brothers exchanged a glance. "I'll be looking for you," said Zeke. "We'll wait for you up at the land."

"I'll be there," Eli promised. For a moment Zeke's hand grasped his, then he was gone—and so was Anne-Marie, heading resolutely for the nearest tent.

"Good evening, Captain!"

Before Massey could lift his head, General Burgoyne had breezed past him into Carleton's office and shut the door behind him.

The door might have been open, since Massey knew Burgoyne's purpose—the same purpose Burgoyne had been pursuing since he'd stepped off his ship at Quebec. Burgoyne wanted Carleton to let him at the Americans. Gentleman Johnny was a man after Massey's heart, especially now with the crippled American army in laughably easy reach. If Carleton would permit it, Burgoyne could have them today. If Carleton would permit it.

Massey looked out the window at the main street of Saint John, a town with nothing more to recommend it than Three Rivers or Sorel—nothing save the proximity of the Americans. Then again, he was lucky to be here; when Carleton had left Quebec a month ago he'd left Massey behind. Although Carleton hadn't said so, Massey understood that the general had been worried that after what had happened with Brownell, Massey might let personal grudges interfere with his work.

He'd been in Quebec when Carleton had forwarded the letter from Anne-Marie to Saint Vallier. Massey had read it, which had been a mistake, since it brought back all the humiliation of that day the fleet had arrived and she had left him tied to a bedpost while she ran off with Brownell. She didn't explicitly say that they were still together—she probably wouldn't to the sieur—but Massey imagined they were. That was the trouble; he could imagine too much. If Carleton hadn't known that the letter existed, he would have burned it, but instead he'd been obligated to deliver it to the sieur. He'd still been seething with resentment when Carleton's summons had come, ordering him to join the reinforcements rushing to Three Rivers to confront the Americans.

Although he'd arrived after the fighting was over, the rout of the Americans had been balm for his wounded pride. But the balm had been short-lived. Carleton had released the captured Americans on their parole, and though he could have nabbed all of Sullivan's forces, instead he let them go.

Now Carleton was in position to nab the army again. If he moved fast enough, he could catch them at Île aux Noix and hold them there in a vast prison camp while the main force of his army marched south to Albany. Carleton's army now numbered ten thousand men, including the five thousand soldiers who had come with General Burgoyne and another four thousand crack German troops under General Riedesel. From what their intelligence had gathered and what Massey himself had observed, there was no reason those troops could not march from Saint John straight through to New York—so long as they did it now. That, in essence, was what Burgoyne was saying to Carleton, and he was saying it with such force that Massey could hear him through the door.

"Opportunity!" Burgoyne was saying. "Before they get away!"

Carleton replied more calmly, but Massey could guess what he said. Carleton was worried about the American presence on Lake Champlain and the number of reserves General Schuyler might be holding at Albany. He was afraid to move down the lake for fear of being trapped. But damn it, the Americans had crumbled every time the two sides had met, and there was no reason to expect it would be any different with Schuyler's reserves—if in fact they existed, and Massey doubted that they did.

Suddenly the door sprang open and Burgoyne appeared, looking as though he'd just been kicked in the gut. "We are moving, but slowly, and without orders to attack! Ten thousand soldiers and we are sitting on our guns!"

Massey stood at attention as Burgoyne strode from the room. No sooner had the door closed than he was out from behind his desk and in with Carleton.

Carleton, who'd clearly expected him, smiled tiredly when Massey came in. "Don't tell me, Captain. You want to move up with the advance guard. But even if Brownell has been on the island, the chances are good that he's already left. Men have been moving south for the past month."

"Yes, sir. I understand. But I'd still like to go. According to intelligence, Mademoiselle Doucet has been acting as a nurse in the American camp. If she's there, maybe Brownell is, too."

"And what will you do if you catch them?"

"Make them prisoners."

Carleton gave him a long look. "You know that the Sieur de Saint Vallier has begged me to be kind to the *mademoiselle* if she is caught. He is an important friend of England and it stands to reason that we'd lose that friendship if we harmed the *mademoiselle*."

"Yes, sir. I understand. But what about Brownell?" He would be satisfied to take his revenge on Brownell, especially if he could do it in the presence of Anne-Marie. The image of them together had fed his hate for the past six weeks.

"Brownell is another story," said Carleton. "He misled us intentionally." Carleton looked disappointed that Brownell had let him down. "But we're counting our chickens before they hatch. For all we know, both Brownell and the *mademoiselle* are both long since back at Crown Point."

"Even so," Massey persisted, "I'd like to go with the advance guard."

Carleton nodded slowly. "All right. Tell General Burgoyne that you have my leave. But take care of yourself. Even with ten thousand soldiers, a good aide is hard to find."

"Yes, sir, and thank you." Massey bowed his head, mostly so that Carleton wouldn't see the eagerness in his eyes. His sense of justice told him that Brownell would be on the Île aux Noix, and unless he was greatly mistaken, so would Anne-Marie.

He only stopped to change his uniform and load his pistol before reporting to Burgoyne. In his sixteen years with the army he'd never been with active troops and he'd always wondered how he would feel under arms. He felt on edge and excited and not afraid of anything, apart from the possibility that he might somehow miss Brownell.

Thanks to Carleton's order, he was able to move up with the very first of the troops. It was dark by the time they left, a short string of canoes, each carrying three soldiers and paddled by two Indians. Their orders were to reconnoiter and report back. The tacit understanding was that they wouldn't land.

In a matter of minutes the island came into view, the light of the campfires illuminating the starless night. Even before they rounded the north shore, they could hear the splash and clatter of boats being shoved off from the rocky beach.

Massey's throat constricted with anxiety. Anne-Marie and Brownell could be aboard any one of those boats and he'd miss them if he didn't get ashore. The lead canoe was drifting noiselessly along. They could see enough from the water so there was no point in going ashore. Massey realized grimly that he was going to have to disobey orders and strike out on his own—and unless he meant to swim ashore, he'd have to take his canoe along.

He leaned forward to the Indian at the bow. "Drop back until we're last in line, then turn into the shore. Do what I tell you—I've got my orders directly from General Carleton."

He wasn't sure how much English the Indian understood, but he must have understood the most of it because he did as Massey said, communicating in sign language with the Indian in the stern.

"What's going on?" the other two soldiers grumbled, but Massey shut them up. This might be his only chance at Brownell and he'd knock them both unconscious if they tried to stand in his way. At the moment he didn't care what Carleton thought.

They landed in a stretch of underbrush, which would be hell to wade through, but there wasn't too much choice unless he wanted to waste time persuading the Indians to land them somewhere else.

He took along the soldier named Gordon and left the other behind to eliminate any chance of their disapproving what he was up to and ganging up on him. One man could protect him, but two could hold him back. The mosquitoes attacked them with a vengeance as they beat their way through the brush—one branch forked Massey's wig and almost dragged it off. At least they didn't have to worry about being quiet, since the Americans were making more than enough racket to wake up the dead.

Slapping bugs and dodging springing branches, they made their way forward until they were within sight of the farthest row of tents. Without any apparent order, some of the tents were being struck, while soldiers were carrying stretchers out of others and heading toward the beach. The scene was less chaotic than he'd expected, given the noise, but it lacked the coherence of English discipline. While he was watching, Massey saw a soldier stop in the midst of breaking a tent to rush off to do something else, leaving his companion gaping after him. As he looked after the first man, he caught sight of Anne-Marie.

She was standing in profile, wearing a terrible rag of a dress and her hair pulled back in a braid. She looked harassed and weary but nonetheless beautiful. Her beauty touched his resentment like a personal affront; he remembered all too clearly how she'd refastened his gag and how he'd felt when the servants had finally found him hours after she and Brownell had gone. That had been a black hour, but this one would make up for it.

He kept his eyes on her, not wanting to chance her slipping away. She was standing in a clearing between two rows of tents and doing her best to direct every soldier within range. Brownell wasn't with her, which immediately worried him. But he was being overanxious. What did he expect—that Brownell would be standing next to her, holding her hand? More likely he was seeing to his own affairs. Maybe—

Before Massey could complete the thought, Brownell suddenly appeared, stripped to the waist and looking like a drover, and a disreputable one at that. Massey tensed and his fingers found their way to his gun as Brownell strode straight toward him, then stopped at the half-struck tent to help the soldier who'd been deserted by his partner. As Brownell bent to the crumpled canvas, Massey's lips curved in an icy smile.

Beside him, Gordon whispered, "What are you going to do?"

Massey raised his hand to tell him to be still. The spot where Brownell was working was screened from the rest of the camp by other tents. If they sneaked up a little bit closer, they could grab him and drag him into the bushes, where they could knock him out. What about the other soldier? They'd have to get him, too. If they both moved at the same time—

Then, as if fate had intervened, Massey heard Anne-Marie's voice raised, calling a name. She was calling the name of the soldier Brownell was working with.

"I'll be back," the soldier said to Brownell. He trotted over to Anne-Marie, who gave him an instruction that sent him off toward the wharf.

As Anne-Marie walked toward Brownell, who was now working alone, Massey leaned close to Gordon and whispered in his ear. Gordon nodded briefly to show he'd understood.

Anne-Marie stopped less than two yards from where Massey crouched, her back to the bushes. "There's still no sign of them. Maybe they're not coming."

"They're coming." Brownell paused to wipe his sweaty forehead with his arm. "My guess is that Carleton is still trying to be our friend. If we ever win this war, we'd better erect a monument to him."

Thunder rumbled above them. Anne-Marie looked up. "Just what we need right now—another storm."

"More likely it's from the heat," he said, bending back to the tent.

"I hope—" she began, but the rest of her words were lost in a grunt as Massey's arm clamped around her middle and his pistol touched her cheek.

Brownell reacted in the next second, but by then it was too late.

"Go ahead," Massey taunted, holding her against his chest. "Take one step toward me if you want to see her die. Tie him up," he added as Gordon emerged from the brush. Triumph surged through him as he saw realization darken Brownell's eyes.

Anne-Marie spoke for the first time. "He won't hurt me," she said. "Run, quick, Eli!"

Before Brownell could do that, Gordon's pistol was at his ear.

"This way and quickly." Massey jerked his head in the direction that they'd left the boat. If they were in the bushes no one would notice them, and in all this confusion no one would miss either of his prisoners.

He kept his grip on Anne-Marie as they waded through the brush, though she kicked and struggled and fought him every step of the way. When they'd gone twenty paces, he stopped and tossed Gordon a rope so that he could tie up Brownell. He was concentrating on Gordon's progress, so he didn't notice Anne-Marie bending her head until her teeth were sunk deep into his arm.

Bright red flashed before him. "Damn!" he cried, and
let her go. She'd been waiting for her moment and was off
and bounding through the bushes before he fully realized
what she'd done. His cry had distracted Gordon, who
looked up from his rope. As he did, Brownell's fist came
up, pushing his stomach into his lungs. Gordon doubled up
with a grunt and Brownell raised both arms and brought
them down hard on Gordon's back.

Anne-Marie was long gone. Massey turned the gun on
Brownell, but Brownell's fist was already flying and caught
it as it came around, knocking it out of Massey's hand. As
Massey swiveled to retrieve it, Brownell knocked him in the
chin. He felt himself reeling but he refused to fall. Instead
he brought his own fist up and caught Brownell in the jaw.
He heard him grunt at the contact but the triumph was
brief, for Brownell's next blow sent him crashing to the
ground. As he went down he reached out for the gun, but
what his fingers closed on was the toe of someone's shoe.

"Stay where you are," a cool voice commanded. "Eli,
are you all right?"

Anne-Marie was standing above him, holding his gun.
Without thinking of what he was doing, Massey grabbed
her foot. This time surprise was in his favor and she went
down heavily. He grabbed her by the ankle as he scrambled for a better grasp. She fought him, but he held her, but
by then Brownell had the gun.

"Let her go," he ordered.

Massey shook his head. Behind him, Gordon was
groaning. "Shoot me," Massey said.

"Too messy," Brownell said flatly. He also had Gordon's gun. "Cleaner to knock you out. I'll do it if you don't
let her go."

Bile, thick and bitter, rose up in Massey's throat. It
would be better to be knocked unconscious than to surrender to Brownell.

"Let her go," Brownell repeated, pushing off Massey's wig. Grabbing a handful of his short hair, he twisted it and pulled back hard.

The pain made Massey's eyes water. As much as he hated to surrender, he knew he couldn't win; he let Anne-Marie go and rose slowly to his feet when Brownell told him to. Anne-Marie held both guns while Brownell wielded the rope, tying up both Massey and Gordon, who was still moaning on the ground.

"What are you going to do with me?" Massey asked.

Brownell shrugged as he checked his knots. "Turn you over to headquarters and let them deal with you. When Carleton gets over being angry about tonight's peccadillo, no doubt he'll trade to get you back. Time to go," he added, pulling Gordon up.

"Saint Vallier's ruined," Massey said to Anne-Marie. "He never got the letter you left at Deschambault. I found it and destroyed it." Even in the darkness he could see her face go pale, and that gave him satisfaction despite everything else. "I hope whatever you get from Brownell is worth what you did to the sieur."

"He's lying," Brownell said. "Carleton needs the sieur's support. Beyond that, he's jealous."

"Ha!" Massey sneered. "Of what?"

"Oh, stop it!" Anne-Marie cried, her eyes flashing in the dark. "I don't want to hear any more. Let's take them to headquarters and get back to work."

The way to headquarters took them past more rows of tents full of skeletal soldiers being helped along by other soldiers who weren't in much better shape.

"You're a fool, Brownell," said Massey. "You can't win a war with men who look like these. You'll fall back and fall back until your backs are against the wall. Then you'll wish you'd taken the deal Carleton offered you in Quebec."

"And I suppose you'll be there to remind me. We turn here." Brownell gave him a nudge to the right.

"I can't imagine a greater pleasure," Massey said as he turned.

A minute later they were at headquarters, the island's only house. The place was in chaos, so instead of waiting for Sullivan, they left Massey and Gordon in the charge of one of his aides.

"It's true about the letter," Massey said to Anne-Marie, and saw her go pale again before she turned away.

"You'll be whipped by autumn!" Massey called after them.

"Thanks a lot," muttered Gordon, sinking down on a rickety bench.

Chapter Eleven

Dawn was a milky line on the horizon when Eli said to Anne-Marie, "All that's left is tearing the last of the tents down. It's time to leave."

She was too tired to protest, and besides, he was right. The island looked as forlorn abandoned as it had teeming with tents. "I hope General Burgoyne likes mosquitoes," she said as she followed him. Then, noting that they weren't headed for the beach, she asked, "Where are we going?"

"I figured there wouldn't be any boats left when we'd finished, so I put one aside."

He'd stowed it in a little cove near the spot where Massey had tried to ambush them. The boat he'd set aside was a worn canoe, which began to ship water as soon as Eli dragged it out of the bushes and pushed it into the river. It also rocked violently as soon as Anne-Marie got in. "There wasn't much of a selection," Eli explained, climbing into the stern. "But if I can get her rigged, hopefully she'll sail."

He rigged the canoe with a blanket tied to two pieces of wood and a paddle for a rudder. After he finished, the boat was even unsteadier than before. "Can you swim?" he asked.

"A little, if I have to."

"Let's hope you don't, but you will have to bail." He tossed her a tin cup and she set to work, though what she really wanted was to curl up, water or no water, and go to sleep.

When they came around the island, they joined the motley procession in its splashing, uneven way south. Zeke must have been right about Schuyler sending every craft he had, since the boats carrying the retreating army were as ragtag as the army itself: bateaux, canoes and longboats all loaded to the gunwales with men. Those with the strength were rowing, while those too weak lay packed like salted mackerel at their feet.

The sight of the sick men gave Anne-Marie a pang. "I ought to be with them."

"You will be soon enough. Why don't you rest for a while? I doubt you'll get much chance for rest once we get to Crown Point."

She nodded distractedly, her eyes still on the boats they were passing rather neatly with the benefit of their sail. "Do you really believe Massey was lying about the sieur?"

Eli nodded. "The only reason Carleton would punish him for what you did would be out of vindictiveness, and Carleton's not vindictive."

She knew that was true, but there was also the letter, which Massey claimed to have destroyed. "I should have written the sieur another letter before we left. I could have left it at the farmhouse." She looked back past Eli.

"Don't worry," he said. "Even without a letter the sieur will know why you did what you did and he'll understand."

She stopped looking at the horizon and looked at Eli instead. Until this moment she hadn't realized how nice he was being to her. At first she'd been too tired, and after he'd woken her up she'd been too distracted trying to organize the men for the evacuation. When they'd left Quebec he had done things for her out of duty or because Zeke had forced him to. But now he was being genuinely nice.

She felt an increasing dampness beneath her: she'd forgotten to bail. She picked up the cup and continued, but she was still thinking of him. "You washed my dress, didn't you?" she asked, glancing up.

"Not me. I gave it to a soldier who had nothing better to do. And your stockings," he added, and they both looked down at her bare feet. She'd taken off her shoes and stockings when they were pushing off the boat and now they were lying nearby, muddy and soaking wet.

She bit her lip. "I'm sorry," she said, and began to laugh. Once she started laughing she couldn't stop, though the motion was making the boat jerk around like a lopsided top.

Eli wasn't laughing, but he was smiling.

"I'm sorry," she repeated. "For laughing."

"I don't mind." He continued to smile until he caught himself. Then he looked away.

She looked away, too. Dawn was coming fast, drab and sunless in a sky thick with clouds. The thunder she'd heard last night was still rumbling to the east like some huge hungry animal prowling along the shore, growling in anticipation as it followed the clumsy boats. Even without the sun shining, she could feel the heat. She thought again of the sick men and hoped that those with them would give them something to drink.

"How far is it to where we're going?"

"A day, maybe more, depending upon the wind."

"And to Crown Point?"

"Maybe another two."

She wanted to ask him what he would do when they arrived, if he would stay with the army or go back to his farm, but she was afraid that if she pressed the matter, this truce between them would break and he would start treating her coldly again. The mugginess was oppressive despite the river breeze, and her eyes felt as if they had sand under the lids. She leaned back a little and closed her eyes. She was too near sleep to retrieve the tin cup when it slipped from her hand.

* * *

She didn't know how long she slept, but when she opened her eyes she saw that they'd left the flat green floodplain of the Richelieu behind and plunged between deeply folded mountains that shared a common palette of colors with the sky. The thunder was still growling and the sky was low and gray. Eli was guiding the rudder and boom with his left hand and bailing with his right.

"Sleep well?" he asked when he looked up and found her awake.

"I must have. Where are we now?"

"We're just coming along the islands at the top of Lake Champlain. We're making good time. If our luck and the daylight hold, we'll be there before dark." He looked up at the lowering sky.

"If you want to sleep for a while, I'll steer."

"I'll sleep when we get there."

"You think I'll sink us or run us aground."

"It wouldn't be hard to do," he said, but not unkindly. "The fact is, I'm enjoying myself. This is the most pleasant of all the retreats so far."

She laughed ruefully. "That's not saying much. At least pass me the cup and let me bail. What do you think will happen to Massey?"

"Sooner or later he'll be exchanged."

"He hates you." She emptied the cup and looked at him.

"After last night, I wouldn't say you're his best friend, either. Speaking of last night, can I give you some advice? Always remember to hold on to the gun. That's twice you've forgotten."

"Twice?"

"Last night with Massey and at the magazine." He grinned. "But the biting's effective."

"Thanks. I'll keep it in mind," she answered, grinning back at him, not because she found what he said funny, but because after living in a nightmare for weeks, she felt almost lighthearted with Eli, which was remarkable.

They were grinning at each other when a sudden gust of cold air swooped down out of nowhere, filling the sail with such force they would have capsized if Eli hadn't let out the boom and shifted his weight in time.

The gust was followed by another. "Stay low," he advised. "If this keeps up we'll be at Zeke's in time for supper."

"That sounds wonderful!" she said, or rather shouted, over the force of the wind. To be anywhere for supper sounded wonderful. She was so used to being hungry she hadn't noticed until now that she was ravenous. She shouted to Eli, "Do you have anything to eat?"

Letting go with one hand, he reached into his pocket and pulled out a handkerchief, which he passed across to her. She untied it and found a piece of bread.

"It's for you," he shouted. "I've already had my share."

She broke it in two and gave him one piece. "Take it. I can't eat it all."

"I'll bet," he said, but he took it, and as he did they both grinned again, because she knew he'd been lying and he knew she'd been lying back. In the next moment he almost lost his share as the wind gusted again. He took a bite and crammed the rest into his pocket, using both hands to steer.

The wind was coming from the north, gaining force as it was funneled between the islands and the shore. When they rounded the foot of the islands, the wind shifted to the west, pushing them like two great hands toward the eastern shore.

Eli pointed toward where they were going. "That's the Grants. Those are the Green Mountains."

They looked more purple than green and the tops of the tallest were lost among the clouds. The thunder sounded as if it were behind them, growling at their heels.

"You ought to see it on a clear day," Eli shouted above the wind.

She didn't bother to shout back that she wished she could. She wondered if they'd make it ashore before the storm hit.

"Is Zeke's house near here?"

"Right there. In that grove of birch trees on the top of that bluff."

She saw the birch trees tossing in the wind but she couldn't see the house. That didn't matter, since the trees were straight ahead, and unless the wind died, they'd be there very soon.

If anything, the wind blew stronger, shooting them at the shore so swiftly that in the end Eli dropped the sail and paddled so they wouldn't crash into the beach. When the bow touched, Anne-Marie jumped into the water and helped pull the boat to shore. They hauled the canoe to a stand of trees and turned it over.

"Didn't Zeke bring a boat?"

"I don't see it. Come on, let's check the house."

The force of the wind almost carried her up the bluff, but at the top it changed abruptly and almost blew her back down. Eli grabbed her hand and pulled her ahead to the house, of which she got only the vaguest impression through her wildly blowing hair. She stood on the front porch while he knocked up the bar on the door. The door flew open and she flew through it. When Eli slammed it shut behind them, she heaved a deep sigh of relief.

It was dark inside, partly because the windows were shuttered and partly because of the storm. He found a lamp and lighted it. As soon as he did, Anne-Marie saw the note.

It was from Zeke, explaining that Sally had already gone ahead to Crown Point and he was following. They should make themselves welcome and he'd see them when they arrived.

"What should we do?" she asked. As if to respond to her question, the wind shifted again to the north, and the first handful of raindrops clattered against the roof. Within no more than a minute, rain was pouring down as hard as its hardest on the Île aux Noix.

"I think we should stay." Eli raised his voice to be heard. He was checking all the windows to be sure they were secure. Meanwhile, Anne-Marie located the wood box and laid a fire in the hearth. She found steel and a flint on the mantel and in very little time the fire was blazing healthily.

"Not bad for a rich girl," Eli said approvingly.

She held her hands out to the welcome heat. "I wasn't always rich."

He didn't answer. Though the wind was howling and the thunder was rumbling, she felt his silence like a prickling up her spine. She sensed that he'd stopped and was watching her, and suddenly she imagined his arms slipping around her waist—not hard, the way that Massey's had, but slowly and sensuously. He would pull her back slowly against him and nudge her braid aside so that his lips could find the nape of her neck.

"Are you hungry?" he asked from behind her. "There ought to be everything we need to make a meal."

"Salt pork and biscuit." Banishing images of seduction, she turned around and laughed. "When all this is over I hope I never have to eat salt pork and biscuit again."

"If I had a bottle of wine, I'd drink to that."

"Wine," she said wistfully, thinking about all the times she'd declined the sieur's offer to take a glass of wine. She watched as Eli pushed the trapdoor back and disappeared down the cellar steps. When he reemerged with his arms full, her mouth started watering. "What have you got?"

"Salt pork and biscuit."

"You do not, you're teasing me!" She came forward to help him and he surrendered half the load to her. Cornmeal and molasses.

"And dried pumpkin," he said. "Too bad we don't have milk."

"Maybe I ought to go look for a cow." She carried the food to the table while Eli opened the door long enough to fill the kettle with water. "You know how to cook," she observed, watching him measure and stir.

"It's been either that or go hungry for years."

"You could have gotten married. Lots of people do."

"I tried, but she wouldn't have me."

"Why not?"

He shook his head. "It's a long story."

"I don't think I'm pressed for time." She pulled out a chair at the table and sat, cupping her chin in her hand.

Eli looked at her. His mouth was open to tell her that the tale wasn't worth repeating, when the look in those silvery eyes made him change his mind. He was seized by the urge to tell her—to sit down and explain everything while she listened with that half-grave, half-witty look.

He finished mixing his concoction and tapped the excess off the spoon. To buy time, he covered the kettle and carried it to the hearth, but when he'd hung it over the fire, the urge to speak was still as strong.

"You don't have to tell me," she said from behind him.

He shook his head slowly. "If you want to hear it, I don't mind. But you'll have to stop me when you get bored."

"I promise." She smiled as if he'd made a joke.

He went to sit at the table but ended up standing behind his chair, the way he did in court when he was trying a case, while she kept on watching with her hand cupping her chin.

He said, "I was twenty-one. I'd read law with a lawyer in Northampton. That's the Massachusetts Bay Colony. There was a girl I thought I loved—a girl from a good family. I proposed marriage and she accepted me. At the time I was considered to be the most eligible young man in town, but soon after that something happened that lowered my status, whereupon my fiancée decided she didn't want me after all."

"What happened?"

Outside the wind gusted, hurling another sheet of rain against the house. He walked back to check the kettle, which was boiling too high. He did these things in the present, but his mind was in the past, snarled in the dark web of events that had changed his life.

"The man I read with was a prominent lawyer in town. A very proper man. He had a daughter who was the apple of his eye. Before I became engaged, he'd made it clear to me that he'd be glad if I married his daughter, and he was disappointed when I chose someone else. About that time, Zeke came to visit me. He and the daughter laid eyes on each other and immediately fell in love. The lawyer was dead set against marriage, so they eloped."

"And that's why people disliked you?"

"No, it got worse. The lawyer wasn't an unreasonable man—at least at that point he wasn't. At that point he might have accepted Zeke if he'd agreed to settle down in Northampton and live what the lawyer considered a productive life."

"But he wouldn't?"

"Not by a long shot. Zeke didn't want to live in Northampton. He was set on living up here. After they eloped, he brought his bride up here and they lived in a tent while he built the house. Then she got pregnant so he changed his plans. He meant to take her back to Northampton for the baby to be born, but there was a storm, then the baby came early, before they could leave. He had a midwife and he knew what he was doing, but there was a problem."

"The baby died?"

He shook his head slowly. "No, the baby survived. Zeke's wife—the lawyer's daughter—was the one who died. Of course her father blamed Zeke. When Zeke brought the baby back to Northampton, her father had him thrown in jail and charged with murdering her. It took me almost a year to get the charges dismissed, but in the meantime the damage had been done. By the time I got Zeke out of jail, both of us were unattached, so when he gave me some land up in Bennington, I left Northampton and moved up there."

"What happened to your fiancée?"

"She married someone else. He's a judge in New Haven. I've managed to avoid her all these years, but I hear she's gotten very fat."

"So you were lucky." She smiled.

"Yes." He smiled back. He was back in the present; that dark web had disappeared. He didn't even feel bitter. He didn't even care. After all these years, finally, the story seemed far away.

Anne-Marie was still smiling.

"What about you?" he said.

"Me?"

"You and marriage."

"Oh." She leaned back and waved one hand, dismissing the subject as if it were ridiculous. "Who would I marry?"

"A man," he said logically. "They must have been lined up asking for your hand."

She laughed. "Lined up for a mile, but I turned them all down."

"Why?"

Suddenly serious, she said, "Because I didn't care for them."

Their eyes met. He wanted to ask her if she cared for him. That urge to hold her that he'd felt before came flooding back again. He turned to check the kettle, which didn't need his help. Outside the thunder was creeping closer, but here inside it was snug. Anne-Marie was still looking at him, but he was afraid of what would happen if he returned her look, so he gestured to the window. "It's too bad we have to keep the shutters closed. When they're open, sitting at that table, you can see the lake in one direction and the mountains in the other."

She looked at the shutters, trying to imagine it. Then she asked, "What's your house in Bennington like?"

"Nothing special. Just a farm. Zeke's always called it mine, but the truth is he mostly built it and he and Archie lived there until after Zeke married Sarah and they moved up here."

"Archie was the baby who lived?"

"He's not a baby anymore. When I stopped here on the way north last fall, he was almost as tall as me. He's probably taller than me by now. And the baby is probably talking." He shook his head as a crack of thunder broke directly overhead and lightning flashed through the cracks in the shutters.

Anne-Marie made a sound. Turning from the window, he saw that she'd turned white and was hugging herself with both arms, sitting up very straight.

"What's wrong?"

"Nothing." She gave her head a jerky shake.

"Tell me." He moved to the table and saw her cringe and grimace as the thunder cracked again. "Are you worried about the storm?"

"I—I don't like thunder. Wh-when I was a little girl we spent some time in the woods, and when there were storms I thought it was big monsters c-coming after me."

"You're shivering!"

"No, really. I'll be all r-right."

Without thinking of the consequences, he moved around to her chair and raised her so that she was standing, then wrapped her in his arms. She leaned against him, shaking like a leaf.

"It's so s-stupid," she muttered.

"No. No, it's not." He held her, his cheek resting on her hair. Her hair, which he'd combed out so carefully, was a thousand tangles again, but she smelled of the scented soap and a day in the open water had blown away the smell of Île aux Noix. In Quebec her body had been fuller because she'd had plenty to eat, but none of that had stirred him as deeply as holding her stirred him now.

He shifted in an effort to keep her from noticing, but there was no way to lower his body heat, which was rising steadily, as if the fire he imagined were really burning beneath his skin. She stopped shaking and went very quiet, and he held his breath, which was when he realized that she was changing, too.

"I want you," he whispered. He rubbed his cheek back and forth over the tangles of her hair. He felt a gentle movement; she was rubbing her cheek on his chest. Thunder cracked and she pressed closer. He lowered his head and nuzzled against her hair until he'd pushed the mass away and he could feel the smoothness of her cheek.

"Want you," he repeated, his lips touching her ear. In response he felt her shudder and one or the other of them groaned.

He was on fire. Just the gentle friction of their cheeks was almost more than he could stand as the months of pent-up desire all came crashing against the dam. Whatever he'd told himself about her these last months had been a lie; he still wanted her as deeply as he had in Quebec, and if she didn't stop him, he wouldn't stop himself. He rubbed his cheek across her forehead, then against her other cheek. Their bodies were so close together; hers was branded on him through his clothes. When he could stand it no longer, he bent to taste her lips.

He found them open and eager. There was no thought or planning here, and when the thunder cracked and rumbled she gave no sign that she'd heard. Now it was he who was shaking as if he were coming apart.

Her hands were working, rucking up his shirt then thrusting up beneath it to rake along his skin. He shuddered, pressing forward until she was curved like a bow. Now his hands were also working, pulling up her skirts while their mouths stayed locked together, both of them too inflamed to require air.

Her thighs were as long and silken as he remembered them. As his fingertips grazed their smoothness, he understood that he'd been thinking of this since that night in Quebec. His need for her was greater than any he'd ever known.

She muttered hoarsely as his hands slid farther up. He wondered if she would try to stop him, but she only twisted and groaned. Close to bursting, he ripped at the fall of his pants, popping the buttons when they wouldn't come loose. His pants fell to his ankles and he didn't stop to kick them off but took her against the table, thrusting deep inside, battering down her barrier as if it had never been.

The heat of her was stunning. If he hurt her, she gave no sign. She wrapped her legs around him, whimpering in pleasure and frustration. His head was hard forward, hers fallen back, his kisses on her forehead, her cheek, her neck, her throat. Deeper and deeper he thrust until she cried out. Her nails dug into his bare flesh and he plunged into the core of life, deeper and more enduring than he'd ever known before.

His body was racked with shudders, his breath came in great sobs. Beneath him, he felt her soften as her fingers loosened their hold.

"It's all right," she whispered, as if he'd been the virgin here. He tried to answer, but he couldn't catch his breath. His skin was still burning and his body was dripping with sweat. She pushed back his damp hair and kissed his forehead and the lids of his eyes, then laid her cheek against his—the same way they'd begun.

He was still inside her. He didn't want to let her go. He gathered her up and held her to him until they were chest to chest. "I'm sorry," he whispered.

"For what?" she whispered back.

"It should have been slower the first time. Better..."

To his surprise, she laughed, deep and throaty with delight. "I can't imagine anything being much better than that!"

With a sigh, he let her go so that she was sitting on the table with him standing at the edge. Her legs were still around him, but now they were loosely laced and her hands rested lightly on his shoulders while his rested on her waist.

She was still smiling and looked mightily pleased with herself. He almost wanted to laugh. A minute ago he'd been desperate, but now he was light with joy. "It can be better," he said softly. "I'll show you."

She laughed again. "What about dinner?"

"Are you hungry?"

"Are you?"

"Not for pumpkin and cornmeal." His eyes scanned her face, recalling the heat and the feel of her skin.

"Me, neither," she murmured in a different voice. "I want you to show me."

His hands cupped her cheeks. He lifted her face and kissed her lightly and lingeringly until he felt her shoulders heave in a deep gentle sigh. His camp-roughened fingers traced the line of her jaw. He pushed her hair back from her forehead and touched it with his lips. As he did, he felt the whisper of her lips against his chest and then the light tugging of her fingers on the buttons of his shirt.

His lips curved in a smile. Another woman might have waited passively for him to pleasure her, but Anne-Marie would never be passive about anything. For a moment his thoughts moved backward to the Île aux Noix and he saw her standing ankle-deep in mud, promising a man being carried away on a stretcher that she'd see him in Crown Point. He bet there were soldiers who'd live just to see her again. He bet she knew it, too, and that she'd used the knowledge shamelessly when the medicine gave out.

The last button yielded and her hands smoothed across his chest. He felt the softness of her lips again.

"Easy," he whispered, pulling up her head until he had her lips. "If you're not careful, you'll set me off again."

She was grinning but her eyes were dreamy. "You know I'm never careful and I don't think—"

He kissed away her words, then traced the shape of her mouth with the tip of his tongue. His hands rested on her shoulders as his lips moved down her throat to the edge of her bodice. She sighed and shuddered as his tongue traced the rise of her breasts, then his fingers addressed her buttons as hers had done his.

Beneath her bodice she wore a light chemise. He caressed her gently through it with his fingers and his mouth until he had her quivering, then he pulled it up and touched her skin directly.

At his touch she cried out, curving up toward him as he had curved her to him before. She was growing restless and he was beginning to burn. Her legs had unhooked from behind him and were hanging loose, her thighs shining whitely beneath her bunched up skirts. The sight of them made his heart lurch as it had before. He kicked his own pants loose, then sank down to his knees.

"Stop—where are you going?"

"Somewhere nice. You'll see." She shivered as he touched his lips to the inside of one knee and ran them slowly down to her ankle then back up again, first with light kisses, then with a teasing tongue. He did the same to the other leg. She was silent, alert. He felt her muscles tensing as his fingers moved farther up. She didn't protest or try to stop him, but she instinctively drew backward when he touched tender skin.

"Be still. I won't hurt you."

"It tickles."

"Is that so? And what about this?" he murmured, touching her with his lips.

"Oh...!" Her answer was a deep intake of breath and a moment later he felt her fingers in his hair.

He went slowly, advancing, withdrawing, nudging her toward the edge until she was too close for teasing and, her fingers dug in deeply, demanding he meet her need. He met it squarely and she cried out from the intensity; when she bucked against him, it was all he could do not to take her in the moment as he'd done before.

This time he held back. He waited until she'd stopped moving, kissing and stroking her legs.

"Oh, my!" she whispered when he raised his head. Her eyes were enormous and her face looked lovely and wild. "What now?"

He smiled. "Now I take you to bed." And lifting her up from the table, he did exactly that, pausing only to unhook her skirts and let them fall away.

She lay before him naked on the clean sheets of the bed. She was too skinny from the past months but still beautiful, long-legged, high-breasted, with hips that would look fuller when she'd had enough to eat. He was also naked and her eyes raked over him with no fear, only desire and deep curiosity.

She reached out her arms for him. "I'm cold. Make me warm."

It was all he wanted. Without a word, he went to her.

They never did eat that night. After it was over, Eli, who'd been awake for three days straight, fell into exhausted sleep, while Anne-Marie lay nestled against him, transfixed with wonderment. Her body was sated but her mind was wide-awake. She'd lived all these years in her body and until tonight she'd had only glimmerings of what it was capable of.

Until tonight she'd had only glimmerings about a lot of things. Even the moments with Eli in Quebec hadn't prepared her for this, for the depth and the sweetness—the shattering completeness of it all. There was a looking glass hanging above the dresser at the end of the bed, and if she had the energy to get up and look in it she believed she would see another face. She felt totally different, so how could she look the same?

Eli stirred against her. She lay still, holding her breath, but a moment later he uncurled from around her and turned onto his back. She propped herself up on one elbow, looking down at his face. It was dirty, lined with fatigue and darkened with the stubble of three days' unshaved beard—with scratchy stubble, she thought, ruefully rubbing her cheek—but for all that, he was still the handsomest man she'd ever seen.

And the dearest. She'd been wrong about him; not just about his values but about the way he was. He acted cool and distant, but underneath he was as caring and gentle as a person could be. She remembered the story he'd told her tonight, about the girl who'd turned against him when Zeke had been wrongfully accused. No wonder he was leery of showing how he felt. He had shown that girl he loved her and she had betrayed him just when he had needed her the most.

I wouldn't, thought Anne-Marie. If the whole world accused him, I'd say they were wrong. She remembered the struggle with Massey, an episode so lost in the blur of events that it might have been a dream. She remembered how Eli had kidded her about needing to improve her grip on a gun. He had a carefreeness about him despite his seriousness. He was also a wonderful lover, perfectly wonderful. Her lips curled in a smile and she leaned down to touch her lips to his forehead.

He muttered in his sleep and reached out one arm for her. She went to him willingly and curled up against the hard warmth of his side. She closed her eyes and filled her senses with his scent. Had she ever been happy? She was happy now. She loved him. She loved Eli Brownell and after tonight she was certain that Eli loved her, too. Suddenly the future seemed smoothed out like a freshly ironed sheet. Whatever happened would happen and it would be all right because they loved each other.

She thought about François and even that thought made her feel peaceful. Eli would help her find François. Eli could do anything. And when they'd found him, François could help convince Eli to go to Acadia. And if they couldn't convince him—well, they'd work it out. And every night Eli would make her body sing.

At some point a little later, she got up to add water to the pudding, which had boiled dry, and to bank the fire for the night. She was ravenously hungry, so she filled herself a bowl and brought it back to bed, where Eli would keep her warm while she ate. After that, full and contented, she fell straight asleep, hardly aware of the flash and thunder of the storm.

Chapter Twelve

"As promised," said Eli, referring to the view. They'd brought their chairs outside and were sitting on the front porch drinking coffee and looking out over Lake Champlain and the mountains beyond. The storm had moved on at some point during the night and Eli had awakened in time to watch the sun rise over the mountains to the east. He'd wanted to wake Anne-Marie to show her, but she was dead asleep, and from the empty bowl under her side of the bed, he guessed she'd been up and had eaten during the course of the night and probably needed her sleep.

He hadn't really minded. He'd been content just to have her there. Feeling content was a whole new experience, and one he hoped to keep. Instead of waking her up, he'd gone down to the stream behind the meadow to catch some fish. When he got back he'd meant to crawl in bed and wake her up with love, but coming up from the meadow, he'd found her fully dressed and watching from the porch, so he had contented himself with grinding coffee while she fried the fish, and after they'd eaten breakfast they had come out to enjoy the view.

There was a shyness about her this morning he'd never seen before and he found it another facet of her charm. She had found a comb of Sarah's and teased out the mess of her hair and tied it back at her neck. But the dampness of the storm had infused it with a life of its own, and every time she moved another curl slipped loose from the ribbon to halo her head. She looked adorable. At any given moment he was tempted to sweep her into his arms and shower her with kisses—then take her to bed. The entire British navy could appear on the lake, but he wasn't leaving for Crown Point until they'd made love again.

Even so, he was in no rush. The coffee was hot and bitter and the sun was warm; he tipped his chair back against the front of the house and savored the change from the weeks' lost ground and hectic activity. Without even looking at Anne-Marie, he could tell she was feeling the same.

"Comfortable?" he asked her.

"It's a wonderful home."

"It is," he agreed, wondering what she'd think of his farm. Would she find it plain and common after what she'd been used to in Quebec? No, he didn't think so, not after what she'd been through in these past months. Thinking of her at the farm felt very good. Her presence there would make it the home it had never been.

He glanced at her, feeling happy. She was looking out at the lake, sitting forward with her chin cradled in her hands. She looked wistful.

"What are you thinking about?"

"Nothing." She dropped her hands and sat straight.

Her posture told him what she was thinking about: her childhood in Acadia and the ordeal that she'd endured. His instinct was to drop the subject, then it struck him that after last night things between them had changed. "Why won't you talk about it?" he asked in a gentle voice.

Watching her, he could almost see the struggle going on between her old defensiveness and a new inclination toward trust. She bit her lip and released it as she glanced at him. "I guess it's habit. I'm used to keeping it to myself."

"It's yours to keep if you want to."

"No, I want to talk. I want to tell you." But still it was a struggle. She looked into her cup, frowned, looked up and cleared her throat before she could begin.

"There isn't much to tell. I was so little and there were so many months and places. Most of the time until we reached Saint Vallier is a blur. But the one thing I'll never forget is the day we left. I was very little but I remember everything, and not because of my mother or anyone talking about it as I was growing up. As long as my mother was alive, we never talked about that day. Never," she repeated, looking at the lake. "We talked about what came before it, but not about that day.

"It was terrible. The soldiers had come to our village and told our mayor to call all the men to the church. They told him General Lawrence wanted everyone to take an oath of loyalty to the king. At that time everyone was afraid of what England would do. The British had been passing laws, forbidding Acadians from trading or traveling or owning guns. When they heard about the oath, people felt relieved. They thought that if they took it, England would let them be. So all the men went willingly to the church.

"My father was dead by then, but all my uncles went and all the boys over sixteen. They all wore white shirts and their Sunday suits, but when they got there the soldiers locked the door and the captain told them they were being sent to America and if they went quietly they'd be sent with their families. But if they made trouble, their families would be sent on another ship and maybe they'd never see them again."

She spread her hands, cup and all. "Well, what could they do? They begged to take the oath, but the captain said it was too late for any oath. Since they had no other choice, they agreed to go quietly. So they sent word to the women to pack up their things and that the next morning the ships would come to take them away.

"I remember my mother saying, 'They don't mean us. I will tell them about your father and they'll let us stay.' She left my brother and me with a neighbor and went off, but she was back pretty soon. I was too young to know that she was in shock. All I knew was that she looked different, and that after that day she never looked the same again. I remember her sitting in a chair in our kitchen, saying, 'But how can I pack everything, and who will carry it?' As it turned out, she had more than one day, since the ships didn't come for almost a week. That whole time they kept the men locked in the church and the women would go there to bring them clean clothes and food.

"It was like living in a dream. No one believed that it was happening. No one really believed that we'd be sent away. Our families had owned the same land for over a hundred years. We were as deeply rooted as the trees. Besides, the English had been trying to get us to take an oath for the past twenty years. They'd made threats before but the threats had always come to nothing in the end. People told each other that the same thing would happen this time.

"But General Lawrence meant what he said. On the seventh day after the men had been called to the church, the ships sailed into the harbor and everyone was told to gather with their possessions and prepare to board."

She stopped and closed her eyes. She shook her head.

"What then?" coaxed Eli.

"It—it was terrible. So many people, so many boxes and crates, and everything spilling and getting all mixed up. Babies crying, children getting lost and soldiers yelling, threatening people with their guns. Pushing people up the ladder, pushing other people away.

"Things got worse and worse. There was so much pushing and yelling, everything got confused. People were knocking us over without meaning to, so finally my mother took my brother and me and led us to the side and told us to wait there while she went back for our things. We begged her not to go away. We were scared she'd disappear, but she promised she'd be back.

"We'd only been there a minute when the soldiers began to shout that it was time for the people near us to get on the ship. They were pushing the people around us. Everyone began to move. My brother, François, was older. He took a hold of my hand and said, 'Come on. If we stay here, they'll put us on the ship before Mama gets back.'

"I was afraid to go with him and I was afraid to stay. I was crying so hard from fright I could hardly breathe, but François was dragging on my hand and I was stumbling along. Then all of a sudden his hand let go. People were yelling and pushing and I was all alone. 'François!' I screamed his name, but he didn't come. I stood there screaming and crying and being pushed and shoved by the crowd and everyone was so frantic they scarcely noticed me."

Her eyes were still closed. She put her hands over her ears as if that could block out the sound of her remembered screams. Eli reached out to touch her but he doubted she felt his hand.

She continued. "Then my mother came. 'Where's François?' she asked me, but I was crying too hard to say. Her arms were full of our things, but she dropped them and picked me up. She used me as a battering ram to get through the crowd. But it was no use. We searched for him all day but he was gone. They'd loaded him on a ship and sent him away.

"My mother wanted to take the next ship and go after him, but my uncle told her he'd heard the soldiers talking and the ships were going to different colonies. My uncle said our best hope was sneaking away into the woods when the soldiers were too busy to notice us. My mother didn't want to. She wanted to find François, but my uncle made her. He practically dragged her off, and of course he dragged me, too. We left all our things behind except for a little food."

She opened her eyes and looked at him. "For years I had that dream. I was holding on to François's hand and then he let go. I would wake up screaming his name. I believed it was my fault."

"What could you have done? If you'd held on, they'd have taken you away, then your mother would have lost you, too."

"Yes, I know. But thinking that doesn't help, because whatever happened would have been just as terrible. Instead of imagining François all alone, I'd have imagined my mother screaming for us on the wharf. Screaming for her children." She shivered despite the sun. Sitting back, she remembered her coffee but by then it was cold.

"You never found your brother."

She shook her head. "The sieur tried, but then he gave up." She took a breath, then added, "He believes François is dead."

"He could be," Eli said gently.

"He's not!" She hurled the word at him like a weapon. Her eyes, wistful a moment ago, were flashing fire. "He's alive and I mean to find him! If I have to go to every colony, I'll find François—if I have to cross the whole British army and visit every town! And when I do find him, we'll go back to Acadia. That's why I wanted the British to be thrown out of Canada—so when I find François we can go back to our farm."

"But they haven't been kicked out," he said reasonably, though the truth was beginning to dawn, a cold fist of suspicion clenching his chest.

"No, not yet," she admitted. "But there's still a chance. And if the time comes when there isn't, we'll think of something else. It's what I've always intended, ever since my mother died. Before the British came I couldn't see how to do it, and I was reluctant to leave the sieur. But the way things have turned out, it's almost as if fate finally intervened. It gave me the push I needed to go look for him."

"America's a big place."

"I don't care. I'll look until I find him. I know he's there. I know he is," she repeated, sitting up very straight, as if daring him to challenge her most cherished belief.

He wanted to challenge it. He wanted to tell her to forget her brother and the past and to make her life with him. He wanted to tell her how he'd been feeling up until a few minutes ago. He'd felt complete and really happy for the first time in his life. She had brought the happiness and she had made him complete; he'd felt that everything else in his life had happened just so that this moment could be. In short, he felt about her the way she felt for her brother, François.

If only he hadn't asked her to tell him about her past. If only he had let it go. But ignoring the truth wouldn't have made it disappear. The best he could have expected was a few more hours of blissful ignorance. More likely he would have ended up completely embarrassing them both by asking her to marry him, and her having to say no and then explain that she had other plans and that what had happened between them had a whole different meaning for her.

He was sitting in the same place he'd been sitting five minutes ago, but he was looking at the same scene from a whole different point of view. Her shyness this morning, for instance, hadn't been shyness at all. It had been her way of putting distance between them and letting him know that what happened had only been for last night. Whatever her feelings for him, she was willing to put them aside, and if she could do that, her feelings couldn't be all that deep. She felt passion; yes, he knew that, but not a deeper love.

He gripped the arms of his chair and fought a wave of bitterness. It wasn't fair for him to be bitter. She hadn't made any promises. He'd asked for her passion and she had given it to him. They were two people whose paths had come together, but very soon their paths would part. She would go look for her brother and he would go home to Bennington.

Looking out at the sunlit water, he recalled a conversation he'd had with Zeke on the day they'd left Deschambault. He'd recounted Anne-Marie's history and Zeke had asked if her brother was named François, but then Zeke had refused to confide what he knew. He remembered Zeke's expression. Zeke had known all along. If only he'd asked him, if only he'd forced Zeke to tell him, then maybe—

Maybe what? Maybe he wouldn't have made love to her last night? Did he wish he hadn't? Did he honestly? Even knowing that he couldn't have her, would he want to have forgone the magic and the fire that they'd shared—and the sweetness of this morning before she'd told him the truth?

No, he wouldn't have forgone it, but he didn't want to give her up. He was bitter, damn it. He was bitter clear through to his soul. He wanted to grab her and tell her that her brother was dead and that he, Eli, was alive. He wanted to change her mind by making love to her. He wanted to hold her until she forgot. But if their time together had taught him anything, it was that no amount of grabbing and shaking, or even passion, could sway her when she'd made up her mind. He might be able to trick her or coerce her, but if he did that, she'd only hate him again, and he'd had enough of her hate. Her love was what he wanted, and that he couldn't have. All she meant to give him was a memory.

She had been watching him this whole time, still sitting very straight. She said, "I won't believe you if you tell me it's no use."

His mouth twisted in a bitter smile. "Why should I tell you that? What could I tell you that would change your mind?"

"Nothing," she said softly.

That said it all. He picked up his mug from the porch floor where he'd set it down. "We ought to get going," he said, coming to his feet. "If you want to rest a while, I'll clean up the house."

"I'll help you," she offered, but he shook his head. They'd be together in the boat all the way to Crown Point, and for the present, he wanted to be alone.

There wasn't time for washing so he remade the bed, holding his breath as he lifted the covers so he wouldn't catch her scent. But there was no way of shutting out the memories. They were too recent, too powerful and sharp. If he hadn't asked her about her brother they could be in bed right now, wrapped around each other with him buried deep inside of her. If only he'd asked her later, they could have had that much.

"Here, let me help you," she said, coming through the door.

"If you're so eager, you can do it by yourself," he answered, dropping the covers as she came to the far side of the bed. He saw her hurt, surprised expression as he turned away, but that only fed the anger that had begun to build inside. Let her breathe in her own damn scent. Let her breathe in his and think of her brother and her damn farm, which, after a hundred years of cultivation, was probably played out anyhow. He snatched up the dirty kettle on his way through the door. He'd take it down to the water and wash it. That ought to cool him down enough to get her to Crown Point. After that, it didn't matter. He'd never see her again.

The trip down the lake was silent and stiff, with Eli giving his full attention to the sail while Anne-Marie did her best to pretend that she wasn't hurt by the change in him. Starry-eyed as she'd been when she had fallen asleep last night, she had been sage enough to realize that whatever had happened in bed, people acted differently when they were dressed and standing up. She had known that this morning as soon as she had opened her eyes, which was why she had gotten up and dressed while he was out catching fish. She would have felt foolish lolling there naked in broad daylight when he came back.

During breakfast and even afterward, she'd thought it was all right. He hadn't acted like a crazed lover but he had been very nice, encouraging her to talk about her brother and the past. Then all of a sudden he'd shut up like a clam. He had stormed into the house as though he were angry, and when she had followed in puzzlement, he'd been downright cold. Just like the old Eli at his very worst.

She wasn't dumb. She got the message loud and clear— she wasn't supposed to read any deep meaning into last night. What happened had happened, neat and self-contained, and now he'd retreated behind his defenses and expected her to do the same. From the way he was acting, she could almost believe that he was feeling angry that last night had happened at all.

She looked at the glorious scenery and felt her spirits droop. Last night he had seemed to love her. She'd curled against him in the darkness, so happy and so full of hope. But today she was even worse off than she had been before, because before she hadn't known what being with him was like.

A sudden rising gust of wind caught the blanket sail and their bow cut like a pair of shears through the glittering cloth of the lake. There was no point in moping. What was done was done, and she would go on. After all, she had been through worse. Being rejected by a lover was nothing compared to losing a brother and an entire world. She'd go to Crown Point, where there was plenty for her to do. At Crown Point there would be more soldiers she could ask about François. She would keep on asking until she found someone who had heard of him and could tell her where he was. Then she'd go find him, just the way she had planned.

Although they had taken a detour, they had done it in good time, and four hours out of Crown Point they caught up with the convoy of boats they'd seen off at Île aux Noix. The lucky ones had managed to reach shore for the worst of the storm, but even those had taken a buffeting and the sick men were in terrible shape, half sodden, half sunbaked, thrashing their scarecrow arms and calling weakly for something to drink.

Every man whose eyes could focus recognized Anne-Marie, and those who could called out to her as Eli guided the canoe past. She returned their greetings, feeling ridiculously grateful to be wanted. Eli might not care about her, but she was glad to show him that there were plenty of men who did. Had there been an inch of space in any of the other boats, she might have considered having Eli pull up alongside so that she could change crafts. At least now there was a diversion, which increased steadily until they came, bow to bow, into the chaos of landing at Crown Point.

Crown Point formed the hand of a broad arm of land that gestured north toward Canada from the bottom of the lake. By the time their canoe rounded that hand, the bay formed by the crook of the elbow was hopelessly clogged with boats. Every new arrival only added to the press. With a great deal of skilled weaving and bumping, Eli got them up to the shore, where things were as crazy, or crazier, than they'd been on the Île aux Noix.

She shouldn't have been surprised. She'd seen the army operating under stressful conditions before, when panic and disorder habitually drove out all hope of common sense. The landing at Crown Point was no exception. Bateaux loaded with sick men fought one another to reach the shore, thus preventing those already unloaded from moving out to clear space for more to land. Everyone with a voice left was shouting directions and no one was listening. As for the fort, it looked more like a ruin.

Eli scanned the scene briefly and said, "Here we go again."

Anne-Marie heard her name called. Looking up, she saw a corporal she knew from the Île aux Noix.

"Gosh, I'm glad to see you!" he gushed, elbowing his way to where she stood. "Have you ever seen such a mess? Nobody knows where to put the men, so they're putting them all together, the ones who are just getting well all mixed up with the ones who're just getting sick."

"Who's in charge?" She was already on tiptoe, trying to see over the crowd.

"A captain from Fort Edward. General Schuyler sent him, but if you ask me, he hasn't got much sense."

"Can you take me to him?"

"You bet! Follow me." He turned and set off trotting up to the lines of tents that carpeted the rising ground like grimy daisies in a field.

She looked back at Eli, who was still holding the canoe. "I'd better go with him."

"Don't let me stop you."

His tone made her wince. Couldn't he at least be civil now that she was taking herself off his hands? It wasn't as if she'd forced him to be with her last night. What right had he to treat her as though she were to blame? Anger flared up in her, shouldering aside the hurt. She had more than half a mind to tell him what she thought of him, right here in the open with the whole world jostling past.

But before she could tell him anything, a familiar voice boomed out.

"Ho there, Mademoiselle Annie, I see you got away!"

It was Zeke, barreling down the hill, swatting away clusters of toiling soldiers as if they were mosquitoes circling a swamp. "Ho, little brother!" he boomed, as Eli turned his head.

No, she thought firmly. Zeke would make things worse with his uncanny knack for reading her mind. He'd take one look at her and bellow, "Are you two fighting again?" or something equally as humiliating, and of course Eli wouldn't answer, so it would be up to her.

She started moving before Zeke got to them. "Hello, Zeke. We got here safely. I'll have to talk to you later. Right now I'm supposed to be following Corporal Grimes." She pointed up the hill where the corporal was ambling along, and before Zeke could answer, she was safely past.

"What's her rush?" Zeke grumbled, joining Eli, who was pulling his few possessions out of the canoe.

"If she doesn't tell them, they won't know where to put the men. Nobody else is capable of doing it except for her."

Zeke made a noise in his throat. "I guess I don't have to ask if you two had a lovely trip."

"We had a lovely send-off anyway, arranged by our old friend Massey."

"What happened?" Zeke's eyes lit up.

"He tried to jump us. Last I saw of him, he was at headquarters on Île aux Noix, offering good advice."

"I'm sorry I missed him."

"He must be somewhere around here if you want to do some catching up. Where are Sarah and the children?"

"In a tent up the hill. We were waiting until you got here before we left." Zeke gestured vaguely behind him but made no move to leave. "That was a whopper of a storm. We were hoping you two had managed to get to the house before it struck."

"Just barely. We had to stay the night."

"Ah." Zeke was many things, but subtle wasn't one of them. His look told Eli exactly what was on his mind. "What did Annie think of the house?"

"She liked it," said Eli. "She thought it was very nice. Will you take me up to Sarah, or do I have to find her myself?"

"I'll take you, I'll take you," Zeke grumbled, shouldering Eli's pack. "I just don't understand. From the way you were acting on the island I'd have thought—" At that point he stopped because he was talking to himself. Eli was past him and halfway up the hill.

"Brownell!"

Zeke had just caught up to Eli when somebody hailed them from up ahead. He craned his neck. "I thought so. It's Northridge Wells. He came over here yesterday from the Grants, and when I told him you were coming, he said he reckoned he'd stick around to talk to you. Damn coward," he added, not quite under his breath.

"Be charitable," said Eli. "Someone's got to stay at home and see to politics."

"A lot of hot air and excuses!" Zeke said loudly enough to be heard by Wells as he bustled up, mopping his round face with a handkerchief.

"Brownell!" He greeted Eli, ignoring Zeke, who glowered at the affront. "You're finally back from Canada. Bad luck up there."

"Not enough soldiers," Zeke put in. "We could have easily taken Quebec if everyone had served instead of amusing themselves yapping worthless politics."

"You won't think it's so worthless when Congress declares that your land's your own because the Grants are independent and not part of New York!" Wells retorted, jabbing his chin up at Zeke's chest.

"You can stay home from fifteen winter campaigns and Congress won't say that!" Zeke lowered his face into Wells's. "Besides, between me and Sally, we own the land free and clear. She's got the New York title and I've got the Grants, so I don't need the damn Congress to tell me anything!"

Wells, who was accustomed to Zeke's ways, gave up with a shrug and addressed himself to Eli. "I don't know how much you've heard about what we've done. We had a convention in Dorset at the beginning of the year. The Yorkers sent some of their people, but we voted them down. We voted that we won't be governed by Yorker rule and we elected agents to wait on Congress on various matters—including independence," he added with a meaningful look at Zeke.

"Who are the agents?"

"Heman Allen, Dr. Fay and James Breakenridge. Allen's all for declaring independence outright, but some of the others are still leaning toward New York. We're reconvening in two weeks and I guess we'll have it out. You'll be there, won't you?"

"I'd like to be."

"If he hasn't got more pressing business—like fighting Carleton's ten thousand redcoats!" Zeke snapped.

Wells looked Zeke up and down before he said, "Zeke, do you mean to tell me you can't take on ten thousand redcoats by yourself? I'll see you in Dorset," he added to Eli before he hurried off.

"See you in Dorset!" Zeke mimicked, glaring after Wells. "Some good independence'll do us if the redcoats wipe us out!"

"Never mind," Eli said. "When Carleton gets here you can see that Wells and the others fight. Now what about taking me to Sarah and my niece?"

They found Sarah sitting outside the tent watching as thirteen-year-old Archie trailed the wanderings of little Elizabeth. Sarah was holding a new baby in her arms.

Her face lit up when she saw Eli. "You're safely home!"

"Almost," he answered, squatting for a closer look at the baby in her arms. "Where did you get this?"

"Where do you think?" bellowed Zeke. "With all your squabbling with Mademoiselle Annie and the squawking about independence, I didn't get a chance to tell you. Say hello to little Sam."

"Hello, Eli." Sarah smiled, leaning forward to receive his kiss. Then she handed him the baby. "What fighting?" she asked.

"Nothing," Eli answered.

"They were fighting again," said Zeke. "By the time I got there, they weren't even talking."

"That's not true," Eli said, looking down at the baby in his arms. "He's a strapper."

"Like his father." Zeke swelled out his chest. "If you weren't fighting, then why did she run off?"

"She told you that herself—to see to the sick men." He put his finger out and the baby's little fist curled around it tightly.

"I'd like to meet her," said Sarah. "I'd like to thank her for looking after Zeke."

"Then you'll have to run her down in the hospital wards. She's devoted to her work." After he said it, he could have bitten his tongue, especially from the way Sarah's eyebrows rose.

"Maybe I will," she said mildly. "There ought to be time later on. When we didn't know when you were coming, we decided we'd spend tonight here, then first thing tomorrow we'll leave for Bennington. I hope you won't mind the company."

"Not a bit." He extracted his finger from the baby's fist and handed him back. He considered trying to dissuade Sarah from seeing Anne-Marie but quickly gave up the idea. For all she looked like a blue-eyed angel, Sarah had a mind of her own, and the best he could hope for in asking was to see her eyebrows lift again. Stretching his legs, he added, "It'll be good to get home."

It would be good, he was thinking, looking down on the city of tents. He'd been away long enough, beyond which there was no reason to stay at Crown Point. His enlistment had run its course four months earlier and he'd only stayed on because . . .

In any event, if the army needed him, it could call him up from Bennington. If and when Carleton threatened, he'd come back to fight, but in the meantime he would go home and tend to his own affairs. He'd go to the convention in Dorset and hear what had been happening since he'd been gone. Away from Anne-Marie, he'd be able to forget. Love was nothing but trouble, and desire was just as bad. Maybe this time he'd learned his lesson for good and for all.

Anne-Marie was supervising the arrangement of pallets in an empty tent when an orderly told her that there was a woman up the row who was wanting to talk to her.

"What woman?" she demanded, but she already knew. She was still angry enough at Eli to send a message that she was too busy to come, but in the end curiosity nudged her out of the tent and up the hill to where Zeke's wife, Sarah, was waiting for her.

"Miss Doucet?" Sarah stepped forward with both hands extended. "I'm Sarah Brownell."

She was blond and very pretty. From the way she was smiling, for one mad moment Anne-Marie thought Eli had sent her to make peace. But she knew that was wishful thinking. If Eli wanted peace made, he'd come and make it himself, and he wasn't coming.

Sarah squeezed her hands. "I've heard so much about you from Zeke. According to him, you saved his life at least twice, and I wanted to tell you how deeply grateful I am. I never doubted that he would come back alive, but there were times when not doubting took every bit of my strength and then some."

Anne-Marie forgot her anger as tears sprang into her eyes. "I should also thank you for the hospitality of your house. I—we stayed there last night."

"Yes, Eli told me. I'm glad you were able to take shelter from the storm."

"It was very lucky," Anne-Marie agreed hurriedly, herding her mind away from the images that were still seething just below conscious thought. "You live in a very beautiful place."

"Yes, we do," agreed Sarah. "I didn't want to leave, but with a new baby and the British coming . . ."

"You have a new baby?"

Sarah smiled broadly. "A little boy named Sam. Zeke had no idea until he got here two days ago."

"He must have roared with pleasure."

At that Sarah laughed. "I can see you've gotten to know him very well." Sobering, she added, "I don't want to belabor the subject, but the hardest part of having Zeke gone was imagining him in trouble and not being there to take care of him. Knowing you were there eases that burden— even after the fact. Can you understand?"

"Yes, I do." She nodded, thinking of François. If she knew there had been someone to care for him, she would feel better about what had happened, even after all these years.

Sarah continued, "There's something else I wanted to say. I know there's plenty to keep you busy here right now, but hopefully when things get straightened out there won't be so much. Or even before that, if you just feel like you need a rest, I'd be very happy if you'd come and stay with us."

"You're going back to your house?"

"No, for the moment we're going to Bennington to stay at Eli's farm. It'll be a bit crowded, but there's always enough room for friends—especially friends to whom we owe our lives."

"You're very kind." Anne-Marie looked away so that Sarah wouldn't see her reaction to Eli's name. She could imagine his reception if she turned up at his farm.

"You'll come then?"

"I—no, I don't think so. Now I am very busy, and later I—I have other plans. But thank you for the offer."

Sarah looked at her thoughtfully. "I don't mean to interfere or embarrass you, but are you sure there's not something else that would keep you away?"

"Something—"

"I meant Eli," Sarah said quietly. "You don't have to talk about it, but if you want to, I'd be more than glad to do whatever I can to help. As you know, Zeke isn't the epitome of discretion or tact, but he does notice things, and from what he told me I wondered if there wasn't some trouble between the two of you that might benefit from a sympathetic ear."

Anne-Marie felt two urges—to run and to stay. Although they'd only just met, she liked Sarah and she trusted her, and after all she'd been through, she would have loved to let her hair down to a friend. But she was afraid that if the conversation went much further, she'd burst into tears, and she wasn't anxious to do that in the middle of the camp with enlisted men and officers milling all around. So she sighed and said, "You're very kind to offer, but there's nothing you can do."

"Why is that?"

Anne-Marie clenched her jaw. Then she unclenched it and said, "There's nothing you can do to help because he doesn't care. You can't make him, and I wouldn't want you to try."

"But you care for him?"

She nodded silently. "It isn't any good. We're two different people. Even if he was willing to try, we'd never get along."

"I know how that feels," said Sarah. "That's exactly what I thought about Zeke, but it turned out that I was wrong. Differences have nothing to do with love, and if you love each other—"

"We don't," said Anne-Marie, her voice husky from the tightness in her throat. "Eli doesn't love me. Zeke might dispute it, but believe me, I'm right."

"Are you sure?"

"Completely." Sarah looked so troubled that Anne-Marie reached out and took her hand. "I know what you're thinking—that often Eli doesn't show what he's feeling and so I might not know. In the past I have made that mistake with him, but I'm not making it now. Believe me, even underneath he really doesn't care."

"I'm sorry," Sarah said very quietly.

"So am I, but there's nothing to do about it. And besides, there are so many people who have problems worse than mine." She turned to look down the endless row of tents. "There are as many men here sick with smallpox as there are men in all of Quebec, and the ones who aren't sick aren't paid and don't get enough to eat."

Sarah smiled. "You can tell yourself love's extraneous, but it's not. I'm glad we've finally met and I wish you good luck. If there's ever anything I can do to help you, please don't hesitate to ask.''

"I won't." For the second time, Anne-Marie took Sarah's hand. She held it briefly before she let it go and she walked away quickly before she thought of a reason to stay.

It was easier with children, Sarah reflected as she watched Anne-Marie walk away. With children, you knew what they needed and you gave it to them if you could. If only all of life could be that way.

Chapter Thirteen

" "We, therefore, the representatives of the United States of America . . . do, in the name and by the authority of the good people of these colonies, solemnly publish and declare that these united colonies are, and of right ought to be, free and independent states!' "

James Breakenridge looked up from his reading of the Declaration of Independence he and Heman Allen had just carried all the way from Philadelphia.

"It's dated the fourth of this month and it's signed by President Hancock and every damn one of the delegates. We're an independent country," he added unnecessarily.

Northridge Wells shot to his feet. "Three cheers for the United American States! Hurrah! Hurrah! Hurrah!"

All of the men in Cephas Kent's tavern in Dorset stood to repeat the cheer. Thomas Gwinnet, who was standing next to Eli, pounded on the tabletop.

"I have a proposal!" Wells shouted to make himself heard. "I propose that we members of this convention form an association to defend the United American States against the English fleets and armies—and I propose that we associate not as subjects of New York but as independent citizens of the New Hampshire Grants."

This brought another round of cheering, though by no means a unanimous one.

"That ain't necessarily a smart thing to do," objected Jeremiah Grey. "Congress ain't made no secret that if it comes to a showdown, it's siding with New York. We all know Carleton's got ten thousand redcoats up at Saint John, and it's only a matter of time till they set sail south. When they do that, we're going to need Congress's help to defend ourselves. You know we ain't got the money to arm more'n a small company, and that's just with muskets. We ain't got the funds whatsoever for artillery."

Heman Allen shot a look at Breakenridge, who made a face. "Pshaw! Congress has barely got the funds to pay the rent on Independence Hall! I say we form this association, and what's more, I say we require every man in the Grants to sign it or be declared our enemy."

"Hold on, now, James." Jeremiah held up both his hands. "You and I might agree with that, and so might most of the men in this room. But there's plenty of others around the Grants that's leery of taking on New York, 'specially with all those redcoats breathing down our necks."

"He's right." Heman Allen spoke from his seat. "Before we lay down conditions, we've got to be sure of our support. I say we form this association among ourselves, then we take it back to our own towns and we explain to our constituents why it's in their best interests to sign."

Jeremiah still looked doubtful. "What if our con—what if folks don't agree?"

"They will with the right inducement."

"And what kind of inducement is that?"

As Heman considered an answer, Eli raised his hand. "If I'm not speaking out of order, I'd like to propose something else. I suggest we petition General Schuyler to defend the northern boundaries of the Grants against Carleton's attack."

Jeremiah's face puckered in frank bewilderment. "Not to be disrespectful, Eli, but what's that got to do with what we're discussing—and what's the point of it anyway?

Carleton's building warships at the top of Lake Champlain and what's Schuyler got to put against him but a bunch of leaky bateaux. He's also got Fort Ticonderoga, but the shape that was in when I last saw it, it wouldn't have stopped a herd of cows on their way into the barn. Schuyler's already got his hands fuller'n he can handle, so how's he going to spare the men and arms to take care of us?"

"He isn't," Eli said. "It's a foregone conclusion that he'll have to refuse our request. Where does Schuyler come from?"

"Everyone knows that—New York. He owns a couple of miles along the top of the Hudson above Albany."

"Yes, on the New York side. The same side as Crown Point and Ticonderoga and all of the troops. So Schuyler, a New Yorker, will refuse our request in order to pour all his resources into defending his own colony. I can't think of anyone in the Grants who's going to be pleased about that, not with all those redcoats congregated at Saint John."

There was a moment of silence as faces began to light up. "I get it!" said Jeremiah. "When we speak to people about signing, we can tell them that New York may be glad to tax us to fill her own treasury, but she won't lift a finger to defend us, so what choice have we got but to defend ourselves! Pretty clever!"

"Thank you," Eli said. "I take it no one objects to me drafting the petition to Schuyler?"

Not a single delegate did, so it was agreed that Eli would draw up the petition and pass it around for suggestions and approval before he wrote the final draft. After that they voted on the association, which was almost unanimously passed.

"Smart move, Brownell," Heman Allen murmured as the meeting was breaking up. "It's good to have you back."

"It's good to be back," said Eli, and if it hadn't been for Anne-Marie, that would have been the truth.

* * *

The first of the sumac was already turning red five weeks later when Eli rode through Castleton on his way to Larrabee's Point on the Grants shore of Lake Champlain. From there, he took a ferry across the narrow strait to Fort Ticonderoga, the venerable, if neglected, British fort that the Green Mountain Boys had seized from its masters well over a year before.

Ticonderoga lay a dozen miles south of Crown Point, at the spot where the lake narrowed into a river, twisting to the south until it gave up on even being a river and turned into Wood Creek, meandering down to the Hudson just above Albany. Also at Ticonderoga was the river to Lake George: a one-mile carry, then smooth water all the way south. These were the only two feasible routes for an army the size of Carleton's moving south. If Carleton meant to invade New York, he had to get past the fort, and if Schuyler meant to stop him, he'd have to do it here.

Schuyler had known that two months ago, when the bedraggled troops had streamed into Crown Point from the Île aux Noix. After the initial chaos, Schuyler had sorted out the troops, sending the sick and the wounded to Fort William Henry at the bottom of Lake George. He'd sent the fit—loosely speaking—to Ticonderoga with orders to transform the fort into an insurmountable obstacle in Carleton's path.

Had they done it? Eli squinted through the shimmering late summer heat, scanning the fort and the hillsides as the ferry approached the shore. From this distance the most obvious difference from the year before was the sea of dingy tents sprawling up and down the hills. He could see gangs of soldiers digging breastworks all around the fort; more were digging on the hill they'd dubbed Mount Independence, across the channel to Lake George. But for every soldier who was working, there seemed to be two more fishing or swimming from the shore as if no one had bothered to tell them they were in the middle of a war.

He saw plenty of officers who could have put the men to work, but they seemed too busy prancing their horses up and down the hills and stirring clouds of dust up for the men who were working to breathe. In the weeks since he'd left the army, Eli had almost forgotten the way things were done, but now, as the ferry landed, it all came back to him. Could these officers stop the British? Would these men follow them?

As he scanned the hillsides, he wasn't looking for Anne-Marie. She wouldn't be at the fort, she'd have gone south to the hospital on Lake George. For all he knew, she could have already gone in search of her brother, François. Her absence ought to relieve him, but instead it left him depressed—a familiar feeling that hit him at least once a day and some days a lot more than that. He'd be minding his own business, and then for no reason she'd pop up in the midst of his thoughts and he'd feel as if someone had kicked him in the gut. He was grateful to have Sally and the children around; without them to distract him, he knew it would be even worse.

Schuyler's headquarters was in the oldest portion of the fort, but Schuyler wasn't there.

"He's down at Fort Edward, but he'll be back this evening," the lieutenant in charge informed him sourly. The lieutenant's collar was stained dark with sweat, which wasn't surprising since the office was like an oven, despite the thick stone walls. "If you've got a message you can leave it, or you can wait—and if you're going to wait, you might as well find a place up the hill. Whatever breeze gets past the mountains is most likely to find you up there."

"I'll do that," said Eli. He was fairly sure that if he left the petition it would become conveniently "lost." In Schuyler's position, he'd lose it rather than let himself be manipulated for the purposes of the Grants. "Is General Arnold here?"

"If you want Arnold, you'll have to go down to Skenesboro." The lieutenant jerked his head toward the south.

"They've got a sawmill and a bunch of ships' carpenters down there and Arnold's trying to scrape together a fleet. I hear Carleton's got two fifty-gun frigates he's building up at Saint John. That's why he's taking his time—because he knows that when he does sashay down here we won't have anything but a handful of galleys and schooners to stop him with, so he figures when he's ready he can sail right on through!"

Eli declined to answer as he left the fort and found a trail leading uphill as the lieutenant had advised. He'd heard rumors that Carleton's frigates numbered four, but he wasn't especially inclined to accept either number as true, since he'd also heard that Carleton had a hundred ships and twenty thousand men. As the waiting stretched out, so did everyone's nerves, and at this point rumors were flying more thickly than wood pigeons in June.

Knowing Carleton's habitual caution and philosophy, Eli guessed that the commander had greatly overestimated the American strength and believed he needed all those warships to control the lake. The best the Americans could hope for was for Carleton to take so long that by the time he made his move it would be too close to winter and he wouldn't get through to Albany before the cold and the lack of provisions forced him to turn back.

Right now, however, the cold seemed a long way off. The sun beat down furnace-hot on the open trail and Eli took his time climbing up the hill. He figured he'd go until he found a spot with both shade and a view and wait there for either evening or Schuyler's return, whichever came first.

He'd gone about half a mile when he saw a likely spot under a huge old oak. He had left the trail to reach it when he saw Anne-Marie.

She had been sitting with her knees drawn up, looking out over the lake. When she'd heard him coming, she turned her head, and now she was staring at him as if she'd seen a ghost.

"Eli? What are you doing here!" She scrambled to her feet so quickly he thought she might bolt away through the brush. But she didn't; she stood there, clutching her skirts with both hands and looking pale.

"I brought something to General Schuyler but he's at Fort Edward, so I'm waiting until he gets back." His voice echoed strangely, as if he were speaking through a tube. For all that he was speaking calmly, he knew that he was in shock. "I thought you'd be down at the hospital."

"I was for a while, but they don't really need me anymore. General Schuyler ordered anyone even suspected of self-inoculation to be quarantined. There hasn't been a new case in two weeks." She turned her head as if she meant to look away, but her eyes stayed on him. "I came here because someone suggested that General Schuyler might be able to use a translator."

"Can he?"

"Enough to keep me occupied, but not as much as he needs a lot of other things."

"Such as?"

She rolled her eyes as if what Schuyler needed was too voluminous to name. Since the last time he'd seen her, she'd lost that scarecrow look. She looked as she had in Quebec, but she also looked different: tanned and healthy. She was beautiful.

"Such as blacksmiths and tinkers and carpenters." She ticked them off on her fingers. "And anyone who knows anything about building ships."

"Arnold's at Skenesboro?"

"He's doing the best he can, but he could do ten times better if people would only cooperate, and not just the soldiers. The officers are just as bad. Everyone knows that any day Carleton may attack, but they waste time in petty jealousies—even the generals! How can General Schuyler prepare for the battle when he's got to be writing volumes of letters to Congress explaining why command of his army shouldn't be given to General Gates! But General Gates is

from New England and the New Englanders prefer him
over a New Yorker, even though that pettiness may end up
losing the whole war!''

Then she realized whom she was speaking to. Her eyes
narrowed. ''I suppose you're in favor of Gates?''

''Gates may be from New England, but he's also a fool.''
He wasn't about to mention the business that had brought
him here today. After her outburst, he knew what she'd
think of that.

They were both still standing and she was still holding her
skirts. He didn't bother trying to tell himself that he ought
to say goodbye and keep going up the trail. Instead he
asked, ''May I join you?''

''If you want to.'' She bit her lip warily and took a step
backward, toward the far edge of the shade.

''I'll go if you want.''

''Suit yourself.'' She shrugged, then she shot him a quick
look to see what he was going to do. ''What are you bringing to Schuyler?''

''A petition from the Grants. You'd probably consider
it another example of petty jealousy.''

''Is it?''

''To a certain extent.'' She made no comment when he
moved into the shade of the tree. She stood at one edge and
he stood at the edge opposite. From here he could see the
men swimming in the lake. The sight of their bare arms
flashing brought a sharp twist of jealousy. Whom did she
spend her time with when she didn't have work to do?
There would be no dearth of contenders, and at that instant he hated them all. ''But also necessary,'' he added,
looking back at her.

''Necessary!'' she repeated. ''That's what they all say!''
Her eyes flashed with disdain. She let her skirts go and
scowled down at the lake. ''I suppose you know they sent
Massey to Philadelphia?''

He didn't. ''How long ago?''

"A few weeks. Because of his connection to Carleton, they're treating him as an important man."

"He must like that. Did you see him?"

"Once or twice. It was unavoidable. He asked me to pass on his regards to you." Their eyes met as she said this and suddenly she grinned, but when he let down his guard and grinned back, she sobered and looked away.

"You didn't expect to find me here, did you?"

"No."

Her shoulders squared. "If you had known that you might see me, would you still have come?"

He caught his breath and released it. "I don't know. I suppose if I'd known you were here, I would have tried to stay away."

When her head swung back toward him, her eyes were hard and glittering and her lips were pressed together as if she were struggling to hold something in. In the end she couldn't hold it. "Damn you!" she cried. "It's been years—years! Won't you ever forget that stupid girl?"

Whatever he'd been expecting, it hadn't been this. He stared at her blankly as her cry echoed down toward the lake. What was she talking about? One possibility struck him but he dismissed it out of hand. She couldn't think he was still obsessed by his fiancée? He couldn't recall the last time that he'd thought of her. Then again, yes he could: that night at Zeke's house, before they had made love. But why would she think he was dwelling on that now? He shook his head slowly. "I have forgotten her."

"I'll bet." Her mouth tightened again and she looked away. "If it's not her, then why do you have to be so mean?"

"When was I mean?" he asked, thoroughly confused.

"When? You know very well! That morning at Zeke's house and when we were coming down the lake."

"I was being mean?" he said slowly in disbelief. "But what about you—what about your brother? What about your finding him?"

Now it was her turn to look confused. "What does my brother have to do with this?"

Eli spread both hands, palms up. "What doesn't he have to do? That morning at Zeke's you told me you had it all worked out. You're going to find your brother, then you're going to go back to Nova Scotia to try to get your farm. You've got your whole life figured out, so why the hell don't you go and do it instead of hanging around here and acting as if—"

He let his hands fall. "Forget it. It doesn't matter."

As Eli looked out at the water, Anne-Marie continued to stare at him. She knew what he was saying, and she knew that he was right. How was it possible that she hadn't understood before? But she hadn't, she really hadn't. She hadn't even thought—not even after that morning at Zeke's house when she'd told him about François and all of a sudden he'd turned cold.

She had gone back over that morning a hundred times since then, but she'd never seen the connection between the two events. Why hadn't she seen it? Why hadn't she realized?

He glanced back at her, his eyes unforgiving and hard. She tried to find comfort in the fact that they weren't blank. "You may not believe this," she said slowly, "but that morning out on Zeke's porch, when you got up and walked away, I thought it was your way of telling me that, as far as you were concerned, that night didn't mean anything."

He shook his head incredulously. "How could you have, when you'd just told me that nothing that had happened between us had changed your plans, and you still meant to find your brother and go spend your life with him? After you told me that, what was I supposed to do—clap my hands and act glad?"

She hung her head, feeling hopeless. "I can't explain. I know what I said about François, but I didn't mean it the way you thought I did."

"You didn't intend to try to find him?"

"I did and I didn't...I can't explain." She shook her head, searching for the words to make him see, which was hard, since she herself barely understood. But she knew that if she didn't try now, there wouldn't ever be another chance.

"Ever since my mother died and I swore I'd find François, everyone I told said it would be impossible. I kept telling myself I'd do it—how could I not? He was my own brother—how could I give up on him?" The question hung between them, but rather than respond to it, Eli let it fade.

When it was gone, she continued. "Even though I insisted, I think that deep down I began to believe that everyone was right. America was so far away, so big and so full of strangers, and I had terrible memories of being on my own. When I told you the story that morning at Zeke's, I expected that you'd react the same way everyone had. And you did—you agreed with the sieur that François was probably dead."

"But you swore that he wasn't and that you meant to look for him."

"Because I believe he isn't! How could I not believe? If they told you to believe that Zeke was dead, wouldn't you want to prove they were wrong?"

"Up to a point," he said slowly.

"Yes, you can say that when it hasn't happened. But when it has, it's different." Her eyes implored him. Why couldn't he understand?

His eyes told her he didn't want to, whether or not he could. "Your situation here is different from what it was in Quebec. America isn't far away anymore. It's right here, all around you, and you have powerful friends. General Schuyler's a very influential man, he can give you an introduction to just about anyone. You can go looking for your brother if that's what you really want."

"And if I don't go looking?"

He was silent for a minute, then he said quietly, "If you don't go looking for your brother, you could stay here with me."

Down in the water the men were swimming, but up here the world stood still. "Stay—how?" she asked him.

"Stay and marry me. If you give up on finding your brother, you could stay and marry me. Unless—"

"No," she said quickly, turning to meet his eyes, knowing her own showed plainly how much she wanted him. Every night since that one at Zeke's she'd been aching with loneliness, and the only time she was happy was when she was dreaming that she was with him. But when she woke up to her empty bed, she felt even worse. In her dreams, he forgave her and he wanted her. But now she wasn't dreaming. This was real. Eli was offering what she'd been aching for, and all he was asking was that she give up her dream of François.

All. She looked down at the soldiers swimming in the lake. She had probably asked every one of them if they had heard of François. In the four months since she'd left Quebec, she'd probably asked five thousand men, but not one had even heard of him. Everyone wanted to help her, but nobody could. Common sense and experience suggested that the sieur was right and that François might have died twenty years ago. Eli was living. He was here, five feet away. He could give her a lifetime of nights and mornings like the wonderful ones at Zeke's, and all she had to do was give up her dream of François.

Give it up, then, she told herself. As hard as it is, give it up, because if you don't you're going to lose the man you were born to love. She looked out over the water and she heard a little voice, the voice of a child calling from very far away. She knew what the voice was calling because it had been calling that one word for years. "François!" the voice was screaming, and if she curled her hand, she'd feel the pressure of his fingers slipping away from hers.

She turned from the water to Eli, who'd been watching her throughout. "What if I promised that even if I did find him, I wouldn't go to Acadia? What if I just wanted to meet him and to tell him that I was alive?"

His eyes darkened at her question and his voice was low. "What if you found him and he needed you? I'd always be wondering if you were going to leave."

She knew what he was saying and she knew that he was right. All she had to do was to reach out; it was all up to her. She could reach out to Eli or reach out to François. She had to let one go, but which one would it be? She wanted Eli so badly. Please stop! she begged that voice. But she couldn't stop it. She didn't know what to do.

She felt him waiting, balancing on that fine line between bitterness and hope. She didn't want to hurt him, but she couldn't stop that voice. She closed her eyes and whispered, "Eli, I don't know. Forgive me. I just don't know."

Tears stung beneath her eyelids, but when she opened them she was alone on the hillside and Eli had gone.

Schuyler rejected Eli's petition as Eli had predicted he would. Also as Eli had predicted, Schuyler's rejection did a great deal to arouse support among Grants residents to declare themselves independent from New York. Like the other delegates to the convention, Eli spent September trekking backroads and wood trails from farm to farm and hamlet to hamlet, drumming up support. Being busy didn't help take his mind off Anne-Marie. He felt her presence at Ticonderoga pulling him to the west, but he vowed he wouldn't go back unless she summoned him. Still, hardly an hour went by that he didn't wonder if she'd made up her mind whether to go after her brother or to stay with him. Whenever he came home from his journeys, he looked for a letter from her, but September passed and the summer ended, and still no letter came.

No letter and no Carleton. Carleton was still at Saint John and some people were venturing the opinion that he'd waited too long and now he wouldn't come at all. Eli thought that was wishful thinking, and Arnold must have thought so, too, since he'd left Skenesboro and was somewhere up the lake, scouting out the best possible position for his ragtag fleet to meet the superior forces of the British when they came. He'd left his shipbuilders working on the last of the crafts and had put out a general call for men who could serve on his crews.

At the end of September, the Dorset convention reconvened. Although everyone's mind was on the looming confrontation, they managed to focus on the business at hand long enough to vote that every Grants man over sixteen be required to sign the association of independence or be declared a public enemy. They also voted to build a jail in which traitors would be held. Finally, they voted that Eli be named to the committee whose job it was to present the Grants' cause to Congress in Philadelphia.

This last, Eli respectfully declined.

"But why?" demanded Northridge Wells. "It's the greatest honor—and you'd be good at it."

"Because the committee already has three members and at this moment Schuyler needs every man who can fight."

"There may not be any fighting," Wells pointed out.

"There will be," Eli said. "I'm going, and if you've got nothing better to do, you ought to come along. Zeke would like that. He's coming up here to meet me on his way to the fort, and he specifically mentioned that he hoped we'd be able to convince you to go."

Wells blanched at the prospect of being convinced by Zeke and changed the subject fast. No one else mentioned the coming fight after that, but later, after adjournment, a dozen of the delegates stopped by as Eli was gathering up his things to say that if he was going over to join the fighting, they reckoned they might as well go with him.

They came out of Kent's tavern to find Zeke waiting in the yard. He was pleased at the number of men who'd decided to go. "But what about Wells?" he bellowed, already starting for the door. A minute later he was back, toting Wells by the scruff of the neck.

"I haven't got a gun," Wells was saying.

"Don't worry, we'll get you one—and I'll walk right beside you so's to make sure you don't get lost in the woods." Zeke looked delighted.

Wells looked terrified. "I've got to let my wife know."

"Send her a letter," said Zeke. "Speaking of letters..." He reached into his shirt and tossed Eli a small sealed envelope. "This came yesterday."

It was from Anne-Marie. Eli's hands were shaking as he broke the seal. It was a short letter, one sentence to be exact. She wondered if he could spare the time to see her at the fort.

The men were waiting, kicking up dust in the tavern yard. "What are we waiting for?" he said gruffly, swinging up onto his horse.

They spent the night in Castleton and by the following midday were at Larrabee's Point, which was where they heard the news that Carleton had left Saint John and was sailing down the lake.

"Well now, that's news, ain't it!" Zeke gave Wells a wallop on the back that almost sent him flying off the ferry and into the lake. "You see, Northridge, you didn't make the trip in vain! I hope it's not too late to join Arnold," he added worriedly.

It wasn't too late as it turned out. Their ferry pulled into the landing beside the last of the Skenesboro galleys, which was in the process of being rigged by an entire company of soldiers who were trying to make up for inexperience with speed. They were tripping over one another and doing everything wrong, while the galley's captain looked on in despair. When Eli told the captain that he and Zeke had some experience on the lake, the poor man almost went down on his knees, begging them to sign on as crew. They were leaving within the hour whether they were rigged or not. Eli left Zeke with the captain and went to search for Anne-Marie.

He found her in the barracks, binding the arm of a soldier who'd been working on the galley until he'd been hit by a falling beam. He paced the gallery outside until she had finished and joined him there.

"You've heard that Carleton's coming?"

He nodded. "We heard at Larrabee's Point." He was reading her face for her answer, but without very much luck. Could he have been mistaken about her reason for calling him here? "I hope Arnold's ready."

"I guess he's as ready as he can be, but everybody knows that he's way outnumbered. It would take a miracle for him to stop Carleton."

"We're about due for one," said Eli, but he wasn't thinking about that. "If Arnold doesn't stop him, you won't be safe here."

She smiled bleakly. "I'll be all right. Don't forget I've had experience with an army in retreat. I—I take it you got my letter?"

"Yesterday." He stopped and waited. Now it was all up to her.

She bit her lip and released it. "I wanted to see you to ask if—if you'd changed your mind."

"Changed my mind?" he repeated, baffled.

"About what you said. About marrying me," she stated firmly. Her color was very high. "Because if you haven't—have you?"

In silence he shook his head.

"Because if you haven't, I know what I want. I want to be with you. Forever." There were tears in her eyes.

For the first few seconds he wasn't sure of what she'd said—not sure whether she'd spoken or he'd imagined she had.

"What about your brother?"

She dashed at the tears with the back of her hand. "It's hard to let him go. A part of me will always be that little girl who lost hold of his hand. That memory will never leave me, but now I've grown up. I'm not that little girl anymore. I'm a woman and I need other things. I told you that François was a dream and that's what he was. But you're not a dream. You're real, and it's your face I see when I close my eyes."

"I see your face, too." His voice was hoarse. They were standing in the open; he took her hand and drew her back into the shadows where they'd have some privacy.

He put his arms around her and held her close. He closed his eyes and murmured, "I'll die if you change your mind."

"I won't change it. I love you," she murmured against his chest.

"I love you, too." He raised her head and kissed her forehead and her eyes. Her eyelids tasted salty so he kissed them again.

"People will see us." She laughed shakily.

"They'll think that we're in love."

"When can we be married?"

"As soon as I come back."

"Back?" At the word, she stiffened and drew away. "Back from where? Where are you going?"

"To meet Arnold, wherever he is. Zeke and I just signed on to that galley down there." He pointed down toward the landing where the men were still scrambling.

She didn't turn to look. Her grip on his shoulders tightened. "If you're going, I want to be married first. Right now, this afternoon. We can do it before you leave."

She was trembling; he gathered her close and stroked her hair and her cheek. "There isn't time. Besides, Sarah would kill me if she wasn't there. When I get back I'll take you home and we'll have the biggest wedding Bennington has ever seen."

"How many has it seen?" she quavered, trying to be brave.

"Oh, two or three." He kissed her ear and murmured, "Don't worry, I'll be back."

"How do you know?" she whispered.

"Because you'll be waiting for me." He touched her beneath the chin, and when she looked up, he closed his eyes and kissed her until he knew that he'd better stop. They were both breathing hard when he let her go.

"If Ticonderoga is threatened, I want you to go to Bennington, to Sarah, and wait for me there."

"Don't worry about me," she said staunchly. She bit her lip to stop it from trembling and even managed a smile. "When I first knew you, you wouldn't have rushed off to fight. You'd have held back until you'd thought everything through. You've changed."

"Are you sorry?"

"Not as long as you come back to me."

"I'll be back," he promised.

"I'll be waiting for you."

Chapter Fourteen

Anne-Marie stood on the landing watching the galley pull away, flying its white flag with red rattlesnake and the warning Don't Tread on Me. At first she could see Eli, then she could only see Zeke, so she kept on looking at the space next to him until finally all she could see was the ship. That's when she grabbed her skirts in both hands and took off up the hill, nearly running to the oak tree where Eli had found her—and left her—a month ago. Her lungs were burning by the time she got there so that she could barely draw her breath, but from that height she could see much farther than she could have from down below.

She kept her eyes on the galley, grateful they didn't blur. She didn't feel like crying; what she felt was too deep for tears. That day she'd stood here with Eli, he'd been balanced between hope and loss, waiting for her to make up her mind. Now she was standing exactly where he had stood. If he came back, her life would be magic, but if he didn't, her world would turn dark.

Watching the white sails in the distance, she remembered that day. If only she'd chosen him then, they would have had a month together before he'd left. Thirty days of sweet anticipation and thirty nights of bliss. Then, if anything happened, at least she would have had that to look back on instead of a lonely month of soul-searching and growing up.

It had been hard to give up François. In a way it had been harder than anything she'd ever done, because letting him go had been breaking the last real connection with her past. She supposed that people went through the same thing when they grew up and moved away from home. Even the sure knowledge that where you were going would be better than where you'd been didn't make the break any easier. The human heart was unreasonable and it wanted both.

In letting go of François, she'd learned something about herself. She had realized that for years she had been clinging to the childish belief that finding him would let her go back and change history. She might be searching for him as an adult, but in her mind she was still that three-year-old child lost and screaming in the crowd, and believing that if she found François, everything would be different. She'd believed that he would help her to erase those nightmare years and construct a happier past in which they were all together: she, her mother and François.

The hardest part of the last month had been admitting to herself that even if she found François she couldn't change the past. But after some of the pain had abated, she had found comfort in the truth. She'd remembered the sieur saying that until you had let the past go, you couldn't find peace or happiness. Now, finally, she knew what he meant. She couldn't really love Eli until she let go of François, because so long as she clung to him, she would always be half in the past, brooding and bitter about things she couldn't change.

She shielded her eyes against the water's reflection to follow the smudge of white that was all that was left of the galley. Then the smudge disappeared. She felt a wave of panic. It had been easier to be brave when she could see where he was. Now, squinting at the emptiness, she knew that if he didn't come back this was all there would ever be: a great glittering emptiness and insufficient memory.

To distract herself, she imagined him standing on the galley, gazing back at the fort. No, he wouldn't be looking back. He would be looking ahead and thinking about the battle that he was rushing to join. Not for the first time she reflected to herself that, despite the greater dangers, it would be easier to be a man. She'd rather be heading for battle than waiting here on this hill—especially knowing as much as she did about the coming fight.

She knew where Arnold was. He was at a place called Valcour Island, toward the northern end of the lake. He had his ships tucked inside the channel between the island and the New York shore and his plan was to hide from Carleton until he'd sailed past, then to lure him back, hoping that in turning, Carleton's fleet would drift apart and come into the channel piecemeal so that the American gunners would be able to pick them off one by one.

She knew that Arnold had seventeen gunboats, and that whatever rumors one chose to believe, Carleton's fleet outnumbered his by at least two to one. Carleton also had sailors, while Arnold did not. Most Americans with any nautical skills were too busy making a fortune privateering to bother themselves with defending their country against the coming British attack. Many of the men Arnold was counting on had never set foot on anything bigger than a bateau and they'd be going against some of Britain's best naval officers.

Of all the unequal battles fought thus far, this one promised to be the most unequal of all. Arnold's two strongest weapons were the lateness of the season and Carleton's cautiousness. Even Arnold, with all of his arrogance and superiority, didn't believe he could win. His hope was to do enough damage to the British fleet to make Carleton doubt that he could master the lake and establish his supply lines before the winter struck. If Carleton couldn't do that, he would be forced to retreat to Canada for the winter, then try again next year.

Anne-Marie had heard Schuyler say in private that it would take a miracle for Arnold to succeed. Schuyler was hoping for a miracle, and now so was she as she scanned the horizon for something that wasn't there.

The days dragged by. The waiting was terrible, and not just for Anne-Marie. If Arnold couldn't stop him, Carleton would sail down the lake and descend on Ticonderoga with his frigates and his schooners and his ten thousand crack troops. After a summer of bickering and rumors, now the fort was enveloped in a sense of dread. The generally held belief was that Carleton would knock Arnold out of his path like a pesky mosquito then swoop down upon the fort. Suddenly the defenses seemed hopelessly inadequate and a new wave of frenetic activity swept up and down the hills. Men alternately dug breastworks and squinted at the lake, and every day brought sightings, all of which—after a half hour's panic—turned out to be gulls.

Just after eight o'clock on the morning of October 14 the familiar cry of "Ships coming!" rang out across the fort. Anne-Marie, who was eating breakfast, ignored the shouts, but when they were repeated ten minutes later, she dropped everything and ran. The walls were already crowded but the men made room for her, and by that time she could easily see the sails.

Her heart sank. It wasn't Eli's galley. It was the schooner *Revenge,* which had been built at Skenesboro and had sailed north with Arnold almost a month earlier. When she'd sailed, she'd been freshly painted and her sails had been whole. Now they were ragged and flapping, and as she limped toward the shore, Anne-Marie could see where her side had been shattered by artillery fire. By that point everyone was rushing down to welcome her into harbor—and to hear her news.

Anne-Marie stayed a minute longer, scanning the men on her deck. She didn't believe she saw Eli but the men were so ragged and filthy she couldn't be sure. There were also fewer of them than when the *Revenge* had sailed. Her chest tight with fear and her hands cold, she made her way down to the shore.

By that time General Schuyler was on board conferring with the captain, while what members of the crew who weren't needed for berthing had been dragged into the crowd, where each was in the process of babbling his tale.

"A big black ship," one man was saying. "Biggest ship you've ever seen, with guns bristling out of her like quills on a porcupine! When she came into the channel she got her head stuck in the wind and couldn't turn around. She just hung there and we gave her everything we had, but we couldn't touch her—it was like she was protected by a spell." The man looked exhausted and his eyes were wild.

"What then? What happened?" The crowd urged him on.

"Then more of the ships came up and they managed to tow the black ship out of our reach. But that isn't saying much, since most of our gunners hadn't ever fired their guns before. And meanwhile, the damned redcoats are raining down iron on us. They got a schooner and a galley and shot the rest of us up pretty bad. You can see for yourself," he added, looking back toward the *Revenge*.

"Which galley?" Anne-Marie called out, but he didn't hear because everyone else was shouting, "What happened then?"

The man dragged a filthy sleeve across his mouth. "I could do with a drop of something, if anyone's got some?"

Nobody had, and though a boy was hastily dispatched, he moved off a few feet then crept back to hear the rest of the tale.

"Then it got to nighttime and the fighting had to stop. Carleton had us bottled up in that channel, and all of us knew that first light the next morning, he'd come in and finish us off—except that General Arnold thought to send out a dinghy to check and he found out that Carleton wasn't blocking the whole channel, he was only blocking one side. So when the fog rolled in, General Arnold took the notion that we ought to leave.''

His eyes rolled with admiration. ''So that's just what we did. We stretched out in a line, and every ship had a hooded lantern in the stern to lead the one behind it, and the first in line just sort of felt its way along. I'll tell you, for a while there, it was nip and tuck. But we made it, every one of us—only then the real trouble began, because the wind was against us and more'n half of the ships weren't in shape to make any kind of time. So Arnold gathered us all together and sent the halest of us down here—and that ain't much. Just us and the galley *Trumbull* and a couple of the gondolas.''

Eli's galley wasn't the *Trumbull;* it was the *Washington.* Anne-Marie's whole body went cold. She wanted to ask about the others, but someone else in the crowd asked for her.

The man drew his arm across his mouth again. ''The last I saw of them they were all headed this way, but at the rate some were going, I can't see how they're going to stay ahead of Carleton—not with those schooners of his.'' He stopped speaking and looked hard up at the fort, and it was clear to every one of them what he was thinking about.

Anne-Marie pushed her way up closer until she could catch the man by his tattered sleeve. ''Did you see the *Washington* galley?''

The man turned at the tug on his arm. When she repeated her question, he gave her a long sober look. ''She was afloat when I last saw her, but she wasn't doing very well. She got shot up pretty bad in the battle.''

''What about her crew?''

The man opened his mouth to answer, then seemed to change his mind. ''I wouldn't fret about them,'' he said. ''Even if Carleton does take them, they say he's good to prisoners.''

''Eli Brownell?'' She spoke his name quickly, but the man shook his head.

"Sorry, I don't know him. If you'll excuse me, ma'am, I ain't wet my whistle in longer'n I can recall, and if I don't wet it soon, it's likely to close down on me for good."

"Of course," she murmured. He'd told her all he knew, and the best she could do was to see who came on the other ships.

Half an hour later the galley *Trumbull* came in, but Eli wasn't on it, or on the gondola that limped in after it. She questioned the men who straggled off both ships, but they had little to add. One man thought he'd seen Eli after the battle, but he wasn't sure. Another assured her that the *Washington* would get home safely, but she knew he was lying, so after that she gave up.

She spent the rest of the day at the landing, watching the horizon for the sight of sails. When darkness had fallen and no more ships had appeared, she walked to headquarters to see if there was any news. There wasn't any more than what she'd already heard, but there was a letter for her.

"A letter?" She turned it over. It bore Massey's name over a Philadelphia address. She put it in her pocket unopened; she could imagine the sort of letter Massey would write and she could easily wait to read it until she knew that Eli was safe.

October was half-over and the night was cold, but she spent it on the landing, wrapped in a warm woolen cloak. Morning found her half-numb with sleeplessness, but she knew she wouldn't have rested if she'd been in her room. Her eyes ached as she scanned the water, but the sun rose on the same empty horizon on which it had set. She was still watching at half-past nine when a single mast bearing a tattered sail wobbled into view.

A crowd had gathered around her by the time the boat was close enough to be identified.

"It ain't one of ours," murmured one of the sailors from the *Revenge*. "And it ain't one of Carleton's. Must be some settler from the Grants—'less our men borrowed it after they lost theirs."

At the suggestion, Anne-Marie's heart gave a wild leap. This could be Eli. It could be, she thought stubbornly. She stood on tiptoe, squinting to see, though the ship was still too far away.

It drifted in closer. She saw him then, standing in the front, shielding his eyes and searching—

"Eli!" She raised her arm to wave, jumping up and down and calling his name, oblivious to the men all around her.

"Eli!" Her arm hit something solid and she heard someone grunt. She didn't care, she kept on waving—then she saw him wave back. After that, nothing could hold her back. Heedless of her skirts, she waded out into the water as the bateau nudged in, and he leapt over the gunwales and caught her in his arms, pressing her against him amid the cheers of the exhausted men.

"I'm next!" someone shouted.

She only laughed and felt him laugh against her.

"I'm filthy," he murmured against her lips.

She laughed again. "I don't care!" But she loosened her lock around his neck and he let her down. Standing face-to-face in the water, she got her first good look at him. He looked awful, all torn and tattered. He looked wonderful.

"Come on." She caught him by the hand and pulled him to the shore.

"Where are we going?"

"Wherever you want!" She laughed. She felt absolutely weightless. She felt as if she could fly. "You lost your ship?"

"We scuttled it yesterday to keep it away from Carleton. After that, we came most of the way on foot until we got about level with Five Mile Point, then we borrowed this boat."

"Is Carleton coming?"

"He'll stop at Crown Point. Unless I miss my guess, he'll stay there for a couple of weeks, then go back to Canada."

"Then we're safe?"

"For the moment. At least until next spring." They'd come to the stone staircase leading up to her room, which was in the main building of the fort. "Where are we going?"

"Up to my room. If we're about to be married, I don't think anyone will object."

"I don't care if they do." His teeth flashed white against the gunpowder that darkened the skin of his face. "I am filthy."

"I'll get some water. You can have a bath." She flashed him a brilliant smile as she led him up the stairs to her room, which was hardly big enough for her dresser and her bed. She closed the door behind them. "I'm afraid it's very small."

He closed his eyes and breathed deeply. "I love it. It smells of you." When he opened his eyes again, he took her in his arms.

"What about your bath?" she murmured.

"Later." He nuzzled her ear. "You smell delicious."

"You don't," she said. His hands slid down her legs then slid back up again underneath her skirts. She shivered as his fingers grazed her naked skin; when he gripped her and pressed her against him, she went willingly.

"I was so worried," she whispered. "Yesterday, when the first ships came back and told us what had happened, I was afraid that you'd been killed."

"I gave you my promise."

"Yes, I know." His hands were moving, coaxing her to open to him. It didn't take much coaxing; she was trembling with eagerness and his skin was burning through all the layers of their clothes. "I love you," she whispered.

"I love you!" he whispered back, and dropping his head lower, he showed her just how much.

They clung together, stifling their cries in each other's shoulders and hair as they tossed among the covers and the rumpled pile of their cast-off clothes.

Afterward, they lay with their limbs entangled and their bodies shining with sweat. She lifted one finger and drew a lazy heart in the soot that stained his cheek. When she'd finished, he caught her finger and held it to his lips. He kissed it, then he drew it slowly into the heat of his mouth.

Her laugh was low and shaky. "What—again so soon?"

"I could make love to you forever." Still holding her hand, he rolled onto his side and raised himself on his elbow so that he was looking down at her. "All through the fighting and afterward, when we were running, I kept thinking I must be going to die. I couldn't believe I was going to have you, so all I could think of was that I was going to die."

"But you'd promised me you wouldn't."

"That's right," he said, and he smiled. He brushed her hair back and traced the lines of her brows. "I'd promised and here I am. Are you glad to see me?"

"What do you think?"

Instead of answering, he bent to kiss her breast. She sighed and arched against him. He kissed her lazily, tickling and coaxing the way she remembered from that night at Zeke's.

Footsteps passed outside on the gallery. He raised his head. "Does everyone know we're in here?"

"Do you care?"

"Do you?"

She linked her arms around his neck and pulled him down again. "I care this much," she whispered just before they met. "Ouch!" She shifted abruptly.

"Did I hurt you?"

"No, I must be lying on something." She rolled aside and he reached beneath her and pulled out an envelope. "Where did this come from?" she said when he held it up. Then she remembered. "It came for me yesterday but I put it in my pocket because I was watching for you. I forgot I had it."

"Who's it from?"

"Your old friend Captain Massey." When he stiffened in reaction, she smiled chidingly. "Don't tell me you're jealous!"

"Has he written to you before?"

"Never." She looked at the letter. "I wonder why he did now."

"You can find out if you read it." He edged sideways to give her room.

"I'll read it later."

"No, you should read it now. Otherwise you'll be wondering what it's about and you won't be able to concentrate."

At that, she laughed aloud. "You are jealous! All right, if you insist." To please him, she opened the letter and read. She only meant to skim it, but the first sentence caught her eye. She read it and sat up. "My God—he's found François!"

"What do you mean he's found him?"

Still reading, she tapped the page. "He says here that he's found him. He's living near Baltimore."

"He may be lying."

"I don't think so. He's written the whole thing here. He happened to tell my story to a man from Maryland and the man recognized the name. Imagine!" She shook her head in amazement. "Massey found François!"

"The bastard!" Eli muttered.

She looked up. "What do you mean? After what happened, I think he was nice to tell me."

"Oh, sure. Very nice. What are you going to do about it?"

She laughed. "I don't really know. Should I write him a letter or drop in unannounced? Imagine—François is living. The sieur will be surprised!" She pushed her hair back and looked down at him. "Eli? What's the matter? Why are you looking at me like that?"

He pulled away when she touched him and shook his head. Seeing his breeches nearby, he reached down. "I'd better go."

Her hand shot out to stop him. "Eli, tell me what's wrong! Are you angry about my brother?"

He looked up. "What do you think? Did you make me a promise a few days ago, or am I thinking of somebody else?"

She felt her whole body contracting at his words. "This doesn't mean I don't love you or want to marry you. Eli, I've found my brother! Can't you be happy for me? Can't you be happy that I'm not an orphan—that I have some family?"

"Of course. I'm ecstatically happy."

It was no use explaining or begging. She let go of his arm. "I can't believe you. I can't believe you're doing this. You're acting as if I've let you down just because I'm happy to find out that my brother's alive. I can't believe you're so selfish."

"Selfish!" He laughed bitterly. "I'm surprised you're not already packing to rush off to Baltimore."

"I want to see him. Is that so terrible? You could come with me—I wish you would come along. I want you to meet each other."

"And what if when you get there, he needs you for some reason? What if he wants you to go back to Acadia. What then?"

"Then I'll tell him that I'm staying with you."

"Right. Just the way you told me you weren't running after him."

She opened her mouth, closed it and slowly shook her head. "I can't believe you can love me and talk to me this way. Nothing's changed since the first day we met, has it? You didn't trust me then and you don't trust me now. And if you don't trust me, how can you love me?"

He looked away. "Maybe I don't." Her chemise was lying on the covers at his feet. He picked it up and handed it to her. "Maybe we're wrong for each other."

She snatched the chemise from him and threw it back on the floor. He could break her heart if he wanted, but he wouldn't make her feel ashamed. "Is that what you want?" she demanded.

"It doesn't seem as if I'm the one making the choice." He swung his legs over the edge of the mattress to put his back to her.

She watched as he pulled on his trousers and reached for his boots. "You said you loved me, but I don't believe you ever did. You care more about your pride than you've ever cared about me."

"Maybe that's because my pride's more reliable."

"Ha!" She gave a bitter laugh. "Why shouldn't it be, when you've spent your whole life nurturing it? I hope it makes you happy."

"Thank you, I'm sure it will. Give my regards to your brother and have fun in Baltimore."

Chapter Fifteen

June 1777. Bennington.

"Not in the washbasin, Betsey. Give the stockings to Uncle Eli, that's a good girl." Zeke nodded with approval as little Elizabeth took the stockings out of the basin and brought them across to the bed, where Eli was in the process of packing his saddlebags.

Eli thanked her gravely and added them to the pile of things he was taking to Philadelphia. He had a good suit of clothing, a couple of books and a thick packet of papers well bound in oilcloth. The clothing he packed quickly, but before he added the packet, he weighed it in his hand.

Zeke was watching. "You've got a heap of signatures there. Probably pretty close to every man in the Grants—and you probably collected most of them yourself."

"Thanks to New York's help." Eli moved the packet to keep it out of Betsey's reach. "If New York hadn't adopted a constitution declaring that she intended to collect taxes from every landholder in the Grants, a lot of people in these parts would still be hemming and hawing about whether or not we ought to be an independent state. Now it's up to Congress either to let us join the party or to keep us out." He gave the packet a final look. "If this won't convince

Congress that we're serious about independence, I don't know what will."

"Hamstringing a company of Yorkers?" Zeke grinned nostalgically. "Don't you ever get lonely for the good old days when we could fight battles on our own and win them, instead of having to trip over a bunch of birdbrained generals who muddle everything up?"

Eli considered the question. He got lonely all right, but not for chasing down stray Yorkers with the Green Mountain Boys. He got lonely, so he'd spent the winter tramping the length and breadth of the Grants, collecting signatures on the petition he was about to take to Philadelphia to deliver to Heman Allen and James Breakenridge, who'd spent their winter drumming up congressional support.

He dropped the packet into the saddlebag and put the books on top. "If Congress grants us independence, you'll never hamstring Yorkers again."

Zeke's grin broadened. "Don't be so sure about that. Congress or no Congress, I can't reckon the Yorkers giving up so easily. Maybe they'll organize some Green Mountain Boys of their own."

"They don't have the Green Mountains."

"The Hudson River, then. Maybe a company of Hudson River Boys'll come riding across the river to stir up trouble in Vermont." He rolled the new name off his tongue experimentally. "I still don't know if I like it. It sounds foreign, sort of French."

"Would you prefer it to sound English?" Eli buckled the saddlebags and looked around the office for anything he might have forgotten to pack.

That is, this room had been his office in former days, before Zeke and his whole family had come to stay. Now this was both his office and his sleeping room, while Sarah and Zeke and the children squeezed as best they could into the rest of the house. He was glad to have them; they were his family, and beyond that, Zeke had practically built the house himself.

But since he'd come back from Valcour Island it had been hard to be around Zeke and Sarah, because seeing the way they were together made him think of Anne-Marie. That was why he'd spent most of the spring and winter away from home, and that was why he was glad to be off to Philadelphia. Not that he'd be any better off if Zeke and Sarah left; he knew if they left him alone, he'd probably stay here and brood.

"I was thinking," Zeke said offhandedly as Eli hefted the saddlebags. "Philadelphia isn't all that far from Maryland...."

"Thanks for the suggestion, but I have no intention of running after her."

"I didn't mean—"

"It doesn't matter." Eli set the bags back down and looked at Zeke. "In the first place, she's probably not even there. By now, she and her brother are probably in Nova Scotia moving heaven and earth to reclaim their precious farm."

"Not with the place seething with British, they aren't. Unless her brother's a raving madman, they'll still be in Maryland."

"Maybe they are," Eli admitted, "but I don't plan on taking the time to go and see, not with Burgoyne and ten thousand soldiers at the top of Lake Champlain. You know as well as I do that Schuyler's even more desperate than he was last year. Carleton learned his lesson. This time he won't waste time at Saint John. This time he'll come straight down here, and I mean to be here when he does."

"Right." Zeke nodded, pushing off the wall. "Rush down to Philadelphia and then rush back up, and if you're lucky you can get here in time to catch a bullet through your brain. That'd be a whole lot quicker than trying to kill yourself with work."

"I'm not trying to kill myself with work." For the second time, Eli shouldered his bags.

Zeke watched impassively. "Then what are you trying to do?"

"I'm trying to serve my country the best way I know how, and I'm sorry if you don't approve. Now, if you'll excuse me—"

"In a minute." Zeke shifted his huge frame to squarely block the door. "A few years back when I needed it, someone gave me a piece of good advice—something about swallowing my pride and going after the woman I loved."

"I know you're trying to help, but this isn't about pride."

"What's it about, then?"

"About choices," Eli said. "She could have had me, but she chose her brother instead."

"I doubt it was that easy."

"It was," Eli said. He didn't want to think about it. Just thinking about it hurt.

"What if she regrets it?"

"That's her problem, not mine. My problem is getting these papers to Philadelphia and hoping I can get back before Gentleman Johnny Burgoyne and his Hessians make our independence a moot point. I'm not going to see her and that's final, so please move aside."

Zeke shook his head. "I should have let Sally do the talking. She could have made you see sense."

In spite of his bitterness, Eli smiled at his brother's distress. "Sally couldn't have done any better. What happened between you and her was different. From the first time I saw you together I knew that you belonged. The only problem was whether you'd ever wake up and see it yourselves. You're happy together, but we could never be." As he said that he remembered the morning after they'd made love, the way the sun had come up on a newly made, glorious world.

A stab of pain sliced through him. "I've got to go. Take care of the farm—I'll be back as soon as I can."

Zeke and Sarah watched him as he rode away, Betsey perched on Zeke's shoulders and little Sam in his arms.

When horse and rider had vanished, Zeke heaved a mighty sigh.

"It's not you, it's him," said Sarah. "You can't change someone's mind. You can only try."

"I could have tried harder."

"I doubt it," she said. "What's more, you never can tell. He's got a long trip ahead of him. Maybe by the time he gets there, he'll see things differently."

"He's a Brownell," Zeke said.

"I know, but so are you and you finally came to your senses."

"Me!" He threw back his head and bellowed, "Ho, woman, what about you?" Then he realized she was teasing and he began to laugh.

"Do horsey, Papa." Betsey tugged on his ears. Still laughing, he gave a whinny and pranced about the yard, both of the children shrieking with delight. Sarah smiled distractedly, her eyes still on the road. She was thinking less of Eli than of the British massed at the head of the lake, maybe even at this moment plundering her house. She loved that house and what it represented almost as much as she loved Zeke, and she hated the thought of the British defiling it. Everything hung in the balance, and all she could do was wait and hope that when the dust settled they'd all still be able to find cause for happiness. She wondered if a country had ever known such a difficult time.

It had been a rough winter for Philadelphia. Alarmed by the fighting in New Jersey, Congress had bolted the city for the greater safety of Baltimore. In March, bolstered by Washington's brilliant defense, Congress had returned, but now, three months later, everyone's nerves were still on edge.

"Howe's got ten thousand troops in New York City and Burgoyne's got another ten at the top of the lake." Heman Allen summed up the situation to Eli after dinner in his rooms. "I know that Grants folks believe that Howe means to march up to Albany while Burgoyne comes down the lake, but Washington believes that's a hoax. He believes that Burgoyne's real plan is to sail around and attack Philadelphia.''

"But that would leave New York and New England intact.''

"Relatively speaking,'' Allen said. "But you know that New York and New England are always at each other's throats. Look what's happened with Schuyler and Gates. Last year when Carleton was on his way, New England and New York were fighting over whether Gates or Schuyler should command the troops, and this year it's the same. Maybe Burgoyne's smart enough to realize that if he leaves New York and New England alone, the chances are better than even that they'll do each other more damage than he and all of his Hessians could do.''

"Maybe,'' said Eli, but he was far from convinced. "What about our petition?''

Allen shook his head. "New York will feed us to the lions before she'll let us break away, and with this new campaign beginning, Congress doesn't dare take a stand. They're not even impressed when we threaten to negotiate a separate peace with Carleton and Howe. We've half decided not to present the petition right now.''

"You've got to present it,'' Eli said earnestly. "People in the Grants are angry. Ever since New York published her constitution, they've been ready to take a stand. If we move now, they'll be with us. If we don't, I'm afraid we'll lose our support.''

"What if Congress rejects us?''

"Then we'll be forced to stand on our own. It won't be the first time and we ought to be used to it. If Congress won't let us be one of the United States, we'll declare ourselves an independent republic and invite Congress and the other states to form diplomatic ties.''

Allen's brows rose. "But will they do it?''

"Will they relate to us? They won't have any choice. They can't do without us and they haven't got the men at arms to take us against our will. They may fuss and threaten, but there's nothing they can do. As long as we're fighting the British, I believe they'll let us be. There might even be certain advantages. For one thing, we won't have to put up with Congress's shilly-shallying to get things done. And once Grants folks get used to being free of New York, you know they'll never go back."

"If that's what it comes to, will the convention support us?"

"I believe they will. Our next meeting is scheduled for the second of July."

"We won't have an answer from Congress by then."

Eli spread his hands. "Then they'll go forward on their own. Under the circumstances, that may be for the best."

The two men regarded each other in comprehension and accord.

Allen's eyes narrowed. "You ought to stay here, Brownell. We could use your help wooing Congress."

"Thanks for the offer, but Schuyler can use me, too."

At that, Allen shook his head, looking half-amused. "I don't recall you being such a red-hot soldier when all this began. What happened?"

"Ten thousand redcoats sailed into Quebec," Eli answered, thinking of Anne-Marie. The day he'd left to join Arnold, she'd also said that he'd changed. He was hit by a wave of yearning and a wave of bitterness.

A week later he was back on the road, riding north toward New Jersey through a magnificent summer day. The sun was hot and golden and there had been enough rain the last month to keep the road free of dust. He was thinking that the corn at home must already be up to his knees, and he was thinking about the cow that was getting ready to calve and hoping that if there had to be fighting at Bennington it would miss his farm.

Then all of a sudden he was thinking about Anne-Marie, not thinking but being overwhelmed but a rush of images. She was sitting on the bed in Quebec and shaving him while she pretended not to notice how close he was. She was turning to look up at him in the tent on the Île aux Noix, her face smudged and dirty and her hair in that tangled braid. She was wading through the water to welcome him back after the battle against Carleton for Lake Champlain. If he closed his eyes, he could feel her arms locked around his neck and the sweetness of her body pressing into his. If he closed his eyes he could remember exactly how they'd made love.

His horse had stopped and was agreeably cropping grass from the side of the road. Even with his eyes opened, he was still in her room, warm from the warmth of her body, enveloped in her scent, all the aches and exhaustion soothed from his muscles and bones. He was watching her smile as she traced a design on his dirty cheek.

He shook his head to drive out the image and pulled up on the reins. "You'll have dinner at dinnertime. Hey-up!" Still chewing, the horse started off. As they went, Zeke's voice was saying, "What if she regrets it?"

"That's her problem," he said aloud.

Her problem. Her problem. The horse's hooves kept time as they traveled northward, away from Baltimore. Her problem. Her problem. She was probably already gone. She had chosen her brother. It was too late.

This time it was he who stopped. Pride was a hard master, but he was unhappy and he wanted to see her. He wanted to see her so much. If there was a chance in a million—even if there was no chance at all. He turned back in the opposite direction and began to ride.

It was ironically easy to find her brother's farm—ironic after all the years it had taken her to find him and what finding him had caused. The countryside was pleasant and the farm looked prosperous, fields plowed and fields fallow, orchards thick with young fruit and a dairy herd grazing in a pasture on a hill. There was no one to greet him as he rode into the yard, so he tied his horse up and knocked on the door.

He heard a baby crying as if in response to his call. The crying grew louder and Anne-Marie appeared, standing in the open doorway with the baby in her arms and two older children clinging to her skirts. His shock when he saw her was almost as great as hers. The memories hadn't come close to recreating her, and it was all he could do not to grab her and wrap her in his arms, not to pull back her head and kiss her—

"Would—would you like to come in?" Her voice sounded as if it were coming to him from far away, and she was still staring at him as if she wondered if he were real.

"If you don't mind."

He followed her into a parlor that faced the fields. The baby had stopped crying, and when she laid it in a cradle that stood beside a chair, the older children let go of her skirts and squatted to coo to it.

"Your brother's children?"

"Who else's?" she replied.

"You must be a great help to your brother."

"We help each other." She seated herself in the chair, clearly waiting for him to tell her why he'd come. Had she changed since he'd last seen her? She had, but he couldn't say how.

"Your brother's got a fine farm."

"What are you doing here?" She asked the question calmly, but he could sense the tension rising beneath the calm.

"I had to carry some documents to Philadelphia, so..." He found that he couldn't tell her, so he gave up and said, "I wondered if you'd already gone to Acadia."

She looked away for the first time as she shook her head. "As it turns out, François had a very different experience from mine. The ship he was put on sailed to Baltimore.

Many people died during the voyage, but François survived. When the ship arrived at Baltimore he was indentured to a man who had an estate very close to here. All of the Acadians who were able to work were indentured to people here. Some of them had cruel masters and suffered very much.

"François was fortunate. His master and mistress were kind and they treated him well. They even taught him to read and write. In exchange for their kindness, he worked very hard. Toward the end of his indenture, his master took ill, so François stayed on. The illness lasted for several years and in the end he died, but in gratitude for François's loyalty he gave him a grant of land.

"For as long as he can remember, François has considered Maryland his home. He has no desire to return to Acadia. He has a different name and he scarcely remembers his French. His name here is Francis. Francis Perkins." She said this as matter-of-factly as she'd told the entire tale. From the tone she was using, she might have been talking about someone else.

It wasn't hard for Eli to feel the disappointment behind that tone. She'd chosen her brother and he'd let her down. Maybe he ought to feel vindicated, but he didn't; as he looked at her averted face, all he could feel was her hurt.

"I'm sorry," he said softly.

"Don't be." She raised her head. "I don't want your pity."

"I didn't mean—"

"Never mind." She glanced at the older children, who had been listening. "Come on. I'll get you each a cookie, then you can play in the yard. I'll be back," she added to Eli as she left the room, pausing to check on the baby, who was fast asleep.

Left alone, he went to the window to look out over the fields. He had wanted to see her, but he didn't think she was glad he had come. She seemed tense and still angry—and he knew the reason why. He could feel her disappointment

at the way things had turned out. She didn't want his pity—
did she want him at all, or would she have preferred that he
hadn't come? Would she be relieved to come back to this
parlor and find that he had gone? It suddenly occurred to
him that that might be why she'd left the room—to give him
a chance to go. Could he do that, knowing that he'd never
see her again? The idea gripped him like a cruel hand
around his heart.

A sound caught his attention. The baby was starting to
fuss. He glanced back at the cradle and saw its face screw
up. From here it looked very little; he moved up for a closer
look.

"It's all right, she'll be right back," he murmured, leaning down to rock the cradle. As he did, the crying increased. Where was the baby's mother? Probably upstairs
resting, and meanwhile Anne-Marie was holding down the
fort. She'd come all this way to find her brother and she'd
ended up working like a servant for his wife.

The baby was very small. It was also very unhappy. Eli
cocked an ear toward the doorway where Anne-Marie had
gone, and when he didn't hear her, he leaned down and
lifted the baby. It was like holding a feather. He'd never
held one quite so small. Even Betsey as a newborn had been
bigger. But tiny or not, it was working itself into a fit.

"Hey there, little fellow—or gal," he clucked to it. When
he rocked it, the baby stopped crying and puckered up its
mouth, but a minute or so later it started up again.

"You're hungry," murmured Eli. "I can't help you
there, but if you hold on just a minute your auntie'll take
you up to your mama. But you've got to be patient. You've
got to—"

"What's wrong?"

While he'd been talking to the baby, Anne-Marie had
come back and was standing there, looking at him as if
she'd had a shock.

"What's wrong?" she repeated.

"Nothing ten minutes with his mother won't fix," he answered, holding the baby out. "Or her mother," he added as she took it in her arms.

"His mother," she said flatly. The baby had stopped crying again. She looked down at its puckered face.

"He's very small," said Eli.

"He was born early. But he's a scrapper." Still looking down, she smiled.

As she did, Eli felt a chill run down his spine. There was something—what was it? She looked back up at him, and in the instant that their eyes met, suddenly he knew.

He felt as if someone had kicked the air out of him. He felt as if his body were hollow and his head were filled with bells. Alarms were ringing and he knew what they were for. He tried to look down at the baby, but for the life of him he couldn't stop looking at Anne-Marie.

She knew that he had guessed. He could see it in her eyes, but he couldn't read them. He was in too much shock.

She spoke quietly. "You don't have to stay. I don't know why you came here, but you don't have to stay."

Don't have to stay! Without thinking, he put his hand to his eyes, as if to shield them from her reflected pain. He thought he felt moisture before his hand dropped away. "Why didn't you tell me? Why didn't you let me know?"

"I thought it would make things worse. I thought it would be better to—to do this alone." She looked down at the baby, who was crying again.

"You'd better feed him."

"Yes." She looked toward the door, as if she were debating whether to do it here or go somewhere to be away from him.

"Please stay," he murmured, and her eyes came back to him, but it was still impossible to read what was in her mind.

When she unbuttoned her bodice, he couldn't drag his eyes away. That's why she looked different; he'd been a fool not to see. Her breast was swollen and blue-veined, her nipple dusky brown. She guided the baby to it, and when the tiny mouth clamped down, Eli had to clench his fists against the power of the sensation that surged up through him.

"What—what did you name him?"

"Henri. Henry," she said in English. "I named him for the sieur." Her eyes came up, searching.

He nodded. He felt numb. There were too many feelings, and but for the shock, they would have ripped him apart. But the numbness was already fading and his face was beginning to burn. He murmured, "Do you hate me?"

She bit her lip. "I did," she admitted when she let it go. "Until I had the baby. Then I didn't anymore. How could I hate you and love him?" Looking down, she shook her head.

Lifting a gentle finger, she eased her nipple from the baby's mouth, tucked it back in her bodice and raised the baby to her shoulder to burp. She had her hair braided as he'd once braided it. Suddenly he couldn't stand another moment of being apart from her.

The floorboards squeaked in protest as he crossed to her chair and sank down on his knees before her. "Will you forgive me?" he asked.

Still patting the baby, she nodded. He saw the tears in her eyes. He put his arms around her and the baby both and held them gently. He'd never felt so much—guilt, relief, gratitude, pleasure. Love. There was a small eruption between them as the baby belched. Surprised, he released her.

"Is he all right?"

She looked up, laughing—or crying. "He's perfect, can't you see? Oh dear, I'm afraid I'll drown him." She held him in the crook of one arm as she swiped at her tears.

He released her to pull out his handkerchief. After he'd dried her tears, she put the baby to her other breast.

"You're crying," she said softly.

"I know." He wiped his eyes. "I never imagined—I wish that I'd been here." He thought of Zeke and Sarah when Betsey had been born.

"I did, too," she whispered. "That's when I stopped being angry." She watched as he took her free hand and held it against his cheek.

"Will you come home and marry me?"

She drew in a quick breath. "I don't want you to think you have to do this because of the baby. My brother's wife died two years ago and he'd be more than happy to have me here."

"If he wants you, he can come to Bennington." He held her hand against his lips before he gave it back. "I love you, Anne-Marie. I loved you long before this baby existed and I almost lost you once."

"More than once," she whispered.

"More than once," he agreed. "I won't leave here without you—without you and Henri," he added, and she smiled at his speaking French.

For a moment her smile faltered. "François—Francis, can't speak French. He's forgotten."

"I won't let you forget yours," he promised. He slipped his fingers into her open bodice to touch her free breast.

She caught her breath. "Don't do that."

"Why not? Does it hurt?"

"No. Not exactly." She smiled in spite of herself. When he leaned forward to kiss her, she raised her head to kiss him back.

"Will you come home and be married?"

"Anytime you want."

But of course, there was a problem with that. He was in a rush to get back before the fighting began, but he couldn't subject Anne-Marie and the baby to the rigors of the trip—not to mention the dangers they'd face once they arrived.

Anne-Marie tried to argue, pointing out that she wasn't afraid of the British and that she'd nearly regained all her strength. She joked that long trips were her specialty, but Eli was adamant. They hadn't come this far to risk everything. On the other hand, as much as he wanted to be there to greet the redcoats, he had an almost superstitious aversion to leaving her behind, so he accepted her brother's invitation to stay. As for the brother, he was predictably glad not to lose Anne-Marie.

Her brother was nothing like her. After meeting him, Eli guessed that he had gotten all the English and Anne-Marie had gotten the French. Francis Perkins was light-haired, complacent and very American. Watching them together, Eli was tempted to laugh that this potbellied farmer was the force that had almost pulled them apart. But he was still too tender to laugh about that yet.

Although he wouldn't leave her to go back to Bennington, after they'd spent ten days together, he did make the two-day journey up to Philadelphia. When he arrived, Heman Allen greeted him with two pieces of news.

"We put our petition before Congress."

"Yes?"

"They turned it down. So far as they're concerned the Grants are a part of New York, and if we want it any different, we're on our own. Speaking of New York, you were right. Burgoyne never did intend to sail to Philadelphia. He's already come down the lake. We got the news the day before yesterday."

"Ticonderoga?"

"Gone," Allen said. "Schuyler couldn't hold it. That'll be the last dance for him. The redcoats are at Fort Edward and Gates is in."

"Gates!" repeated Eli, thinking of Bennington. Fort Edward was a day's ride from Bennington. If the British needed food and fodder that was most likely where they'd look for it, and an army the size of Burgoyne's would need a great deal of both.

"There's more," Allen said. "Howe has loaded his troops onto ships and sailed out of New York. No one knows where he's going—maybe here, maybe Chesapeake Bay. Maybe Virginia—it's anybody's guess.''

Chesapeake Bay meant Anne-Marie would be in jeopardy. "But why would Howe leave now, when Burgoyne must be counting on him?''

"Beats me." Allen shrugged. "Maybe Burgoyne thinks so little of us he's convinced he can take New York all by himself. Speaking of which, if you're on your way up to join the fray, you can deliver Congress's message."

Eli took the papers that Allen prepared for him and walked back to his rooms lost in sober thought. He wanted to be at Bennington, but what about Anne-Marie? And what if Howe's armada landed in Chesapeake Bay? He hadn't answered his own questions by the time he got back to his room—and found Anne-Marie sitting on his bed.

The baby Henry was sleeping in her arms. "We're going with you," she said calmly.

"I'm not going anywhere."

"Of course you are. I just heard that Burgoyne captured Ticonderoga."

"Is that why you came?"

"No. I thought it was time to go, but I knew if I told you, you wouldn't listen, so I decided to show you instead. We've been traveling for two days and we're perfectly fine." She looked down to include the baby, then she looked up again. "If you tell me I can't go any farther, I'll keep going on my own, so you might as well let me go with you."

"What if I said I was staying, too."

She smiled as she answered, "Then I'd say you were a fool." She stood. "Are you coming?"

"Have I got any choice?"

The easiest route from Philadelphia to Bennington was by water to Connecticut then up through Massachusetts, except that they had to avoid anywhere the British might be, and since no one knew where Howe was, they had to go by land. They went up the Delaware River into New York, then east toward the Hudson, north of where the British controlled. Their route added time and discomfort to the trip, but despite Eli's worries, Anne-Marie did fine. As for baby Henry, he was growing before their eyes.

They went up the Hudson as far as Albany, then struck out to the east on the road to Bennington. As they went, they heard rumors about the British whereabouts. Burgoyne was at Fort Edward with the main body of the troops, but he'd sent out columns in search of provisions in the surrounding countryside. One such column—the largest—was said to have marched to the Grants.

They felt the presence of the army more strongly with every mile they rode. Farms appeared deserted, their windows shuttered, their herds nowhere in sight. The farmers were either lying low or had hidden in the woods. They were within two miles of Eli's farm when they heard the faint popping sound.

Gunfire! They drew up the horses and stood, listening.

"Where is it coming from?" she murmured.

He shook his head. "I'm not sure." Looking around, he added, "You'd better stay here while I scout around."

"You don't think we can make it to your farm?"

"It isn't worth taking the chance. There's a thicket in the woods here. You ought to be safe."

He left both horses with her and continued on foot, avoiding the main road for a path in the woods. He'd gone about a quarter mile when he heard the strangest sounds—like a tinker's wagon clattering down the road. He crouched down, watching; the thudding and jangling increased until all of a sudden ten men came into view. They were soldiers and they must have been Carleton's, because a dozen of Schuyler's men didn't possess the amount of equipment any one of them had strapped, hooked and otherwise attached to his uniform. They wore tall black hats and heavy green breeches and coats. They were sweating rivers as they jangled past.

Eli stood, looking after them when they'd gone. They were jogging away from the gunfire, which could mean just about anything, including that they were lost, since they didn't strike him as men who knew their way around the woods. He was about to go on when he heard another sound, this one so soft he might have missed it if he hadn't been listening. He crept soundlessly back into his cover and held his breath, and a moment later, who should come padding along the trail but his brother, Zeke.

"Zeke!"

"My God, you scared me!" Zeke jumped as Eli appeared. "Where'd you spring up from?"

"Philadelphia. Where's the fighting?"

Zeke jerked his head behind him. "The Walloomsac hills, but you're too late. It's just about done."

"Who won?"

"We did." Zeke gave him a resentful look, then he added, "You didn't happen to see any Indians passing this way?"

"None. Just ten soldiers with a lot of canteens."

Zeke grinned. "Those'll be the Germans. They carry sixty pounds of equipment each. It makes for slow going, especially in these hills." His grin faltered. "We ought to go round 'em up and bring them back, but I was set on tracking those Indians."

"What Indians?"

"I can't say rightly. One of the northern tribes. The redcoats brought 'em down by the hundreds and turned 'em loose. Some of 'em scalped a girl name of Jane McCrea over by Fort Anne a couple of weeks ago. I don't like to think of them roving around in these woods."

Neither did Eli, who was thinking of Anne-Marie. "Which way were they going?"

"That's hard to say. We could split up and make a circle—"

But before Zeke could finish explaining his plan to find the Indians, the Indians found them, rising up from the bushes as if they were made of air. There were four of them, all painted in ways that Eli had never seen, and they all had muskets, two pointed at Eli and the other two at Zeke while they stripped them of their weapons and pushed them against two trees. When they spoke, Eli couldn't understand their dialect. He wondered if they spoke English, or if he could talk to Zeke.

Zeke must have had the same thought. "Look at old Rooster Head," he said, referring to the Indian who was bald except for three feathers stuck into a tuft of hair. Old Rooster Head raised his fist and punched Zeke in the jaw.

Zeke's head snapped back; when it snapped forward again, he muttered, "I guess they speak English."

Rooster Head and the Indian with his nose painted black continued to point their guns, while their two companions searched the brothers for weapons and valuables. They found twenty dollars in gold on Eli, which they immediately began to argue about.

Without even glancing at Zeke, Eli could read his thoughts. If the Indians were distracted, it was time to make a move. Two to one wasn't easy, but it could be worse, and they couldn't count on having another chance. He tensed for action; when Zeke sprang, so would he.

Zeke sprang with a bellow, launching his body into Rooster Head and knocking away the gun before he could fire it. Eli did the same thing, lunging for Black Nose's legs and hoping he could fell him before the other two got to him. He shut his eyes as he connected, hurtling to the ground and rolling over so that Black Nose was on top of him like a shield. He could hear Zeke yelling. He had Black Nose by the throat, then all of a sudden the other Indian was there, holding a tomahawk in one hand and reaching down with the other for a handful of his hair.

He couldn't release Black Nose—all he could do was squeeze hard and pray he'd go limp in the next second, which was about all he had. But he knew that it was hopeless. The fingers grasped his hair and the tomahawk swung higher—

An explosion filled the air. The tomahawk faltered and tumbled to the ground; with a startled expression, the Indian followed it, just as Black Nose gurgled and slumped over him. He pushed away the inert body and sprang to his feet. He was face-to-face with Anne-Marie, who was looking very pale and still pointing the pistol she'd fired at the dead Indian. Meanwhile Zeke was rolling around in the grips of two Indians.

Eli grabbed the nearest musket and jabbed it into Rooster Head's back, disengaging him from the tangle, while Zeke dealt with his friend.

"Not bad work," he panted a moment later, staggering to his feet. When he saw Anne-Marie, his face split in a grin. "Eli never said you were coming!"

Her face was still very white.

"Give me the gun," said Eli.

She handed it to him. "It isn't loaded—not any more, that is."

"I know." He smiled gently.

Relaxing, she smiled back. "I guess I held it that time."

"I guess you did."

"I guess you did!" Zeke echoed, but they were still smiling at each other and hardly noticed him.

Then Eli thought of something. "The baby!"

"He's all right. Come on. I'll show you."

They left Rooster Head and the other Indian tied up to two trees, and Anne-Marie led them back to the thicket, where she'd slung the saddlebags over a branch and put the baby in one side. He was sleeping soundly when she lifted him out. She also took out the packet of papers she'd stuffed in to keep him snug.

"What's this?" Zeke was gaping.

At his expression, Eli grinned. "The one that's folded is Congress's rejection of our independence. The one that's not is Henry Brownell."

Zeke held out his arms for the baby. "He's little, but he'll grow."

"He's already growing." Eli held out his arm to Anne-Marie and she slipped into its curve.

After a bit, Zeke looked up from the baby. "About Congress," he said. "They're too late. Three weeks ago the convention unanimously declared us an independent state." He grinned from one of them to the other. "Welcome to Vermont."

Anne-Marie smiled up at Eli. "It's good to be home," they murmured in unison.

* * * * *

Author's Note

The Battle of Bennington took place on August 16, 1777. Two months later the Americans defeated Burgoyne at Saratoga in the battle that brought France in as America's ally and changed the course of the war. It also marked the end of fighting between New England and New York. Although Vermont had declared her independence in July 1777, Congress did not grant her petition for statehood until 1791. Until that time she existed as an independent republic, governed by the first constitution to allow universal manhood suffrage and to outlaw slavery. On March 4, 1791, after an already colorful history, Vermont became the fourteenth state.

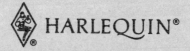

THE TAGGARTS OF TEXAS!

Harlequin's Ruth Jean Dale brings you
THE TAGGARTS OF TEXAS!

Those Taggart men—strong, sexy and hard to resist...

You've met Jesse James Taggart in FIREWORKS!
Harlequin Romance #3205 (July 1992)

Now meet Trey Smith—he's THE RED-BLOODED YANKEE!
Harlequin Temptation #413 (October 1992)

Then there's Daniel Boone Taggart in SHOWDOWN!
Harlequin Romance #3242 (January 1993)

And finally the Taggarts who started it all—in LEGEND!
Harlequin Historical #168 (April 1993)

Read all the Taggart romances!
Meet all the Taggart men!

Available wherever Harlequin books are sold.

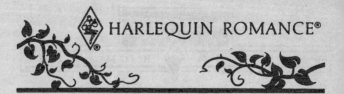

HARLEQUIN ROMANCE®

• STORIES • 1992 •

Capture the magic and romance of Christmas in the 1800s
with HARLEQUIN HISTORICAL CHRISTMAS STORIES
1992—a collection of three stories by celebrated
historical authors. The perfect Christmas gift!

Don't miss these heartwarming stories, available in
November wherever Harlequin books are sold:

MISS MONTRACHET REQUESTS by Maura Seger
CHRISTMAS BOUNTY by Erin Yorke
A PROMISE KEPT by Bronwyn Williams

Plus, this Christmas you can also receive a FREE
keepsake Christmas ornament. Watch for details in all
November and December Harlequin books.

DISCOVER THE ROMANCE AND MAGIC OF THE
HOLIDAY SEASON WITH HARLEQUIN HISTORICAL
CHRISTMAS STORIES!